RICH LI

The photogra
glossy page wa
Carol thought
pose was stu
erotic and the lighting was breathtaking in its artistry. It had made the face heart-bending in its angled shapeliness, its lights and hollows, curves and planes; the sculptured mouth challenged the imagination, the spectacular blue eyes were backed by visions, the hair was a blaze of white gold.

She stared at it, mazed with admiration even as a second dawning of consciousness filtered into her mind. It was a picture of her! An impossible, fantasised image, but undeniably she.

RICH LITTLE POOR GIRL

Terence Feely

Hamlyn Paperbacks

RICH LITTLE POOR GIRL

ISBN 0 600 20201 1

First published in Great Britain 1981
by Hamlyn Paperbacks

Hamlyn Paperbacks are published by
The Hamlyn Publishing Group Ltd,
Astronaut House,
Feltham,
Middlesex, England

Printed and bound in Great Britain by
Cox & Wyman Ltd, Reading

1

Carol Blair's knee came up almost as a reflex. The hands abruptly left her breasts, like two mechanical grabs with the power cut off, and 'Ike' Palmer crumpled to the ground in agony.

She stepped over him out of the doorway in which he had cornered her and ran on down the alley as if nothing had happened. By her standards, nothing had. It was a fairly routine aspect of coming home from school in her part of town.

Except that she wasn't going home. She had something else on her mind. An unusual obsession for a girl barely sixteen years old. Less unusual, perhaps, in her part of town. Running with the wiry stamina of someone who had hardly ever been on a bus or a train in her life she jinked left at the next alley to avoid Frankenstein, the local urban equivalent of the village idiot. He haunted these 'back jiggers', with his tramp's clothes and his slobbering grin, waiting to flash himself at anything female that might come his way. The police knew all about him, but they had more desperate men to fight in this city than Frankenstein and in any case nobody in the district ever lodged a complaint. He was a part of their lives, like street fights and mildewed mattresses.

She leaped over the dog turds, skirted the festering rubbish that people tipped out of their baikyard doors despite all the pleas of the local council: on and on she ran, down the long, interlocking passages that honeycombed the back streets of Liverpool, pungent with the urine of cats, dogs, small boys, and Saturday night drunks who admired, maudlin, the great jewelled vault above them while they pissed away half their week's wages against the wall.

On she hammered, catching a glimpse of two lovers in a doorway, locked, Laocoon-like, in a standing embrace, the girl's legs grapevined round her lover's waist, suspenders at bursting point.

Her father would half kill her should he find out she'd disobeyed him and come down the back jiggers again, but she was in a hurry and it was quicker this way. How could she know that some other girl had not had the same idea and was even now speeding along some parallel course towards the same destination?

On the streets you had to contend with other people, crowds, knots, blockages. Here, along the backtracks of the jungle, you were on your own - apart from the Ike Palmers and the Frankensteins and she reckoned she could handle them.

Ahead lay another hazard. Mad Ma Luther, lurking in her back yard, apparently twelve hours a day, waiting to spring out, flailing a broom, at any youngsters who happened to pass. She had an uncanny, radar-like ear, Mad Ma Luther. No matter how you tip-toed, or varied your speed, she heard you and judged her strike with the precision of a rattler. Carol had perfected an approach, however, that Mad Ma was not flexible enough to counter. Thirty yards from the old witch's back door she jumped, caught the top of the wall, hoisted herself up and ran past Mad Ma's, sure-footed as a cat, along the top of the wall. Moving as fast as she was and concentrating as hard as she was, all Carol saw as she sped elevatedly past was a camera-click image of Mad Ma, crouched by the door, broom in her hand, one frustrated eye glaring upwards as she realised she'd been wrong-footed again by the same tow-haired urchin.

Apart from speed, there was another reason why she had chosen the back tracks. There was less chance of her being spotted. Her mission was, in a sense, illicit and this was a city of nosy parkers. The most dread expression among the city's long catalogue of guilt-inducing phrases, uttered always with a deeply accusatory and doom-laden cadence was, 'You were seen.' Well, she was not, if she could help it, going to be seen this time, although she was rapidly nearing the point where she would have to break cover. She was approaching the posher end of the city, where the big stores, the offices and restaurants were. The back jiggers ended here and in another fifty yards she was out.

As always, she was elated when she reached this part of the city. She had no idea it was run-down and grimy. To her it signified a lighter, sparkling air, a luminosity. People wore smooth cloth and their clothes fitted. Shop windows glittered and plastic models looked out at her with flawless faces she wished were hers. When she was younger she would stand and stare at them for twenty minutes at a time until the shopkeepers, disconcerted by the rapt immobility of this strange ragamuffin in front of their shop, would chase her away.

As she reached London Road she slowed down for the first time. On the run she'd had no chance to put her thoughts in order. Now it was vital that she should think clearly. She stopped and looked at herself in a shop window. Her hair was like a burst straw bale. With her fingers she combed it into some kind of pattern that the human eye could identify. She ran her hands over her sweater and skirt, both cast-offs from Martha, her older sister by nine years, so that the clothes, too, were at least nine years old: and it showed. Her pale, rather severe little face was smudged with dirt from her scramble on to the wall and she hastily scrubbed it with a grubby sleeve. She rehearsed what she was going to say, then slowly walked a few yards further and into the modestly imposing premises of Andrew Marshall & Nephew, Photographic Suppliers. She looked far worse than she realised.

The interior of the shop smelled of expensive things. A customer, on his way out with one hundred and twenty pounds' worth of camera and lenses, looked at her curiously. The breeze from his choice tweed suit vaguely excited her as he wafted past. Mr John Mackenzie, manager, large, florid and with the beginnings – just like

Father O'Donnell, she thought – of a whisky nose, looked at her even more curiously from behind the barricade of his spotless glass counter.

She fixed him with her disconcertingly blue stare. 'My name's Carol Blair,' she said. 'I've come for the job.'

Mr Mackenzie, something of a connoisseur, he reckoned, of the nuance, looked upwards at the ceiling, sideways at Jeremy Knackford, his pale freckled assistant, and then at Carol. '*For* the job,' he said, the lilt of Inverness-shire in his voice. 'Not about the job, or concerning the job, or *is* there a job: but *for* the job. What makes you so sure, missie, that there's a job to be had?'

'Because Sister Ignatius said so,' she replied firmly.

'And what did Sister Ignatius say about this wee job?' enquired Mackenzie.

'She said it was to do with taking in films to be developed and giving them out again when they was ready.'

Her heart had been steadily sinking. This man was toying with her, not taking her seriously. She caught another glimpse of herself reflected in a glass case behind him and thought she couldn't really blame him. She looked about as right in this shop as a rag doll in a march-past.

Mackenzie was speaking again. 'Did Sister Ignatius say anything else?'

Carol clenched her hands and determined to stick to it. 'She said she knew about the job because the girl you've got now got herself knocked up and she'll have to leave to have the kid and you sent her to Sister Ignatius to sort her out.'

The faint smile that had been patronising her up to now disappeared from Mackenzie's face. The directness of this funny little scrap in front of him was beginning to refashion his response to her.

'I'm sure she didn't put it quite like that,' he said, 'but the details are, in essence, correct.'

'I thought they would be,' said Carol, equably.

Mackenzie felt faintly reproved. 'Tell me, d'you always dress like that?'

Carol looked down at herself, bewildered: 'I put on what's give me,' she said. 'Me dad can't afford a school uniform.'

He felt obscurely ashamed of himself and tried to make amends. 'Given your own free choice, how would you dress?'

Carol unexpectedly smiled and the effect was like sunshine suddenly flashing on a stream. Against all the odds of calcium deficiency in the rest of her diet, free school milk and some indomitable gene had given her beautiful teeth. 'Oh, like them models you see in the windows,' she said.

Mackenzie grunted. 'We wouldn't want to go quite that far here.'You do understand,' he went on, 'that the lassie who's to be replaced has to leave immediately?'

'Yes,' said Carol openly,' Sister Ignatius did say it was next week the girl was due to drop her bundle.' She saw the look of incomprehension on Mackenzie's face and added, helpfully: 'Have her baby, like.'

'Would you be able to start immediately?'

'Oh yes,' she said with a hopeful, helpful little grin. 'The only reason I'm back at school is because I couldn't get a job when I left in July. I've done my time,' she added, with another of her quick, flashing grins; 'the Sisters would let me go straight away.'

Mackenzie knew the youth employment situation in Liverpool in 1960 as well as anyone. 'Aye, I take your point,' he said. There was something about the wee mudlark that made you take her increasingly seriously. 'You realise,' he said, 'that when I mentioned this to Sister Ignatius I intended that she should tell all the girls, give the whole class a chance.'

'The whole class isn't here,' said Carol.

She could feel herself beginning to sweat, around her hairline, through her palms, down the nape of her neck. Part of it, she realised, was her cooling off after her run through the chill October city, but part of it wasn't. That part was because she knew she was coming to the crunch. And how it came out, she knew instinctively, depended on what kind of man this was. That she didn't know. But she wasn't too heartened by the lilting precision of that Inverness-shire voice. 'Are you the only one who's interested, then?' it was now asking.

'I'm the only one who's come,' she answered evasively.

'Yes, I was wondering about that,' said Mackenzie. He looked at his watch. 'What time d'you get out of school these days?'

Now it was coming. 'Four o'clock,' she said.

'It's only five past three.'

'Yes.'

'How come you're here, then?'

'I left school early.'

'Ah! Sister Ignatius gave you permission.'

'No.'

'Oh?'

She took a deep breath and abandoned evasion as a bad job; it was bound to come out sooner or later, anyway.

'As soon as she told us about the job I asked to leave class to go to the toilet, but I came down here instead.'

There was a pause. Carol watched, fascinated, as Mackenzie's face became congested in an alarming manner, seeming to increase steadily in size and in depth of colour until the pressure was relieved, as by a safety valve, by his mouth. His laugh was the explosive wheeze of a sixty cigarettes a day man.

When he'd recovered, he asked, 'Don't you think you're being unfair to the other girls?'

'If they'd wanted the job as much as me they'd have done the same,' said Carol.

'Don't you think you're being unfair to me, then, trying to pressure me into taking you when there might be someone I haven't seen who might suit me better?'

'When it comes to taking in films and handing them out again we're probably all even Steven, but at least you know I'm the keenest and, honestly, do you really want to slog your way through seeing all the others?'

Mackenzie smiled. 'Never let it be said a good Scot discouraged enterprise. Come here, lassie.'

She obeyed his beckoning finger, going through the gap he magically opened in hi gleaming glass barricade. He presented her with a pad and a ball-point pen. 'Let's see you write.'

'What shall I write?'

'Your name and address will do for a start.'

Dutifully, she wrote down Carol Blair, 16 Mugsley Street, Liverpool, Lancashire. She had a good, strong schoolgirl's hand with powerful, generous loops on her l's, y's and g's. It was a surprising script, both characterful and classless.

'Yes, I see,' said Mackenzie thoughtfully. 'Now supposing a customer comes in here with six films he wants developed at one shilling and ninepence a time. What would that amount to?'

Carol's strong suit had never been her arithmetic, but she knew this was a crisis point and the adrenalin pumped into her bloodstream and her brain responded. 'Ten shillings and sixpence,' she said, with a promptness that startled herself.

Mackenzie's eyebrows lifted. 'Good, good. You know what the job pays?' He couldn't know the essential meaninglessness of the phrase to Carol, who had never even had pocket money in her life.

'No.'

'Three pounds five shillings, less your income tax and national insurance. Well?'

Some deeply buried instinct took over and Carol, to whom the figures were merely figures, heard herself saying, 'I thought it was three pounds ten shillings.' She had, in fact, heard nothing of the kind.

Mackenzie's eyes narrowed; was it something like stifled approval she read in them? 'Three pounds seven shillings and sixpence,' he said, 'and that's my last word.'

Something she had read in some dim, distant Library Period at school echoed in her mind. 'Done!' she said, her flat Liverpudlian accent lending the word even greater comic finality.

The alarming symptoms heralding another laugh started to show themselves, but this time Mackenzie managed to suppress it. He didn't want to give the child the impression he was some sort of simpering clown. 'Start tomorrow morning, nine o'clock sharp,' he said.

'I'll be here, chief,' said Carol.

She marched out, feeling light-headed, and Mackenzie pulled out the stopper on his laughter. Knackford joined in. He was going to enjoy working with this kid.

Where, before, Carol Blair had run, now, on her way home, she walked, slowly, in a haze of glory. Even the most commonplace objects seemed to have an aureole of light outlining them. She took her time, wanting to savour her happiness. Passers-by going the other way turned to look after her, so extraordinary was the radiance in her grubby little face.

Had they known the cause of it, most of them would have understood. For this was a community where unemployment had touched most families at one time or another. Certainly, her own kind would have known how she felt. Living where they did, sounding the way they did, dressing off market stalls and hand-me-downs, they were last in the queue when jobs were handed out, in a city where jobs had been shrinking for years.

Approaching home, she ran into Ike Palmer again. He was walking rather gingerly, trying to avoid heavy footfalls that might jar a certain recently tenderised portion of his anatomy. 'Hi, Car,' he said, without rancour, 'everything AOK?'

'Yeah,' she said. 'Sorry about that, before.'

''S'all right,' he replied, 'I asked for it, messing you about. It's just . . . with you . . . I can't help it.'

It was true. He was a studious boy, physics star of the sixth form of her younger brother Tony's school. He looked gentle, Carol thought, and a bit vague, like a very young version of Henry Fonda whom she'd seen in old movies on the telly, with steel-rimmed glasses. But with her – she couldn't understand why, she knew she was a funny little thing – something hard and demanding emerged in his nature and he couldn't keep his hands off her. It was as if he became older and more flinty.

'See you,' she said, turning into her own street.

She drifted up Mugsley Street, the glamour of her secret

making even this pinched little huddle of hutches glow, trailed hazily to number 16, hugging herself at the thought of what they'd say when she told them, and knocked.

Her father opened the door, dragged her into the hall and felled her with one blow to the side of her skull.

'Where the hell have you been?' he snarled.

Her head ringing, she didn't at first understand. 'What d'you mean?' she asked, trying to struggle to her feet, one hand to her throbbing ear. She didn't cry. It had been a long time since she had cried.

'You know bloody well what I mean,' said big Jack Blair. 'Sister Ignatius has been here.'

Instantly, Carol got the picture. She should have expected it. Naturally, when she didn't come back from the toilet at school, she had been missed. And in the great Liverpool tradition it had naturally been assumed that she was off somewhere, committing mortal and – what was worse – hugely pleasurable sins.

'I've been downtown,' she said, 'I—'

'You've been with some bloody lad,' said Jack.

'No—'

'Don't bloody lie to me, you crafty little git! Come here !' His voice seemed to fill the cramped little space. She knew he was going to hit her again.

There was the rattle of a key in the lock and Janet, stepmother to Carol and her brother and sister, came in, a thinly provisioned shopping basket on her arm. Her patient, worn brown eyes filled with concern, even though this was a tableau she'd seen a hundred times before.

'Jack! Carol! What's the matter?'

'It's this little cow,' her father replied, 'skived off from school and ended up God knows where – behind some shed with some lad.'

Janet looked from one to the other. She knew Carol hadn't been off with any lad. Where Jack got this rooted suspicion about his daughters from, she would never know. He'd been exactly the same with Martha and still, to some extent, was, even though she was twenty-five and looked the way she did.

'Don't be daft,' she said, 'she hasn't been with any lad. Come on, we can't stand here in the hall like three fried eggs. Let's go in the kitchen.'

They passed the front parlour, which was never used. Jack kept it locked. In the kitchen, Jack turned to Carol. 'Right, let's have it,' he said.

Carol burned with rage, an icy fury that she should have been too young to know, but which she had learned at the hands of a master.

'I've got a job!' she said. 'A sodding job! This isn't how I wanted to tell you. This isn't how I wanted it to be at all. I was excited about it, thrilled, knocked out. Now you've ruined it, like you ruin everything you put your sodding hands on! You're like the bloody plague we read about at school – I'm amazed we haven't all got bleeding boils under the armpits from you living in the same house—'

He lashed out at her again, but Janet shrieked and interposed her shopping basket. It went flying, food exploding out of it all over the room, including a half-dozen precious eggs. Janet ignored it. She hugged her beloved stepdaughter. 'A job! Carol, how marvellous! How clever of you, love!' She, more than anyone, knew Jack's power to blight. She also knew how to counter and cope with it. And she protected his children from it as best she could, with as much fervour as if they'd sprung from her own body.

'What job? Where is this job?' demanded Jack.

'Get stuffed!' said Carol, from the cover of her mother's embrace.

He tried to rip her from his wife's arms. 'Give her here!'

'Leave her alone!' shrieked Janet. 'Leave the kid alone!' She turned her face to Carol. 'You shouldn't speak like that to your father, it's not right. He is your father, no matter what. Tell him what he wants to know, there's a good girl.'

'Andrew Marshall & Nephew, London Road,' she blurted out, sullenly, not looking at him.

Jack Blair slammed out of the house. He walked three quarters of a mile until he found the nearest unvandalised telephone box. He rang up the shop to check his daughter's story, using all the considerable charm he could switch on when he needed it, so as not to jeopardise her job if she really had one. Then he walked the three quarters of a mile home again.

When he got back to the house he found that Janet, the peace-maker, thinking ahead as usual, had spared him the humiliation of the grunt he had steeled himself to make to Carol as an apology. She had given Carol her tea, then packed her off hastily to the public baths with her towel and her soap. All the family went twice a week at twopence a time each. This wasn't one of Carol's days, but it was a means of getting her out of the house in a way of which Jack could not disapprove.

She was halfway across the ruined site between Edon Street and Preen Road on her way home when they struck. Two of them – Linda Oakley and Noreen Pratt. They appeared in silence from behind a fragment of wall which was still standing. They came towards her, menacing, taking their time.

Carol looked quickly behind her, prepared to run. But at her back, emerging from behind another stretch of torn wall, appeared Loretta Minter and Siobhan O'Brien. She was surrounded by four of the biggest and heaviest girls in her class.

Desperately, she looked about her for a weapon, or at least a wall against which she could get her back. There was no weapon, no wall. They were tacticians, these girls, junior urban guerrillas, impossible to visualise as the wives and mothers of five or six years hence. They came on, still in silence, until they had encircled her.

'Who's a clever little girl, then?' opened Linda Oakley, poking her painfully in the left breast with a stiff forefinger.

'Who's a crafty little bugger?' added Loretta Minter, kneeing her between the buttocks from behind.

'Who sloped off and nicked the fucking job?' said Noreen Pratt, welting her across the face with the back of her hand.

'You foxy little fart!'

'Nasty cow!'

'Stinking little whore-face!'

'Shitting pig!'

They were hitting her now, punching her, pulling her hair, the violence escalating.

Carol knew the pattern. She had to break out of the circle before it was too late. She exploded, arms and legs flailing right and left, her lean body alive with the energy of desperation. But they were experts, these four, falling back, holding the ring, letting her expend herself. Then closing in again, hitting her from all angles.

She knew she mustn't go down. To go down was fatal. That was when the kicking began. And once the kicking started, it was goodbye to her turning in for her first day at work tomorrow. So she stood there and took it, getting in a blow herself whenever she saw the chance – she had the satisfaction of winding Noreen Pratt and making Linda Oakley's nose bleed. But the end was inevitable. They closed in. Siobhan O'Brien's arm went around her throat from behind and her knee went into her back and she was down, surrounded by feet.

She did the only thing experience had taught her could be done in straits like this: she curled herself into a ball like a hedgehog, protecting her head and her ribs, and prepared to ride it out. The kicks started coming in and she resigned herself to pain and damage.

Then dimly she was aware of a change. The kicks had become sporadic. There were shouts. Siobhan O'Brien suddenly landed on the ground beside her, her mouth bleeding. Carol unwound and looked up and there was her younger brother, Tony, like an avenging archangel in his fury, ripping into her attackers.

Tony was under-developed for fifteen, fine-featured, fine-boned. Normally, he would walk miles to avoid violence, but in defence of his sister he had more than once proved himself a tiger. He hit them like a whiplash, thin but precise, and they were crumbling.

Generally speaking, to be a boy in a fight with girls in this neighbourhood gave the boy no physical or psychological advantage. The girls could fight as well and as savagely as the boys, and apart from those lads – there were always some – who had grown a man's bone and muscle almost before they could spell, there was little difference in strength and the girls feared no male of their own age.

But the delicate-looking Blair lad, fighting alongside his skinny, tough sister, who was now on her feet, was a different matter. He fought with his brain, he hit you in places you didn't know you had. It was rumoured, incredulously, that he got it all from books. He used his elbows and heels as well as his fists.

Within two minutes it was all over. Linda Oakley and her three accomplices were off, confused and bleeding, stumbling unevenly over the broken bricks and cavities of the derelict land, shouting abuse and threats as they went.

'We'll get you, Carol Blair!'

'Little creep-arse!'

'Your brother won't always be around!'

Tony grabbed up two quarter bricks, flung them with all the springy leverage of his willowy back. One caught Noreen Pratt thunderously in the small of the back and the other took Linda Oakley behind the left knee, making it buckle momentarily. They broke into a run. It was a rout.

Carol looked at Tony gratefully. 'Thanks, Tone,' she said. 'How come?'

'Mum told me when I got home from school,' he said; 'about the job and how you got it. Well, bloody hell, it didn't take Einstein to work out they'd be laying for you. What did you expect – a medal from the neighbourhood?'

'I didn't think,' she said.

'Come on,' he said, 'let's get home before they come back with tanks.'

As they went on their way, Carol dusted herself down and inspected for damage. What neither of them wanted was questions from their father. They both knew what the consequences of that would be. Jack Blair's philosophy was both eyes for an eye and a mouthful of teeth for a tooth.

But Jack Blair already knew. A little potato-nosed Irishman called McGowran had seen the whole thing. He was one of Jack's runners, feeding him titbits of news. In return, Jack got him jobs on the docks. Not being of strong build, he had no business on the docks at all, but if you kept in with Jack Blair, he'd always find you a corner. It wasn't that he was a union man, nor a bosses' man, nor even a foreman: in fact there was no official reason why he should have so much influence. It was just that he was Jack Blair and where Jack Blair walked, men got out of the way. If he said you were on a cargo, you were, come hell, high water, bosses or unions all. When he'd heard the story, it never occurred to Jack Blair to reproach McGowran for not having gone to his daughter's aid. In this ghetto adults did not interfere in juvenile wars. Kids had to be toughened up for what lay ahead of them. This was not to say, however, that accounts could not be settled between their elders and betters later. The laws governing the situation were immutable. Which was why George Pratt, five streets away, and John O'Brien, Bill Oakley and Bob Minter all knew that Jack Blair would be calling on at least one of them before the night was out.

Two streets away from the Pratt house, Jack Blair and McGowran ran into Carol and Tony on their way home.

'This way,' said Jack.

Carol and Tony knew from experience what business their father was about. 'We were just going home,' said Tony.

'I said this way,' repeated Jack.

'It was nothing,' said Carol, 'honest!'

'I won't tell you again,' said her father.

McGowran whispered to them persuasively: 'I think you'd better come along.' They looked at the little Irishman contemptuously and sullenly fell in behind.

A few minutes later, Jack Blair knocked on George Pratt's door like the hammer of doom. Pratt, almost as big as his caller, opened the door, took one look at Jack Blair with his children behind him and wasted no time on words. He launched a steel-tipped kick straight at Jack Blair's testicles. Had it connected, the whole matter would have been concluded there and then.

But Jack Blair's formidableness came as much from his speed as from his size. He jerked back just far enough to evade the kick, then seized the foot, heaved, and sent Pratt crashing back into his own hallway. He leaped in after him and dragged him, dazed, to his feet. He hit him in the solar plexus, knocking every cubic inch of air out of his body. As Pratt jack-knifed, doubling up in agony, Blair brought his knee up to meet the descending face and Pratt catapulted backwards to land, split-nosed and bloody, at the feet of his wife, who had just appeared screaming at the door into the hallway from the kitchen.

'You bloody animal!' she screeched at Jack Blair.'You should be put away. You're not fit to live with human beings!'

Pratt, groggy, but still conscious, looked up at her and spoke through rapidly ballooning lips: 'Shut up, woman!' He rose to his feet slowly, as if beaten, and then without warning lowered his head and charged like a bull, his cannonball skull smacking into Blair's stomach, bearing him backwards along the hallway and out of the front door into the street, where they both went sprawling.

'Kill him! Kill him!' Pratt's wife was screaming.

Carol was shivering. Fighting among youngsters was one thing, but violence among grown men horrified her. The thud and crunch of big fists against flesh and bone and cartilage, the thump of big bodies on stone, sickened her and gave her a kind of hysteria. She turned away, whiter than ever, and Tony put his arm around her.

The fight went on. Pratt had landed on top and chopped for Blair's throat; but Blair blocked him and struck him like a hammer, just under the nose, with the iron-hard heel of his hand. Pratt couldn't believe the pain. He felt himself being hauled to his feet, a hand grasping his right shoulder to steady him and set him up, then an explosion to the side of his jaw that totally unplugged him. He went down with a crash, his limbs disconnected from his brain. He lay there, panting.

'Get up!' his wife shouted. 'Kill him!'

'You kill him,' he said.

Pratt looked up at Jack Blair: 'There'll be another time,' he said.

'Aye,' said Jack.

The light was going, the Panda police cars had started patrolling and Carol and Tony turned homewards again. The violent jungle village purred like a tiger as it waited for night. Old folk got themselves safely indoors and anyone who didn't have to be out did likewise.

Carol and Tony, weathered old Indian scouts in Apache country, picked their way through the gathering murk and the crumbling ambush-inviting terrain without fear. She told her brother about her epic run downtown and how she had outwitted Mad Ma Luther and they giggled together as they rubbed shoulders and jostled each other along the pavements in the thickening darkness.

Carol Blair had got a job and like most things in her life up to then, it had ended in blood and bitterness, touched with laughter.

2

Next morning she lay curled in bed, her hands clamped warmly between her thighs. Her sister, Martha, with whom she shared the room, was already up. She was always up half an hour before anyone else.

Carol looked out at the metal-grey skies. For once they didn't depress her. Today they were tinted by the colours of her expectations. She savoured the taste that was in her mind. The sense of independence, the knowledge that she wouldn't have to go to school ever again, the thought that maybe now she'd be able to buy at least a couple of the things she wanted.

She slid out from under the old topcoats and macs that did duty for an eiderdown over her bed and clothed her skinny frame. The process did not take very long. The arctic temperature of the bedroom did not encourage sensuous dalliance with her underwear. The wind whistled through the rotten window-frames, making her nipples stand out like bits of coral and her Woolworth's bra scratched them as she shrugged into it.

The root of her elation was something at the back of her mind: something she knew in that strange little way she had of knowing things.

Carol didn't know much. The nuns who had schooled her in the grimy little barracks the Victorians had left behind four streets away had been more interested in keeping her mind off Hell and her hands off her clitoris than in any enlargement of her general understanding. But she did know this: that she was different and that she had been boxed in.

She wasn't quite sure how she was different: she had

never heard of divine discontent. But she was sure how she was boxed in, doubly, maybe triply enclosed, and that the boxes fitted one inside the other. She had to escape from school, out into the second box, which was the slum where she lived, then out of that into Liverpool at large, then out of that into . . . what?

'Get weaving, will you!' This, her father from downstairs. 'You'll lose that bloody job before you've even started!' To Jack Blair, to lose a job was life's cardinal disaster, obliterating illness, injury and even death in its enormity.

'Coming!'

She wrapped a paper-thin dressing-gown around her and tumbled, shivering, down the coffin-narrow stairs to get washed.

In the back-kitchen Tony was in possession of the sink, the only place in the house where her father allowed hot water – an Ascot gas heater. Her stepmother, Janet, was at the gas cooker, frying bread, with that weathered patience that characterised everything she did.

Carol kissed Janet on the cheek, although this was not, generally, a kissing household.

'Morning, Mum.'

'Hello, love.'

She did not kiss her father, who was shaving with a cut-throat razor at a cracked mirror over by the door to the backyard, his big, hard-muscled stevedore's frame, in undervest and trousers, seeming to take up all the oxygen in the cramped little space, his man-smell overpowering.

'About bloody time!' he said.

She slipped out of her dressing-gown and tried to shoulder Tony aside.

'Come on, Tone, I'm going to be late!'

'I can't go to school with BO,' he answered, shoving back. 'I think I've got it made with the geography mistress.' Janet turned round from her frying pan. 'Tony!'

'Oh, come on, Tone, it's my first day!'

Tony made room for her at the sink. They were the only household in the pinched little street that had not taken advantage of the government grants towards installing bathrooms and inside lavatories. In vain the family had pleaded with Jack Blair. 'They pay half, out of what they grab from us, then we pay the other half out of what they leave us with,' was his answer. 'They must think we're bloody soft in the head.'

But that wasn't the real reason. The real reason was that Jack Blair was mean. There wasn't an electric fire in the house. Stamped out in iron, he never seemed to notice the cold; in winter, the rest of them waddled around the house looking like bulky woollen ragbags.

He had removed the electric light fittings from his children's bedrooms: 'You don't need light when you sleep in the dark.' All her life Carol would remember the smell of the paraffin that fired the tiny lamp by which she and Martha undressed for bed, as did Tony in his room next door. That camphorish, curiously disturbing smell had permeated her earliest erotic dreams. Much later in life she was to have occasion to remember that.

'Give us the soap, then!' Carol grabbed at the bar of plain green carbolic that was all Jack would allow as an aid to hygiene.

'If we had Martha in here mixing it with us every morning, too, we wouldn't know who was washing what,' grinned Tony.

He missed the warning sign of the half-turn of his father's razor-rasped face towards him and, fatally, went on: 'Good job she's such a Virgin Mary!'

The blow came from out of Tony's field of vision, the back of Jack Blair's left hand, a tap by his standards, but enough to send Tony spinning until he crashed into the far wall. Blood trickled from the corner of his mouth. Jack turned back to his shaving, unconcerned. 'I've told you,' he said, muffled by the razor, 'save it for your pansy mates at school.'

There was always a casualness about his violence to Tony which was infinitely shocking to Carol. When her father beat her, he formalised it almost into a ritual. But, whenever he hit Tony, he managed to do it in such a way that it seemed unimportant to him.

Tony scrambled to his feet, Janet and Carol rushing to help him.

'Leave him alone,' Jack snapped, not turning his head.

'Why don't you try leaving him alone?' Janet snapped back, in one of her rare moments of revolt. 'You're at him twenty-four hours a day!'

Jack was unmoved, a statue, shaving. 'He needed a smack in the gob, he got one.'

'That's your answer to everything, isn't it – a smack in the gob? The world would be a better place if everyone started the day with a smack in the gob from you!' She dabbed at her stepson's split lip with a clean rag.

Jack caught and held his son's eye. 'Like to have a go at me, wouldn't you?' he taunted.

'No,' said Tony, simply, knowing it was the answer that would displease his father most. He had the satisfaction of seeing the rock-like face darken.

'Maybe when he's more your size, he will,' said Janet.

'He'll never be my size,' said Jack, dismissively. He turned back to the mirror.

Carol, scrawny in her tired little bra and pants, wheeled on her father. Only the thunder behind the blue irises prevented her from looking comical. 'He's bigger than you are now, you lousy, bullying bastard!'

'You'd better keep your trap shut, girl, or I'll shut it for you.'

'Yeah, go on, why don't you? I'd love to turn up to work on my first day with a black eye – and I wouldn't tell them no yarns about walking into a door, either. I'd tell them it was my dad, big puncher, undefeated champion of the Blair family against three women and a lad–'

'You cheeky little bitch!' He said it almost with satisfaction. He started to unhook the wide strap on which he stropped and sharpened his razor. This, the deliberation, was the first part of the ritual. 'There won't be no black eyes for anyone to see.'

Janet threw herself in front of him. 'Jack, for God's sake! The kid's got to get to work! Her first day! D'you want the money coming in or not?'

Unerringly, she had gone for the vulnerable heel of this Achilles whom she hated and worshipped in bewildering alternation from day to day: sometimes, it seemed, from minute to minute.

Jack paused and slowly put the strap back on its hook.

'It'll keep till tonight,' he said.

Upstairs, Martha, in front of the only decent mirror in the house in her parents' bedroom, trudged with fortitude through the unrewarding job of making up her face. It was dull and pudgy. As was her body. As were her eyes. Mendelian theory had blown a fuse on Martha. Her eyes had missed out on the incandescent blue blaze of the Blairs. Some errant gene had put green eyes in her head. Not the blazing, tigerish green of a Barbara Cartland heroine, either, but the dull, slate shade of a Welsh quarry in the rain. She sighed gently and smoothed on more jade eye shadow.

She had, of course, heard the row of which she had been the absent and innocent occasion, but it hadn't upset her. She knew it was true. She was prudish. She never had been able to take part in the warm, ammoniac-scented, underwear-clad scramble to get washed in the back kitchen, tumbling and rubbing over each other like puppies in a basket. Therefore she got up half an hour before anyone else, so that she might have the sink and the soap and the hot water heater to herself.

She looked solemnly at her solemn face and sighed again. Carol's pale, pointed little pixie face was solemn, too, but when she smiled it was transformed as if a light had been switched on inside. When I smile, thought Martha ruefully, it's like one of those earthquake movies where you see splits opening in the ground.

She had had one chance at a man and her father had rubbed it out. Fred had been no Paul Newman. He wore trousers that streamed downwards from lower chest to ankle – just above the ankle – in twin waterfalls of broad flannel. His wrist-bones protruded from his tweed jacket sleeves and he had his hair clipped short right up the back of his head and over the tops of his ears, so that he always seemed to be taking off perpendicularly, like a rocket, out of his own body. But he was a clerk with the Water Board and he was better than nothing and he could have been hers.

Jack said nothing about him one way or the other. But one night he took him down to the local pub and poured pints of beer into him until he was sloshing like a perambulating water bed. Jack supported him back to their house on one marble-hard arm and prevented him, by sheer force of character, from throwing up until he had got him inside and into their kitchen, when Fred did – an exploding, sulphurous geyser, all over the floor. Then he slipped and fell in it. Martha never saw him again.

She had simply concentrated harder on her work. When she'd left school she'd got a job as a filing clerk with the Inland Revenue and had instantly enrolled for a free council evening class course in accountancy. Figures and their relationships had always fascinated her. Born into a different sort of family she'd have been a mathematician or a physicist, a cheerful, ugly bluestocking at some university, attracting a mixture of respect and affectionate amusement.

As it was, her remorselessly improving qualifications, despite her accent, despite the clothes Jack's meanness with her own wages forced her to wear, had pushed her up the establishment ladder until now, at twenty-five, she was a Tax Officer, Higher Grade.

The street regarded her with both awe and revulsion. The revulsion was a natural reaction to anyone who worked for 'the Tax'. The awe was an equally proper response to the fact that someone from Mugsley Street was actually in the Civil Service.

Jack's voice came booming up the stairs. 'What're you doing up there, painting the bleeding Mona Lisa? D'you know what the time is?'

'Of course I do,' she yelled back, 'I'm not an idiot!'

'Cut the backchat and get down here!'

'I'll be down when I'm ready.'

'Get down here now.'

'I said when I'm ready. I'm not ready yet. It's very simple.'

'Don't you schoolmarm me, you toffee-nosed bugger! If I have to come up there–'

She heard Janet's voice: 'Jack, for God's sake! She's a grown woman. She knows the time.'

Jack came back into the kitchen from the door to the stairs, returned to his fried bread. His had a piece of bacon on it, the only one. He'd never asked for it, he wasn't a greedy man about his stomach. His women – Claire before Janet – had always given it to him.

'She doesn't know her arse from her earhole,' he said, his mouth full. 'She sits in a fancy office all day and thinks she's God Almighty's elder sister.'

'There's nothing fancy about it,' said Carol, gulping the last of the powerful, thick tea that made up in stimulants what the breakfast lacked in protein. 'I've seen it, it used to be an old house–'

'You'd better dry up,' said Jack. 'You've got enough coming to you already.'

Carol got up abruptly and went to the outside lavatory in the back yard. She didn't need to go. When she got there she just sat, shivering, in the primitive structure. She needed privacy and this was the only location in the house where it could be found, although even then it couldn't be fully guaranteed.

Her eye rested on the bunch of torn-up squares of the *Daily Mirror*, impaled on a nail, which served as toilet paper to the household. The top square showed a sleek and gilded girl galloping a white horse almost as pretty as herself across white sands. 'Get Away From It All With Kerry Travel–'

She thought she'd pop in somewhere and get the brochure. It could join the others, glowing with glamour in their hiding place under her mattress.

They were there because she had learned her lesson. Two years ago she had brought the first one into the house.

She had sat in a corner of the kitchen by the fire, feasting on the colour and sunshine in it. Jack had come home and found her with it. Without a word, he had ripped it from her hands and thrown it on the fire.

'Dad! What's up? Why d'you do that?'

'This country's always been good enough for my family,' he said.

Martha had been sitting in the opposite corner reading a book called *Corporate Finance Structures*. Armoured by her job, her twenty-three years and her ugliness, she had chipped in: 'This country? What have we ever seen of this country? New Brighton, a tatty little strip of dirty sand the other side of the Mersey – and you practically strap on your gunbelt to go there!'

Jack's answer was a flick of his thick fingers, sending her heavy book flying from her hands. Carol, bewildered, had looked at her brochure, twisting and blackening on the fire, and she'd wondered vaguely if the incident had had anything to do with the glistening, golden young man on the front cover. He looked as if he were charring in the fires of everlasting damnation. From then on she had smuggled her holiday brochures into the house like pornography and read them by the light of the paraffin lamp before she went to sleep.

Her reverie was interrupted by the heavy, familiar footsteps in the yard. 'How long are you going to be stuck in there?'

She ran indoors, through the kitchen where Janet, last of all as usual, was now having her own meagre breakfast, and up the stairs to her bedroom.

She discarded her dressing gown and slipped on her Sunday best, the skirt and blouse she wore for church. She tried to rub some colour into her pale cheeks. She wore no make-up. Jack wouldn't allow it. He had beaten her mercilessly the time he caught her wearing Martha's lipstick.

She looked in the mirror. Her cheeks remained immutably ivory. She sighed and put on her Sunday topcoat.

She still looked like a ragamuffin. But she looked like a ragamuffin who had made an effort.

At the bottom of the stairs she met Janet and Martha, who was just leaving for her tax office across the river.

Janet's heart went out to this spunky scrap of a girl. Ever since she had taken the family over from the beautiful, dead Claire fourteen years ago, she had seen this child fight the poverty, the deprivation, the lack of love from her father, his violence, the harshness of the nuns at school; and the girl hadn't been downed. In the early years, she had seen her cry and had dried her tears. She hadn't had to dry them for a long time now. And here she was, having got her own job by her own initiative, her severe little face showing the apprehension of the unknown that she was trying so hard to hide.

Much the same thoughts were going through Martha's head. On an impulse, she took off a hyacinth blue chiffon scarf she was wearing and tied it around her sister's neck. It was on the same wavelength as her eyes. Then she kissed her quickly and went. 'Good luck, kiddo!'

Janet hugged her hard. 'Good luck, Carol, love. Here's your flask and your sandwiches. Mind you eat them all now.' She hugged her again. 'I'm proud of you,' she added.

Carol thought how much she loved this feminine woman, whom she had always thought of as her mother, although she knew she was not. 'I've always been proud of you,' she answered and fled. Displays of the softer emotions were rare in the Blair family.

She started her long walk to Marshall & Nephew, trying to feel grown-up and not just a schoolgirl in masquerade. The shock hit her round the first corner. Perhaps she should have been expecting it, but she wasn't. Her stomach reeled. This time it was not just four of them, but a whole gang. And they weren't girls, they were boys. She saw that four of them were the brothers of her attackers the night before, the Pratt, Oakley, Minter and O'Brien boys. The rest were their school cronies.

They were blocking her way. There was no way past and if she ran the gauntlet, she knew she would end up with her clothes in strips and her face a horror story. She hesitated, totally without resources.

'Come on, smart-arse,' shouted the Pratt boy, 'mustn't be late for work!'

'We've come to wish you luck, fuck-face,' shouted another.

'We want to see how fast you can run on a broken leg,' jeered a third.

She stood there, frozen, trying to think of a plan. She hadn't got much time. They weren't going to wait for her to come to them: any minute now they were going to come for her. Her best chance was to turn back and run for it.

She looked over her shoulder, making sure her escape route was clear, and her heart plummeted. Coming round the corner for which she'd planned to make was a bunch of the hardest cases the boys' school had. The roughest, toughest villains in St Michael's, an academy which did not grant such superlatives lightly. She watched them, slouching towards her like some collective rough beast and suddenly she almost jumped for joy.

There, in the middle of them, diminished by their hulking silhouettes, was Tony. He was grinning at her.

Her second surprise was the gangly presence among them of Ike Palmer, who had never been one of the tough mob.

They surrounded her like big, friendly dogs, while her enemies looked on in dismay.

'Hello, Car – hear you got a job', 'Member of the bleeding working classes now', 'You don't half look good, Car', 'You look the gear!', 'Here – can you – er – touch up my positives?'

They ignored the gang at the corner, ambling forward with Carol in the middle of them as if it were the most coincidental meeting in the world. They strolled at and through the opposition as if completely unaware of its presence. And the opposition, although outnumbering the hard men, dissolved away into the morning like so many Disprin in water.

The lads walked her out of the ghetto and into respectability at the beginning of Dale Street. Then they left and ran back to school to face a whipping for being late, always supposing there was a teacher on duty that day who was even rougher than they were.

Carol walked on, glowing with the pleasure of the knowledge of her brother's love for her, of his resourcefulness and protectiveness. And of the help so effortlessly extended to her by the young gorillas he had somehow rounded up. She wondered why her father always pretended to regard Tony as a cissy: maybe it was because he always got top marks for art.

She looked down proudly at her Sunday clothes. It really was as if everything were starting to be different. The world had a lustre on it like when you sometimes got a new pair of shoes for Easter and you walked all the way to church, glancing down at them, terrified to see the first wrinkle. She was due for a rude reassessment when she reached Marshall's.

She got there at two minutes past nine, despite running the last two hundred yards. Mr Mackenzie was standing in the exact geometrical centre of the shop, a big gold hunter watch resting flat on the palm of his hand like a hamburger with an egg on it. 'What sort of time d'you call this?' was his greeting.

What could she say - 'I was attacked by a gang of boys and rescued by a gang of toughs?' Long ago she had realised that, whatever it read in the newspaper, the rest of the city refused to believe in the kind of things that happened in her corner of it. She said, 'I didn't realise all the buses would be full, so I had to walk.' It was half true, anyway. He wasn't to know she'd have walked in any case.

'That's no excuse,' said Mackenzie. 'In future get up sooner. The earlier buses are less full. There's one thing you have to learn about this establishment, lassie. Excuses for unpunctuality based on the breakdown or non-availability or internal congestion of buses are not acceptable.' He lowered his head, gazing at her from under bushy eyebrows. 'I hope that is clear?'

'Yes,' she said.

'Yes, sir, would be more appropriate, don't you think?' Oh, Christ, it was going to be just like school, after all!

'Yes, sir.'

Now he raised his head and tilted it backwards so that he was gazing down the pitted moon-landscape of his whisky-eroded nose at her: 'I hope I haven't made a mistake with you, lassie.'

For the second time that morning, her stomach rocked on its shock absorbers. 'Oh, no, sir. I'm sure you haven't, sir.'

'We'll see. It is now five past nine. Knackford will show you where to put your coat, then you'd better start making up for lost time.'

Knackford, his pale freckled face looking more than ever like breadcrumbs scattered on milk pudding, took her to the staffroom at the back and showed her where to hang her coat.

'Don't worry too much about Mackenzie,' he whispered, 'he's much better after lunch.' He reached down a pale blue nylon overall. 'Here, you have to wear this.'

She put it on. It was too big. Especially too long in the sleeves. 'Listen,' said Carol, 'I know the girl before me was up the stick, but that only swells your stomach, it don't do nothing to your arms. Her knuckles must have brushed the floor!'

'She was a big girl all over,' said Knackford, 'if you know what I mean, like.' His eyes rested contemplatively on her breasts. They were beginning to be round and full, quite out of keeping with the rest of her.

'You can keep your eyes off Tom and Jerry,' said Carol flatly, 'they're not on the market.'

'I was just looking,' he protested, 'to see how the overall fitted.'

'It makes me look like a bloody pole holding up a tent,' she said, rolling up the sleeves until her hands emerged, as if gasping for air.

Mackenzie shouted from the body of the shop: 'When you're quite finished in there!'

'Yes, Mr Mackenzie!' shouted Knackford, making a face

for Carol's benefit, waiting for her to laugh.

'Yes, sir, coming, sir,' shouted Carol, not laughing at all. This might all be a yawn to Knackford, but so far as she was concerned it beat the hell out of school and she wasn't going to jeopardise it by playing silly buggers.

At home, Jack had been down to the docks and come back. There wasn't a cargo for an hour. He had excess energy to work off and Janet knew how he wanted to do it. She wasn't complaining. Janet was a passionate woman, though few people would have guessed it to look at her – only those who noticed the unobtrusive fullness of the lower lip, the well-cut wideness of the upper, the slight flair of the nostrils which the pinching of deprivation had somewhat disguised.

She watched him undress. She loved his body. The broad, deep shoulders tapering down to the narrow waist and hips that fitted so snugly between her thighs. The soft, curling hair on his chest with one skein of it crisping its way in a straight line down the centre of his flat, hard stomach, a gap for his navel, then on down again to meet with the animal fur that grew round his balls and penis.

She loved rippling gently around in that with her finger-tips and he loved her to do it. It was one of the things that roused him most quickly. 'We have lift-off!' she'd joke to herself in her mind – Jack didn't like her to talk while they were making love. He made enough row for two, anyway, she thought fondly.

The first time she had laid eyes on Jack a charge had rippled through her body, seeming to start at her toes, up the insides of her thighs, into her vagina, swirled around briefly in her stomach then into her breasts and face, which turned scarlet. To her intense embarrassment she had discovered that she was instantly lubricated, ready for him: to such an extent that she was glad she was not sitting down.

It was to take five years and the intervention of tragedy to bring him to her at last.

She lay on her stomach on the bed now, waiting for him. He liked to start this way. He knelt beside her, lifted her not exactly sylph-like body effortlessly in his arms and rolled her on to her back, almost as if he were rolling a carpet about. For a big, violent man he was astonishingly gentle most of the time in his love-making, showing his strength only in the effortless way he could manipulate her body.

He ran his mouth over her nipples, holding them tight between his lips when they hardened, pinning her arms with his hands when she tried to pull him away: he liked her to struggle a little at first.

Still pinning her hands, he kissed her all the way down her body to the mistiness – her hair had never been very thick there – between her legs. She clamped her thighs together, bending her knees and raising her legs. She laughed as he forced them apart with his head, starting at her knees then pushing, sliding downwards until he buried his face in the heart of her. There his tongue played havoc, flickering around her clitoris like a flame, penetrating her like a gentle dagger, withdrawing to caress the surrounding clefts and gullies.

At the moment when she felt she couldn't wait a pulse-beat longer he entered her: slowly, conscious of his size, pushing, retreating, pushing upwards, inwards, ever upwards until he filled her totally, his weight compounding the feeling of fullness and completeness; and all the time talking, shouting, groaning as a rough man might and yet he was not rough: until he came like a warm mountain torrent and she was full of his sperm, which was fragrant, like that of a very young man.

And what she had never been able to do was to connect the man with the lover. It was as if two people inhabited the same magnificent body. The miserly, misanthropic lout which, for the most part, she and his children saw and the tender, considerate bringer of Eros in the bedroom.

If Jack had been a man for self-analysis it might have occurred to him that the intense pleasure he derived from sex was the only charm powerful enough to exorcise temporarily the demons that normally rode him. They were memories of things that had happened to him and his parents and brothers and sisters during the Depression of the thirties. The bellies literally swollen from starvation, the eating of roasted rats, the feeling, when gleaming motor cars splashed you in the rain without its occupants so much as noticing you were there, that you were less than human.

Two of his sisters had gone on the streets and he had watched his big father cry the first time they brought home the food for the family that he couldn't provide. Watching him, Jack had nearly choked on the food himself, ravenous though he was.

He still hadn't got a big appetite.

But in the bedroom, when the glory flowed through him, memory was drowned.

At the shop, it was lunchtime. Carol declined Knackford's invitation to the local pub and took her flask and sandwiches down to the Pier Head, according to the nuns the largest floating landing stage in the world, stretching for half a mile on ninety pontoons. She'd always loved the place – the smell of the sea, mixed with tar and hemp, the muddy slate-green of the Mersey, just like her sister Martha's eyes, and the way the floating runways sloped perilously downwards or upwards, according to whether the tide was in or out. When they sloped down, she liked to run, letting the momentum mount perilously, stopping just short of plunging into the river.

Today she thought that unworthy of a working citizen, so she walked down demurely and found herself a bench in the lee of the wind.

She unwrapped her sandwiches as she watched the chunkily muscled ferries churning to and fro, spewing out and swallowing up passengers. She loved all the rope-throwing and making fast and the smell of hot engine rooms they brought with them – a smell, in the curious pattern of her fate, that was to reach forwards and backwards, always able to touch the most powerful capsules of memory. She bit into her sandwich and was happy.

What she didn't know was that she had attracted the attention of 'The Vicar'.

'The Vicar' haunted the Pier Head at lunchtime like a gaunt incarnation of mono-tracked lechery. Others of his general type, but lookers rather than doers, frequented Water Street on the way to the river, where its powerful gusts of wind, straight from the Mersey Bar, could usually be guaranteed to lift a few typists' skirts all the way up to their ripe bottoms. 'The Vicar', however, preferred the frail-looking weediness and lack of finish of immaturity.

And when he found it, he liked to touch it. Perhaps, even, to have it touch him.

He found it in Carol, sitting minding her own business, eating her bread-and-dripping sandwiches in what 'The Vicar' decided was a delightfully secluded corner of the Pier Head. He watched her covertly for five minutes, building his excitement. Then along he came in his clerical grey and dog collar, to which he had about as much right as a Dobermann Pinscher, and sat down with modest gravity next to her. He was humming a snatch of *Greensleeves.*

He had found that *Greensleeves* had a reassuring, tranquillising sound, redolent of country rectories dozing in the sun, their gardens full of wallflowers and petunias, their interiors gleaming with wax polish and the smell of scones in the oven. To Carol, the tune was like that bleeding Morris dancing she had had to do at school and she sighed internally.

'What a very pleasant day,' said 'The Vicar', in what he fondly imagined was a genteel accent, but which, in fact, sounded as if someone had attached his adenoids to his uvula and put them in a state of perpetual tension.

He spoke the phrase as if to the world at large, not looking at Carol, and Carol was perfectly happy to leave it that way.

'The Vicar', however, was not a man to be put off by silence. 'On such a day as this,' he continued, still addressing his words to an invisible congregation of thousands and one seagull, 'one feels the all-pervading presence of the Almighty, even in the breezes of our own beloved Mersey.'

Carol thought privately that the breezes of our own beloved Mersey were bloody cold. She wore no stockings:

for some reason, her father had never allowed them. All she had between her and the shrewd blasts from over the water were the short woollen knee socks she'd worn to school, another small detail that had the testosterone bucking in 'The Vicar's' veins. Now he turned to her. Subtlety was wasted on this child. The direct approach was the answer.

'Don't you think so?' he asked, looking her straight in the eye for the first time, slightly disconcerted, like most people, by that blue dazzle.

'You what?' was her elegant rejoinder.

Not encouraging, thought 'The Vicar'. Nevertheless. 'Doesn't this God-given freshness,' he perserved, 'bring you to an awareness of another reality beyond our own?' He had often found that blinding them with word power brought a most gratifying response. As if someone who talked such high-flown crap couldn't be all bad. He shifted slightly towards her.

Carol realised that he was out of his league. The poor bugger had probably been pulling this line successfully with posh kids from Queen's Drive and Calderstones Park and Heswall for years. From Scotland Road's point of view he should have been in a glass case.

'How d'you mean?' she asked, pulling out another bread-and-dripping sandwich and ingeniously contriving to drop a blob of grease on his trousers. He swallowed his irritation and pulled out the handkerchief he always wore on show in his top pocket, a powerful item in his armoury of respectability totems.

'I mean,' he said, squeezing away at the grease spot with the dedicated expertise of a lifelong bachelor, 'that the Lord resides in all things for those who have eyes to see.' He again bunked up another six inches nearer to her.

'What about,' she asked, biting with careful relish into her sandwich and trying to drop another grease bomb on his trouser, a move which he deftly deflected, 'what about that muck they're sucking up over there?' She pointed to a dredger, scooping up ooze from the bed of the Mersey.

'Who knows what God sees in it?' riposted 'The Vicar',

rather neatly, he thought, sidling up another three inches. Once you had them chatting, you'd got it made.

'God sees shit like anyone else,' said Carol easily, unscrewing the top of her flask.

Sophisticated as she was for her age, there were aspects of human nature that were still a closed book to Carol. She couldn't yet understand that the contrast between her deliberate crudeness of thought and her slightly green and sickly delicacy of physique was an incitement to him.

He slid even closer. Now they were sitting hip to hip.

'You mustn't think like that, my dear,' he said, the unction in his voice almost as oily as her sandwiches, 'nothing is distasteful in the eyes of the Lord. Everything that is, everything we do, all our desires are part of the glory of His Creation . . . '

Absent-mindedly, his hand rested on her bare, bony knee. 'Everything is precious to Him and He is pleased when we take pleasure in it.' His hand slid casually up the pale young thigh. He thought it was the smoothest and the most vulnerable surface across which his spatulate fingers had ever slid. There was a romantic quality about the flesh of young girls, which was not to be found later. His hands, his thoughts and his penis drifted upwards.

'Get your bleeding hand off my leg,' said Carol, almost casually.

'I beg your pardon?'

'I said get your bleeding hand off of my bleeding leg,' she repeated, still with dangerous nonchalance.

He did not remove his hand. Indeed, he insinuated it an inch or two higher and towards the inside, where the skin became even finer and smoother and slightly damp.

'Come now, my dear,' he said, 'we are all God's creatures. I am sure the friendly intimacy of touch between His children is something He intended and approves of.' He smiled reassuringly. 'You can touch me if you like.'

'Oh, yes?' she responded, her face unreadable. 'Where had you got in mind, like?'

'Well, I should think about here,' he said. He took her hand and placed it over the throbbing pouch of his straining flies.

With the casualness that had characterised her attitude to the whole encounter, Carol took her hand away and tipped the entire, scalding contents of her flask over his wildly pulsating private parts. He leaped to his feet with the soundless agony on his face of a character in a silent movie.

A second later the sound came. The kind of yell that can only emanate from a man whose tumescent member and tightened scrotum have been engulfed and enveloped by a flaskful of sugar-sticky tea at something approaching boiling point.

'You bloody little cow!' In his voice the sacred had given way to the profane with a vengeance. Desperately, he hopped about, trying to pull the still-scalding trousers from his crutch. All pretence at dignity had been abandoned: he twitched and wriggled like an ant on a hotplate, his language Biblical only in its variety and picturesqueness.

And his activity and his noise were his undoing. For he attracted the attention of PC Banks.

PC Banks, large and measured in his manner, had been watching the crowds pushing off the ferries for pickpockets. He had a particular down on 'dips', having once had his own whistle and watch nicked from under his nose, a fact they had still not let him forget at the station. He had been there an hour and felt bored and frustrated.It was therefore with all the joy of a man meeting a long-lost friend that he now moved towards Carol and her molester.

'Well, if it isn't Charlie the Vicar! Back in your old haunts, are you, Charlie? Get fed up with the benches in Sefton Park?'

'I am an ordained minister of the Church of the Universal Brotherhood of Christ the Compassionate, of Phoenix, Arizona,' boomed Charlie, 'and I have a diploma to prove it.' His trousers were now turning icy cold in the breeze.

'Aye,' said Banks, 'well you'd better stick your diploma down your trousers before you get frostbite.' He turned to Carol. 'Now then, love,' he asked, as a pure formality, 'has this man been molesting you?'

She had to think quickly. There were so many unknowns in the situation. And as always when she needed to think fast, her brain seemed to freeze. 'Yes . . . er . . . no – er . . . what does molest mean?' she stammered. Her experiences at school with those accomplished black-wimpled descendants of the Spanish Inquisition had taught her the value of stalling, if only for a moment.

'Did he have his hand up your drawers, love?' Banks explained kindly.

Carol felt suddenly as generations of women had felt in her place before her. That, in some obscure way, the fact that it had happened at all was her fault. In that second, she saw clearly the dreadful truth which up to now she had only sensed and knew the kind of trouble she was in. She had to stamp on it now – and quickly.

'Nothing happened,' she said firmly. 'He never done nothing. My flask slipped and I spilled my tea on him, that's all.'

But Constable Banks had had a thin week – a sneak thief and a parking on a pedestrian crossing. He wasn't going to let this one go without a struggle. He got out his notebook. 'Still hanging out the same place, Charlie – Ma Bernie's in Upper Parliament Street?'

'Yes,' said Charlie, sullenly.

'Don't leave the bishop's palace without telling me,' said Banks.

Charlie scowled.

Banks turned to Carol. 'And your name and address, miss?'

And it was then, in blind panic, that Carol made her fatal error. 'Jane Lucas, 43 Queen's Drive,' she said and from that utterance onwards never knew another moment's peace.

A fortnight later, it happened. One night, after tea, there was a knocking at the door which was different in rhythm and authority from all the others. And Carol knew, as surely as if she could see through it, who was waiting on the other side.

Her father answered the knock and a second later Constable Banks clumped into the kitchen behind Jack Blair, the two of them together seeming to fill the room from wall to wall.

The ghetto didn't like coppers. It was a disgrace to have one in your house. Jack Blair liked them less than most. It was with a face like a thunderhead that he said to Carol: 'This copper reckons he's got business with you.'

Banks had his helmet off, looking like a dog with no collar on. 'You've given us a right old runaround, miss.'

Martha and Tony were out, but Janet was there, her face like a mask, her eyes two dark pools of fright.

'She gave us a false name and address,' said Banks. Carol felt sick, her flesh hot, but her skin clammy cold. 'Your name's Blair, Carol Blair – is that right?'

'Yes.' Her head was swimming.

Jack butted in. 'What business did you have taking her name and address anyway?' he demanded.

Then Banks told them the story and with every ponderous word Carol could see how the picture looked worse and worse for her on the poisoned photographic plate of her father's mind. She had a feeling of suffocation. She felt guilty of something and the fact that she wasn't only increased her mental turmoil.

Jack's eyes were fixed, not on the policeman, but on her.

When Banks had finished, he turned to her. 'Now then,' he said, 'nobody's accusing you of anything – apart from the false address and we'll come to that in a minute. But we have to know the truth. What happened? Did he indecently assault you or not?'

And at that point, when she heard that ugly legal term, it came to Carol what she had to do. She had to lie and lie and lie. Earlier, she had thought that the easiest way would be to tell the truth – after all, she hadn't done anything to be ashamed of. But now she saw that it wouldn't stop there.

If she told the truth, there would be more questions, more precise and intimate details to be given. It would end up in court with scores of strangers salivating over it.

And then at the end of it, when Charlie the Vicar had been found guilty, if he was found guilty, which wasn't a certainty, there would be the knowing voices of the women in her street and all around, over the backyard walls and the washing lines: 'It takes two to tango!' Nudge, nudge. 'I'll bet the little hussy led him on', 'You can't tell me he didn't get the come-on from that little madam.'

'So he didn't approach you in any way?' Banks was asking.

'He did say something about God's creation and what a nice day it was,' said Carol.

'Was it a nice day?'

'No, it was very blowy.'

'Didn't you think that was odd?'

'I thought he was odd altogether, but he never done nothing.'

'You're sure of that? It only takes the slightest touch.'

'No, nothing like that.' She could feel the vibrations from her father.

Banks dropped it for the moment, his manner kindly. Indeed, he did feel kindly towards this waif. He looked at the fires in the eyes of her disturbingly quiet father. He weighed up his size – a six-man job if ever he had to be arrested and didn't want to go, he reflected. And he thought he knew the reason for the terror in the kid's eyes, which matched the fury in her father's.

'Why did you give me a false address?' he asked, gently.

'I've never had nothing to do with the police,' she answered, 'I was frightened.'

Yes, frightened of me-laddo there, thought Banks, looking at Jack Blair's clenched hand and whitened knuckles. Christ, the damage some parents do!

He turned back to Carol. 'You realise that technically you've committed an offence, love?' he asked. 'Obstructing the police in the performance of their duty.'

'Yes. I'm very sorry.'

She did look very pale and frightened and contrite and Constable Banks was aware that it was not he who inspired her fear. 'And you're sure he never touched you?' he asked once more. 'Remember you're talking to a policeman and that's very serious – like being on oath. Do you give me your word that he didn't touch you at any time?'

'No, he never,' answered Carol.

'That'll do me,' he said decisively; 'that'll do the police force.' He rose with deliberation. 'As for the false name and address, well, I dare say you had your reasons.' As he said it, he looked directly at Jack.

Jack's eyes blazed arrogantly back at him. If ever you do have to be arrested, I hope I'm there, thought Banks. Janet showed him out down the hallway.

And now came the moment Carol had been dreading for what seemed like years, the encounter that all her lies and wrigglings had been designed to avoid. Jack picked her up bodily by the armpits and literally threw her into an armchair. 'All right, let's have it, you little slut!' he shouted.

'It's nothing,' she protested. 'It's like I told the scuffer.'

'Well now you're telling me,' said Jack, 'not some thickhead from the nick.'

Janet came hurrying back from the front door. She'd been expecting trouble. 'I said let's have it,' Jack repeated.

Janet hastened in. 'Jack, the poor kid's had enough. Do we have to go into it all again?'

'Yes, we bloody well do! The penny hasn't dropped with you yet, has it? This all happened two weeks ago and we didn't know a thing about it. If this crafty little bitch's lie about her name and address had worked, we'd never have known anything about it at all.'

'Why should we have?' asked Janet, 'when nothing happened?'

'Nothing happened, my arse! Her first day at work and she lets herself be mauled by a filthy old sod on a bench!'

'I did not, you dirty-minded bastard!' screamed Carol, her Blair blood ignited at last, all the tension of the last fortnight exploding. 'He put his hand on my knee and I poured my tea over his prick. That's all there was to it. Anything else is in that creepy bloody mind of yours!'

Janet intervened, alarmed. God, the passion in these Blairs, especially these two! 'Carol, love, don't! You'll make things worse.'

But Carol was past it. The chemicals her anger had poured into her bloodstream had taken over. 'Things couldn't be worse!' she screamed. 'My own father thinks I'm some kind of . . . dirty . . . sick . . . thing, who likes being touched by old men! Well, it's just come to me: I can't understand why I've never rumbled it before – he's the one who's sick. He's got worms in his head!'

Her father had gone white. Janet tried to drag her from the room. She held on to a table, grimly determined to finish. 'Why can't I wear no make-up? Why do I have to have my skirts halfway down to the ankles? Why can't I wear no scent? It's all because he thinks they're sinful. He's a bloody nun in trousers! He thinks they're sinful because they turn him on, that's what it's all about!'

Jack Blair got up without a word and went out into the back kitchen where he kept his razor strop.

'Get out,' said Janet to Carol, urgently, 'get out; I'll handle him.'

'And leave you to get beaten up instead of me? No, thanks, Mum.'

Her father came back into the room, the heavy strop in his hand. He advanced on Carol.

She snatched up the poker, something she had never done in her life before. She couldn't have explained why she did it now: she had always taken her beatings mildly, as part of the pattern of things. She backed away, the poker held high. 'Don't touch me,' she threatened.

'Don't you raise your hand to me, you blasphemous bitch!'

He came at her swiftly and she brought the poker down wildly at him with all her force. He sidestepped with a massive grace which she noted even while she was hating him, held out the flat of his hand and caught the poker in his saddle-hard palm as if it had been a lollipop stick. Nevertheless, she saw the pain of it stain his eyes. That and a fractional deepening of the creases that ran down the sides of his cheeks to his jawbone were the only indications he gave. Then he clenched her by the back of the neck with one huge hand.

He dragged her over to a chair, brushing aside his pleading wife. He sat down, bent her forward over his knee and trapped her head under the other knee. Then he started the steady, merciless strokes of the strop.

Now that she was growing up, he no longer bared her bottom. But he did lift her skirt and for Carol the humiliation of that was almost as great.

It was as the blood started to ooze through Carol's knickers that Tony and Martha came in. Tony was into the kitchen first. He took one look at the blood on his sister and reached a bottle of milk from the kitchen table. He had picked the spot behind his father's right ear and his arm was drawn back when Martha came in.

She was cool and swift. She used the one weapon against which she knew Jack had no defence - her irony. 'What's up, Dad?' she asked. 'Dull night on telly?'

He looked up at her, arrested, a glaze dispersing from his eyes. 'You want to watch that mouth,' he said, 'you're not too old to have your own arse tanned.'

Martha spoke mildly, unslinging her handbag from her shoulder and masking Tony while he replaced the milk bottle. 'Yes, well let's have tea first, shall we?' she said. 'What have we got, Mum?'

'I'll get it,' said Janet eagerly, wondering what it was that gave this puddingy girl the courage to stand up to Jack Blair like that, while Martha sat down swiftly to disguise the fact that her knees were trembling.

'I'll get it,' said Tony.

Carol, using every ounce of willpower she had, straightened her back and stood up, instead of slumping to the floor as her body desperately wanted to do. Her stepmother took her out to the back kitchen with a clean piece of rag and the only bottle of antiseptic in the house.

Carol, on her way out, in agony as she was, saw the expression in Tony's eyes as he looked at his father. Things might have turned out very differently later that night if she hadn't.

3

Carol awoke suddenly. She was curled foetally on her side. She could not, at first, place what it was that had woken her; she normally slept fathoms deep. Perhaps it was the pain in her buttocks.

Then a strange thing happened. She was sure that Martha was asleep; there she was, in the bed next to hers. But she found she was equally sure that Tony was not asleep, but very much awake. What was more, that he was not in his room next door.

Now it was starting to filter back – what had woken her in the first place. It had been noises – furtive noises. She wasn't sure how long ago. Someone opening a door with infinite caution – like that story *The Tell-Tale Heart* she'd read at school. She had the same feeling of terror now as the story had conveyed to her then.

Tony wasn't in his room, she knew it. So the person opening his door like that horrible man in the story had been Tony. But why would he want to open his door like that? He could be going to the backyard, to the lavatory, of course. But he'd done that before tonight and the noise he made was usually enough to awaken the dead. Why the eerie quietness?

Moving as furtively as she believed Tony to have done, she slid out of bed and opened the bedroom door a millimetre at a time, a pounding iciness around her heart.

In the moonlight that shone through her window, dimly illuminating the landing, she saw Tony. His back was to her and he was reaching for the handle of the door to her parents' bedroom in that same, slow, horrible way as the man in the story. What was worse – oh, God, please let her be dreaming! – the moonlight was glinting on something in his right hand. It was a carving knife! Held the way Tony was holding it, she had never seen anything look so evil in all her young life.

As she stood, frozen with shock, he eased open the bedroom door and went in. Released into action, she slipped through her door like a wraith, ran barefoot and silent as a mist-patch along the four yards of landing that separated her from her parents' bedroom and slid silently in.

In the dim light she could see that Janet was on her side, deeply asleep. Jack was on his back, the clothes thrown off him, snoring gently. Tony was standing over his father, the knife glittering in his hand, gazing down on him. She could not see his face.

She skimmed towards him soundlessly and threw her arms around him from behind, pinioning his. At the same time, she pressed her blanched, cool young cheek against his burning face.

He could have broken free without effort, but his sister's gift of loving, unspoken communication and compassion was so powerful it was as if his murderousness dropped from him like a coat falling from his shoulders. The hand holding the knife slackened and Carol caught it just before it would have crashed to the floor.

Silently, she urged Tony out of the bedroom and back down the landing. He did not resist, moving slackly, like a puppet. She guided him into his own room and sat him on his bed. Then she held him for a long, long time.

In his bedroom, Jack finally opened his eyes fully and relaxed. Contrary to what Carol believed, he had caught the look in his son's eye. He had seen it once before, in the eyes of a crane driver he had thrashed in some dockside brawl. Half an hour later a cable had mysteriously slipped on that driver's crane and a two-ton crate of machine parts had missed Jack by six inches.

He had lain in bed, knowing Tony was going to do something about it, wondering what he would try. He had listened to his own son come creeping along the landing to kill him and prepared his counter-move. Then he waited.

He was not shocked. Jack didn't judge violence in the normal way. To him, a son determining to kill his father was a practical consideration, not a moral one.

When Carol intervened, his primary emotion was one of disappointment. He would have liked to have known for certain that his son had the guts to do it. However, he reflected that he would have to watch the little bugger. The next time he might have his back to him. Jack went to sleep almost with a sense of satisfaction.

In the last of the three tiny bedrooms, also with her quota of old coats piled on top of the bed to keep out the cold, Martha slept in ignorance of the drama that had just been played out in their crumbling snail's shell of a house.

Her eyes flickered to and fro beneath her lids as she dreamed of a huge, pretty plant that had reached out for her with its tendrils and lifted her gently, but irresistibly, towards its central stem. Now her thighs were sliding around the stem, through no act of her own, but because there was no resisting the imperative pull of the powerful tendrils. Her body was pulled tight against the slippery, smooth, yet gently abrasive stem and held there. Then something else was happening that was not quite clear yet. She made a small noise and rolled, in her sleep, towards the edge of the mattress, on her stomach, one hinged-back thigh sliding over, her knee slung in the hammock of the tucked-in sheet.

Martha had a rich dream life. She sometimes looked at her colleagues in the tax office from behind those muddily opaque green eyes and wondered what they'd say if they knew what wild, impossible sensualities happened to her each night in the recesses of her mind.

The building had been an old mansion before it was converted for the Inland Revenue. Each office was more like a cosy reception room, increasing in size and grandour according to the seniority of its occupant. Martha occupied what was once probably a sitting room, a small one. Beautiful little fireplace in honey-veined marble, probably not

Adam, and panelled walls, duck-egg blue, the panel surrounds picked out in white.

At that point all aesthetic considerations ceased. Four desks – Ministry of Supply Regular Issue – had been bunged in and four tax officers slammed behind them. The carpet, also, was regulation issue for their grade, beige – by merciful accident matching the fireplace, but stopping far short of the walls. However, they did have a lovely old silver-haired retainer to top up all the fires in the building. It was rumoured that he had nothing to do with the Inland Revenue at all, but had managed to hide, like the old servant Firs in *The Cherry Orchard*, when the owners had left, only to re-emerge from his cupboard when the new masters took over.

Certainly, the whole ambience was so much grander, more gracious, unimaginably more sweet than the hovel to which she returned each night that Martha was always the first to offer to stay late, if that was necessary.

It was into this environment, into her very room, that George Ironstile had clumped that afternoon and demanded to see her by name. 'Which of you lot is Martha Blair?'

'Well, you can rule two of us out, can't you?' answered Peter Taylor, office wag and one of her two male companions in the office. He nodded across at the other one, John Atkins. 'That leaves you two, then,' said Ironstile, looking at Martha and the other girl, Isabella Moore. He had a strong Lancashire accent and he was wearing bulbous-nosed, short-ankled boots under his shortish trousers. He was as square and chunky as a tugboat and his hair looked like a black-bristled, thick-pile scrubbing brush. 'Come on,' he said, small brown eyes smoking in his ham-red face, 'I haven't got all day to fuck about!'

'I'm Martha Blair,' she said, 'and if you use language like that to me I'll have you chucked out on your bloody ear. Who are you, anyway, you great tub of lard?'

He'd been expecting some pale-blooded, grammar school milksop. Her directness, her accent and her bloody-mindedness hit him between wind and water. He took a second or two to recover, but the blood of the Ironstiles was in him and he recovered well. 'My name's George Ironstile,' he said, 'and you've had your hand in my bloody pocket long enough!'

Martha's face cleared as recognition dawned. This was the thick-head she'd been having trouble with for years. He ran a small scrap-iron business in Preston, employing about seven people, three of them casuals. He hadn't filed a CT61 in two and a half years, he never seemed to have heard of an employer's responsibility to deduct Pay As You Earn tax from his workers' wages on behalf of the government. And national insurance contributions – both his as an employer and his workers' as employees – appeared to mean to him some obscure method of forcing him and his men to pay for the nation's false teeth – both upper and lower sets – single-handed.

He systematically ignored every communication she sent him: every letter, every demand, every request for information. Periodically, she would have recourse to the Red Demand, threatening court action and peremptory seizure of his possessions unless he paid a certain sum. The sum would then, at the last hour, be forthcoming: Martha always had the feeling the cheque must have been written in arterial blood, somehow blackened by exposure to heat. Then the struggle to establish some form of rational contact would recommence.

She finally had recourse to the taxman's ultimate weapon, the Speculative Assessment: better known as the think-of-a-number-and-double-it or 'So They Get a Coronary?' ploy. You smack a mind-numbing figure into the box provided for it on the demand form and somewhere approximately near it you put a tiny E.

A footnote in miniscule type on the other side of the demand, which the recipient is not particularly encouraged to read, explains that the E means it's only an estimated assessment of the tax due, because the information on which to base an accurate one has not been available.

The bloodshot eyes of the recipient of this psychic stun-grenade fail totally to notice the little E, much less the even smaller footnote, but read only where it says – it seems to him – his heart is to be cut out in some public place to the accompanying jeers of the populace if he does not pay up the equivalent of the whole cost of maintaining the country's educational system for the next six months.

It was just such a bureaucratic surprise attack that had fetched George Ironstile reeling into Martha's office that afternoon.

His visit was not entirely unforeseen. It had been preceded by a letter, badly handwritten on unheaded writing paper, which read:

> Dear Madam, I have been a native of these shores for twenty-eight years. I have never asked nobody for nothing and nothing is what I've been given. Whatever I've got, I've worked my arsehole off for.
>
> I don't believe that the money you keep asking me for is being spent on defending this country from the Red menace, or keeping a load of layabouts' bellies filled while they squat in other folks' houses.
>
> I'll tell you what I think. I think the people above you know sod-all about what's going on and it's all slipping into your fucking pocket and the pockets of the fucking rest of you parasitic pisspots. I shall be coming in to sort you out at my convenience.
>
> I remain, Your Favourite Milch Cow, George Ironstile.'

Martha had read it, grinned and put it with the rest of the documentation in the George Ironstile file. Now here he was, a chancer who would think nothing of punching everything on her desk into the four corners of the room – and perhaps send her in the same directions. It was definitely a case for proceeding with caution. Martha's idea of caution, however, was not everyone's.

'Mr Ironstile,' she said, in what she considered to be a very reasonable tone, 'don't be a bloody imbecile. The tax cheques you make out, when you make them out, which is about once every blue moon, are made payable to the

Inland Revenue. How the fuck do you think I could convert them to my own use?'

'You what?' said Ironstile.

'Nick them, pay them into my account, use the fucking money,' explained Martha.

This gave Ironstile pause for thought. It was not the first pause for thought he had taken since he walked into this bloody wasps' nest. In the first place, he'd expected to be confronted by something crushable in crisp and delicate female attire, not this apprentice battleaxe in her second-hand woollens and battered tweed skirt that looked as if it had been woven out of hawthorn twigs. And in the second place he'd expected to shock her with his language, not find himself shocked by hers.

'How the hell do I know?' he said finally and feebly. He felt he hadn't done himself justice: more was needed. 'That's the whole point about you lot,' he added, 'you're bloody jugglers. You can make figures jump through crapping hoops. All I do is try and keep myself and the bloody country going; and I can't do that with you trying to cut my cock off.'

'Mr Ironstile,' said Martha, in what she imagined was a warm and sympathetic tone, 'all those forms and things I send you. I don't make them up myself. I'm just doing a job. If I didn't do it, I wouldn't eat. I pay tax on what I earn, too, and I don't like it, either. Everybody pays taxes, nobody likes it, but there's no way of getting out of it.'

He watched her face carefully; if he could only get behind those muddy-green eyes. He was beginning to decide that this was a human being he was dealing with after all, not some officially-sanctified rip-off artist. But he wasn't going to soften that easily.

'What about this, then?' he demanded. He produced from his pocket her speculative assessment on him for Corporation Tax and slammed it on the desk in front of her. 'Does everybody pay this kind of millionaire's bloody ransom?'

Martha hesitated and decided to tell this man the truth: 'That was just to get you in here,' she said.

He looked at her for a long time, the brown button eyes unwinkingly on her face, his colour steadily rising, whether from relief or anger she couldn't tell. Finally, he blinked and made a noise halfway between a seal's bark and an impression of someone being strangled. 'You brass-faced bugger,' he said, equably.

The other occupants of the room, who had never heard a conversation even remotely approaching this in a tax office in the whole of their professional careers, had now frankly abandoned all pretence of not listening and sat transfixed.

'Compliments aren't going to help you,' said Martha. 'What you need is to sit there on your backside and listen to me.'

George Ironstile, who wasn't accustomed to listening to anyone much, opened his mouth. Martha promptly shut it for him. 'I don't know how good you are at what you do with your scrap iron, but your acquaintance with figures is pathetic.'

'Listen, big mouth—'

She talked right over him. 'For instance, d'you know what I mean when I talk about Corporation Tax?'

'I know I started in my own back yard with three rusty bicycles,' he said.

She decided she had to shut him up once and for all. 'Corporation Tax,' she said, 'is chargeable on the profits of a company, generally any body corporate or unincorporated association – excluding a partnership – resident in the United Kingdom, on the amount arising in the company's accounting period.' She drew a breath. 'To arrive at the profits it is necessary to compute the company's income in accordance with income tax principles, make certain adjustments required for the purposes of Corporation Tax and add to the total a fraction of any chargeable gains computed in accordance with capital gains tax principles.'

George felt himself drowning. This bitch could keep this up all day. He made one last effort to regain ascendancy: 'Is that your own mouth you're using,' he asked, 'or are you breaking it in for an idiot?'

'Vulgar abuse,' said Martha, 'is a waste of your bad

breath and a sad drain on your limited brainpower.'

Christ, she hadn't finished yet! Martha was rolling relentlessly on. 'If you've got any land whatever and you sell it, the whole or part of capital gains from the disposal of interests in land with development value—'

There was one great virtue about George Ironstile. He knew when to cut his losses. This fat hen held all the cards. She was on her own territory, she knew her stuff and she had the power to make his life a bloody misery, she'd already proved that.

He also knew the theory of charm, although its practice was a totally different proposition altogether. He composed his bulldozer features into what might, with imagination and goodwill, be construed as a smile, his rough white teeth looking like stalactites in a pink grotto.

'Help!' he said.

Martha stopped in her flow. 'How d'you mean?' she asked, determined to make him go the whole way.

He nudged his chair six inches nearer her desk. 'I'd never get the hang of it by myself, not in a hundred years,' he said, 'and I can't afford an accountant.'

She sat watching him, her face expressionless, silently admiring this brazen-faced turnabout.

'Bring your chair round here,' she said.

He did. It was the best move George Ironstile had ever made in his life.

Spring and summer were the busy times at Marshall & Nephew as people came in with their lobster-faced images of themselves, photographed on hot and alien islands between one dash to the lavatory and the next. Carol's workload increased.

Just at this moment, she was enjoying her mid-morning tea break in a particularly curious fashion. While Mr Mackenzie and Knackford were indulging in a prim cup of tea, stiffened by a digestive biscuit, she was twisting herself, with her knickers down, into strange contortions in the Ladies' Lavatory. She had earlier knocked back her tumbler of a proprietary mixture full of carbohydrates and vitamins and other goodies, guaranteed to turn skinny little scarecrows like her into miracles of firm-fleshed curvaceousness.

Something was starting to happen to her figure. Gradually, almost imperceptibly, the millimetres, the half-ounces had started to add themselves. She was still a skinny kid, but not now so noticeably so. But there was still, she noted anxiously, a disproportion between her breasts, which had never been as skinny as the rest of her, and her torso, because although her torso was gaining substance, so were her breasts, so that the ratio remained the same.

Her consolation was the cause of her contortions in front of the cloakroom mirror. There were no full-length, or even half-length mirrors at home, so that it was here that she viewed with interest the cute little crease between her buttock and the top of her thigh, a phenomenon she had noted with interest on other girls, but never until now owned herself.

'Shop, Miss Blair!' It was Mr Mackenzie, indicating that break was over and there were customers to be attended to. She pulled up her pants and went out to the counter. She had a stern little efficiency that the customers liked. She also had the very rarely displayed blinding smile, which few ever saw.

Of the few who had seen it, one was Stewart Crown. He was tall, slim, and had that heavy, dark hair that seemed to fall straight back into shape whatever happened to it. She knew that because the first time she ever saw him, he stepped off the street out of a gale, his hair flying; and as he closed the door behind him it all magically re-arranged itself on his head as he was walking towards her, his honey-coloured eyes on her face. And he had a beautiful voice.

He came in every few weeks to have films developed. In his case, she had broken one of Mr Mackenzie's strictest rules and sneaked a look at some of them. They were mostly to do with sailing and girls with rich-daddy faces in dinghies, although there was one of him in a rather new-looking lawyer's wig.

She knew from the very first moment those rich, golden eyes rested on her that he fancied her. But she knew also, by instinct, that he fancied her in a particular way. Here was a lion who was used to the best, the choicest. He fancied her as a touch of the roughs, an amusing diversion. She noticed that his interest increased when he heard her voice and accent, as raw as crude oil.

In one important sense she was right. Stewart Crown had been used to the best. In his time at Cambridge, with his lion's eyes, his slender musculature and his delicate ruthlessness, he had parted more glossily tremulous prime thighs than the banisters at a girls' school. His reputation had grown by what it fed on: there came a time when he didn't have to try any more. The banks of the Cam were lined with maidens competing for the honour of impaling themselves upon him and then going back and writing it all up in passionate analysis in their diaries.

And when he came down, with the double first he had always been expected to get, there had been no interruption in the supply of luminous, well-bred pussy. At the parties his proud father – king glass manufacturer of the North – gave to celebrate his triumph, he found the rich young Cheshire beauties he had remembered as schoolgirls, cool-frocked, hot-clefted and just as experimental as the beautiful blue-stockings under the willows on the Cam.

Perhaps it was satiety, the urge for something different, that had thrown the switch in his well-shaped head the first time he saw Carol. Undoubtedly, the sexual flares had been fired in the brain. He put it down to a jaded palate, collected his pictures and left.

But mysteriously, he found he had used up his new roll of film with remarkable rapidity and found himself, much sooner than usual, back in the lens-loaded, camera-smelling premises of Marshall & Nephew. He couldn't be sure, but he thought it was more than just tired taste buds. He did find her earthiness, some indefinable aura of the slums, her unbelievable accent, fascinating – yes. But there was something else – that solemnity on the plain ivory face, the astonishing eyes, the sudden, stunning smile. There was something that evaded him in the skinny little creature and he wanted to find it and possess it.

And in her confused way, she knew that, but mistook it for the crude desire to fuck a slum girl and so she swerved away from his beautifully flighted arrows of enquiry as to whether there was anything doing and kept her eyes down on her records book. Nevertheless, she still felt the bang in the heart and the quiver in the crotch whenever he walked in and she hoped he was the reason she had been summoned now.

It wasn't Stewart Crown. In fact, it wasn't anybody. It was just Mr Mackenzie in the act of putting down the telephone receiver and picking up a yellow duster. 'Come on, girl, come on! Mr Robert's to pay us a visit.'

'Who's Mr Robert?' she asked, the Liverpool lilt that accents any question making her sound impudent.

Mackenzie, in his agitation, took her by the ear, making her feel as if she were back at school under the iron clutch of Sister Theresa, and towed her over to the window, pointing at the legend on it. 'Marshall & Nephew! Marshall & Nephew, girl! A chain of shops all over the North. Mr Robert is the nephew!'

Mr Robert, when he arrived, proved to be a brown-haired, chunky, rugged-looking man of about thirty in a black cashmere blazer and cream slacks. He arrived in a convertible Rolls Royce Silver Cloud and, despite his look of openness, generated a faint unease. Maybe it was the button-down collar. Or it could have been the rub-off from two years at the Harvard Business School. Carol felt something clenched and secret in him.

From the moment he came in, he had eyes for nothing but her. He made a pretence of examining the stock, looked cursorily at the books, but spent most of his time on Carol's ledgers which recorded the intake and output of films for development. Mackenzie and his assistant looked on in bafflement and even Carol knew that there couldn't be much to interest him in that lot.

'Mr Mackenzie,' he called, 'd'you suppose you could find me the comparative turnover figures for the branch for the last three years. I'm sure Mr . . . er . . . will help you.'

'Certainly, Mr Robert. Right away, sir. Come, Knackford.'

Mackenzie fussed off into the nether regions, followed bemusedly by Knackford, who knew as well as Mackenzie that Head Office already had the information. Robert Marshall watched them go, then turned immediately to Carol.

'You're doing a good job, Miss Blair.'

'Thank you.'

'Are you interested in photography?'

'I wasn't when I started, but I am now.' She tried to get behind the hot brown eyes, which seemed to see a lot more of her than was actually on view.

'Ever done any?'

'I haven't got a camera.'

'I don't mean behind a camera, I mean in front of it.'

'You what?'

'Have you ever had any pictures taken of you?'

'No, nobody at home's got a camera.'

'The brown eyes seemed to get hotter. 'Photography is my hobby as well as my business. I'd like to take some shots of you.'

'What, now?'

'No, not here. I've got a fully-equipped studio at home, the proper lights, props, everything. I'd like to do it there.'

'Again Carol was aware of the tenseness in him beneath the easy, debonair manner. 'I don't know,' she said, 'I mean . . . where d'you live?'

'Helsby, in Cheshire,' he said.

To Carol, he might as well have said Russia. The fat, green, buttercup-studded plains of Cheshire were as remote to her as Moscow. To get there she imagined you practically needed a package tour. He saw the expression on her face:

'It's near Chester,' he said encouragingly, 'just the other side of the Mersey.'

'I couldn't get away,' she said, happily resolving the problem. 'My father doesn't let me out much at night.' It was true. She'd never even been to any of the clubs that were springing up like couch-grass all over the city.

'We could go now,' he countered, his aura of tension almost palpably increasing. 'It's only thirty miles away if we take the Tunnel. I could have you back home at your usual time.'

She was intrigued. He was the boss . . . well, the boss's nephew, but she had a fair idea that he ran things and it would be something new to be photographed and she'd never seen Cheshire. She nevertheless found herself putting up one last obstacle. 'I'm supposed to be working here,' she said. 'I can't just float off whenever I like.'

'That's easily arranged,' said Robert Marshall. He called: 'Mr Mackenzie!'

Mackenzie came out from the rear, flapping papers, his incendiary nose ablaze with the desire to please. 'Yes, Mr Robert, sir?'

'I think we'll leave those figures until next time. I'm impressed with Miss Blair's bookwork – a fine piece of recruitment on your part, Mackenzie.' Mackenzie shuffled with pleasure. 'In fact, I'm going to steal her for the afternoon,' Marshall continued. 'I'd like her to get some order into my photo-library at home.' He smiled. 'I'll let you have her back tomorrow.'

The smile appeared easy, but the muscles around his mouth were tight.

Without further discussion, Carol found herself being escorted outside, Marshall helping her on with her coat as they went. Behind them, Mackenzie and Knackworth exchanged a look.

Marshall ushered her into the royal blue Rolls parked outside. As she sank into the leather armchair, thicker and more deeply padded than she had seen in anyone's house, much less a car, she thought she had never smelled anything quite so delicious before. It was the scent of luxury, and it instantly took its place in her catalogue of formative smells, along with her bedroom lamp, her first river breeze and the body-steam of the back kitchen first thing in the morning.

From the Mersey Tunnel they emerged into the murk of

Birkenhead. The car, carrying its own climate and environment with it, took most of the misery out of the soot-stained, crumbling images that unrolled across the windshield. Then, with a burst of breath-soft speed they were through on to the A41, into the clipped, groomed lushness of the Wirral Peninsula with its immaculately lawned village suburbs and hamlets, its meticulously polished and painted houses, its Renoiresque riot of roses.

Carol, who had seen nothing but visual garbage for most of her life, looked at it all through the tinted glass as another kind of girl might view the bay at Lindos or the arches of Porto Cuervo for the first time.

Then lakes and meadows streamed past her window, glossy cows rotating jaws full of rich Cheshire grass; woodlands full of lady fern, dogwood and columbine seemed to brush the glittering haunches of the car. To the left she could see Helsby Marsh, the shrubby marsh-mallow herb dusting it with green and beyond that the majestic, reflective sweep of the Mersey as it pushed on out to sea.

They skirted Helsby Hill, novice climbers crawling all over it like soft-backed insects, whispered through a small wood in a swirl of leaves that had already started to fall and turned abruptly into an avenue of oaks, which Carol eventually gathered was a drive leading to a house.

As the wide façade of the house slid into view she had the sensation of being in a movie. It was pretty beyond belief: white, criss-crossed with age-blackened beams and window frames, built in the fourteenth century, lovingly improved in the fifteenth, sixteenth and seventeenth, then sprayed by the glaze of Time, fixing its beauty.

The drive finally cut through broad breasts of velvety greensward, flanked by borders glowing with late summer colour, ending eventually in golden gravel before the front door, which seemed to Carol to be about the size of that of a church, spattered with great iron studs. Marshall's manservant had heard the Rolls's crunching arrival on the gravel and was already out, a stocky, black-suited figure, opening her door. If he felt any surprise at her unexpected arrival, he didn't show it.

Marshall took her elbow and steered her through the door into the great hall, its old pictures and occasional tapestry like sombre jewels on its walls. She reflected that it could contain about a quarter of her street. 'D'you live here all alone?' she asked with frank incredulity.

'I have one wing, my uncle has the other,' said Robert Marshall, 'and I do have people to stay quite a lot.' They were on their way up the broad stairs. 'Would you like tea now or when we've finished?' he asked.

'I think after.'

Marshall nodded to the manservant, who'd been silently awaiting the answer at the foot of the stairs, one hand on the bottom pillar of the banisters, and who now turned and silently disappeared.

Marshall led the way up on to the broad, golden-carpeted gallery that ran around three sides of the hall and opened one of the doors that led off it. Carol followed him in to find herself in a completely equipped studio. It was enormous. There were spotlights and cycloramas – great sheets of paper that could be drawn down the walls from rollers to make neutral or figurative backgrounds. There were rugs, rocking horses, animal skins, artificial little gardens, sofas, a giant bed with silk coverings and wild profusions of artificial flowers. And everywhere cameras, filters, light meters, lenses, all the shiny technological toys of the rich photographer fanatic.

Marshall's tension had been increasing steadily as they got nearer his home and now, Carol thought to herself, if he had a pressure gauge in the middle of his forehead the needle would definitely be in the red. He tried to play it matily. 'All right, Carol,' he said, 'let's just see how your face lights. If you could just sit on the stool there for a moment.'

Carol perched up on a high stool while Marshall arranged lights this way and that. 'Don't worry about the dazzle,' he said as she screwed her eyes up, 'you'll soon get used to it.' He fiddled with light meters, looked at her through the viewfinder of a camera. 'Beautiful . . . beautiful,' he murmured. Carol had hoped that playing with his expensive toys would perhaps tranquillise him, but the reverse was happening. He seemed to be getting more agitated than ever.

Finally, he bent over a camera, examining it minutely and – with a heroic attempt at casualness – said, 'Fine, fine – now if you'd just go behind that screen and strip off.'

Carol thought perhaps she'd mis-heard him. 'You what?'

'If you'd just take your clothes off,' he repeated off-handedly.

'Piss off,' said Carol.

The cool, if taciturn, skipper of his lovely big cool car had suddenly started to sweat and a vein filled just by his temple. He came over to her, his control suddenly gone.

'Listen,' he said, feverishly, 'd'you like your job or don't you? D'you need your job? How would you like to be out on your ear tomorrow? How would you like to be out on your ear now? I could throw you out of the house this minute – how would you get home? What time would you get home? What would you tell your father?'

'Listen, cock,' snapped Carol, 'you're not throwing me out, I'm going. And you'd better pray I don't tell my father nothing. Because he's bloody King Kong and if he ever got hold of you he'd pull your fucking head off!'

She turned and headed for the door. She hadn't the faintest idea what she'd do once she got outside. She'd no idea where to get a bus or even if there were any, nor where they went if there were. So far as topography was concerned she might have been in Tibet.

'Look, wait a minute, I'm sorry.' Robert Marshall was taking her elbow. There was a look of contrition in the hot brown eyes. 'I shouldn't have come on like that,' he said. 'It's just that when I get a . . . compulsion . . . to photograph someone, I . . . well . . . I suppose I lose control a little bit.'

'A little bit!' snapped Carol. 'You were coming on like a Number Ten tramcar running downhill with its brakes shot!'

'I know, I realise that. I'm sorry. It's just that I've never seen anyone I wanted to photograph so much.' He was leading her imperceptibly away from the door. 'I was too abrupt.' The eyes bored into her, willing her to believe him. 'I swear to you my only motive for wanting you to take your clothes off was artistic.' She gave him a sardonic look out of her slanting azure eyes, but his fervour was beginning to reach her.

He pressed on, desperate to make his point. 'Haven't you been to art galleries? Museums? Have you never been to the Walker Gallery in Liverpool? A lot of the most famous pictures that have ever been painted are of the nude female body! Look, look here!' He took her over to a large cabinet and started to open drawers. From the drawers he pulled big, blown-up photographs of beautiful girls. They were all naked. The pictures were works of art of their kind, superbly posed, exquisitely lit, a joy to the eye and a celebration of female beauty. 'This is what I do,' he said. 'Would you be ashamed to look like that?'

She looked down at the pictures again. They weren't what she'd call dirty pictures. In fact, they were really sort of . . . classy. 'You haven't seen me,' she said, 'I'm just five matchsticks stuck together with a head on top.'

'You're slim,' he agreed, 'but you're not skinny and you've got something the camera likes.'

'Oh? What's that?' she asked sceptically.

'I can't tell you, I don't know myself. But I recognise it when I see it and the lens sees it, too. Look, I'm asking you again – would you be ashamed to look like these pictures?'

She had to be frank. 'No.'

'Well then, have we still got a problem?'

She hesitated for one last second. Then, 'No, I don't suppose we have,' she said. She moved towards the screen. 'But one wrong move out of you and I'll stuff a tripod up your arse.' She went behind the screen and started to undress. 'And another thing,' she shouted through it.

'What's that?'

'Wherever you want me to pose, you turn your back till I get there.'

'Agreed.'

She took off her last garment. 'All right, where d'you want me?'

'I think, to start with, on the bed.'

'All right, I'm coming. Eyes off!'

She peeped around the screen, saw him dutifully turn his back, and scuttled across the deep, shag-piled white carpet to the gleaming silk bed. She adopted a pose which was excruciatingly uncomfortable, but which had the virture, to her, of obscuring both her cunt and her tits. 'Okay, you can turn round.'

He turned and the chocolate eyes – hot chocolate again now – surveyed her judiciously. 'I knew you would have,' he said.

'Have what?'

'A natural talent for posing, for arranging your body in patterns.'

'This pattern, cock,' she answered, 'is to keep my you-know-which and my you-know-whats away from those prying, roast-chestnut eyes of yours.'

'That may be so,' he replied, unabashed, 'but you happen instinctively to have chosen a very pretty way of doing it.'

He pointed a seven hundred-pound Rolleiflex at her and peered into the view finder and she saw an extraordinary thing happen. He instantly got a hard on. Her head spun. When he looked at her in the flesh – nothing: that she had noticed. Looking at her in the viewfinder – a hard.

In an odd way, the discovery emboldened her. A hard at one remove sort of made it art, didn't it? In the viewfinder, he wasn't looking at her, he was already looking at a picture. It was pictures, not people, that turned him on.

She relaxed. She began to flirt with him through the viewfinder. As he took shot after shot, lighting her, re-lighting her, rushing about in a state of priapic excitement, she felt herself challenged by the throbbing bulge of that inflammatorily stimulated cock doing its erectile best to burst through the twenty-two-ounce worsted of his trousers. She became inspired, throwing herself into pose after beautiful pose, while he sweated and shot and re-lit until she thought the thing must burst out like a Sam missile and fire a starburst of come at the ceiling, leaving it dripping, viscously, like stalactites forming on the roof of a cave.

When it ultimately did happen, she didn't know whether to feel sorry or glad for him. Without being aware of it, she had struck what was, for him, an infinitely exciting attitude, which he had deliberately heightened by highlights and shadows into the ultimate, exquisite, cock-teasing trigger.

He came, like a New Zealand hot geyser, at the precise moment he hit the button to capture it for all time.

His face suddenly contorted, she saw the straining bulge in his trousers twitch convulsively and then he was down on his knees, his back to her, racked by his sexual seizure and helpless to hide it. The minute it was over, he hurried from the room with a strangled 'Excuse me' and without turning round. Carol's nerves were leaping with excitement. She lay back on the bed, electrified and, clasping both hands in and around all those places that the nuns had forbidden her ever to touch, she blew her mind, her vagina and her clitoris all at the same time.

Then she found a bathroom, which opened off the studio through an almost concealed door and by the time Robert Marshall had returned, in a sweater and a new pair of trousers, she was fresh, dressed and ready to go.

'I'll drive you home,' he said.

'Near home,' she corrected him. 'If you dropped me at our house in that Buckingham Palace on wheels, there'd be a riot. They'd think I'd been had by Prince Philip.'

'When do I see the pictures?' she asked, as they drove back into the Wirral.

'Oh, there's a great deal to do yet,' said Robert. 'I handle all my own developing and printing. I've got to get out some pages of contacts – they're very small prints that I can examine. Then I can choose the ones I want and enlarge and develop them to perfection – you can waste a lot of paper doing that. And even then I might be able to add improvements.'

'You mean make me look better than I am?' asked Carol.

'If you like to put it that way. I prefer to regard it as bringing out your full potential,' he explained.

'But it's still only on paper,' she said. 'It's not really me.'

'Who are you?' he asked. They were hurtling fatly and softly into the Mersey Tunnel from the Birkenhead end.

She knew what he meant, but not so that she could have explained it to anyone else. 'I know who I am, Mr Marshall,' she answered, with a flat finality. 'Let's know as soon as the pictures are ready.'

Marshall's brown eyes flicked back to the road, acknowledging a small defeat. Carol was reflecting, with interest, that there were certain people you could dominate.

Marshall dropped her halfway along Dale Street, held up a hand in a brief wave, moved out from the pavement with a silent surge of power and disappeared, making once again for the Mersey Tunnel.

Carol wandered up Dale Street. She had no intention of going back to Marshall & Nephew that day, even though it was only the middle of the afternoon. She could have gone home, but Janet would inevitably ask why she was home so early and she didn't want to lie. She turned into a record shop. Once again, in the hushed vaults where Carol Blair's fate was kept, one might have heard a tumbler click.

At that moment, Jack Blair was about two miles west of her, in the river at King George's dock. He was on a gang unloading a cargo of Chinese spun cotton from Hong Kong.

Jack was down in the ship's hold where his strength was needed. As they roped and hooked the bales, he and his gang chanted. The air was thick with a fine, fibre-based dust. The men sang to help keep it regularly expelled from their lungs, although if you'd explained that to them, they wouldn't have believed you.

The tune they sang was a weird one, of which none of them knew the derivation, although they had a theory that it was a corruption of a wharfside chant from the days when the city was the centre of the black slave trade;

'One hammer on a black meenah, miner,
One hammer on a black miner man,
Tippety can, blow Billy blow,

Fire away laddie and arnie so.

'Two hammers on a black meenah, miner
Two hammers on a black miner man—'

The second verse ended in a scream of agony. It came from Long Billy McGrath. The merchantman they were unloading had wallowed in the wake of an outgoing freighter, being snatched and worried towards the Bar by its pack of tugs. The movement had been enough to topple a bale, badly stacked in Hong Kong.

It had rolled on to Billy, seven hundred pounds of it, trapping him by the legs against a bulkhead. After the one scream, Long Billy shut up. You can't help the first one, but anything after that and you're indulging yourself. Besides, you get on the nerves of the lads who are trying to help. Thirdly, you've got other things to worry about, in this case two other bales, next in line to the one that fell, threatening to follow suit and if they do, they're going to land right in the middle of your long spine and it's curtains.

You've got one chance and it's big Jack Blair and what he's doing is climbing on to the bale that's got you trapped, ignoring the extra weight he knows he's putting on your crushed legs because he knows you've just got to put up with it, and spreading his back under the forward bale, the one that's teetering on its edge, threatening, with the next lap of water, to come down on you and bring its companion with it.

The very next second, a lurch of the tide has, in fact, slowly brought all seven hundred pounds down on to Jack Blair's back – instead of Long Billy's spine – and Jack is taking the strain, though how he can be, Billy doesn't really understand.

And Jack Blair's language has to be heard to be believed.

He's directing his gang. Officially there's another man who's the foreman, but any gang that Jack works on automatically becomes his and he's even got the foreman jumping about like a chimpanzee in his total, bloody-minded dedication to save Long Billy's life.

'Get up there, you pox-ridden twats and get those fucking ropes round this fucking bale before it turns me into pressed arseholes! For Christ's sake, you shit-faced schoolgirls, get on to it!'

The sweat was pouring off him as he yelled and Long Billy could see the sinews starting to quiver, the veins standing out on Jack's muscles as the lactic acid started to build up in the tissues. Still Jack held on, his language radiant in its obscenity, and his gang worked like inspired maniacs, shifting bale after bale at a speed to make an employer kiss their feet and a union negotiator weep, until they got to the one that was slowly crushing the life out of Jack and they lifted it and all he said was, 'About bloody time! Now get this one off Billy's legs!'

They took Long Billy off to hospital, cushioned by morphine. They wanted to take Jack, too, but he told them where they could put their stretcher and he and his gang went off to the Blood and Sawdust, a dockside pub, and it would have taken more than the combined efforts of the Mersey Docks and Harbour Board, the chairman of the Trades Union Council, and the whole of Liverpool's and Everton's football teams on their knees to get them back on to the wharves that day.

In the record shop, Carol was browsing through the sleeves. She felt a hand on her left shoulder, looked around, saw nobody, looked the other way and saw the circular, battered, grinning face of Pat McGrath, a boy from the next street to hers. He'd left school the year before her and landed himself a job as a delivery boy. Sometimes he brought film stock to Marshall & Nephew from their suppliers.

'Hiya, Car,' he said, 'how's it go?'

'All right. What about you?'

'The gear. They're letting me use the delivery bike at week-ends now. I've been on loads of trips.'

'Next time you go to Paris, take us on the crossbar.'

'Gerroff!' He scuffed the toe of his right shoe, a sure sign to Carol that he was going to ask for something: 'Hey . . .'

'What?'

'I've got a new Cliff Richard, only my record player's broke. I'm going Doo lally waiting to hear it. 'D'you think your kid would give us a lend of hers?'

By 'your kid' he meant twenty-five-year-old Martha. In this city any brother or sister was 'your kid' or 'our kid' until they were lowered into the ground, whatever the relative seniorities of the parties concerned.

'Yeah,' she said, carelessly, 'come round after work. We'll have a listen.' With such nonchalance did she trigger off a chain of circumstances that would reverberate into the future like an eternal series of railway wagons, buffering up to each other, one by one, along an infinite stretch of track.

Down at the Blood and Sawdust Jack was putting away prodigious quantities of Guinness. One of his black moods was coming down on him.

And when he finally strode home, without a falter in his stride, that evening, he was a State of Emergency, waiting for someone to declare him.

Carol and Pat McGrath were in the bedroom Carol shared with Martha when Jack got home. It was where Martha kept her record player and the plug on it wouldn't fit anywhere else. Fatally, they had the door closed because Janet had shouted up the stairs to 'Keep it down, for God's sake!' and there was no point in listening to a really good beat unless the volume had you pinned to the wall.

Jack strode in through the front door like the wrath of God. He was looking for trouble and, Lucifer help them, they'd presented it to him gift-wrapped. As he entered the hallway, the noise hit him. 'What in hell's name is that ?'

Janet, who had heard the key in the door, came out of the back kitchen, her hands covered in flour. 'They're just playing a record,' she said, nervously.

'They?' thundered Jack, 'who the shit are they?'

He ate up the stairs three at a time like an ogre in a fairy tale and burst open the door of Carol's room.

The sight that met him would scarcely have stirred most father's adrenal glands by more than a micro-micromillimetre. Pat McGrath was sprawled on one bed, Carol on the other. Her skirt had slid up slightly, displaying an inch or two of thigh just above the knee, but that was all. They were lost in the music, as disconnected from each other as two hung-up telephones.

Such distinctions, in his state – probably in any state – were too fine for Jack Blair. All he could see was his daughter in a bedroom, with a boy, with the door closed.

'You shameless little cow!' The words, spoken at a roar, were directed at Carol. But the terrible actions were directed at Pat McGrath.

The boy found himself lifted bodily from the bed, smashed against the wall, then literally thrown, like a sack of flour, down the stairs. He hit them halfway down, then bumped and cannoned the rest of the way to the hall.

Jack followed him down, an ogre anxious to finish the job by crunching his victim's bones. Pat lay there in the hallway, his limbs at unnatural angles. It was only then that Jack Blair, looking down on the boy, recognised him.

He was the nephew of Long Billy McGrath, whose life he had saved that day.

What would happen now was as fixed and immutable as the rituals of an ancient tribe, just as it had been when Carol had been attacked. Young Pat McGrath lay in hospital with two broken arms and a broken leg – all clean fractures, at least – and multiple bruises. 'Vengeance is mine' saith the Lord, but the word had never reached Scotland Road. Jack prepared himself. The women of the house, Carol and Janet – Martha wasn't home yet – knew better than to try and interfere.

The police knew what was going to happen, too, but they proposed to do nothing about it, either. If it weren't going to be here and now, it would be somewhere else another time. They had no basis, either, for legal action against Jack. Young McGrath was conscious, but had refused to say a word about how he came by his injuries. All they could get out of him was, 'Will I ever play the violin again, sergeant?'

Jack lay on his bed in the hope of retrieving some of the strength he had left in the hold of that ship and waited for the knock, as the rest of the street was waiting for it. Janet and Carol sat in the kitchen, their tea untouched.

The knock came at the door. 'Blair! Jack Blair!'

Out in the middle of the street stood Jimmy McGrath, the boy's father, and Benny McGrath, Pat's uncle. They were big men, but there was a lot of flab and puffiness on them where Jack was hard and solid.

In every door and window, heads crowded, turning the mean little street into an arena. Lowry could have painted the onlookers, but not the combatants. Jack came out, rolling up his shirtsleeves. Tonight he needed all the tricks he knew and he used the first of them straight away. He walked casually up to the McGraths as if to have a word in view of the peculiar circumstances. 'How's the lad?' he asked Jimmy.

'He'll live,' said Jimmy tersely and – unforgivably taken off guard – was instantly felled by Jack's hammer-like right hand. Benny, however, had spotted the sinews stiffening in Jack's right arm and his brother had hardly hit the ground before he had exploded a left to Jack's belly and a right to the side of his head.

Jack went down on one knee, As he struggled to his feet he was knocked down again by a left hook from Jimmy, who was now back on his feet, and took a knee in the face from Benny as he crumpled. Thus started the fight that was to become part of Scotland Road mythology, rivalling the tales of the titanic battles to be King of the Tinkers, which took place as often in arcane Liverpool as they did in Ireland.

At first, Jack's heart didn't seem to be in it. He was fighting from pure skill and experience and he seemed to be tired. It was while he was down on the ground yet again, from a barrage of punches from both brothers, that it happened. Passions were at fever level, and the McGraths had taken a pounding from Blair's iron punching which neither of them would have been able to withstand alone. Jimmy's heart was filled with fighting hatred and he thought Blair was finished. 'Anyway,' he spat as Jack lay panting on the ground, 'I'll bet I know who shut that bloody bedroom door.'

It was the biggest mistake McGrath would ever make in a fight in his life.

Jack Blair rose slowly from the ground as if, like Anteus, he had drawn strength from the earth itself. From looking like an exhausted, beaten man, he became an impregnable, vicious, inexhaustible engine of war, swinging with arms of bronze, connecting with fists as heavy as gold. He knocked the McGraths impartially from one side of the street to the other, brushing their best efforts aside as if they were boys. At the point where he was starting to pick them off the ground with one hand so as to knock them down again with the other, the crowd, knowing when enough is enough, moved silently between them and the fight was over.

Jack lurched back into his house, pushing past his wife and daughter as if not seeing them, managed to get upstairs, threw himself on the bed and fell instantly, unwakeably asleep. He slept for twenty-four hours. And it was during that time that McGrath made his second mistake.

Jimmy McGrath was a bad loser. He sat, he brooded, he poisoned his blood with the chemistry of hate. Then he marched down to the police station and preferred charges for assault and grievous bodily harm against Jack for what he had done to his son, Pat.

When they told Long Billy in hospital what his brother had done, his attentuated frame had to be held down in the bed. That action of Jimmy's, apart from its other consequences, caused one of those famous Liverpool intra-family estrangements that was to last for twenty years.

The first thing Jack did when he emerged from his massive draught of sleep next evening was to call for Carol. She had been waiting for the call and she was ready. He had the razor strop already in his hand.

This time he punctuated the strokes with a verbal commentary: 'This . . . will . . . teach you . . . not to bring. . . randy little . . . sods . . . into this house . . .

and. . . take them . . . up to . . . your . . . bedroom.'

The blood had begun to ooze again and the same devil in Carol that was in her father had at last, in her pain and anger, begun to formulate what her revenge was going to be, when there was a 'Ran-tan-tan' on the door knocker and Janet fled thankfully to open the door.

On the doorstep, headed by a sergeant, stood the three largest policemen the local force could muster. One of them was PC Banks, the constable who had been there before about the assault on Carol by Charlie the Vicar.

Sergeant Llewellyn led the way in, and informed Jack that Jimmy McGrath had preferred charges.

'Crap! Jimmy McGrath wouldn't do a thing like that.' And, indeed, the stigma of having done it was to stay with McGrath for the rest of his life.

'He's done it,' Llewellyn answered smugly. He started ponderously to produce some kind of document.

Jack brushed it aside. 'You know what you can wipe with that,' he said. He was thinking furiously. He had his left hand behind his back. Sergeant Llewellyn wished he knew what he was doing with it. 'McGrath wasn't even around when his son was here,' said Jack, buying time.

'That can all be discussed down the station,' said Llewellyn, 'if you'd just come along with us.'

What Jack Blair was doing with his left hand was confirming, with a sinking heart, that he had broken it. At some time during the battle with the McGrath brothers, he must have struck a blow with the knuckles open and snapped a bone. Now, testing it behind his back, he was sure he couldn't hit with it. He couldn't even slap with it. Normally, he'd have given this lot the shock of their bloody lives and cheerfully paid whatever the price would be.

He sighed and stood up. 'All right, then,' he said, in that typically half-childish, half-impudent Liverpool accent, 'what are we waiting for?'

Janet, incredulous, breathed out for what seemed to be the first time in five minutes. She threw her arms around Jack's neck in a fierce, mute hug and Jack slung on his old jacket and went, flanked by the three policemen. Outside, the whole street stood and watched the solemn procession in silence. Not one of them that wasn't on Jack Blair's side. Whatever he'd done, it was no concern of the scuffers.

Inside the house, Janet sank on to a stool and cracked into a torrent of tears, profound, wrenching sobs that brought Carol rushing in from the back kitchen in alarm.

'Mam! Mam! Don't, please don't!' It seemed inconceivable to her that anyone could be crying for that black-souled sod who had just been taken away – she hoped for ever. She crouched down and threw her arms around this beloved stepmother of hers, rocking her gently, as if she were the woman and Janet the child.

'You heard what they said,' sobbed Janet. 'Grievous bodily harm. That's jail. They'll put him away. Oh, Car, they'll put your father away!'

If only she knew, thought Carol, how much more she thought of Janet as her real mother than she did of Jack as her undoubted father. As so often before, she wondered bewilderedly about the varieties of human affection. Janet loved that awful bastard. She could feel that love for him now, pulsing through her shaking frame, communicating itself to Carol in some inexplicable, visceral way; she could feel the anguish of Janet's losing him. Yet the man was a shit, a vicious, sadistic, mean-minded monster!

'It's all right, Mam,' she said, helplessly, 'it's all right, honest. They won't put him inside. You'll see.'

Janet just went on sobbing. Carol desperately wanted her to stop. 'Mam!' she pleaded.

'You don't know,' stammered Janet, 'he won't have a chance!'

Why the hell should he have a chance, thought Carol, when he'd chucked a lad half his size down the stairs for nothing? What chance had he given Pat?

Janet was still talking, in between gasps. 'I know he done wrong, but it's nothing to what goes on in some places around here. But just because he's the one who's been reported, they'll come down on him hard. And there'll be no one to speak for him. There are things to be said for him and there's no one to say them.'

'What sort of things?' asked Carol, trying desperately to make the question sound interested rather than hostile.

'There are things to be done in court, things – like – to be put in certain ways. You've got to think and you can't do it yourself. Jack needs someone to think for him and he's got no one.' Her sobs burst out again, intensified.

Carol remembered her television programmes – 'There's legal aid, Mam, they give you legal aid!'

'People like us,' said Janet bitterly, 'they give us some deadbeat old drunk or a kid just out of school. What he needs is a proper lawyer, a man, someone who knows his business. Then Jack might have some kind of a chance. We don't know no one like that.'

And a bloody good job, too, thought Carol.

Janet's sobs deepened, almost as if she'd read Carol's thoughts. 'Aw, come on, Mam,' Carol begged. This darling, vulnerable, womanly woman with her soft, lilting Welsh voice and her brown, embracing eyes, who seemed so full of love that her flesh was always warm with it, this was her mother. She was unique. When she was a child, it had been enough just to stand next to her to feel enveloped in love.

She hugged Janet tighter, as if she could squeeze the pain out of her. And then it came to her, as if someone had written it in her mind. She released Janet and stood up, slowly. 'Mam . . . '

Something in her manner impressed Janet, momentarily arresting her sobs. 'What is it?'

'I think we do know someone. A real man. A proper lawyer, like you said.' Still her manner mesmerised Janet, willing to clutch at any straw.

'But where—?'

'I'll be as quick as I can, Mam. It mightn't work, but it's worth trying.'

Janet was at the point where she wanted to believe that maybe her children could work miracles. She made no further resistance, simply looked up at Carol with a kind of childish hope in her red-rimmed eyes as Carol kissed her lovingly and ran out.

4

Janet, the Celt coming out in her, sat keening quietly to herself on the stool. She had had a premonition of something like this for years. This didn't, as those who weren't fey thought, make it any easier. It made it much worse. What was it she'd read in the little village school in Flintshire, that elvishly lovely corner of Wales for those who could see it? Something about a coward dying many times, a brave man just the once.

From the day she had first set eyes on Jack twenty years before, she had known that a time must come when the demon in the man would drive him too far.

She saw him first as he got out of the coach at the Women's Voluntary Service hall in her little village of Dyserth. The Second World War had just been declared and the children of the big cities of Northern England were being evacuated to pastoral Wales, in which the bombers of Hitler's Nazi Germany could have no possible interest.

Jack and his lovely blonde wife Claire were the only parents in the coachload. The rest were children on their own, their names on cardboard plaques slung around their necks on strings, clutching bags of broken biscuits and dried-up oranges.

She had been a very young nineteen in those remote days and she certainly was not used to the shocking sensation she felt between her thighs at the first sight of Jack Blair's eyes, that made even the deep Welsh summer sky look pale, and the contours of his body.

He had with him a pasty-looking little girl of about four or five. Normally, Janet's shyness would have made her run for the nearest hedge, from behind which she might inspect him at her leisure. But today she was in charge of this shipment of evacuees, and she was obliged to deal with this unexpected parent.

She advanced along the pavement towards him, her clipboard constituting a kind of shield against his masculine radiation. 'There must be a mistake,' she said. 'Parents aren't allowed.'

'I see,' he said. 'That's a new rule, is it, to do with the war? No more parents allowed. Children to be produced by machine, like bombs and fighter planes?'

Thank the Lord he was abrasive and Bolshie. She knew she couldn't have handled charm on top of everything else. 'No, I mean that only children are being evacuated,' she said. 'We're not taking adults.'

'Well, that suits me great, sweetheart,' said Jack, 'because I wouldn't stay in this sick-green, sheep-ridden hole for five minutes. I'm just here to see that my daughter isn't billeted in a cow shed.'

It was at this point that Claire had got out of the coach. She was about the same age as Jack and Janet thought her the prettiest girl she had ever seen. She was pale blonde, with creamy-white skin like a magnolia and eyes of pure, transparent hazel.

She had a soft Lancashire accent. 'Come on, Jack,' she said, 'there's no call to be rude.' She turned to Janet with a sweet smile. 'You know what they're like about daughters,' she said confidentially. 'If it were a lad, he'd let him climb Everest on his own without boots on!'

Then Janet had the inspiration that was to turn out to be the hinge of her life. Matter-of-factly, she consulted her clipboard and said 'She's staying with us, with me and my family. We run the village store.'

Jack grunted with cautious satisfaction. He had taken to this dark-eyed little Welsh thing, with her funny accent and her thick hair that looked as if every strand had been polished to that glinting blue-black. 'Oh, aye?'

'If you'll just wait here, I'll help see to the rest of them, then I'll come back and take you home myself.'

And off she had marched, with her tiny waist, her clipboard and her neat legs and Claire had smiled at Jack, knowing that they'd encountered treasure. Janet, on the other hand, simply wanted to go somewhere and do something about the dampness between her thighs, which the first thudding impact of Jack's physical presence had triggered.

When Jack joined up in 1940 it was questionable who was the more heartbroken, Claire or Janet. Janet had only seen him half a dozen times altogether, when he came down with Claire to visit little Martha; but during those times she fell in love with him, hopelessly and irreversibly. His physical effect on her remained shattering. With her Welsh arts of discretion and secretiveness, she managed to prevent both Jack and Claire from ever guessing. Even when he used to lift her, squealing with protestations, over stiles and fences on the green and jewelled walks she showed them around her perfect little village, he never knew that when he put her down again she was as helplessly open and moist as a flower turned to the sun. She was glad of Claire's sobbing the first time she came to see Martha on her own after he had gone to the war. It gave her an excuse to let loose, as if in sympathy, all the sense of desolation she had been holding back.

In the five years Jack was away, Claire and Janet had grown as close as sisters. Martha had gone back to Liverpool after nine months when the government, lulled by the absence of the expected bomber blitz, decided it wasn't coming after all and sent the children back to the big industrial cities.

They were wrong, the Germans starting their 'hell from the skies' offensive two months after the children were back in the centre of the target areas. But there was no further attempt at evacuation. Nevertheless, Claire and Janet continued to see each other, and in the end they finally came together under the same roof in a manner as ironic and unexpected as it was tragic.

Late in 1943, Janet's parents were killed by a stray German bomb. Although Janet could have gone to stay with an aunt in Llangollen, Claire arrived like a pale flame to whisk her off to Liverpool.

Jack wrote sporadically, his letters so heavily censored that it was impossible to make more out of them than that he missed Claire and was giving both the enemy and his own side a fair idea of hell. He finally came home just after Victory in Europe Day. Typically, he hadn't even bothered to write to say he was going to be demobilised.

Janet was in the house on her own, ironing Martha's school blouse. There was a 'Ran-tan-tan' at the front door. Janet opened it and her heart turned inside out. There he was on the doorstep, his demobilisation suit too tight across the shoulders, too baggy round the hips, his face more devastatingly creased than ever, the indescribable blue of his eyes ablaze.

He grabbed her by the shoulders, lifted her off her feet, kissed her on the cheek and put her down again. 'Hello, kiddo,' he said, as he would to a sister, 'you've grown into a right little cracker! Where's Claire?'

She had the familiar sensation of physical dissolution, the instant vibrations in her clitoris. Her knees would hardly support her as she followed him into the kitchen, fighting off the hopeless jealousy she felt because the whole thrust of his being was to find his wife. 'I'm glad Claire had you,' he said. 'All the time I was away I was glad of that.'

'I'm glad I had Claire,' was all she could answer. 'It was Claire who took me in, not the other way round.'

'You're sweating,' he said, casually. There was one thing about this man: whatever other virtues he may have possessed, refinement wasn't one of them. Nor sublety. Which was why she felt safe to answer with the simple truth.

'It's the excitement of your being home.'

And he shouted with laughter as she grabbed for her powder compact and then there was a rattle of the key in the front door and Claire standing in the kitchen doorway and Janet just caught the shopping basket in time from her nerveless fingers as she half-collapsed into Jack's arms.

5

Carol was running, as always, unknowingly building on to her gangling limbs the smooth feminine muscle that would one day mould itself into a pair of legs that would stun men from Alaska to Acapulco. She was running because she believed she could console the stepmother she loved by helping the father she hated.

This time she was out in the streets. There were fewer people to impede her than during the day and the back jiggers became dangerous at night, even for her.

She was making for Marshall & Nephew.

She reached London Road and slowed down to a walk. It was important from now on not to attract attention. She walked slowly past the shop. It was padlocked and shuttered.

At the back of the shop there was a yard, separated from the alley by a wall. Jumping like the little alley-cat she was, she grabbed the top of the wall and hoisted herself up. She dropped down into the yard as neatly as a gymnast, and made straight for the window of the stockroom. It had a loose catch, but nobody had ever bothered overmuch about it because it was so small. Carol was surprised to find it was harder to squeeze through than she'd imagined: she wasn't as skinny as she thought.

Eagerly, she went to the drawer where she kept her records books and scrambled through the pages until she came to the name she wanted. Stewart Crown. Hastily, she noted his address, a flat in Rodney Street. She went out again the way she had come in, dropped down into the alley and broke into her tireless, native runner's stride until she reached the flawless Georgian terrace that was Rodney

Street. Prime Minister Gladstone had been born at Number 62. It was now a kind of Harley Street of the North, studded with the consulting rooms of famous and fashionable medical specialists, but there were still some private flats. Stewart Crown's was one of them.

Panting now, she rang the doorbell next to his nameplate.

There was a pause, then a voice boomed from the entryphone, making her jump.

'Who is it?'

'It's Carol Blair.'

'Who?'

'Carol Blair. From Marshall & Nephew. Where you get your photos done.' There was silence. 'Its life and death,' she added, desperately, remembering a television play.

There was a further pause, then the voice – the curiosity in it almost palpable – spoke again: 'You'd better come up.Third floor.'

The door buzzed and she pushed it and ran in. It smelled expensive inside. There was a lift, but she ignored it, running straight up the mushroom-carpeted, white-banistered stairs.

Stewart Crown was standing just inside his handsome door, its brass gleaming against mahogany. He had one hand on it, holding it open by its edge. He was wearing a white Terry-towelling robe and his heavy black hair was damp. She noticed that he was both slim and muscular. He smelled sweet and sharp. The honey-coloured eyes rested on her. They were full of intrigued speculation as he surveyed this quaint little solemn-faced thing, the straw-coloured hair plastered over her forehead with sweat, which ran on down her face. He wasn't smiling, but, somehow, she felt that he was.

'Well now,' he said. 'Come in and tell me about this life and death emergency of yours.'

She went past him into the flat, vaguely aware that there wasn't a lot of furniture, but what there was was of the kind you saw in antique shops, the sort of things that looked as if they'd been polished four times a day for hundreds of years. The air smelled of leather and books and the lights in the room glowed rather than shone. There was a spicy, masculine flavour about it all that gave her an excited feeling in her stomach.

There was a sofa, gold like his eyes, to which he pointed. 'Sit down.' He gestured at his robe. 'Sorry about this. I was taking a shower.' He sat on another sofa, lighter gold, opposite her. 'First of all, how did you find me?'

'The ledger at the shop.'

'The shop's closed.'

'I broke in.'

The extraordinary eyes widened. 'You did what?'

'I had to. You weren't in the phone book – I looked, in a kiosk–'

'No, I'm ex-directory.' He contemplated her, black lashes going up and down like shutters over his eyes. There had always been something about her from the first time he'd seen her in the shop, something he couldn't identify. But it had sent that old black magic coursing through his balls in a way there'd been no mistaking. Don't say he was getting an urchin syndrome! Even as he studied her now he was obliged to draw his dressing gown more discreetly around his knees. He had to admit that if any other little slum girl had come ringing his bell, he'd have sent them packing.

'What is it you want from me?' he asked.

'My father's in trouble,' she said. 'He's been arrested by the police.'

'For what?'

'My mam says they'll say it's grievous bodily harm and it's jail for him. We don't know anyone to help us and then I thought of you.'

'Why me?'

'Because you're a lawyer.'

'How do you know that?'

'I took a dekko at some of your snapshots once and I saw one of you in one of them wigs and them black gowns.'

So his instinct hadn't let him down. The little beggar had been interested in him, too. Now the smile did break through his eyes and there was nothing he could do to stop it.

She exploded with anger. 'Listen,' she said, 'it's nothing to grin about. People like us don't have much chance when we get messed up with the law. My mam's destroyed, just sitting there sobbing like a little kid, and we don't know what to do. D'you know what the worst thing about living in Scottie Road is? That you don't know nothing about nothing. You don't know how to deal with the fucking world because you don't know the kind of people who run it. Well, I don't know you, but I did know how to find you and I'm asking you now, please, to help me, to tell me what to do.'

He listened to her with respect. Before, she'd been a possibility for an intriguing screw, of a type he hadn't had. Now she had become a very real person, slightly formidable in that she wore no masks. She was just there, very intensely, like an elemental force.

He leaned forward. He wanted to take her hands in his, but he was afraid of being misunderstood. 'I'm sorry,' he said. 'I didn't mean to smile. And I certainly wasn't smiling at your predicament.' He saw the incomprehension cloud those startling eyes. 'I mean the fix you're in. But the question is what we can do about it.' He realised, with surprise, that he was already committed in his mind to doing something about it. 'First of all, tell me exactly what happened.'

She told him, with a surprisingly graphic eye for detail, watching his stern, beautiful face settle into chiselled lines of concern. At the point where she started to describe how Jack grabbed Pat McGrath and threw him down the stairs, he made a note on a scribbling pad on a table next to him.

He waited patiently until she had finished the whole story, then he fixed her with the amber eyes, from which he had carefully excluded all expression. 'Now then,' he said. 'I want you to go back to the bit where you say your father threw young McGrath down the stairs. Are you absolutely sure about that? Are you quite sure you actually saw it happen? After all, you must have been in a state of some confusion. You couldn't actually see what was going on outside on the landing. How wide is the landing, by the way, between the bedroom door and the stairs?'

'About a yard,' she said, transfixed by that gaze, trying to understand what it was he was telling her.

'Well, there you are,' he said. 'Very easy to lose one's footing in a little space like that, especially when one's trying to get away from an angry father.'

And then she got it. In one. 'No,' she said, 'you're right. I didn't actually see what happened after Pat McGrath dived out of the door. I just heard him fall, a second before my father went after him.'

'Just before your father went after him,' Crown repeated slowly. Jesus, she was quick, this kid.

'Yes, that's right,' said Carol. 'That's all I can tell you in the court when you ask me what happened.' And she tried to put into her eyes the message that she'd got the rules of the game.

Crown hesitated. 'I'm not sure I can be in court,' he said.

Her face became tragic: 'But you've asked all these questions. I thought— You mean you can't help me after all?'

There was genuine pathos in the voice and the young head had bent in a resignation that tweaked at that hardy organ that was Stewart Crown's heart. He knew he was going to help her. But it was going to be done according to Hoyle. Again he leaned towards her. 'I didn't say I couldn't help you,' he said. 'It's just that there are certain difficulties in the situation.' He tried to put it to her as simply as he could. 'There are two kinds of lawyers – solicitors and barristers. Now for some stupid reason you can't go straight to a barrister and ask him to act for you – I mean, to help you. You've got to go to a solicitor first and ask him to help you and then he can send you to me, as it were, and I can help you. D'you follow me?'

Carol had been studying his face and listening closely. 'It sounds like a rip-off to me,' she said, shortly: 'jobs for the lads, just like down the docks.'

'I don't propose to argue the structure of the profession

with you,' said Crown. Christ, thought Carol, he's treating me like a real person! 'It's just that things have got to be done in a certain way. Now what I'm going to do is to telephone a solicitor and refer you to him. You tell him all the details and if he thinks your father should be represented by a barrister, he'll recommend one. It may well be,' he added airily, 'that he will recommend me. If he does I shall be happy to take the case.'

By the book, Crown, he thought cynically, strictly by the book. But it wasn't only in order to put a knowing kid in her place. He'd been winning a lot of cases recently; he was rising fast. And those who rose fast left enemies below. He wanted no chinks in his professional armour.

He rose from the sofa. 'I'll see if he's at home.'

Carol watched his tanned, muscular calves, as he went into the small study which opened off the room they were in. Vaguely, she wondered what it would be like to bite them. A few minutes later, Crown put the receiver down slowly. It wasn't an easy one. But they wouldn't be expecting him and he intended to hit them out of a clear blue sky before the case could gather momentum. He was beginning to get fully engaged on a professional level. It was a tactical problem now, divorced from human considerations. He turned to Carol. 'Tell your father I'll be in to see him first thing in the morning, before he comes up before the magistrates. And he's to be a deaf mute in the meantime. And now you'd better go.' He was suddenly acutely conscious of his nakedness beneath his robe and he had an idea that she was, too. He led her to the door.

'Thanks,' said Carol. 'I mean really thanks. I know you didn't have to do this.'

His amused, protective smile rested on her serious little face. She looks like a small, plain elf, he thought. 'What do you know about what I have to do?' he asked. 'You just run along and cheer your father up. Tell him the Fifth Cavalry is on its way.'

'There's something you should know about my father,' she said, 'I hate his guts. I did this for my mam.' And she was out of the door and gone – almost, he could have sworn, in a wisp of smoke.

At the Bridewell police station they tried to flick her away like a bothersome gnat at first. They weren't used to pale little girls demanding as of right to see a prisoner in custody. They quickly discovered that they'd better get used to this one. 'Either I see him, or I call his lawyer,' she said, drawing extensively on her acquaintance with television crime series.

'His lawyer?' laughed the desk sergeant. 'Who's he, Perry Mason?' He raised a gratifying, if sycophantic, laugh from his inferiors.

'No, Stewart Crown,' she answered, wiping the smile off every face in sight.

Jack Blair was sitting like a graven image, big hands interlocked. 'What the hell are you doing here?' was his surly greeting as the police constable let Carol into the visiting room. The constable stayed in the corner, out of earshot.

She could make her face as granite-like as his. She did so now. 'I've just come to tell you that you've got a lawyer. He'll be in to see you first thing tomorrow before you go in front of the beaks.'

'That's ale-house talk,' he growled. 'I can't afford no lawyer.'

'It's being done on Legal Aid,' she said.

'How? Who worked that one out?'

'I did.'

'You!' he snorted, without humour. 'If you think you're going to buy your way out of what's coming to you for sprawling around your bedroom with Pat McGrath—'

She hissed at him, her face like marble: 'If I had my way, you'd rot in jail for the rest of your bloody evil life! It's just that Mam seems to need you – God knows why. But, then, I read in school about these bugs that think cyanide's the most terrific stuff they've ever tasted—'

He made a threatening move towards her, then remembered the police constable in the corner and managed to master himself. 'You'll wish you'd taken some when I get out of here—'

'If you get out of here.' she flashed back. 'This lawyer geezer is clever,' she lowered her voice to a vibration of hatred that only he could hear, 'but after all, you are bloody guilty!'

That view of things, which had never even occurred to him before, set him sagging thoughtfully back in his chair. The fact that it was not lawful to throw somebody down a flight of stairs just because you'd found him in a bedroom with your daughter was not part of his thinking.

She pressed home her advantage. 'The lawyer said to keep your big gob shut and say nothing. He'll be along tomorrow morning to see you before you go to court, remember, so until then, shut it. Right?'

She luxuriated in her position of dominance over her father. For the first time in her life, he was in her power and the headiness of it sent her pulse thumping.

Jack simply looked at her. By God, he thought, at least there's no mistaking the little bitch comes from my side of the family – the Blairs, fighters all and fighters ever. There was no fear of him in those eyes that were mirrors of his own – and he was accustomed to seeing fear of him in the eyes of men who could pick up this whey-faced fury sitting opposite him and put her in their pockets.

She got up to go. 'Just remember,' she said quietly, 'whatever I'm doing, I'm doing for Mam.'

The flash of suspicion struck suddenly through his mind and crackled in his eyes. 'How did you get this lawyer?' he demanded.

'I fucked him in the middle of Lime Street and sold tickets,' she said. Then she got up, nodded to the constable, who unlocked the door for her, and she went.

Next morning Stewart Crown carved his way, with a certain dispatch, through the minor bureaucracy of Bridewell police station and demanded to see his client. Since wigs and gowns were not worn by barristers in magistrates' courts, he had taken particular pains with his appearance to emphasise his status. He had on a dark suit with Savile Row showing in every stitch of it, a dazzling white shirt with a stiff short collar and a dark tie; and stretched across his vest a slim gold watch chain.

He wanted to flatter the court and its susceptible magistrates – he'd taken the trouble to find out who they would be – by appearing in his full splendour. Old 'Woody' Woods, an undoubted if non-practising homosexual, would be Chief Magistrate with Dolly Maidment and Cicely Anderson, two gorgon-like battleaxes with hearts of pure marshmallow, flanking him on either side. The Clerk of the Court, who advised the magistrates on points of law, would be John Stenmuir, a dry, sandy-haired Scot who approved of advocates who took the trouble to enhance the dignity of the court.

Crown, as Jack Blair's lawyer, had the privilege of meeting his client in his cell. The lock rattled, the door opened and he stood there, pigskin briefcase in his hand, confronting Blair like a young farrier, called in to shoe a stallion. In the raw morning light, blue eyes met yellow eyes and took the measure of each other. There was too much maleness behind each pair to make the meeting an easy one. Hard old bastard, thought Crown. Dangerous young sod, thought Jack. Neither offered to shake hands.

'My name is Crown. I've been retained to represent you. I'd like a quick word before we go into court.'

'How did my daughter get you here?' asked Jack, abruptly.

'Mr Blair, we've got approximately ten minutes. I'm probably the only man in this city who can get you off, but if you prefer to waste precious time in irrelevancies, I'd much sooner get off to my next case in Chester, which concerns the fraudulent conversion of three million pounds.' He looked at his watch impatiently. Nothing like a touch of pomposity to bring a client to heel.

The pomposity didn't make a dent on big Jack Blair, but the confidence and the shortage of time did. Over a sleepless night it had come slamming home to him what he was facing. Jail. Years of it. Without the Mersey breeze blowing in his brine-hardened face he'd just wither away like a strangled tree. He knew it and he now stared at this arrogant bugger who could be his salvation and he was prepared to listen.

'All right, Mr Mouthpiece, let's have it,' he said.

Crown spoke carefully. 'I take the view that there is no case to answer.

Jack, bewildered, thought he was being sold out. 'No case to—'

'Please don't interrupt,' snapped Crown crisply. 'I feel there is insufficient evidence for the case to go forward. On the other hand, should the Bench not share my view and the case does proceed, I would like to check with you what your daughter – who would, of course, be a witness – has told me about the alleged incident.'

He held Jack's eyes as he said it. Jack fought against being mesmerised by the big cat stare until he realised he wasn't being mesmerised: he was being told to listen. He began to get the feeling that this smooth-tongued hunter was genuinely on his side. He didn't know what the bugger's motives were, but he knew he could trust him.

'What did she tell you?'

'She said you burst unexpectedly into her bedroom while she was listening to a record with young Pat McGrath. He took fright and dodged out past you, then tripped and fell down the stairs.'

'That's what happened,' Jack answered with the grace of a practised liar, which was something he was not. 'He was too quick for me. Not,' he added, 'that I wouldn't have given him a tanning if I could have got my hands on him, but by the time I got out of the room, he'd already gone for a smash.'

Embellishments, too, thought Crown; and unprompted. He was still young enough to be taken aback by untutored intelligence.

'Therefore you will plead not guilty,' he said.

'Well, I'm not, am I?' Jack answered, the mocking complicity bright in his eyes.

'You realise,' Crown explained, 'that the other side will say differently – that you threw the boy down those stairs.'

'That's how you blokes make your money, isn't it,' said

Jack, 'stomping the other side into the ground?'

'The prosecution will try to shake you on details. Just stick to your story and you'll be all right.'

'Aye,' said Jack wryly. 'How's the lad?'

'They're not serious fractures. He's got young bones. He'll be up in no time.'

Jack grunted. 'And how's Long Billy?' he added.

'Who's Long Billy?'

Somehow Jack had assumed that this straight-faced, all-knowing young stag would know everything about everything. Then he realised he'd told nobody about the accident in the hold, not even Janet. Reluctantly, now, in monosyllables, he had the story dragged out of him.

Crown listened, the warm feeling growing in him that there was a pattern to the world and the pattern had ordained that he was one of the winners. He made no comment, paused a moment, then rose to go.

'I may not call you to give evidence at all. But if I do call you, speak clearly and look straight at the magistrates.'

'I don't generally look down at my boots when I'm talking to someone,' said Jack.

'I'll see you in court,' Crown answered and left without ceremony. He'd done all he wanted to do. And more.

Carol, Martha, Tony and Janet were sitting on the sparsely populated public benches. The McGrath clan were sitting across on the other side. Martha, shocked by the story she had been told when she got home late the night before, had taken the day off work to be there. Tony hadn't wanted to come. 'Just send me the good news by special messenger if they send him down,' he told Carol. But Carol had persuaded him that he owed it to Janet to show solidarity.

The preliminaries were swiftly over. Jack had pleaded not guilty and Chief Superintendent Belling, lingering with satisfaction over the villainous unshaven appearance of his captive, decided he could despatch this one quickly despite the formidable opposition of Stewart Crown, with whom he had already had several bruising collisions.

He outlined the case against Jack efficiently, produced a

sworn statement extracted, he was at pains to point out, from young Pat McGrath on his bed of torment in hospital, and sat down.

Crown rose to his feet. 'Your Worships, Chief Superintendent Belling has been admirably brief. I will try to follow his example. I would like to call the arresting officer to the witness box.'

There was a flurry among the police contingent. What the hell was Crown up to now?

Sergeant Llewellyn straightened his tie, smoothed down his hair and tried to collect his wits.

'You are Sergeant Llewellyn and you were the arresting officer in this matter?' He always said 'matter' rather than 'case': it made it sound like some irritating trifle which they had to get out of the way.

'That is correct.'

'What time did the accident to young McGrath happen?'

Belling was on his feet. 'Objection. The prosecution claim it was no accident.'

Crown bowed winningly towards the Bench. 'With respect, that is for their Worships to decide.' He addressed himself again to Llewellyn. 'What time, sergeant?'

'Approximately five-thirty p.m.'

'And what time did Mr McGrath lay the charge of grievous bodily harm against the defendant?'

'About nine-thirty p.m.'

'Four hours. Quite a long delay.'

'A delay, yes.'

'Are you aware that, in the interval, Mr McGrath and his brother challenged the defendant to a fist fight and were severely worsted by him?'

'Yes.'

'D'you happen to know what time that was?'

'I understand it was about eight forty-five.'

'So that we have nothing happening between five-thirty and eight forty-five' – he let the irony creep into his voice – 'presumably because Mr McGrath was waiting for his brother to come off shift before he felt able to call on my client. We then have a fight, which they lose, and three-quarters of an hour later we find Mr McGrath suddenly laying a charge of grievous bodily harm against the defendant. Does the chronology of those events suggest anything to you?'

'No.'

'Do you suppose, for instance, that we should all be here this morning, wasting the court's time, had the McGrath brothers won that fight?'

Woods, the Chief Magistrate, wagged a fondly reproving finger at Crown. 'Now then, Mr Crown, you know better than that – calling for a conclusion from the witness.'

'I beg your Worship's pardon, I stand corrected.' I'm getting to 'em, he rejoiced: he knew from the note in Woods' voice. And from the softening in the features of the two old harridans who flanked him. Now he was going to put in his Sunday punch. He turned to Llewellyn.

'Are you aware that the day before yesterday the defendant saved the life of a third McGrath brother during an emergency in the hold of a ship?'

Out of the corner of his eye, he was conscious of the pencil leaping into the hand of the reporter from the *Liverpool Echo*, sitting in the press bench. Suddenly, this had escalated from a boring case of routine Liverpudlian violence into a good story. Another helpful piece of publicity for the blossoming legal star Stewart Crown, thought Crown: although, to be fair to himself, that wasn't why he had brought it up. He'd introduced it as a piece of totally irrelevant but very powerful emotionalism, a fact of which Chief Superintendent Belling was instantly aware. Why the hell hadn't he been told this? He was on his feet in a flash.

'Your Worships, I fail to see the pertinence of—'

'Agreed, Superintendent,' said old Woody.

Crown, however, had his justification ready: 'All I'm suggesting, your Worships, is that it is hardly credible that a man should save a friend's life in the afternoon, then deliberately set out to wound that man's nephew in the evening.'

In the public gallery, Carol had been watching Crown as if he were some kind of minor god. His authority, his grace, the precision with which he chose and flighted his words, the clear way his mind worked, were a joy to her unconscious instinct for excellence. Now, as he produced a story about her father that not even his own family knew, she was alive with admiration. 'Did you know that?' she whispered to Martha and Tony.

'No,' they said, as astonished as she was.

A policeman frowned at them.

'Proceed, Mr Crown,' said old Woody, benevolently.

'Thank you, Sergeant Llewellyn,' said Crown, 'that will be all.' Llewellyn stepped down to face the empurpled wrath of his Chief Superintendent and Crown turned his handsome attention towards the magistrates.

'Your Worships, in the classic dilemma of "did he fall or was he pushed?" there is no way of arriving at the truth without corroborative evidence. The unfortunate boy says he was pushed, or rather the police say he does – we have had no opportunity of cross-questioning him. My client and his daughter will say that he ran from the room in alarm and tripped. Those are the only witnesses, the count is two against one, all the common sense probabilities are on the defendant's side and the prosecution can produce no corroborative evidence whatsoever. I therefore move, with all respect, that there is no case to answer.'

There was the briefest of consultations between Woods, his fellow magistrates and the Clerk of the Court. Woods sat up straight. 'The court so finds,' he said. 'Case dismissed. The prisoner will be discharged.'

Outside the courtroom, in the corridor, Crown met Carol. She was with Jack and the rest of her family. Carol looked at him shrewdly. She knew very well that Stewart Crown had been fast on his feet in there.

'Ta!' she said.

'Just doing my job,' said Crown with an impersonal smile. He could feel Jack Blair's eyes on them, burning with one crude question.

Janet, who was clinging in tearful joy to her husband's arm, released her grip and came to Crown. 'Oh, thank you,' she said, in her sweet Welsh lilt, 'you're a clever, kind man. We'll never forget you!'

'Your daughter's a very persuasive young woman, Mrs Blair,' he smiled.

Martha looked at him with steady curiosity. To be handsome and clever was one thing. To look like a young king was another. The same thought ran through her mind as was exercising Jack's: how the hell had Carol managed to pull him? She looked sideways at her sister. Carol didn't seem to be paying him any more attention than she would a lad from their street. But then she never had been able to read this beloved, odd little sister of hers.

The McGrath tribe passed, glowering their disgust. Young Pat's father and uncle detached themselves from their wives and cousins and came over to the Blairs. 'You've conned this bunch of berks with your fancy lawyer,' Jimmy McGrath said, 'but I wonder how good he is at mending a smashed knee-cap?'

'What are you going to bring with you this time?' asked Jack, contemptuously.' A Centurion tank?'

Crown put up a hand to stop Jack going further. He spoke to Jimmy McGrath. 'It's not really very sensible to utter menaces within the vicinity of a court of law,' he warned.

McGrath, who had flushed dark red at Jack Blair's taunt, opened his mouth, found nothing to say and was hustled away by his wife.

'Goodbye,' said Crown to Jack. 'Try not to let any more people trip down your stairs. It might be harder to explain next time.' He nodded his swift goodbyes to the others and left, striding away down the corridor, the flawless suit doing nothing to hide the male shapeliness of his body.

Jack watched him go. So the bugger had known all along. He'd been so bloody convincing in court, he'd almost had him thinking he really believed in Jack's innocence. He bloody near had him believing in it himself! He watched the women of his family watching Crown's departing back and he knew he didn't like owing his liberty to Stewart Crown.

They walked back home in silence. Word had preceded them by that mysterious Liverpool bush telegraph, which is a mixture of ESP, all-seeing eyes and fleet young runners, and by the time they got back to their street the neighbours were out in force to applaud Jack all the way to his front door. He showed no sign of noticing and made no acknowledgment. They hadn't expected any; they knew their Jack Blair.

Once in the house, he led the way, unspeaking, through into the kitchen. Then he uttered for the first time since they had left the court. 'Right,' he said to Carol, 'sit down.'

She sat at the bare wooden table, knowing what was coming. He stood over her. 'Now then,' he asked, 'how did you get this Fancy Jack lawyer Stewart Crown to help me?'

'For Christ's sake!' said Tony.

'Shut your gob!' Jack warned, making a mental note not to turn his back on the dangerous young bugger he now knew his son to be.

Martha joined in. 'Dad, you're home and dry! What's the inquest about?'

And Janet: 'Jack, for heaven's sake, love, what does it matter? All we care about is that you're home and safe and out of trouble and we should be thankful to God and Our Blessed Lady for it.'

'But it's not God and Our Blessed Lady, is it? It's smooth-gob Crown, who wouldn't normally use anyone in this street to wipe his arse on. Why is it me who gets the favour from him? What makes me qualify?'

Tony spoke quietly. 'There's something wrong with you, Dad. You need your nut fixing.'

Jack moved towards him, his fist closing, but Tony slid around the other side of the table, putting himself out of range. He carried on talking. 'D'you want to know something? If you ever get done again – and you will, for something, because they'll have it in for you now – I'll give evidence against you. Even if you're innocent, I'll lie you right through the bloody gates of Walton Jail!'

Jack lunged across the table at him, but Martha thrust herself in front of Tony and Janet threw her arms around Jack's neck.

'Please, Jack!' begged Janet, the tears starting in the

bitterness of her disappointment that happiness never seemed to last longer in this house than a cloud of breath in winter. 'This isn't how it should be.'

'Mam's right,' Martha added in her blunt, hammer-headed way. 'You're out of order. You've no right to be grilling Carol, you should be down on your bloody knees to her.'

Jack felt the familiar, ultimate blaze of rage beginning to inhabit him. It seemed to start at the back of his skull and neck, pressing forward until it almost blinded him. For the first time in his life, in that police cell and later in court, he had felt helpless, totally in the hands of others, and it had tormented the demon in him to a pitch of murderousness.

Janet could see it and she was frightened. She tightened her arms around his neck. 'Jack, love, you're tired, you're not seeing things as they are. Come and sit down and I'll make us all a cup of tea.'

He flung her off with a brutal carelessness that hurt her more than the physical pain of it. He grabbed Carol by the hair and pulled her head back so that she was forced to look up at him. 'I asked you a question,' he said.

She gritted her teeth against the pain of his grip. 'What?' she asked sullenly.

'You know bloody well what. Why did I get the treatment?'

'Because I asked him.'

He kept his grip on her hair. 'How did you know him?'

'He comes into the shop. To get his films developed.'

'So how did you know where to get hold of him last night?'

'I got his address from the shop.'

'At half past nine at night?'

'I broke in.'

'You little liar; you must think I'm soft in the bloody head. You knew where he lived, you'd been to see him before, you'd been to his house.' He shook her by the hair, the powerful hand rattling her like a doll. 'Hadn't you?'

'If that's what you want to think, you think it,' she spat at him.

He hit her, then, the back of his hand across her face.

Tony flew at him, hands reaching up for his throat. Jack knocked him aside as though he had been an empty box. He struck Carol's helplessly upturned face again: 'Slut!' he cried. 'Filthy little slut!'

It was Martha who acted. She stepped forward, stocky and square, clubbed her fists together and smashed them across Jack's mouth. His mind came momentarily to a stop. The blow hardly rocked him on his feet, but he had never been struck by a woman before in his life, much less by one of his own daughters. He tasted his own blood as it trickled out of the corner of his mouth. He released Carol and put a hand up to his lips, brought it down again and looked, marvelling, at the blood on it and then at Martha.

'You're a cripple,' she said quietly. 'You've got a sick thing about your own daughters. You've got it about me, but thank God I look the way I do. Yet you still screwed up the only chance I ever had - with Fred. Carol's not so lucky. She looks like Claire. Here!'

She grabbed the photograph of Claire from the sideboard, where it had stood through all the years of Jack's marriage to Janet. It was obvious - the bones, the hair, the beauty in Claire's face, which was perhaps only latent in Carol's. 'Don't you understand why you hurt her so much? Don't you bloody know what you're really doing? You're the bull and this is your field and all the womenfolk are yours and those you're not allowed to poke aren't going to be poked by anyone else, either, not if you can help it!'

He nearly did strike her, then, but Janet threw herself in front of Martha: 'Please, Martha love, no more.'

But Martha kept on relentlessly: 'No, Mam, there are things that have needed saying in this house for years.' She turned her face to Jack again. 'Inside you there's nothing but hate and spite and bloody-mindedness. So you had a hard time in the thirties. Tough turd! So did a lot of other people, but they didn't turn into fucking monsters! So you lost your wife – we lost our mother. You loved her, so did we. We still love her, but we got a miracle in her place. We got Janet. If there's one person in the world that Janet shouldn't have happened to, it's you! You don't deserve a hair off her head, you're not bloody fit to cut her toe-nails. But you got her – God knows how or why. Yet you still go around as if the world is kicking you in the balls sixty times a minute twenty-four hours a day! You're the world's Number One Olympic-class shit and I'm truly, deeply bloody sorry we didn't get rid of you for five years today. If I'd had anything to do with it, Carol would never have gone anywhere near that lawyer last night. I just wish to God I'd got home in time to stop her.'

There was a silence so deep that Carol could hear her heart move. Then Jack, who had been chilled into total immobility by the arctic hatred of Martha's voice, said, simply: 'Get out of my house. You're none of mine.'

'Oh, I'm yours all right,' said Martha. 'I wish to Christ I wasn't. And I'll get out when I'm good and ready.'

'You think so?' he said, moving towards her with the obvious intention of putting her out physically.

'You try and throw me out,' said Martha, 'and I'll go straight to the law about what you've knocked off from the docks in the last ten years.' Every docker stole from the docks; everyone knew it, including the police, who had learned that ignorance was the better part of valour. But if someone laid information, they were bound to act. Jack knew it and Martha knew it. And Martha knew something else. She had seen what nobody else had divined in her father's impenetrable face in the dock that morning – fear: the fear of being shut up.

'The police will be only too happy to listen,' she went on. 'Tony was right - they'll be looking for you now, and if you try to chuck me out of this house I'll hand them your bloody head on a plate.'

Jack said nothing. He simply smashed his way out of the room like a truck and left the house. In his savage, complex way he almost exulted in having fathered such a prize bitch as this square-shouldered, mud-eyed termagant with whom, had she been a man and a stranger, he'd have picked a fight within five minutes of their meeting.

They didn't see him again for twenty-four hours.

Carol and Martha and Tony had their lives to get on with. Janet sat and waited.

6

When Jack had come home from the war, Janet had gone missing. The rapturous lovemaking she hadn't been able to avoid hearing from the next room had devastated her. Next morning, she crept out of bed at five o'clock, slipped downstairs like a ghost, and quietly left the house. She went to the bus station and got on the fist coach to North Wales. She changed to a swaying, loose-limbed local bus at Mold in Flintshire and was carried to Dyserth. It was the same as it had been for a thousand years. She skirted the village, passing the quarry, where gigantic Shire horses were still hauling wagons half the size of houses, filled with stone. She climbed to the top of Cwm Hill by way of its gently sloping southern side.

She sat on a rock by the side of a sheep track, intrigued again by the acoustic phenomenon of the hill, the snatches of conversation she could hear from the High Street, nine hundred feet below at the bottom of the ocean of crystalline air that was North Wales.

It was then that she remembered her pool. Merlin's pool she'd called it as a child. No one else had ever discovered it. It was in a fissure in the rock, just short of the summit of the hill, concealed by bracken and sweet briar and maidenhair. She pushed aside a briar bush and there it was, more overgrown than ever now, but still as pure, as glassy, as immobile as she had remembered it, so clear that it made you feel you could see more clearly looking down through the water at its bed of little pebbles than looking through the immaterial air. A leaf floating on top of it looked as if it were suspended in space.

She pushed through the undergrowth and lay down at the

edge of Merlin's Pool. She put her face into the water and drank. Its icy sweetness made her realise that she hadn't tasted real water for years. She slaked her thirst, then, in a shock movement she could hardly explain to herself, she plunged her whole head under the water.

She came up, numbed by its iciness, took of her cardigan and started to dry her hair with it. And there, rubbing her hair, nine hundred feet up in the diamond-sharp air, with the sweet-scented embroidery of fields and meadows spread beneath her, she found that everything became clear. Harsh but clear.

There was no future for her in Liverpool. If she stayed, she was staying because of Jack, because she wanted to be near him, to see him, perhaps to brush past his hard body in the cramped little rooms. It would be sterile, unhealthy, potentially explosive. Only bitter unhappiness could result.

She knew what she had to do. She knew it, but that didn't mean she could immediately accept it. She wept, she raged, she discovered the liberating luxury of yelling obscenities into the uncaring heavens, knowing that nobody could hear. And when she had finished and had wrestled herself to a standstill, she had reached a kind of tranquillity. It wasn't passive acceptance, but it was a stillness. And she thought she could live with it.

She went down the hill the hard way. The north face was the steep face and if you started to run there was no way, short of a grinding fall, that you could stop until you got to the bottom. She ran. By the time she got to the meadows at the bottom she was exhausted. But something in the physical passion of the run had exploded any residual doubts and confirmed her decision.

People gazed at her as she got to the coach back to Liverpool. She had the look of a woman who had walked through a blast furnace and somehow emerged on the other side.

When she arrived, she found Claire white-faced and almost ill with worry; and the first sight of her friend's stricken face told Janet that she was going to have to be very strong if she were to carry through her resolve.

'Love! Where've you been?' Claire was still in her dressing gown, sitting in the kitchen. Jack was at the docks, Martha was at school. Claire rose as Janet came in, her huge hazel eyes, dark-ringed, fixed on Janet's face, trying to read there what she wanted to know.

Janet kissed the lovely, fragile, concerned face. 'I've been home, love.'

'Your home's here. This is your home. What are you talking about?'

Janet couldn't meet those translucent, troubled eyes just yet. She busied herself with her handbag: 'I mean Wales – you know, Dyserth, my little village. Oh, it was sweet! I'd forgotten.'

Claire knew her too well. 'Janet, you must have left here practically in the middle of the night! To go and see your village? All of a sudden like that? Janet, sit down, love, and let's have it straight.'

'I just felt like it. I wanted to get away.' She felt she was weakening. She called on her Celtic warrior genes, please God, to help her.

'On the day Jack got back, after five years, alive and well?' Claire exclaimed. 'On the happiest day of our lives?'

The Celtic warriors had answered Janet's prayers. At last she found the courage to meet those cider-clear, almond-shaped eyes. 'On the happiest day of *your* life,' she answered.

She left the phrase hanging in the air between them. And for the first time since they had known each other, these two superbly feminine women, who had shared each other's most private thoughts for five years, misunderstood each other.

Claire was still, the hazel eyes clouding, for a long time. Then she shook her head. 'I don't believe that. I don't accept it. You're trying to tell me you were jealous of my happiness? That you didn't feel you could share it with me? After all these horrible years we've been through together when I'd have died if I hadn't had you and I *know* you felt the same? You're trying to tell me you were so jealous of my happiness you had to get away from it?'

'Claire, I'm saying that now Jack's home I've got to leave.'

'No!' Claire gasped. 'Why?'

'It won't work any more, that's why.'

'But why? Janet, you're the best and closest and sweetest friend I've got. You can't just say you're going to go away and leave me!'

'Claire, love,' Janet said, softly, 'what if I said I couldn't stand it?'

'But why shouldn't you be able? You've always liked Jack.'

'Yes.' She held Claire's eyes with her own. Claire tried to look away, to avoid picking up the message the velvety brown irises were insistently sending. But Janet refused to let her look away, saw with a mixture of relief and grief the understanding and the sorrow filter into Claire's eyes.

'I never knew,' said Claire.

'How could you?' Janet smiled without mirth. 'I've only seen him half a dozen times in my life. It's just . . . well . . . it's just that way.'

'Yes,' said Claire,' it was that way with me.'

Then she reached for Janet and Janet reached for her and they wept together, finding a release unknown to men.

The next day, Janet packed her few things and left while Jack was at work and Martha at school.

It was an afternoon in July, 1948, one of those blazing rare blue and white-gold days when the Welsh light rivals Greece's mysterious luminosity. Inside the shop it was cool. Outside, the street shimmered in the heat, the stream glittered like a torrent of gems.

Janet was stock-taking. The shop doorbell tinkled and there, framed in the dazzle from outside, was a black, wide-shouldered, narrow-flanked silhouette that made her clutch the counter for support. Jack hesitated for a second, then came forward into the cool cave of the shop.

His face was leaner, there were new furrows in it. The eyes still made the sky outside pale by comparison, but the skin beneath them was dark with misery.

She tried to speak, but her voice didn't work. Jack, as ever, wasted no words.'You've got to come back,' he said. 'Claire needs you.'

She was disoriented. 'Needs me how? What are you talking about? Jack, I've made my own life here. Claire has got hers in Liverpool. She's got you and the children. There's nothing I could give her.' Her heart had come out of its stranglehold and was now pumping so hard she could feel her body shake.

Jack looked at her, his strong face a mask of despair. 'Claire's ill,' he said.

It was his face rather than the words which brought the chill to her skin. She had to force herself to ask the question she didn't want to ask: 'How d'you mean? How ill?'

'Bloody ill. Bloody, bloody, bloody ill.' He pounded a big fist into his other palm. All the high colour had gone from his face, leaving it like grey stone. 'It's her blood. It's destroying itself or something. They call it leukaemia. They say you can have it slow or fast. She's got it fast.'

She could see the panic in the black-fringed eyes, belying the stolidness of his words.

'Now she's so weak she can't look after the kids. It's terrible to see her trying. Dragging herself out of bed. Hauling herself around the house; saying she's all right. They want to put her in hospital, but she won't go.' He paused. 'Just lately, she's started talking about you. She talks about you all the time. She seems to think if only you were there, everything would be all right.'

She looked at the big man, hurting because all his massive strength was helpless to do anything for his darling Claire.

And she knew what she was going to do.

In Liverpool Jack met her at the coach station. There was a new look on his face as he flicked her suitcase into his hand as effortlessly as if it had been a little purse. 'She's getting better already,' he said excitedly. 'She's been different since she knew you were coming. Really like . . . lively.

You know what I mean?'

'Yes,' said Janet joyfully, taking in the light in his face, 'I do.' She bounced along next to Jack, her mood rising with every step.

When Claire opened the door to them in Mugsley Street it was instantly obvious that she was dying. Janet was totally unprepared for her appearance. Claire had always been slim, but now she had lost half her body weight. Only the sunlit eyes, huger than ever in the sweet, wasted features, showed the old Claire, the love radiating out of them in a warm, all-embracing glow. They threw their arms around each other and Janet's flesh shrieked in silent protest as she felt her darling's frail, uncovered bones under her arms and beneath her touch.

Jack looked on with hope and pride as he witnessed the reunion. Janet could tell he was thinking everything would be all right now. Once two of these strange creatures, women, got together, anything was possible. But Janet knew and through her Celtic feyness sensed that Claire knew, too, that Death was the third and unseen partner in their impassioned embrace.

A month later Claire died, as gracefully as she had lived. But in her dying she demonstrated a ruthlessness she had never shown in life. Three days before the end, just after the doctor had made a final, despairing attempt to get her into hospital, she shook the little handbell that Janet had bought her when she was no longer strong enough to get out of bed.

Janet went up the narrow stairs, her heart beating fast, as it always did now when she heard that tinkle, dreading some final emergency that might face her as she went through the bedroom door. The doctor had told her and Jack what to expect.

But Claire was sitting up, some kind of resolve shaping her lovely, ravaged features. She patted a space on the edge of the bed near to her. 'Sit down, Janet, love.'

There was a quality of quiet command about her that brought Janet obediently to her side without a word.

'He's going to be destroyed, you know,' Claire said, without preamble.

'Nothing's going to happen,' replied Janet stubbornly. 'Nobody's going to be destroyed. You're going to get better.'

Claire laughed a little, her face very fond. 'Oh, Janet, love, you are a marvel! I remember that Welsh eye of yours. You've known what's going to happen to me since the minute I opened the door to you four weeks ago. And I've known for a lot longer than that.'

Janet made to interrupt with a protest, but Claire gave her no chance. 'You think it was all Jack's idea to go down to Wales and fetch you? So does he. It wasn't. I put the notion into his head.'

'But why?' demanded Janet. 'Why didn't you just write and ask me yourself? I'd have come from anywhere in the world!'

Claire paused and gazed steadily at Janet: 'I wanted you to see what kind of man Jack was.'

Janet felt herself begin to blush, but pressed on with what she felt had to be said. 'I already know what kind of man he is. You must remember why I left!'

'I don't mean that. Yes, you were in love with Jack, but that's not the same as knowing him. I wanted you to see that he's not all iron and stone. He feels pain, feels it hard, deep down, doesn't let nobody know. Maybe that's what makes him the way he is. I've been loved by that man more than anyone has any right to ask. That's why, when I go, he's going to go through hell's fire. God knows he's suffered enough trying to get me out of . . . this . . . ' She made a weary gesture embracing the whole slum ghetto into which they were locked. 'He hasn't got the education, so he's tried to do it with his back and his brawn and it's finding out that they're not enough that's made him harder than ever – on the outside. Sometimes I see an expression on his face that's like two hundred years old. So you've got to take over.'

She threw in the last bit fast, so that it didn't register with Janet immediately. Then: 'What was that?' she demanded. 'I've got to what?'

Claire was quite calm. 'There are going to be three kids

to look after, two of them barely able to walk. Jack can't cope. Not if he's going to have to earn a living at the same time. And even if he didn't have to do that, he still couldn't cope, he's just not that sort of man.'

'I don't want to talk about it any more,' Janet said, decisively. 'Anyway, it's not going to be necessary.'

She rose to go. Claire seized her hand in her delicate, now almost transparent fingers. 'Janet, I've got two days, three at the most.' Her voice sounded exhausted, as if it were coming from a long way away. 'I can feel it. I know. Tomorrow, I want the priest, but he's not the one who can help me to die peacefully. It's you—'

Janet tried to push the responsibility away. 'I don't want—'

But Claire, in her new-found ruthlessness, had no intention of allowing her a say: 'I've always had a thing about dying peacefully. I've always known I could – die peacefully, I mean – if everything else was all right; if what I was leaving behind me was how I wanted it to be. But everything won't be how I want it to be if I know Jack's going to be left on his own with three kids to bring up and nobody to help him.' She began to roll her head restlessly from side to side. 'And what'll happen to the kids? What sort of life will they have? Maybe they'll take them away from him, split them up, put them into institutions—'

The head-rolling became wilder, the tears cascaded and spread, like a glaze, down her cheeks.

Janet shouted, in desperation: 'All right, I'll stay, I'll look after them.' More slowly, she added: 'If it becomes necessary. And if Jack wants it.'

'Jack will want it,' Claire assured her. It wasn't until a long time afterwards that Janet realised how quickly the head-rolling had stopped and the tears had dried up.

Three days later, she died, just when she said she would.

Janet was alone in the house with the man for whom she had burned from the first minute she had laid eyes on him and she wished she were anywhere else on God's earth.

7

The day after Jack's disappearance, Carol was sitting eating her lunch, as usual, at the Pier Head. Idly, she watched as a ferry boat thrashed and wheeled, in a storm of foam, to come alongside and disgorge its hurrying passengers.

She still smouldered from the sense of injustice at her father's behaviour the day before. She had known enough not to expect gratitude, but to have the situation so totally turned round on her, so that suddenly she was on trial herself on a charge of whoring! She chomped viciously into a sandwich as she watched the boat-load disembark.

She saw the dark, heavy hair before she saw anything else, in a gap among the other passengers. She felt a catch in her breath and choked slightly on her sandwich. Then the golden eyes flashed in her direction. He had on one of his beautiful suits and he was carrying, of all things, a sort of drawstring sack or bag over his shoulder. He saw her practically at the same time she saw him. He didn't smile and neither did she. As he came towards her, she watched, fascinated, the way the river breeze snatched at that heavy hair, pulling it about, then the minute it let go, the hair dropped back into place instantly as if nothing had disturbed it.

She had heavy, swinging hair, too. She resolved one day she'd have hers cut in that way.

He sat down beside her on the bench. Instantly, she felt the vibrations from him, as she had done the first time he walked into the shop. Her intuition told her that he was conscious of her physically, too. She couldn't think why. Admittedly, she was putting on a bit more flesh now and she seemed to be getting taller, but compared to the birds a top gun like this must know – and she'd seen some of them in the photographs she'd peeked at – she was still Oliver Twist dressed like a girl.

He spoke casually, easily,as if they were old friends. 'How's your father doing?'

'He's scarpered,' she said,' 'disappeared.'

'Good God!'

'Oh, it's nothing to worry about,' she reassured him. 'He's done it before. He'll be back when he's had a few fights, smashed a few people up.'

'Does he drink?'

'Not more than any other docker. He doesn't get pissed and go berserk, if that's what you mean. He can go ape cold-stone sober.'

'Then what did he get exercised about? Go ape about?'

'He thought the only way I got you to help him was because you'd been screwing me.'

Once again, Stewart Crown's composure was chipped by the totally unfenced directness of this odd little girl. Her eyes were on him now, completely unaware of how open and disconcerting her attitude was. 'Why on earth should he think that?' was all he could say.

'I suppose because he couldn't find any other reason why someone like you should help someone like us.' She paused for a moment, the blinding blue eyes giving him nowhere to hide. 'Why did you help us?' she asked, curiously. 'That was what I couldn't really answer when he asked me.'

'Well, you seemed pretty confident I *would* help you,' he said, playing for time by turning the question back on her. 'Why did you think I would?' Thank God he didn't meet many like this in court.

'What's in that bag?' she asked, unexpectedly. Completely untutored in intellectual fencing she nevertheless knew, from her native intelligence, when it was time to make a ninety-degree turn.

'It's my wig and gown,' he said. 'I've just come from Chester Assizes.'

She'd had time enough to think now and she'd decided the best thing was to be straight. 'When I came to see you,' she said, 'it was partly because I didn't know who else to go to. But, as well as that, it was because I didn't think you'd send me away. And why I didn't think you'd send me away was because I had an idea you half-fancied me.'

Crown knew when to meet directness with directness. 'How old are you?' he asked, the legal brain still sweeping for mines.

'Sixteen, going on seventeen.'

'I do fancy you,' he said.

And now she identified the thought that had jumped into her mind the minute she saw that dark hair blowing on the boat. She'd wanted to pull him, but the nuns and her father and the whole air in which she lived had too strong a grip. But if her father had so little faith in her he thought she already had . . . sod them all!

Crown was looking at her curiously, her swift reverie showing, as did all her emotions, in her eyes, while her severe little face remained expressionless. Without warning, she smiled her very surprising smile, the flawless teeth making her suddenly dashing. 'I fancy you, too,' she replied. 'I'd like you to put your wig and gown on and screw me in front of those magistrates.'

Crown laughed aloud. Fantasies were one thing he hadn't expected from her. 'Good God,' he said, 'I never suspected what a hot-bed of vice I was stepping into every time I brought one of my innocent little rolls of film through the sedate portals of Marshall & Nephew.'

'I like it when you rabbit on like that,' she said. 'It's one of the things that turns me on. What are you doing this afternoon?'

Crown laughed again. He was beginning to get the full strength of this weird little dolly's essence and he found it stimulating beyond measure.

'It so happens,' he said, determined to regain the initiative, 'that all I have to do for the rest of the day is to read one brief – that's the details of my next case. But you have to get back to Marshall & Nephew, otherwise their whole empire will be in imminent danger of collapse.'

'They can stagger along without me for one afternoon,

especially when I've got a sudden belly-ache.'

He rose decisively. 'Look,' he said, 'I've got to get back to my flat and make a few 'phone calls. You finish your lunch and then follow me. I'll be waiting for you.'

'I can come with you now.'

'No,' he said, hastily, 'you finish your lunch. You'd only be sitting around while I talked dreary business on the 'phone.'

'Okay.' She knew bloody well it hadn't got anything to do with business. It had to do with him not being seen walking through town with the likes of her. Especially, it had to do with no one seeing them go into his flats together. On her own, with five doorbells to choose from, who was to know whose bell she was pushing? The phrase struck her as obscene and she laughed.

He stopped as he was moving away. 'What are you laughing at?' he demanded, bristling slightly.

'Just a thought,' she said. 'Nothing to do with you.'

Satisfied, he turned and went on his way, a cavalier figure, his bag slung over his shoulder, his stride lordly.

And yet wasn't it to do with bloody him? Carol asked herself. She'd been laughing at the pushing someone's bell gag, yes, but hadn't she been laughing a touch bitterly at him? At his caution? His question about her age hadn't passed her by, either. She looked after him as the shapely back diminished in the distance. She wished those long legs would trip in their majestic, masculine progress and send him flying flat on his face. Fuck him, she wouldn't go. See how he liked that.

But when she said she'd got a sudden belly-ache she wasn't far from the truth – except that it wasn't the kind she'd thought she meant when she said it. She had an urgent, warm glow all down there. It was as if, when she stood up, her upper thighs, her pelvis and her lower stomach would be delineated by a glowing red line. She imagined herself walking along the Pier Head with her crotch outlined in mysterious, pulsating neon light and she couldn't decide whether there would be a male stampede towards her or away from her.

Half an hour later she was listening to the turn-on voice, speaking to her from the Entryphone at the elegant Georgian door in Rodney Street. 'Push the door, Little Miss Muffet.'

She shoved the door and found herself again in the hushed, cosseting and immaculate hall. She rejected the lift again, but this time in order to postpone the encounter for just a few more seconds. Carol Blair had the heart of a young lion, but just now she was so nervous that, as she climbed the stairs, each leg juddered as she put her feet down.

Stewart Crown was standing as he had done the first time, just inside the door, one hand on it. He wore a short crimson silk robe a bit like a karate jacket. It showed his bare legs. Carol was glad to recall they were strong and brown. She hated white, skinny legs. There was something of a pose in the way he was standing, but she had to admit he looked knockout. She advanced slowly towards him, trying to conceal her shaking, wondering, in a lunatic fashion, if her cunt really was burning the carpet like a laser beam.

'Come, Miss Muffet,' said Crown, 'it's not fair to keep your lover waiting.'

'What's all this Miss Muffet bit, anyway?' she asked as she went in, feigning casual indifference. She wished she'd got pretty knickers on like the ones in the shops in Bold Street, instead of the utility cotton jobs she was wearing.

'You remember the rhyme. Little Miss Muffet sat on a tuffet, eating her curds and whey. There came a big spider that sat down beside her . . . '

'You're no spider,' she said, 'you haven't got the legs for it.' She walked past him into the elegant, masculine room with its smell of leather and roses and polished wood, feeling the satisfaction of seeing him look momentarily disconcerted as he glanced down at his legs.

He shut the door. 'Let me take your coat,' he said.

The minute he touched her she knew that the vibrations she had sensed in him every time she'd seen him were in his hands, too. She felt as if her skin had rippled like a nervous horse. Despite her bravado, Carol knew nothing about making love, except for the noises she had heard from the front bedroom and the practical mechanical details she had inevitably picked up during a lifetime in the slums. She'd seen enough couples poking in corners, been tumbled and groped by enough boys to be something of an expert in the cruder aspects of fucking. In one sense she knew everything. In another she knew nothing. She thought it was smash and grab. Nothing had prepared her for what was about to happen.

Somehow, in taking her meagre little coat, Stewart Crown had turned her round to face him. Now he brushed her lips with his, just a fleeting, sliding contact with the insides of his lips, inviting her to open her mouth. At the same time, he buried strong fingers in her hair and massaged her scalp, not gently, but with powerful, insistent pressure. The effect was extraordinary, a warmth spreading down from her scalp through her neck and shoulders right down to her stomach and the whole of her pelvic area. Her mouth opened automatically and the softness of the inside of her lips met the softness of his and a new thrill was added to the tide of sensation running down her body. She felt his hard male face behind the soft lips and just the difference of it, the fresh beard beginning to grow through, giving it a slight harshness, was dizzying.

Now the tip of his tongue was running inside her lips, in front of her teeth, now it was pressing hard under her tongue. And now he had slid his hands under her skirt, cupping her buttocks and he was hoisting her up, still with his mouth on hers, his tongue raking her. She realised with a delicious shock that he was naked under the silk robe as she felt the hard ridge of his cock pressed against her body. She was giving him pleasure, too! The knowledge sent another surge of excitement powering through her. She wanted to give him more, wriggling her firmly muscled young belly against him. 'No,' he whispered urgently, 'not yet.'

Deftly, he changed his grip, cradling her behind the knees and back and lifting her effortlessly. He carried her through into the bedroom, butting the door open with his shoulder, and then those magician's hands were all over her, undressing her with an expertise that defied analysis. It was as though catches, zips and fastenings had ceased to exist. Her clothes slid from her and suddenly she was naked, standing in front of him as he sat on the edge of the bed and he clasped her by the hips and buried his face between her thighs, nuzzling into her blonde fur, as palely golden as her hair. Yet another jolt of arousal ripped through her, looking down on that darkly beautiful head, with all its masculine authority, pressed into her down there. She caught her breath convulsively and grasped the back of his neck; spreading her legs, pulling him into her, trying to swallow him. She reached out and pressed him back on the bed: she was ready now, now! She wanted to engulf him, to possess and be possessed.

'Not yet,' he murmered again. He rolled her on to her back and smoothed her out with his hands, like some precious material, until she was lying straight, flat out.

'I'm skinny,' she objected, as the jungle-cat eyes surveyed her.

'You're like a sketch,' he said,' an exquisite sketch. You mustn't disparage your body.' She wondered hazily what disparage meant, but had no time to ponder it for his powerful, sensitive fingers claimed her again as he kneeled over her, starting at her scalp, then finding leaping responses at nerve centres behind her ears, between her neck and her collarbone, in the articulation of her elbows: all the time talking to her softly in that beautiful, purring voice, telling her how lovely she was, how fine and delicate, how rich her texture, until the gentle outpouring of words and the cunning mastery of his fingers seemed to merge in a haze of golden sensation. He stroked his tongue across and around her nipples as if he were painting them with velvet and she felt her labia swelling and plumping as if her nipples were a kind of switch. Then he pressed his thumbs simultaneously into the soft spot inside each hip bone and she came sweetly there and then.

Finally, he moved on to the insides of her thighs and the

nerve channels between the smooth muscles, now slippery with her own juices, the fingers probing deeply, triggering flashpoints, moving on finally to her velvety lips and her clitoris, now throbbing like a minuscule version of his own penis, which all the time she had watched as it waited, pulsating, like a thing of its own, for its turn. Just as she was ready to scream with the pent-up energy of her arousal, her internal fluids flooding and fleshing her to a peak, he slid on a sheath and went into her.

A faint expression of surprise crossed his face and he withdrew. He pushed in again, a little further this time, and again withdrew. And again. And again. She lost count of the gentle thrusts, each a little deeper, each suffusing her body with sensation. He was big and long and she was small. He knelt up between her thighs and she instinctively raised her feet to his shoulders, pressing on them with her little pink soles, helping him to penetrate her more deeply. By the time he had filled her, she had already come, deeply, three times.

Then he was all in, the hilt of him pressing against her and as he lowered himself and lay full length on her, the passivity his authority had imposed on her dissolved and her strong, runner's legs clamped and unclamped the spare, muscled body between them like twin pythons. Unknowingly, she had inherited from her mother an exceptional ability to control her pelvic muscles. She was as conscious of them as she was of moving an arm or a leg. She moved instinctively to his rhythm, rippling like a serpent outside and inside and as they exploded within seconds of each other, Stewart Crown, who had expected to be the principal pleasure-giver in this encounter, found himself the recipient of some of the wildest, sweetest tastes he had known.

'You didn't tell me,' he said.

'I thought you mightn't go through with it if I did.'

'There's one thing that puzzles me,' he said.

'Yeah?' She was lying, superbly relaxed, her head resting on his thighs, looking up at the slimly ribbed muscles of his brown stomach, smelling the sweet aroma of fresh semen.

'It was your first time,' he said,' 'and yet you were so good.

'You brought out the beast in me.' She smiled her white smile and then started idly to flip his now soft and satiated cock. Instantly, it started to stiffen and regain its appetite.

He sat up abruptly. 'No, you don't, Miss Muffet,' he said. 'I've got a brief to read and you've got to go home. The bathroom's through there – there's a bidet.'

'What's that?' she asked.

It suddenly came to him with a jolt that he'd just fucked an ill-educated, under-privileged, market-stall-dressed slum girl and that it didn't feel like that at all. This strange-eyed stray was more woman than any girl he'd ever met. She felt like an equal who simply happened to have been born in the wrong place.

That night, Jack Blair came home again, as they'd all known he would, his big knuckles bruised, his face cut and battered. He said nothing, wolfed down his meal and went to bed.

While he ate, Carol studied him covertly in quiet triumph. Now he really did have something to whop her for and he didn't know. She supposed she really *was* a slut now. Well, it sure beat the shit out of just being thought one. She rubbed her thighs together in slow body-memory and the corners of her mouth twitched.

Martha watched her from across the room. Martha had no psychic antennae at all. She dealt in solid practicalities, so she merely wondered what was the secret her little sister was quietly, almost triumphantly, hugging.

She had a secret herself. She'd got a new man. But she was damned if she was going to bring him anywhere near Jack this time. He was the unlikeliest beau in the world, really. He was George Ironstile.

That first day, seven months ago, all blag and bluster at first, when he had finally pulled his chair around her side of the desk, had been the start of it. She had taken him, step by step, through the intricacies of his tax affairs, his ruddy face getting redder, like a ripening tomato, as he struggled to follow her, while her three colleagues in the office had watched entranced. She was conscious, after the first hour, when she had neatly unravelled some of the knots and laid out the results for him in rows of neat figures, that he would now and then raise his head from the papers and study her profile with his small, bright, brown eyes.

When it was all finished and she'd straightened him out, he thanked her and left. Her colleagues congratulated her on her handling of an awkward customer. And yet she was conscious of a sense of let-down, almost of disappointment. He was one of the roughest diamonds you'd meet in a day's march – well, wasn't she? – but the energy and drive he was putting into that crude little business . . .

When she left to go home, he stepped out from beside the portico outside. 'I wondered if you'd like to have a bite to eat wi' me,' he asked straight out in his Lancashire accent.

'I don't mind if I do,' she answered, without hesitation. She knew Janet wouldn't be worried at home. She worked late as often as not.

He had taken her to a cheap little restaurant nearby and even though he'd sat down before she had and let her struggle out of her own coat and even though the place smelled of hot grease, it was the first time any man had ever taken her to a proper, sit-down, tables-and-chairs restaurant with nylon curtains at the window. She knew – though there was no regulation about it – that if her Inspector knew she was being dined by one of her victims, he would knit his tarred-rope eyebrows together in disapproval, but she didn't give a damn. There was more to life than wagging your rump after a patronising pat on the head from the boss and she was intrigued by this clumpy, beef-faced George Ironstile, who was man enough to know when he was licked and could surrender with such grace that he made it a kind of victory. Where a scrap-iron thug – and they usually were thugs – got that kind of agile diplomacy from she didn't know. She was interested to find out.

He grabbed a menu from an adjoining table and studied

it without consulting her. 'We've got two choices,' he said. 'Scampi with french fries or scampi without french fries. What'll it be?'

'With,' she answered.

A strung-out waitress with a face like a failed soufflé approached: 'Yes?'

'Two. With,' ordered George Ironstile.

'Anything to drink?' asked the sunken soufflé.

'A jug of white.'

The soufflé sniffled. 'Carafe of the house white,' she corrected. So she was going to be wined as well, thought Martha. Another historic first.

'Whatever you say, sunshine,' said Ironstile to the waitress, 'so long as we don't go blind.'

The waitress departed with all the vitality of a squeezed-flat toothpaste tube and George turned to Martha without guile or preamble. 'You could help me,' he said.

'I thought I just did,' she replied, bluntly.

'You were just doing your job,' he said, 'servant of the public.'

'I could have told you to push off and pay an accountant to unscramble you.'

'Why didn't you, then?'

'Because he'd have bunged you on his compost heap of things to be attended to and it would have been another five months before anything got sorted out. I like things done and I like them tidy.'

George Ironstile studied her with his bright little brown eyes. If they'd been black, thought Martha, he'd have looked like a squat, tough teddy-bear. 'If you want to keep me tidy, you'd best do it yourself,' he said.

'Look,' she said, 'let's get something clear. I'm not anybody's for a plate of scampi and a glass of plonk. I put you straight today, now you can get on with it and keep yourself straight. I'm not wet-nursing you.'

Their meal had been delivered and George was speaking with his mouth full. 'I'm not asking you to do it for nowt. I'd pay you good money. Just a couple of hours a week, that's all I want.'

'Look,' said Martha, 'I'm a tax officer, not a bloody accountant.' She drank some of her wine. Never having had any past her lips before, she didn't know whether it was good or bad. It tasted like boiled flintstones.

'All I know is that you understand figures,' he insisted. 'They mean something to you. They don't to me. What I understand is cash in my hand. All the rest is crap.' He leaned across the table to her, a composition in black, brown and lobster-red. 'I know how to make bloody money,' he said. He dived into his pocket and produced a wad of notes as thick as his forearm, slapping it on the table.

The eyes of the couple at the next table bulged. It was all in five-pound notes. They think I'm a whore, thought Martha. At those prices, I wish I were. The other half of her mind, the computer-figures-tax half, was wondering where the hell all that bare-arsed cash had come from.

'I'm not asking you to teach me how to fiddle my tax,' he went on. 'I'll pay my bloody tax.' He had finished half his dinner and had now forgotten about the rest of it. Martha carefully and systematically went on spearing scampi with her fork and transferring them to her strong, thick-lipped mouth.

He continued: 'All I'm saying is . . . Look—' he arrested her remorseless, scampi-scourging hand ' – all I'm saying is that in my game you have to put yourself about, you have to get out and around and make people sit up and take notice. And you can't do that if you're sitting on your arse, up to your navel in figures. All I want is you to take care of that side of it for me, part-time. I'll pay you cash, no need to declare it – Oh, Christ, I didn't mean that—'

'I didn't hear it,' said Martha. She was impressed by the energy pouring out of this man like kilowatts out of a power station. Anyone else might have been lit up and carried away with it, but she, with her low, rock-like centre of gravity, was able to absorb and withstand it.

'I'll tell you what I'll do,' she said. 'Yes, I'll take you on. I'll give you one night a week to keep your books straight. And I don't want no humpty messing about with cash.

You'll pay me by cheque and you'll claim it as a business expense.' Hell's delight, half the staff in her building moonlighted in one way or another. She was much more excited by the challenge of channelling the massive life-force of this ugly, scarlet-faced bugger sitting opposite to her than by considerations of Civil Service etiquette.

'I'll need to see your operation. Your business lay-out, warehouse, yard, whatever you want to call it.'

'What for?'

'Because I want to see what goes on.'

'What, you mean you think I'd give you bent figures to work with?'

'Damned right.'

'Well, sod you, then!' He made to rise from the table and stomp out.

'Hold your water,' she said, 'you haven't paid the bill yet.'

He subsided into his chair. 'You are, without exception, the most insulting bitch I ever met in my life,' he steamed.

The following week Martha visited George Ironstile's 'operation' for the first time. As she came out from work he picked her up in a rusty old truck and drove her the thirty bone-shaking miles to just outside Preston.

'I knew you collected scrap-iron,' said Martha after the first mile. 'I didn't know you drove it as well.'

'Have you got any kind of bloody transport at all?' asked George.

'No,' she admitted.

'So shut up,' he said.

They rattled into the yard after dark. Martha was at first totally bemused. It looked like a cross between a farmyard and a natural disaster. George Ironstile had seven horses stabled in it and seven carts. Among the horse dung and the straw and the spilled oats was a tangle of old refrigerators, tin baths, lead and copper piping, zinc guttering, antiquated bicycles, and a number of other objects which Martha found unidentifiable. There were three bonfires, burning yellow and orange in different corners of the yard, and a coke brazier glowing like a ruby in the middle.

'This is it?' she asked.

'This bloody *is* it!' George fired back, indignant at the incredulity in her voice. 'What did you expect, the British Steel Corporation?'

He explained that he employed seven 'totters', men who drove the horses and carts around residential areas and touted housewives for anything made of metal that they were thinking of throwing away or wanted to get rid of. Sometimes they paid the women small amounts of cash, but mostly the wives were so glad to be relieved of their junk that they let it go for nothing. At the end of the day, the totters brought it all back to the yard for George to assess and categorise.

'But if it's such a good thing,' asked Martha, 'why aren't there more people doing it? How come you've got the monopoly round here?'

They were sitting in the glass-fronted shed that George called his office, overlooking the yard, drinking tea like treacle. For answer, George looked around the yard at his totters, unloading the day's haul. 'Have you had a look at my lads?' he asked.

Martha looked around at the figures lifting old refrigerators as if they were empty cereal packets and realised that they were almost as big and teak-like as her father.

'Where d'you find them?' asked Martha.

'In pubs,' said George, frankly. 'I go into all the pubs round about and I wait for a fight to start. A big one. The last man on his feet at the end of it – I offer him a job. Two quid a day and if he sees any opposition while he's on his rounds, he's to . . . like . . . discourage it.'

Martha looked down at the men moving steadily among the carts. Some of the carts seemed to have more on them than others. 'Two quid a day,' she asked, 'no matter how much they collect?'

'That's right.'

'What if one of them comes back with too little?'

'I give him a rollicking. If it happens again, he gets fired.'

'What d'you reckon is too little?'

'Whatever I feel is too little' – he slapped himself in the stomach – 'here.'

Martha, with this man, was beginning to learn tact. 'May I make a suggestion?' she asked.

'It's a free country.'

'Instead of two pounds a day, why don't you make it one, plus ten per cent commission on what they bring in?'

'They'd go raving ape on me. They'd just jack it in and I'd never see them again.'

'No, they wouldn't,' said Martha, 'not if the first couple of weeks you guaranteed to pay them their two quid a day anyway, if their new deal didn't give them more.'

Georged shifted about on his chair, unable to locate the precise source of his irritation; but he expressed it as accurately as he could. 'Listen,' he said, 'I brought you in to do the books. I didn't ask you to re-organise the fucking business.'

Martha took home with her the pathetically rudimentary books that George had been keeping and she worked on them over the next few nights in her bedroom. She came to the astonishing conclusion that he was making three thousand pounds a year clear, after tax, and that, with a little rationalisation and simple business management, he could double it. In 1961, that was good money.

She hadn't got a telephone at home – nobody in the street had – so that it was at the office a month later that George Ironstile rang her. 'It's more bloody trouble getting through to you than ringing Buckingham Palace,' was his opening salvo. 'Listen, I was thinking we could have a dose of scampi tonight and see how you were getting on.'

'I'm getting on fine,' she said, 'and I'd rather have Chinese.'

He picked her up outside the office and drove her to a Chinese restaurant.

'Three bloody grand a year in me pocket – never!' spluttered George, choking over his pork sweet and sour.

'I'm telling you,' said Martha.

'Then where's it all going?' he demanded.

'You tell me,' challenged Martha.

'Well,' he started thinking about it, 'I make the payments on a little car for me mam and dad—'

'That's how much?'

'Six quid a week with insurance and everything.'

'That's three hundred a year. And?'

'And I like to give Dad twenty quid in his hand every week – he's all gnarled-up with arthritis, he can't work and he's not due for his pension for another five years.'

'That's another thousand a year. Right. First of all you put your father on the pay-roll as a clerk. That way his twenty quid comes out of the company, not out of your personal take-home. You make the car a company car, so it becomes a company expense. That means you'd have an extra thirteen hundred pounds to spend. Except I don't think you should spend it: you should plough it back into the business.'

'Listen,' said George joyfully, 'there's going to be plenty to plough back into the business without that! You know that idea of yours about putting them on commission? Well, it's worked like a bloody miracle! They've been bringing in more stuff than I can handle!'

Martha privately upgraded him ten points for 'that idea of yours'. A lot of men would have said 'of ours', or simply 'of mine'. She had no intention, however, of showing him he had passed 'Go'. Instead, she said, brutally: 'That's no excuse for chucking money away. Money's for working with. It's . . . like . . . the most precious raw material of all; it's a crime to squander it.'

'I would just remind you,' answered George, with as much dignity as he could project through a mouthful of prawn cracknel, 'that I did build my business up from my old man's one cart and horse to seven horses and carts and that I didn't do it by being daft about money.'

No, thought Martha, you've done it by pure bloody brute force and ignorance. The overkill, in terms of energy expended, must have been horrendous. But then energy was what this man had got. It was driving out of every pore. When he ate, it didn't look as if he were consuming food so much as taking fuel on board. If only it had all been underpinned by an understanding of figures, of money as a commodity, money in the abstract, where might he be now?

Back home, Martha began to draw graphs.

During the next six months they kept in touch, once or twice a month, George Ironside taking Martha to dinner at a series of local Wallasey restaurants, gradually escalating in style and price as George increasingly prospered under the new commission system and Martha's merciless invigilation over his books.

There came a point when her graphs reached a plateau. This time, she called him. 'We have to meet,' she said. 'Dinner's on me.'

'You're not progressing,' she announced abruptly, the minute they sat down in the little Italian restaurant which was their current favourite.

'Not progressing?' was his indignant reaction. 'I'm making three times as much as I was this time last year.'

'But that's your limit: you could stay on it or thereabouts for the rest of your life. Is that what you want?'

'If only I could specialise – that's the secret. If I could specialise in ferrous metals—'

'What are they when they're at home?'

'Well, basically . . . iron and steel. Look—' Warming to his theme he leaned forward, putting an elbow into the spaghetti. 'Look, d'you know, really, where you find most decent scrap – I mean iron and steel?'

'No,' said Martha, honestly.

'You find it on the factory floor. Engineering shops, machine tool makers – what are they doing all day? They're working iron. They're shaving it, cutting it, sawing shapes out of it. And where does all the waste end up? On the factory floor. Perfect metal, only needing to be melted down and used again. It's just money lying around. At the end of the day they're heel-deep in cuttings, shavings, slivers, lumps and bumps that are a pain in the arse to them. All they want is to get shot of it. They'll let you have it for next to nothing if you can guarantee to shift it out of their way efficiently. I met a chap, he's got a fair-sized little steel-turning factory. The bloke who swept up for him, like, has just died. He's looking for someone to make a new contract with, to get shot of all his scrap for him.'

'Then take it on, for God's sake!' said Martha.

'Don't you think I would if I could?' shouted George, the closest she had ever seen him to frustration. 'The things it could lead to, the standing it would give me, the other contracts I could pick up. But I can't! I bloody can't!'

'Why not!'

'It's not a horse and cart job!' he explained, exasperated. 'Trundling about, dropping horse shit all over the place! You need the right equipment – a tipper-lorry, scoops. Personally, I'd like an electro-magnet on a generator; they've got 'em in the States – naturally,' he added bitterly.

'How many trucks would you need?'

'A minimum of two.' She tried to speak, but he carried on. 'But it's not only the trucks. To do the job properly I'd need my own furnace, melting pot, hoppers, billet-moulds—'

'Just tell me exactly how much you think the contract with your factory-owning mate would be worth and what you think it could lead to,' Martha interrupted.

Within three weeks Martha, dragging George – cardboard-stiff and creaking in his best suit – into his local bank and presenting his case for him as his accountant, had got him the money to buy his equipment, secured on the value of his present site, his current profits and his track record thus far.

After the meeting, the bank manager gave them both a glass of sherry and discreetly offered Martha a job. Martha noted George's face turning plum-coloured just before she equally discreetly turned the offer down.

She sipped her sherry. She wasn't sure whether it was that or the colour of George's face that gave her the warm feeling inside.

8

It was Saturday afternoon. It was snowing. Carol was supposed to be out shopping. Instead, she was inside in the warm, watching the snowflakes drift gently down past the window and sitting astride Stewart Crown.

They were both naked and she was wriggling like an eel and gasping with slow lust as she navigated the movements of him inside her. 'Riding St George', the Elizabethans used to call it, according to Stewart: they used to say it was an infallible way to beget a bishop.

Not that she was in the begetting business herself; and neither was he. Caution was his middle name. Still, she thought, as she spread her thighs a bit wider to get him touching that delicious corner just to the side, way, way deep . . . aaah! . . . he didn't half know a thing or two about this lark.

Ever since that first encounter when he had opened to her the Ali Baba's cave of the world of sweet sensation, he had been her sexual guru, bringing her to a knowledge of herself and of men with a steady, tender authority.

Only one thing slightly irritated her. His total control. He had never once come before she had. She appreciated that it was the considerateness of the gentleman-lover, but she wished that just once she could excite him unbearably enough to bring him off first. When, a couple of weeks ago, he had rolled their knotted-together bodies over to leave her on top for the first time, she thought she had the answer. Now she was in control. She could dictate the rhythm, the strokes, pace, friction, her own reactions. But still she couldn't shake his magnificent forbearance. Still he refused to come until he knew she was climaxing or had already done so.

He reached up now and was cupping her breasts, which were fuller and rounder than ever, but seemed, thank God, to have stopped developing any more while the rest of her caught up. He was stroking her nipples with his thumbs, sending that old, unmistakable message down her body through those mysterious electrical connections which he had explained to her was how the nerves worked. 'You're a nymph from old, rough, sensual Greece,' he whispered. 'You drive the satyrs to a frenzy.' He knew how she loved to be caressed with words, even though she didn't always know what they meant, sometimes especially if she didn't know what they meant. In any case, she always remembered them and asked him to explain them afterwards, which very often started the whole gorgeous thing all over again.

This time she was determined to shatter that unshakable command. She squirmed again in a kind of circular motion she knew he loved and leaned back to cup his balls in her hand, to which she knew he also always responded. In doing so, though, she left herself fatally vulnerable. As she stretched back, her clitoris, in full arousal, was pulled proudly forward from its hood. Stewart shifted his left hand from her breast and gave the cheeky, soft little ruby the merest whisper of a touch.

It was all that was needed to light the fuse that seemed to connect every erogenous zone in her body. The ripples came in from every point in the compass, culminating in a sunburst of pleasure and a primitive shout of ecstasy, followed a second later by the feeling of Big John, as she called his penis, leaping and straining inside her like a big salmon in a small net. He'd done it again, the clever, beautiful bastard!

Stewart laughed out loud at his joyously loving outwitting of her and looked up at her. She was nearly eighteen now, with a genius for physical passion that he had never encountered before. She still wore no make-up and all that illuminated the pale severity of the face was the magnificent smile now snarling down on him in love-hate and the eyes which, at the moment, were glinting with mischief.

Suddenly, he realised why. She was trying to lock the mare's hold on his spent penis. 'Oh no you don't, Miss Muffet!' he said. She grabbed his hands and tried to hold him down, but he rolled her over and tickled her on one of her trigger points just inside the crease of her thigh until she unlocked her legs.

Carol traced his profile with her forefinger and sighed. 'I've got to go,' she said, in the naïve Liverpool accent that was beginning to contrast so strangely with her starkly serious face and the way she moved and held herself. And yet already, Crown fancied, the music of her speech had taken on overtones of his own. She had an excellent ear. She couldn't help picking up what she found pleasing. She had once told him what a turn-on his voice was for her.

'Stay,' he said, 'I've got one of those dreadful Beatles discs for you. The least you can do is listen to it.' Before she could reply, the doorbell rang with a stridency that made them both jump.

'I'm not expecting anyone,' he said; 'we'll ignore it.'

But the bell was not to be ignored. It rang again and again with a stridency that seemed not merely mechanical, as if the person at the other end of it were somehow pumping his own urgency through the system.

Stewart cursed, rolled off the bed and strode, stark-ball-naked, through to the Entryphone. In some way, his hard, small buttocks expressed an absurd indignation that totally undermined his familiarly regal stride and Carol had to choke back her laughter.

'Yes?' he snapped.

'Is Carol Blair there?' asked an unmistakable Scotland Road-flavoured voice.

Shaken to the soles of his bare feet – he'd have taken an oath on Carol's discretion – his lawyer's training in mendacity nevertheless came to Stewart's aid. 'Never heard of her,' he said promptly. 'Wrong flat.'

By this time Carol had padded to his side, as nude as a peeled egg. She stood on tiptoe, pushed her head against Stewart's at the receiver and playfully got hold of his cock at the same time. The next words she heard made her forget all thoughts of mischief of that kind. Her brother said loud and clear; 'Aw, don't mess about, will you – it's bloody urgent!'

She snatched the receiver from Stewart. 'Tony, what is it?'

'Let's in, will you!' shouted Tony.

'Give us a minute,' said Carol and hung up. 'It's my brother,' she told Stewart, rushing for the bedroom and her clothes.

'How does he know you're here?' demanded Crown.

'I don't know,' she said. 'I've never told him a thing!' They found they were whispering, even though Tony was still downstairs in the street.

A few minutes later, Tony Blair was hurrying into the sitting room. He was seventeen now, filling out – though he'd never be anything but lean – and very handsome. His girl friends privately treasured the fact that he looked like Montgomery Clift. He had left school, desperately wanting to go on to art college, but Jack Blair had forced him to take a job he had engineered for him as a clerk in the Mersey Docks and Harbour Board, where he was stoically eating his heart out.

'That bastard's yelling murders,' he said, without introduction. 'He's fit for Rainhill,' he added, naming the local mental hospital.

Carol didn't need to be told who the bastard was. 'What's he on about?' she asked.

'You.'

'Why?'

'I don't know. He'd already flipped by the time he got home. He rammed into the house like a bloody bulldozer, yelling for you. We told him you were out shopping – Mam really thinks you are.'

'Why didn't you think I was?' asked Carol. 'How did you know I'd be here?'

'Aw, come on, Car,' Tony answered, almost reproaching her for lack of perception. 'You know how many mates you've got in this city. You were seen.' There it was again, the dreaded phrase – part of the Liverpool litany. God, how she longed to get out of this spy-ridden, guilt-ridden, priest-and-nun-ridden hole, where you were always the prisoner in the dock!

'D'you think he knows?' she asked anxiously. 'D'you think that's what it's all about?'

'No, I don't think so, 'Tony answered with some certainty.

'What can it be, then?'

'With that sod, how can you ever know? But you'd better come home soon, Car. You know him, you know what he's like. If you don't, he'll start asking round the neighbours where you could be, and you can bet your life someone will open his big mouth and he'll be round here like a runaway bloody truck!'

'I'll come now,' she said. Slinging on her coat, she picked up her handbag and went. 'Ta-ra,' she said to Crown.

'Goodbye,' he said gravely. Their relationship had never included little pecks of greeting or farewell. 'If you need me, just call.'

As the door closed behind her, Stewart Crown reflected on just what he'd taken on board when he started an affair with a slum girl. What if Jack Blair had traced his daughter to this flat? What if he had started trying to break the street door down? The scandal of a rumpus like that, the lack of finesse and discretion which important people in his profession would inevitably read into it, what about that? This had been a warning. If the boy was right and this blow-up hadn't anything to do with him, then it was a blessing in disguise. Better to cut loose now in case the next one was, indeed, about him.

And yet, in his balls, he knew that if she were in trouble, if her father were to injure her in some way and she came running, he would lash out on her behalf with every weapon at his command. Stewart Crown had never met a man of whom he was frightened yet. He would see her safe and then he would cut adrift. He'd have to. The future he'd got mapped out for himself couldn't conceivably include Carol Blair, and he realised he was perilously close to being in love with her.

*

In the other world of Scotland Road, Carol was knocking on the door, her stomach sick, her pale face paler than ever.

Janet opened the door, her face chalky. 'Carol, love—'

She was interrupted by a roar from inside the house. 'Is that her? Is that the filthy little slut?' His voice was an offence to the ears.

'Mam, what is it?' whispered Carol.

'I don't know!' Janet whispered back. 'That's what makes it worse!' She turned to Tony. 'Thank God you found her. I don't know what he'd have—'

'Where's Martha?' asked Carol hopefully.

'She's not in,' said Janet. 'She's still over the water.' Carol remembered that Martha had recently taken to spending her Saturdays on the other side of the river.

'Never mind your bloody whispering out there! Get the bitch in here!' came from the kitchen. The whole street could have heard him, but that didn't bother anybody: the street had been living in each other's pockets for years. 'I said bring her in!'

Carol dumped her coat on the hallstand and went on into the kitchen. Jack was sitting there, the Wrath of God carved in stone. He looked at her with a rage in his eyes that made them almost black, so dilated were the pupils. Without further speech, he got up from his chair and went to his jacket, which he had hung behind the door. He reached into his inside pocket and pulled something out, flinging it on the table. It was a copy of the *Amateur Photographer*. On the front were the words 'Grand Prize Competition Winner.' Underneath, taking up the whole glossy page, in colour, was the most striking girl Carol thought she had ever seen. She was completely naked, the pose was stunningly yet innocently erotic and the lighting was breathtaking in its artistry. It had made the face heart-bending in its angled shapeliness, its lights and hollows, curves and planes; the sculptured mouth challenged the imagination, the spectacular blue eyes were backed by visions, the hair was a blaze of white gold. The body was rounded, elegant, glossy, exaggerated in that the thighs were slightly too long, the breasts a little too round for truth, the curve of the buttock too close to perfection.

She stared at it, mazed with admiration even as a second dawning of consciousness filtered into her mind as through a gauze, overlaying her first impression. It was a picture of her! An impossible, fantasised image of her, transmuted by some kind of magic, but undeniably she. It was that last picture that Robert Marshall had taken of her.

As from a distance, she heard her father's voice before the first blow struck her. 'Dirty little cow! Sprawling arse-hole naked for everyone in the country to see!' Then she was reeling across the room under a blitzkrieg of savagery of a ferocity that even she had never experienced before. She was disorientated, hazy, as if everything were happening in a mist. Dimly, she heard Janet screaming, she saw Tony knocked unconscious by a punch to the jaw, then the lashes whistled down on her.

Jack Blair's fury didn't allow him to ritualise it this time: he whipped her anywhere, the leather strap hissing through the air across her back, her arms, her legs, her head, the side of her face, her neck. She was driven to the floor, where her old street-fighting experience prompted her to curl up, instantly, like a hedgehog. But even as the lash crackled agonisingly across her body, she was part-anaesthetised by the euphoric wonder of that magical image of herself that Robert Marshall had managed to conjure from his lights and lenses. Then she slipped into the full anaesthetic of unconsciousness, unaware of the hammering on the door. It was much later before she learned what happened after that.

As she fainted, with Jack, insensate, still laying into her, Janet ran screaming to open the door. Standing there was Stewart Crown, as like a young lord as ever she'd seen.

He took the trembling Janet gently by the shoulders and moved her to one side while he passed her and went down the hall to the kitchen. The sight that met his eyes appalled him. Carol was frozen by unconsciousness into her cowering position on the floor, and the wide-belted, shirt-sleeved, archetypal bully-figure of her father stood over her, brutal right arm raised. Crown's overwhelming instinct was to go for the man like a missile and try to smash him. But he had little doubt what the outcome would be and he had already decided that this battle would be fought on his ground and with his weapons.

'Blair!' Crown had an actor's control of his voice and he gave it the bang of a thunder-clap.

Jack Blair, who hadn't even heard the hammering on the door, froze. Then he turned slowly round to meet the golden eyes. They had a glow in them now like molten steel being poured from a hopper. 'What the hell are you doing here?' he demanded, his mind already darkening with an old suspicion revived.

'Your son called on me,' said Crown steadily. 'He told me he suspected you were going to inflict injury on his sister. He thought you should be prevented. I thought you should be prevented, too.'

'*You* thought!' Blair drew back his fist. He wanted to smash it straight through that structured face. Crown didn't flinch. He was gambling on what Blair saw behind the face, the bewildering thickets of the law, ending ultimately in bars and no sky. He continued, evenly: 'It seems that I'm too late. You have already injured your daughter.' He turned to Tony, who had staggered to his feet. 'Go and call an ambulance,' he said.

'You stay where you bloody are!' shouted Blair to his son. He turned to Crown. 'Where the fuck do you think you come off, walking in here and giving orders like king of the fucking castle?'

'Blair,' said Crown, deliberately omitting 'Mr' in order again to insinuate into the atmosphere the odour of the courts, 'you have beaten your daughter into insensibility. You could well be facing another charge of grievous bodily harm. And this time you won't have me. On the contrary, I shall be against you.'

He stared into the black-fringed, blue, bad eyes, so like Carol's and yet so infinitely different, and watched the words penetrate. 'The longer you leave your daughter without medical attention, the more serious the charge could be,' he added.

He turned to Tony again. 'Go and call that ambulance.'

This time, Blair was silent. Tony went, giving his stepmother a quick, loving, reassuring hug as she stood yellow-faced and shaking in the doorway.

Stewart Crown would never give a better performance in his life – and he was to put on some court spectaculars in the course of his career. Looking down on the crumpled figure of the girl he knew as a gay, loyal, quick-minded and joyously responsive lover all he wanted was to gather her against him, pouring strength into her, kissing her pale, battered face back to consciousness. Instead, he knelt gravely and took her pulse. It was strong and steady. She was durable, this gallant girl, who had come home, without asking his help, to what she must have known was going to be a beating and whom he realised, more forcibly than ever now, that he was going to have to abandon.

He looked up at Blair with death in his heart for him. 'Why?' he asked savagely.

Blair flung the magazine at him. 'That's why.'

Stewart Crown felt a jolt as if someone had jabbed him with an electric cattle probe. He was dazzled by the beauty of the image on the cover, the beauty he had believed only he had been able to discern. He was desperately jealous of the man, whoever he was, who had understood Carol so well. When did he take the picture? Before Crown knew her or after? And exquisite though the picture was, how could she make herself available to hundreds of thousands, perhaps millions, of voyeurs and lechers who would look at her and fuck her in their minds on the way to work?

He could sense Blair's eyes searching his face for some reflection of what he was feeling. Never had he been so glad that he had trained himself to isolate his face from his emotions. Nothing showed in his features. He said evenly, 'It's a beautiful picture. You should be proud of your daughter.'

The blue eyes stared unblinkingly into his. 'You fucking hypocrite!' said Blair.

The accusation maddened Crown, because he knew it to

be true, but his face still remained unchanged. He hit back as viciously as he knew how, going again unerringly for Blair's weak point as the ambulance brayed to a stop outside the door. 'Your freedom is in your daughter's hands now,' he said. 'If she prefers charges, there's not a lawyer in this town who can keep you out of jail. If I were you, I'd be thinking of a way of asking her forgiveness.'

The ambulance men showed no emotion as they gently lifted Carol on to the stretcher and carried her out to the audience that the street had become, at its doors and windows, and loaded her into their vehicle. Scenes like this were not unfamiliar to them in this part of town.

They took her, accompanied by Janet, the dark Welsh eyes like pools of pain, to Mill Road Hospital, bleakly isolated in the middle of the garbage-strewn derelict lots around it. There they treated her for shock, lacerations and contusions and kept her in overnight for observation. She told them some story of being set on by a gang of lads and they asked no questions. Next day she was discharged, but instructed she mustn't go back to work for at least a week.

It was from this point on that a cumulative series of events started to pile up that Carol was to remember for the rest of her life. The first arrival next day was Mr Mackenzie, nose pulsing like a blast furnace against a night sky, a visit that genuinely touched her.

He had, naturally, seen the magazine, received her sick note from the hospital and, from one or two clues which even someone as loyal and reticent as Carol had not been able to avoid giving, in the past, about her father, had put the equation together. She had never, until now, had the faintest inkling of how much Mr Mackenzie admired her guts, her determination and her simple clarity of character.

He bustled into her bedroom, ushered by Janet, all 'Well, well, well' and 'Now, now, now', covering both his embarrassment at revealing how much he cared about the child and his shock at seeing the poverty-scarred ugliness in which she lived. By the time he left he had, by means of an acuteness of observation and sheer worldly wisdom of which Carol had never suspected him, pierced the cloud of camouflage put up by her and Janet and taken in the whole story. Most importantly, he had established that Carol had had no idea that her picture would ever be published.

She was never to know the risk Mackenzie ran for her that night. He was the manager of one fairly average branch of a nationwide chain of camera shops belonging to Marshall & Nephew. But that evening, unannounced, he pitched up at the front door of the magical, fairy-tale house at Helsby and talked to Robert Marshall with the brutal, direct logic that only a Scotsman with his blood up can command. And when he left, he was still manager of his shop and Robert Marshall was a chastened, shaken man.

Next day, the royal blue Silver Cloud, observed from every blinkered window in the street, arrived outside 16 Mugsley Street.

'I didn't know,' he said. 'I just didn't think. Most girls today would give anything to have their picture on a cover. And most parents would accept it – so I thought, anyway. If I'd known it would result in this, I'd never have dreamed of putting that picture forward. Never.' It was the longest speech Carol had heard him make. But he hadn't finished yet. He took an envelope from his pocket. 'I meant to see you in the shop next week and give you this.' He handed it to her.

'What is it?'

'It's the prize for winning that competition. I feel it rightfully belongs to you.'

'Oh, no, that photo was your—'

'My photograph only exploited what was there. I know it sounds childish, but I've always wanted to win a prize with one of my pictures. Without you I couldn't have done it. Please take it.' Carol hesitated. 'If you don't, I'll give it to a dogs' home.'

'Take it, love,' urged Janet softly. 'I know what you're thinking. It's not that kind of money. It's a prize. Respectable. From a respectable magazine.'

'Okay, ta,' said Carol, taking the proffered envelope. 'It's really kind of you, like, it really is.'

He rose abruptly. 'I hope you're better soon.' He allowed himself a faint, sad smile. 'We don't want business dropping off in the Liverpool branch.' The Rolls murmured away just as Jack Blair, out on a lightning unofficial strike at the docks, turned the corner into his street. He saw the car disappearing and ran the rest of the way.

'Who was that?' he demanded as he burst in breathlessly.

'Someone from our Carol's firm,' Janet replied smoothly.

'What did he want?' he asked suspiciously.

'They'd heard the talk about Carol being beaten up by a gang of lads,' said Janet, marvelling at the silky fluency of her own lie, 'and they wanted to put up a reward for information about it to give to the police.' She had learned from watching Stewart Crown handle him how the shadow of the law levelled Jack out these days like turning down the gas under a pan of boiling fat.

'We don't need Marshall's sticking their bloody nose in,' he said. 'They've done enough damage already.'

'It's not them that did the damage,' said Janet, her face tight, knowing she had him on the defensive,' and if you're looking for something to eat, there isn't anything, I wasn't expecting you back.' He slammed out of the house as she'd hoped he would and she found her breathing becoming easier. She'd been terrified that Jack would somehow find out about the prize.

Carol, who had not spoken a word to her father since the beating, now opened the envelope. It contained a cheque, made out to her, for two hundred and fifty pounds.

Janet gasped. It was more money than she'd ever seen at one time in her life. 'You'll have to open a bank account, love,' she said excitedly.

Carol nodded thoughtfully. She'd read the small print in the magazine with more care than her mother. The first prize had been one hundred pounds.

But the biggest surprise was yet to come.

Twenty-four hours later a large, chauffeur-driven Mercedes drew up outside the house. Out of it the chauffeur, who was inordinately handsome, showed a tall, willowy man of about thirty-five, with crisply layered fair hair and a fresh-complexioned, rather serious face. His clothes had an immaculately cut, solemn trendiness which could only reflect a deep commitment to getting them right.

He looked up and down the street not, apparently, in the least dismayed at the surroundings in which his pristine presence found itself, and rapped with commanding confidence on the Blair door.

Janet opened the door. The stranger handed her a card.

'I'm Michael Willoughby,' he said. 'You may have heard of me. On the other hand, depending where your interests lie, you may not. I'd like to see Carol Blair, please. Are you her delicious mother?'

Janet was not so defeated that she couldn't recognise and rejoice in charm when she saw it. You'd have to have your jaws wired together, she thought, not to respond to this man with a smile.

'Stepmother,' she said, the Welsh music in her voice a little more pronounced. 'Carol's in, but she's not very well, I'm afraid.'

'Never mind.' said Willoughby, 'I've been known to make the sick take up their beds and walk.'

Janet smiled: 'Come in, won't you?' This man seemed to have the effect of putting you instantly at your ease. 'Carol,' she shouted, as he followed her up the hall to the kitchen, 'Carol, love, there's somebody here to see you.'

Carol shouted back from her bedroom; 'Give us a minute. Is it someone from the shop?'

'No, I don't think so,' called Janet. She looked at Michael Willoughby enquiringly, then down at his card, where all it said, in embossed gold lettering, was Michael Willoughby. 'You're not from the shop, are you?'

'No,' he said, 'I'm not from the shop, delicious stepmother. What I am, though I do say it myself, is the creator and owner of the most exclusive, certainly the most tasteful and possibly the most successful model agency in London.' As he reached the end of his speech Carol, in her dowdiest clothes, appeared in the doorway. Her right eye and cheek were still swollen, and stained by a livid yellow and purple bruise; the eye was still partially closed. Her upper lip was cut and swollen and there were red weals striping her neck.

Michael Willoughby, unlike Stewart Crown, had never been able fully to mask his feelings. For a brief flash his face now registered genuine distress, then he managed to cover it. 'Oh my!' he said. 'You are a funny little thing! What have you been up to? Experimenting with a new make-up?' He spoke to her as if he'd known her all his life. There was a quality of empathy and warmth about him that almost made her feel he had. She smiled a cracked, painful smile.

'I had an accident,' she said.

'This is Mr Michael Willoughby, love,' said Janet. 'He owns—'

'Yeah, I know,' Carol interrupted. She'd seen his picture in magazines. 'Bloody hell!'

'Well, I can't say it's the most elegant reaction I've ever had,' said Willoughby, 'but it's certainly the most flattering. Can't you guess why I'm here?'

'Well, yeah, I think I can,' said Carol, 'but . . . I mean . . . bloody hell. Anyway . . . that's not really me on that magazine.'

'You mean it was some person or persons unknown masquerading as you, do you?'

'No, but . . . well . . . you know—'

'My dear, solemn, swollen-faced little gnome, all art is illusion. If we insisted on everything being absolutely the real thing, all we'd have left is the wind blowing through a Greek lyre.'

He had, thought Carol, exactly the same way of treating her as a real person and of talking above her bloody head as Stewart Crown. She was momentarily at a loss. Janet, seeing her adrift, stepped in with her infallible answer to pain, problems or awkward pauses. 'Would you like a cup of tea?' she asked Michael Willoughby.

'Beautiful stepmother, there's nothing I'd like better,' he smiled. Janet bustled delightedly out to the cooker in the back kitchen and Carol and Michael Willoughby contemplated each other. Looking the way she did, in the surroundings in which she was, if fate had sent anyone but Willoughby he'd have walked out. But fate had sent her Willoughby, who now asked, politely, 'May I sit down?'

'Ay? Oh! Yeah! Sit down,' said Carol, who had never been asked the question before in her life. Willoughby sat down without examining the chair, which was something he customarily never omitted to do even in the Ritz. It might be a slum house, but his first glance at Janet had told him that everything inside it would be spotless.

'I think, I *think,*' said Willoughby, 'that you have the makings of a quite spectacular model.'

'Me?' Carol's head reeled as if the words were blows.

'Had you ever posed for anyone before Mr Robert Marshall, ace prizewinner of the national *Amateur Photographer* contest?'

'No, he . . . I—'

'Did he tell you what to do? I mean . . . positions, poses, how to hold yourself?'

'No, I just – well, to be honest, I was just mostly trying to hide my crotch and my tits.'

Willoughby's laughter was so deeply felt that it made very little noise, but brought tears to his pale blue eyes. Janet, coming in with the tea, was alarmed to see him delicately dabbing at them with a blinding white lawn handkerchief.

'Did it take a long time to light that shot?' he asked, when he'd recovered. 'The one that won the prize?'

'Oh, yeah,' said Carol artlessly. 'Ages.' She turned to Janet. 'Mam, he says I could be a model.'

'A model! Carol, love, there's exciting!' In her own excitement she'd slipped back into a Welsh idiom she hadn't used for years. Then the possible catch occured to her. 'What kind of model did you have in mind, then?' she asked, cautiously.

'I'm not thinking of nude modelling, if that's what you have in mind, darling protective stepmother,' answered Willoughby. 'In fact, that's the snag. It's possible, you see, that Carol can't wear clothes attractively, that she's only beautiful without any on. Should that be the case, I couldn't use her.'

'Oh, never!' Janet burst out indignantly.

'What I want to do,' Willoughby continued, gently ignoring her, 'is to take her up to London, put her in the hands of one of the best fashion photographers in the world and see what he can do with her. If she looks as stunning in clothes as she does out of them, I shall put her on my books and make her moderately rich and ridiculously famous.'

Janet's hand shook slightly as she poured out the tea to Willoughby's specifications, then poured a cup each for Carol and herself without speaking. Finally, she said, 'We'll need time.'

'In what sense?' asked Willoughby.

'Well . . . ' Janet temporised, 'first of all there's no good taking pictures of her looking like that now, is there?'

'Point taken,' answered Willoughby, looking at Carol's battered little elf-white face.

'And then, you see,' Janet went on, 'there's the question of her father.'

'Ah . . . ' Willoughby's deeply comprehending monosyllable had the heartfelt overtones of a man who had stubbed his toes on fathers before.

'You see,' Carol explained, 'Dad doesn't agree with any of this . . . I mean, you know . . . modelling and that. He's . . . well . . . like . . . funny about it.'

'Yes, all right, dear heart, I know what you mean, you don't have to draw me pictures,' said Willoughby. There was a streak of ruthlessness in Michael Willoughby. It was at the spine of his success. It came into play now. The girl might well turn out to be outstanding. However, there were other girls, scores, perhaps hundreds of them; and if this one was going to be a problem . . . problems were something he didn't need; especially other people's problems. 'I'll tell you what,' he said, somehow including Janet while speaking to Carol, 'you wait until your funny little face has mended and you've dragged your dear father into the nineteen sixties and then you give me a ring. My number's on the card. Just reverse the charges.'

He drained his tea and rose. 'Thank you very much for the tea, Mrs Blair, fairy stepmother.' He turned to Carol. 'I'm perfectly serious. I believe you could be exceptional. Whatever your problems, it's worth fighting them. Don't let life pass you by, darling heart.' With which, and a whiff of exotic after-shave, he was gone.

Each morning, Carol jumped eagerly out of bed to assess how much further the swellings and bruises had faded. And each day she tried to get in touch with the one person with whom, more than any other, she wanted to share the tumult and exultation and confusion inside her.

But Stewart Crown was not to be found. During the week she was off work she called at Rodney Street at all hours. There was never any reply. She telephoned his chambers, but all that his clerk, speaking, she felt, very cautiously, would say was that he was away. She asked if he had left any message for her. The voice became almost indignant as it said that he had not.

It was possible that he was really away. She knew that his work often took him around what he called the northern circuit, fighting cases in cities like York and Leeds. But why hadn't he told her? She was conscious of a deeply probing sense of loss, almost a physical ache. Memories of his smell and texture, the pressure of his lean weight, the superbly sensual things he said when he was deep in her loins, memories would spring into her mind unheralded and bring misery. Only the counter-balancing buoyancy of the offer from Willoughby saved her from total wretchedness during those dreadful days. She thought probably she loved him. Certainly she hated him.

Two weeks later, her face had returned to its customary, smooth-skinned pallor and it was time. The storm broke with an immediacy and a ferocity that took even Janet unawares. She had broached the subject with Jack, as experience had taught her, while they were in the playful preliminaries of love-making that night. She was laughing, tickling the underside of his scrotum with a gossamer fluttering of her fingertips, which she knew he loved and which could always start the first tremors rippling through the magnificent cannon he carried between his Greek statue's legs, no matter how tired he was. Tonight, he wasn't tired.

'Our Carol's going to be famous,' she dropped in casually.

'You what?'

'There was a fellow here from London. He reckons she could make a fortune as one of them fashion models.'

The tremors ceased. the cannon's rapidly rising elevation plummeted. He stared into her face, his colour darkening. 'Are you telling me there's been some ponce sniffing around our Carol in our own house?'

'Don't be silly, Jack. He wasn't a ponce.' She kept her voice soothing, stroked his shoulder lovingly: he shrugged her off. 'He's a well-known man. Famous. His picture's in magazines all the time.'

'I don't care if his picture's in the Walker fucking Art Gallery,' Jack answered. 'Anyone who earns his living selling girls' bodies to be gawped at by wankers is a fucking, stinking ponce!'

'Jack,' she coaxed, still desperately trying to keep the temperature down, 'it won't be that sort of modelling she'll be doing. Fashion models are always decent, they're always in clothes.'

'Always half out of bloody clothes, you mean, sticking their arses in the air, shoving their tits into everyone's face!'

'Jack, that's not true. When was the last time you even looked at a fashion magazine?'

'I seem to remember looking at a photography magazine just recently and seeing my own daughter as bare-arsed as the day she was born.'

'That was different—'

'When was this crap-merchant here?' he interrupted.

'About two weeks ago.'

'Two weeks!' Now he sat bolt upright. 'Two weeks and you only tell me now! Just what goes on in this fucking house when I'm not here? Who else sits in my chair when I'm not around?'

His meaning was clear and Janet's face went white with

hurt and rage. 'Don't you bloody dare say things like that to me,' she hissed. 'Save them for those tarts behind the bar you spend so much time with at the Beggar's Arms!'

'What I do in the Beggar's bloody Arms is drink!'

'And what I do in this bloody house is run it, on no money and no bloody help from you, you great thick pig!'

They were shouting now and the poison of the argument was spreading into old scars, reactivating old battle-grounds.

The bedroom door opened silently and Carol, Martha and Tony came in. Jack's sense of territory was outraged. It was the first time they'd dared invade the parental bed-room in a group like this since they were kids.

'What the fucking hell d'you think you're doing?' he roared.

'Making sure that Mam doesn't end up in hospital like our Carol,' said Tony, calmly.

'All right, lad, you've been asking for it for a long time,' said Jack with grim satisfaction, glad to have a single target on which to focus his fury. He started to get out of bed, then realised he was naked. 'Get me my trousers,' he said to Martha.

'Nothing doing,' said Martha, 'For once in your life you're going to have to think with your concrete skull instead of your fists. You fucking sit there and listen.'

Like most very masculine men, Jack had a horror of being laughed at and a keen sense of the ridiculous. He knew his authority would be totally exploded if he got out of that bed stark bollock naked and made an undignified scramble for his clothes. He was trapped. 'I'll give you the hiding of your life tomorrow, you pasty-faced cow!' he roared, his face looking as if the top of his head were about to blow off.

He paused and made an effort to change down to a quieter level. 'This has all been planned between you, hasn't it? This is your way of ganging up on me to get what you want. Well, it's not going to fucking work. I'm having no daughter of mine going to London as a whore.'

'She's not going as a whore,' said Janet patiently.

'Fashion model is a very respectable job – I've explained.' She turned to Martha. 'Tell him,' she begged.

'He bloody knows,' said Martha.

'It's the old thing,' said Tony, 'like Martha told us once before. It's him, the dirty old ram who can't let his women go, can't stand the thought of anyone else touching them. Especially Carol because she gets to look more like Claire every day. It's not Carol he won't let go, it's Claire.'

'That's a filthy-minded bloody lie!' screamed Jack.

Janet spoke very quietly. 'No, it isn't,' she said. 'You don't even know it, but you've never once made love to me without calling me Claire.' She turned and buried her face in her pillow. The rest were silent. All the blood had left Jack's face.

Carol spoke for the first time: 'It's all right, Mam, you're only hurting yourself. You don't have to fight for me no more.'

They all turned and left the bedroom, leaving two people to their grievous and separate pain.

The next morning, Carol left for London.

When Janet came back from shopping to find the note Carol had left for her, she sank into a chair and wept – for her loss, for her pride in her gutsy stepdaughter, for the pain that Jack Blair was going to feel and of which only she knew him to be capable. Her thoughts winged back to the time, a year or so after Claire's death, when Carol had almost died of pneumonia. During the course of the crisis, Jack and Janet had been thrown together as never before. They had watched over their tiny loved one around the clock. They had chafed their bodies together, rubbed around and past each other. At one point, when Carol seemed to be *in extremis*, they had held hands and prayed. The contact had sent what felt like a filament of thrilling warmth threading right through Janet's body, until her worry for Carol had neutralised it. But all the time, tension had been building: the tension of Carol's desperate sickness; the tension generated by the physical closeness of Jack. And Janet discovered that tension wound up her sexual desire to screaming pitch. She felt inside herself the possibility of an exquisiteness of sensation which was beyond imagination. And it could be liberated only by Jack.

Jack, more elemental than Janet, had felt the same head of steam building up for weeks. He would never forget Claire; she had infiltrated the fibre of him; she was, in a sense, his goddess. But this Janet, this round, juice-smooth pretty with the exciting eyes and the flashing legs, well, she was what being a woman was all about, wasn't she? If you didn't get a hard on just watching her buttocks twitching past you in the kitchen, when you were supposed to be reading the *Echo*, you must be dead from the waist down. Besides, she was so bloody marvellous as a person, like. Even if she wasn't bloody sexy, you'd still want to know her.

Janet had just finished saying goodnight to Carol the day her fever had been down for forty-eight hours and her breathing was as free as a breeze through reeds. She had settled her down and the little sweetheart was sleeping like a squirrel in winter. As she came out of the room, she met Jack, coming up the stairs to say his goodnights, too. 'No,' she whispered, 'she's fast asleep, you'll only wake her.' It was the day Dr O'Mara had pronounced Carol free of infection, told them it was now only a question of convalescence. They were both on a high.

'God, Jan,' said Jack, 'isn't it bloody marvellous? Isn't life . . . I mean sometimes . . . isn't it bloody different and great?

At that moment Janet recognised a childish wonderment in Jack, and before she knew what she was doing she had responded to it by throwing her arms about his neck and kissing him full-bloodedly, with her fruit-rich mouth on his, her body already like a peeled plum.

From there it had been a progression as natural as seed corn and harvest time. He scooped her up with a hand behind her knees and, mouths still locked together, carried her effortlessly into the front bedroom. And there, for Janet, eight years of longing and lust and frustrated chemical compatibility and love detonated with a violence and lack of shame that beautifully ravaged Jack Blair to the uttermost resources of his stamina. She wrestled, she gripped, she felt his tenderly ruthless rod of flesh reaching into the tiny, secret place somewhere in the centre of her where ecstasy lurked, waiting to be tickled and teased and brought to heart-stopping, brain-blowing explosion point. Her inventiveness and litheness re-charged Jack's batteries as if he were plugged into some sexual mains and he realised, between her gloriously merciless thighs, why it was that he could never pass her in the house without his long-gun getting cocked and ready to fire.

The next morning, there was a sense of a purging in the house. A burning-out of disease – Carol was cool and demanding solid nourishment – and a release of tension and emotional imprisonment.

Five weeks later, Janet and Jack were married and Carol, Tony and Martha accepted her unhesitatingly as their new mother.

9

Carol stepped off the train into the great bellowing vault of Euston and made straight for the first telephones she could see. It was 1963, she was eighteen years old and it was the first time she had been on a train in her life. She looked up Michael Willoughby's number and rang him.

'*Who's* calling?' asked the girl who answered, a note of incredulity in her voice at the accent on the other end of the line.

'Carol Blair. Just tell him, will you? He'll know.'

A pause, then another girl's voice on the line, snootier, this one, with overtones of distaste. 'I'm Mr Willoughby's secretary. Can I help you?'

'You can help me by putting me through to your boss,' answered Carol, a hint of exasperation creeping into her voice.

'What's it about?' A wall of ice.

'It's about him coming all the way up to Liverpool a couple of weeks ago just to see me, and if you know what's good for you you'll get off your pear-shaped arse and get him on the line!'

A further, arctic pause, then the unmistakable, ruthless, dancing charm of Michael Willoughby himself. 'Darling, where are you? Why didn't you tell me you were coming? I'd have had you met.'

'I'm at Euston station and I couldn't tell you I was coming because I broke out of Stalag Luft Sixteen this morning without my father knowing.'

'Get straight into a taxi, darling heart, and ask him to deposit you at Willoughby House, Bond Street. We'll pay the fare this end.'

Dazzled by the jewelled mosaic of rich old stone, shape, colour, light, perspective and psychic authority which together make up the world's loveliest capital city, Carol was rattled in her taxi to the opulent windows of Bond Street and to Willoughby House. A commissionaire, ready-primed, stepped forward on to the pavement, paid the cabby, and ushered her in through the marble-faced foyer to the lift.

'Second floor, miss,' he said. 'Mr Willoughby is expecting you.' He treated me like a queen, thought Carol, unused to the sunshine a member of the London Corps of Commissionaires could turn on when he tried.

Halfway up, she realised she hadn't even given him her name. With Michael Willoughby's descriptive powers, she hadn't had to. 'Expect a tallish, roundish, half-clown, half-waif,' he had said.

From the lift, she stepped out into a completely different atmosphere. It opened straight into a lovely room that seemed to be matched by its lovely girls. The room had blue pastel walls panelled in white and a gold carpet. The girls were sitting at beautiful desks, not old like Stewart Crown's but as glowingly rich in their wood. They were mostly talking on telephones and had files and photographs in front of them.

Those who were talking noticeably slowed and lost concentration as the figure with the pale, mask-like face, orphanage top-coat, bare legs and battered cardboard suitcase appeared in the lift doors. Those who were not on the telephone simply dropped everything and stared. The air was full of the gossamer ripples of ridicule. These were mostly girls who, despite their looks, had failed for some reason or other to make it as models, but they'd remained as close to the scene as they could; and you couldn't get much closer to it than working for Michael Willoughby.

Carol stood at a loss, aware of the barely concealed derision. Then she walked over to a desk with a plaque on it reading, 'Jacquie: Reception.'

She said, 'I'm Carol Blair. Mr Willoughby asked me to come.' Her accent, on top of her appearance, caused actual titters to break out. The receptionist, a sweet-faced Cockney with dark curly hair, picked up her telephone. 'Miss Carol Blair is here,' she said. She put down the telephone and indicated a door next to her. 'Go through, love.' Then she jerked her head at the other exquisite occupants of the room, their every finger-nail lacquered to a Rolls Royce finish. 'Don't mind this lot. They're all sitting there with no drawers on anyway.'

As the dazzle of beauties gasped, Carol smiled her thanks at Jacquie and went through the door. She found herself in a small, daintily but efficiently furnished office, occupied by the snooty secretary she had spoken to on the telephone. She was, if possible, even prettier than the girls outside. She looked at Carol with triumphant surprise, as if her worst hopes had been realised. She had, however, no chance to do anything else, since the door that opened into Willoughby's own office was immediately thrown wide and there, just fractionally too graceful in his stance, was the tall, elegant, fair-haired figure of Michael Willoughby.

'Dearest funny-face, do come in,' he said. To the disgust of his secretary, he kissed her on both cheeks, swept her through and closed the door behind them. 'I wasn't quite sure we would ever meet again.'

'I was,' said Carol.

The room was unlike anything Carol had ever seen before. It started with a Chinese silk wall-covering in some elusive shade of green and went on from there. It had, to her, the tranquillity and beauty of something under the sea, pictures she had seen of underwater reefs in the tropics, the same gem-tinted yet serene ambience. She gaped in wonder.

There were two other people in the room: Willoughby had been working fast since she rang up. He introduced the first, a man with the dress, face and moustache of a Greek bandit, whose black eyes had never left Carol's face since she walked in. 'This is Gregoriou. I borrowed him from Elizabeth Arden across the road. I want to see if he can do something for that odd little face of yours'.

He turned to the second stranger. 'And this is Madame

Récamier from St Laurent's ready-to-wear department over here. Oh, yes, he's got one; he's just not trumpeting it too much at the moment.'

He spoke as if he had the greatest confidence that Carol knew what he was talking about. She hadn't, in fact, the foggiest idea.

'Madame Récamier,' he went on blithely, 'is their principal fitter. She's brought a few things along to see if there's anything that might suit you.'

Carol had a vague idea that Madame Récamier must be French and that she should, for some reason, bow to a Frenchwoman of ripe years. She did so, just perceptibly, and was rewarded by a grim little smile, as if a portcullis had been fractionally raised in a castle keep.

'Over here, please,' said Gregoriou, in an accent as fractured as the Parthenon, urging Carol towards one of the long, nylon-gauzed windows and at the same time picking up a chair with a hairy black arm as thick as a club.

'Let the child get her coat off first!' exclaimed Michael Willoughby, peeling it from her shoulders as he spoke.

'I would much prefer my own studio across the road,' rumbled Gregoriou in bad-tempered retaliation.

'Yes, well, we can't always have what we want, can we? Now that I've got her here, she's not leaving my sight.'

Gregoriou grunted, wrenched aside the curtains, plonked the chair down in front of the window, then plonked Carol down on the chair. The daylight hit her full in the face. Gregoriou glared at her, speaking as if he were accusing her. 'The eyes must be one and one quarter inches long. The space between the eyes must be at least one inch. The eyes fully opened must be one half inch from top lid to bottom lid. These things are not always seen by people. They are never missed by the camera. Similar principles apply to the nose, the mouth and the bones. It is not enough to be pretty! It is *ridiculous* to be pretty!'

He seemed to be getting angrier and angrier, until Carol seriously thought he might shake her like a doll. He peered into her face, scrutinised it, studied it from this angle and that and as he did so the bad temper gradually left his eyebrows, his forehead unknotted. He began to hum a little Greek tune to himself. He reached for what looked like a doctor's bag, but much bigger. Inside was an alchemist's treasure of bottles and cases, powder, creams, brushes, pencils and spatulas.

The first thing he did was to clean every crevice of her face with cotton, which he repeatedly moistened from a small jar. When he was satisfied, he patted her face dry with special absorbent tissues and blew on it all over like some human blow-drier. He had sweet breath, like apples. Then he reached for his brushes and his tints.

Michael Willoughby watched, fascinated, as Gregoriou worked. Even Madame Récamier, who had been showing some signs of impatience, gradually drew near and became still. Carol was conscious of a suppressed but steadily rising excitement emanating from the three people surrounding her. She had never worn make-up before, but she had watched Martha and other girls and it had always looked like a fairly heavy process. This Gregoriou seemed hardly to be touching her, caressing her with cloud-soft pressures, a whisk of a brush, a delicate smearing of a fingertip, his humming of the little Greek tune getting gradually louder, the wise, woman-loving eyes getting brighter and brighter, never leaving her face, analysing, creating, appreciating. The feather-light touch became yet more delicate, as if what he was creating got more precious to him by the minute. He finished with a final flourish of a camel-hair brush and an exclamation that sounded to her like a Greek oath.

'Now!' he said. 'For the first time in your life, see your face!'

He led her triumphantly to a gold-encrusted mirror on the wall. She looked and her mind rocked on its hinges. She was disorientated by the feeling that the face looking out of the mirror was not the face that was looking in.

The alien who looked out at her had high, wide cheek-bones; translucent, elongated eyes that seemed to fill her face with blue from side to side. The skin was ivory now rather than white, even though it was not covered with anything. She would have called the short, straight nose sculpted if she'd known how to spell it. The full, flushed mouth might have been considered too wide by some people, none of them men. Above all, there was shape and depth in the features which she had never seen in her face. Even her hair, which she had washed and ironed the night before, streamed in a glittering cascade with a look it had never had before.

And yet there was a likeness to Robert Marshall's photograph of her. What he had done with his lights and lenses, Gregoriou had done with his magic brushes. The girl in the mirror could pass for the sister of the girl in the magazine.

She didn't think it a pretty face, exactly. It was solemn and there was a strangeness about it, some haunting, elusive quality which it was beyond her power to formulate. Gregoriou defined it without knowing he was going to. He flung out a great, swarthy arm. 'The girl from Venus!' he shouted. And Carol recognised instantly that this was the element that had been eluding her; she looked as if she might have come from another planet.

Someone else had recognised it, too: Madame Récamier. With an impulsive movement, she pushed away the wheeled rack on which were hanging the considered elegances of St Laurent and rushed over to a plastic bag lying on a chair. She pulled out a strange, white, geometric garment with holes cut from it here and there. She shrugged apologetically. 'It's something Courrèges was experimenting with in Paris,' she said.

She brought the garment over to Carol. 'Here, my dear, try it on.' She indicated a screen at the end of the room. Mutely, Carol took the dress. She could feel the tension in the room and it made her stomach sing like a violin string. As she was halfway to the screen, feeling as if she were in some kind of hallucination, inhabiting someone else's body, Madame Récamier's voice rang out: 'Stop!' she commanded. Carol stopped. 'Les bas,' demanded Madame Récamier, 'the stockings – where are your stockings?'

'I don't wear stockings,' said Carol uncomfortably. 'My dad would never let me.'

'She has the face of a goddess and the habits of a peasant,' declared Madame Récamier despairingly to the two men, as if Carol were unable to hear her. She turned to Carol. 'It is impossible, my dear, to wear clothes successfully without les bas.' She looked more closely at Carol's legs, polished by eighteen years' exposure to the elements, then grunted grudgingly: 'Well, perhaps just for now. But those abominations on your feet will have to go. Wear the dress barefoot.'

Obediently, Carol went behind the screen, kicked off her shoes, peeled off her pauper's skirt and jumper and climbed into the dress. It was stiff and odd and angular. She felt freakish, with a face she didn't recognise, a dress like a punctured space suit and no shoes. She wished she had a mirror back there to show her what she looked like.

'Come on out, darling,' shouted Michael Willoughby. 'We're not going to eat you!' This is where I blow it, she said to herself, as she finally moved out from behind the screen.

She looked spectacular.

None of the three sophisticates out there, waiting so critically, had ever seen anything like her before. The dress had been made for her in some psychic hinterland where model and maker had met in a dream. There was the extraordinary blue of the eyes, the contoured ivory of the face. It wasn't exactly 'beauty'. It was . . . what was it? Their expressions were masked by the complexity of the analyses going on inside those three professional heads. Carol took it for dismay and her stomach sank like a lead bar. Whatever happened, she thought, there was no going back. She would not return home. A voice was speaking. 'My *dear*, darling girl!' It was Michael, advancing towards her, his arms out stretched so widely they seemed in danger of springing from their sockets.

'You like it?' she asked incredulously, her thoughts somersaulting.

'I wish Courrèges were here!' exclaimed Madame Récamier.

Carol smiled.

'Oh, Christ, the smile! Look at the smile!' shouted Gregoriou and amiably picked up and smashed to pieces a little gilt chair against the floor.

Michael Willoughby picked up the telephone: 'Get me David Hales,' he said. He put down the receiver. 'Madame Récamier, you're a sorceress: Gregoriou, you're Michelangelo!'

'I am not,' said the Greek, considerately picking up the pieces of the chair he had splintered. 'I am Gregoriou.'

The telephone rang. Willoughby picked it up. 'David? I'm bringing her right round.'

He swept Carol through the door and into the outer office. The decorative pride of beauties who manned it froze at the sight of the stunning creature who now strode out, bare-foot and mesmeric, with their boss. Carol had never actually seen people's mouths drop open before. She felt, however, as remote as she looked; she still seemed to be walking about inside a doll.

Fifteen minutes later, Michael's beautiful chauffeur and the big Mercedes had deposited them at the seedy-looking Regency-fronted studios of David Hales in Bayswater. On the way, they had stopped at this shoe shop like a palace, called Charles Jourdan, and bought a bunch of stockings and a pair of short white boots that someone called Jacques had had pushed on to him by Paris – '*foisted* on to me, my dear!' he quivered – and was unsure about.

David Hales was a small, young, scraggy, black-haired terrier with eyes so dark you couldn't see the pupils. He wore immaculately scruffy jeans and a bomber jacket and his fingers were stained with developer. He started to whimper when he saw Carol; she could find no other way to describe the noise he made. Without introductions or preliminaries he rushed her through his courtyard up into the chaos that was his studio. It bore the same relationship to Robert Marshall's studio as did a salt-caked freighter to a luxury yacht, but Carol recognised much of the same equipment. Hales got there first and was already backing away, squinting through a viewfinder, taking his first shot of her as she came up the stairs.

Michael put his hands steadyingly on Carol's shoulders as she threw a questioning glance at him. He indicated a door. 'Go in, darling, and put the stockings and boots on.'

It was a day for discoveries. As she slithered into the stay-up stockings, she found that her polished skin had an affinity with nylon. When the fibre hit the leg fusion occurred, producing highlights that would have sent Fra Filippo Lippi screaming for his brush and palette and a release from his monastic oaths.

There was more.

She had never been allowed to wear high heels at home. She hadn't even been able to try on anyone else's because Martha always wore flat brogues and Janet's were too small for her. The short boots she now slid into had only moderately high stacked heels, but even they threw tensions into the smooth muscle of her legs, rounded and honed by all her running, the effect of which she observed with growing fascination.

When she emerged, striding like a huntress from the dressing room, the transformation from scrappy urchin to almost mythic feminine potency was complete. David Hales, who by personal inclination was a leg man anyway, started to bark. Well, not exactly bark, Carol admitted to herself, but his terrier-like appearance helped to make it sound like that. What he barked was a series of staccato orders, starting from the moment the shock-wave of her emergence from the dressing room hit him. 'Stop right there!' 'Jump in the air, arms and legs wide!' 'Turn your back and look at me over your shoulder! Great! Now stick your bum out!' 'Christ, what an arse!' – this to no one in particular, his hair falling more and more over his left eye. 'Kneel down!' 'Lean back!' 'Run at me!' 'Make the skirt ride up!' 'Feel sad!' 'Want to murder me!' That was easy; she did anyway: she hadn't realised the crack about her arse was a compliment. And all the time click-click-click, squinting at her from halfway up ladders, kneeling on the floor, lying on his back. He was a man in a frenzy.

For her part, she was not. The remoteness she had felt when the compelling stranger had looked out at her from the mirror in Michael's office had neutralised her behavioural censor – never very strong – and liberated and instinctual creature who knew exactly what the manic man with the insatiable camera wanted from her. This was different from the Robert Marshall experience. Then he had created something and someone without her knowledge. Here she was in total collaboration with a man, his mythology and his camera, and the only question to be resolved was who would become exhausted first. In the event, it was Hale's film that ran out. He had used nine exposures on the end of a film he already had in the camera and two new reels of thirty-six shots each.

'When?' asked Willoughby.

'What?' Hales, a man absorbed, was already on his way to his dark room.

'See something; when can I see something?'

'Tonight.'

'Bring them round to the house around nine o'clock tonight,' shouted Michael. 'We'll be eating in.'

'Hey, listen,' said Carol, 'never mind where we're eating. I've got nowhere to kip yet.' They were ensconced again in the back of the Mercedes, the chauffeur's immaculately clipped head beneath its elegant cap in front of them.

'For now, you'll sleep at my place,' said Michael.

'Oh no, I won't,' Carol answered firmly. She felt as if an anaesthetic were beginning to wear off. Her mind was in the process of assimilating her near-miraculous transformation and the powerful young character her life had built was beginning to break through the silken bubble in which she felt she'd been encased. She might have been in the back streets of Liverpool only hours ago and she might now be in a big Mercedes with this famous Michael Willoughby, who must have at least a thousand pounds' worth of clothes on his back, and he might come on like a pansy, but there was a look in his eye that said differently and she wasn't being taken for an idiot by anyone.

As it happened, she was absolutely right. Michael Willoughby found his effeminate manner and his beautiful chauffeur a most effective sedative for nervous girls and anxious mothers. In fact, he and his pretty pilot were two of the biggest rams in town, often hunting as a pair and driving the female prey towards each other. This, however, Carol was not to know until long afterwards. Michael Willoughby did not believe in muddying his relationships with his models by fucking them. If ever he did, it was a sure sign that the girl who slid between his sheets was about to slide off his books.

'My dear Lady Galadriel—' he began.

'You what?'

'I take it you've never read *The Lord of the Rings*?'

'You take it dead right.'

'Lady Galadriel is the Queen of the Elves in the Kingdom of Lorien. You remind me of Tolkien's description of her: 'Beautiful and terrible as the Morning and the Night! Fair as the Sea and the Sun and the Snow upon the Mountain! Dreadful as the storm and the Lightning. Stronger than the foundations of the Earth! All shall love me and despair!'

'Get off!' said Carol.

Michael sighed. 'We really must do something about your vocabulary,' he said.

'What's wrong with it?'

'Well, it *is* rather basic.'

'I know a lot more words than I use,' countered Carol happily. 'I just like to keep things simple.'

'Then there's the question of your accent.'

'It's a good old Scouse accent – what's wrong with that?'

Willoughby pressed his fingertips together. 'You may remember hearing – no, you wouldn't – that when talking pictures came along they completely destroyed the careers of several great Hollywood stars – because they looked like goddesses but sounded like Bowery waitresses. It's a question of incongruity. It's offensive to people's aesthetic sense that a woman should have a lovely face and body and an ugly voice.'

Carol had always had a good ear; she was an excellent mimic, had been the scourge of the nuns at school with her uncanny impersonations of them. During her months with Stewart Crown she had picked up much of the music of that beautiful voice and could, in short bursts, imitate it. She would sometimes do it at a crucial point in their love-making, inducing helpless laughter in him and a tremendous fight to prevent premature orgasm. She decided to use it now.

'If it's a goddess you want,' she said, in Crown's groomed and cultured tones, 'then a goddess you shall have and you may kindly kiss my arse.'

For the second time that day she saw a sophisticated mouth drop open – and she noticed the Mercedes go into a quickly corrected but unmistakable swerve.

'Can you keep that up?' asked Michael Willoughby.

'Of course I bloody can't!' said Carol. 'I've never wanted to, but if that's what you need . . . '

'Actually, that's a bit more than I need,' he said. 'What would be ideal is just a pleasant, standard, classless accent.'

'That'll come,' Carol assured him. 'Give us a month and you won't know me from Julie Andrews.'

'You'll need longer than that.'

'Balls! That's the gaping great hole in *My Fair Lady* for me. I've never understood why it took that dim bird so long to change her voice. Girls do it all the time. I'm more worried about my face. That Greek fellow can't be with me all the time. What happens when it wears off?'

'It can't wear off,' he said patiently. 'It's your face. Get that into your stunning little head – it's your face; all Gregoriou has done is to bring it out, that's his magic. Tomorrow I'll have him teach you how to do it yourself.'

She considered this piece of information for a moment, then decided to show that she hadn't been diverted from her original question. 'I still have to have somewhere to stay tonight,' she said.

'I've told you, you're staying with me.'

'And I've told you I'm not.' They were passing down the rosiness of the Mall towards Buckingham Palace. If the route had been chosen to impress her, well . . . shit, it did! But he didn't live in Buckingham Palace, did he?

Where he did live was in a gem-like, whitely gleaming little square opposite Harrods and she was almost as impressed by its sense of quiet old luxury as she had been by the Mall.

'At least come and have tea,' he had said. 'It doesn't commit you to anything and you can see what my domestic arrangements are. Following that, if you still think I'm after your body, we'll find you a nice bed-sitting room somewhere.'

She was bowled over by the house. Again it had that carefully selected, lovingly polished geometry of which she had first become aware in Stewart Crown's flat, but this was more lavish, more silky, swathed, textured: a small gold room sending its glow out into a large white one, an unexpected soft red suffusing a corner, a table scattered with tiny jewelled eggs, winking in a parchment-coloured light.

'I can't claim the credit,' he said, as he saw her face. 'I had David Hicks do the whole place over. It's dolly, isn't it? There's nothing like Royal connections for giving an interior decorator good taste.'

He had a cook-housekeeper, Mrs Pinkney, who looked as if she'd come off a Christmas card, and a manservant, Farnell, who should have been in a commercial for a stately home. The guest suite had a canopied bed, silk sheets, a teddy bear with a blue satin bow on a corner shelf and its own bathroom. She decided to stay.

Mrs Pinkney had already laid out or put away the pathetic contents of the cardboard suitcase. The threadbare brushed nylon pyjamas were laid across the bed, the exhausted underwear was in drawers, the defeated skirts and blouses and sweaters were on hangers, or folded on shelves down the side of the wardrobe.Carol herself was lying in the bath, up to her neck in soap bubbles but keeping her precious new face out of the water for fear of washing it away, whatever Michael Willoughby might have said.

For the sheer psychological luxury of it, as she lay there cradled in the hot, scented water, she had to keep contrasting it all with where she had been only last night. She had to keep the comparison fresh, not to lose it: she knew it was the start of that thing she had sensed was coming towards her all her life down the shifting maze of Time and she wanted to fix this beginning and hold it. She counted all the firsts she had chalked up that day, things that most other people wouldn't even think about, like trains and taxis. She wished, in a way, it could have happened more slowly, one thing at a time, so that she could have spent, say, a week savouring each one.

Over dinner, cooked and served by Mrs Pinkney, the best part of which Carol privately considered to be the little chops with the white hats on, David Hales exploded into the crimson, velvet-walled dining room with its richness of fair silver and slapped a portfolio on to the table, almost knocking over one of the pink candles.

He opened it, the cover all but obliterating Willoughby's plate. 'Just,' he said with great deliberation, 'take a look at those!'

The pictures were a glory. David had blown them up to twelve by ten. Where Robert Marshall's enhancement of her had been motivated by sexual obsession, David Hales's had been the result of a mixture of things. Certainly, as an ardent lover of women, he had wanted to celebrate this astonishing bird, who had made his cock twitch almost as often as his shutter clicked; but, as a professional, he had also been challenged to master and fix the 'Galadriel' quality that Gregoriou's art had conjured out of her. The creature in these photographs was an explosive cocktail of preternatural sexual promise and utter exclusivity, as if the treasure of the world were to be protected by a force field, which only some new sword of Arthur could penetrate; she blasted off from the glossy paper like an ivory, blue and gold hallucination.

Carol looked at the pictures with her now familiar sensation of disconnection and non-participation. The alchemy which had transferred these images to sheets of paper had nothing to do with her. Willoughby and Hales went through the pictures silently, seriously, a light crackling in Willoughby's pale blue eyes, Hales's like two nuggets of coal about to burst into flame. When they had been through the entire portfolio, light blue met coal black in a kind of orgy of restraint. Then Michael leapt to his feet. 'If that damned geometrician hadn't got in first, I'd yell 'Eureka!' he said.

He broke open a bottle of champagne, wisely restricted Carol to one glass, and they broke up for the night in a wave of euphoria crashing on to a beach of gold.

The next three months were among the most miserable Carol had ever spent in her life. Nobody wanted to know.

Michael deployed the full firepower of his expertise, personality and reputation. He used his best contacts, called in overdue favours, spent a fortune on lubricating lunches. Everyone admitted when they viewed the pictures that they had never seen anyone like this spectacular creature before; and for that very reason, none of them wanted to be the first to take a chance with her. The account executives knew what their clients wanted: what they had always had, the conventional beauties who were the archetypes of the people to whom they hoped to sell. None of them knew quite what to make of this strange and errant seraphim.

Of course he could have got her jobs: underwear, mail order, tatty giveaway advertising sheets – and many good models had got their starts that way. But here it was that Willoughby showed why he was tribal chief of the agents. He refused to compromise; declined to consider anything but the best. He wanted his star to burst upon the world, unforeseen, blinding, unpredictable. He wanted top accounts, top magazines, rocket-launchers who would blast Carol Blair into the orbit he knew was rightfully hers. But those with their fingers on the essential buttons remained stubbornly unmoved.

Carol stayed on in Montpelier Square. She practised the art of minimal make-up, as taught to her by Gregoriou. She watched television endlessly, soaking up the flat, neutral tones that dominated the tongues and larynxes of the nation's electronic gurus, interviewers and documentarists.

At first, the luxury in which she found herself, the translation from Mugsley Street to Montpelier Square, was an occupation in itself.

However, she felt guilt towards Michael, too. Each night at dinner she could divine his impatience, his frustration and anger at the obtuseness of the people with whom he had been dealing all day.

'Listen,' she said to him one night, 'you're not getting anywhere with me, are you?'

'It takes time—'

'I've got two hundred and fifty pounds from that photographic magazine. I can learn shorthand and typing. I can support myself. I'll go out and get a job and when my so-called image finally clicks you can retire to the Caribbean on your ten per cent.'

Willoughby marvelled at the superficial worldliness he imagined this child must be soaking up from the television screen. What he failed to realise was the ultimate sophistication that could only be bred into one by a slum. When daily life is question of pure survival, when privacy is merely a word in a school dictionary, there is very little that a capital city or the ferocity of its flora and fauna can teach you.

It was something the beautiful Francis, failed model and chauffeur extraordinary, had had to learn for himself. Carol had felt his bright blue eyes on her, had read and ignored the question in them for weeks. It was a cold March night when he finally made his move. Unfortunately, he wasn't Carol's type. Like a camera lens she savoured bones, and the reason Francis hadn't made it as a model was that all his beauty was in his smooth flesh and his high colour.

He had dropped Michael at a Fashion Awards dinner at the Dorchester. He wouldn't be needed again for three hours. On the flimsiest of excuses, he came into Carol's bedroom, where she was moist and terry-towelling-wrapped after what she now regarded as the nightly luxury of her bath. The door opened and there he was, dressed in nothing but the tiniest pair of sky-blue nylon briefs she had ever seen on a man. He was sleek, evenly and definitively muscled, but smooth, and she felt not a flicker of response to him between her thighs or anywhere else. He had an electric razor in his hand.

'My electric socket's blown,' he said. 'I wonder if I could use the one in your bathroom.'

'Course you can,' she said. 'You'll find it next to the open packet of Tampax on the ledge.'

He looked at her steadily, then went into the bathroom. The packet was there and it was, indeed, open. He came back into the bedroom. 'Doesn't mean a thing,' he said. 'Like to show me?'

Her face didn't flicker. 'You enjoy that kind of thing, do you?' she asked.

'I just don't believe you, that's all,' he said. She noticed a slight but ominous swelling of the pouch at the front of his briefs as the scent of her, fresh from the bath, started to surround him.

'That's up to you,' she said. 'You can either believe me and get out gracefully, or I can tell you just why I don't fancy you and dent your manly ego.'

He studied her for a long pause, then a slow smile spread across his face. 'I've never pushed for it,' he said. 'Don't believe in it.' He slid more noticeably into his native Cockney. 'And I ain't about to start now, specially against a fit-looking bird like you. But I'm not going to get bent out of shape about it, either. I'm sorry. I was out of order. My apologies.'

He held out his right hand, palm upwards. 'Mates?' he asked.

She spat on her right palm and smacked it down on to his. 'Mates,' she responded.

He smiled and got up. 'I'd better go and get that shave, ready to pick the guv'nor up,' he said.

'What about your faulty razor socket?' she grinned.

'I wouldn't be a bit surprised,' he said, 'if that had put itself right by now.'

'Frankie,' she called as he reached the door. He turned, his face a question mark. 'If ever I do fancy a really handsome blond smoothie, you'll be the first to know.'

He grinned back. 'I won't hold my breath,' he said and closed the door behind him.

She sighed and grabbed a pillow. No, she didn't want Francis. What she did want, had wanted ever since he'd disappeared, was that bastard, lion-heart, lion-cock Stewart Crown. She could summon up the feeling of his hardness and weight on top of her, his hardness and stamina inside her, the lordly face above her. She found she was crushing the pillow between her legs. 'You sod!' she shouted and flung it into the furthest corner of the room.

Two evenings later Michael came back to the house triumphant. 'You're having lunch with Madge Smith,' he announced, beaming.

'Who's Madge Smith?'

'Madge Smith, dearest heart, is editor of *Galaxy,* one of the most influential magazines in town. Her 'Yea' can make you, her 'Nay' can break you. You'd better be sure she likes you.'

'Thanks for the relaxation therapy,' said Carol. She swung her glossy, illimitable legs from the sofa on which she'd been watching some educational documentary on television and stood up, wearing nothing but a woollen sweater and a tanga. Michael Willoughby's years of stern professionalism nearly disintegrated on the spot. Instead, he turned away and got himself a drink. If you could never kill the nerve, you could at least confuse it.

'I'm merely permitting myself a tiny gloat,' he answered. 'She zonked out over your pictures. She's got some idea of giving you the whole centre spread in the June issue. She has a theory that you're the *Zeitgeist* in human form, the incarnation of the spirit of the age that the fashion world has been waiting for as a catalyst.'

'Would you mind putting that lot into Scouse?' Carol requested, reverting deliberately to her native accent.

'She thinks that what you've got is what it's all about at the moment,' Michael explained. 'She wants to have you photographed in a whole range of the new clothes – at least what *she* thinks are the new clothes; and if she thinks it, we'd all better believe it. She wants you to lunch with her tomorrow at "Mary Rose".' He watched her face and saw no reaction there apart from interest. He continued: 'I'm afraid I won't be there to hold your tiny little hand, darling; it's strictly women only.'

'Mary Rose' was less a female executive dining club than a luxurious temple of hedonism dedicated exclusively to women. A little ahead of its time, it was eventually to fail, only to rise again ten years later and become an enduring success. Set in two-thirds of an acre of indoor gardens in the particularly clipped, green and groomed English style, it housed a superb restaurant, sauna baths, a heated swimming pool of a singularly glorious blue and a smaller, emerald-green pool with a jacuzzi that, for tender brutality, was one of the best designed of its kind; it had massage cubicles and a number of luxuriously bedded rooms where the sauna'd, jacuzzi'd, massaged and pleasantly exhausted woman exective could nap for half an hour before going home, out to the theatre or even, in extreme cases, back to the office to beat her male colleagues to a pulp.

Carol, in her Courrèges dress, thrusting boots and shadowed ivory face, had as little trouble getting into one of the best guarded clubs in London as into any establishment she had ever entered in her life. She was welcomed by a ravishing receptionist and escorted straight into the Queen Bee nest where Madge Smith was awaiting her.

Madge had seen the photographs, but was still not prepared for the impact of the girl in the glowing flesh. Her conviction that she had made the central discovery of her life was completely and reassuringly reinforced.

Carol, for her part, saw a pretty woman of thirty-five with a tip-tilted young nose, hyacinth blue eyes, beautiful skin and lovely shape, which she didn't know whether to put down to her exquisite clothes or her celebrated morning runs around Hyde Park. She had a soft, vulnerable mouth that would have made it difficult to hurt her and it was not easy, superficially, to see what made her the formidable force in the shaping of British taste that she was.

'I'm Madge Smith,' she said. 'Do sit down, my dear. What do you like to drink before luncheon?'

Primed in advance by Michael, Carol asked for Perrier water. She sat, her masterfully cut skirt riding up the exact four inches that the designer had intended, showing the perfect line of the leg from the strong, round calf to the chiselled knee to the gradual swelling of the thigh. The sensuousness of the body, opposed to the severe, almost Garbo-esque symmetry of the face, excited Madge's professionally trained eye to the point where she wanted to call for a camera, David Hales and a location-finder there and then.

She wanted something else as well.

Over lunch she asked Carol about her background. Carol, in her new flat Everyman accent, told her the precise truth.

'Tone it down a bit, darling,' Michael had advised her. 'I mean, dress it a bit, d'you know what I mean? After all, *La Vie Bohème* takes place in a slum, but they never let it get too sordid, do they?'

Carol, however, had never been able to tell anything but the plain truth. Madge did not believe a word of it, simply marvelling at the imagination that went into the PR side of the presentation of model girls these days.

Carol, who now that she had achieved the height and weight she had always held as an ideal – that of a somewhat scaled-down Sophia Loren – was determined not to exceed it, ate a steak and salad. Madge, who fought a staunch battle against a metabolism that converted everything that crossed her lips into solid tissue, beamed with approval as she played push-around with her Salade Niçoise. She examined with speculation in her hyacinth eyes the extraordinary face bent over the plate opposite her. Carol looked up and smiled guilelessly. Madge's heart did back flips as she all but counted the perfectly formed teeth.

'Have you started breaking any hearts yet?' she asked.

'In what way?'

'Men. You must have knocked a great many of them

over since you arrived in London. Is there anyone special?'

'No,' said Carol, with her usual candour. 'There was one before I got here, but he dropped me.'

'That's men, my dear,' said Madge. 'Fools. They really don't deserve us. They certainly don't deserve anything like you. Are you still fond of him?'

There was an emphasis of interest behind Madge's questions that Carol was aware of, without being able to pin it down. 'Yes,' she said. 'I have this thing where I love him and hate him at the same time.'

'Odio et amo,' murmured Madge.

'You wh—' Carol just managed to bite off the customary Liverpool interrogatory and change it skilfully: 'You want to hurt him just as badly as you can, yet you know if he walked in this minute your knees would start to shiver.'

'How long has it been?'

'More than three months.'

'Do you still miss him . . . physically?'

'Oh yes,' answered Carol with a ready frankness that triggered an expression on Madge's face that she again found hard to fathom.

'You'll get over it,' said Madge. 'One always does.' She shifted the conversation neatly into the field of fashion. She was curious about the dress. Carol told her the story. 'Michael's a clever boy,' was her fond comment. She shifted smoothly back into Carol's personal life. She was very interested that she had been schooled in a convent. 'Who was your best friend?' she asked, smiling warmly.

'Jenny O'Hare,' said Carol.

'What was she like – dark? Fair? Chestnut like me? Was she a big girl? Little? Was she pretty?'

Carol, a bit bewildered by the barrage of questions, answered as best she could. To her, Jenny was just . . . Jenny. She was a little puzzled by the turn in the conversation. Surely this powerful mover of the nation's tastes couldn't be interested in schoolgirl gossip?

They both finished with a sorbet – 'Just a little naughty because of the sugar, but nice' – and black coffee, which they took in a corner of the country-house-furnished communal sitting rooms, all chintz and warm autumnal colours.

Other women, with shoes and handbags of such spare perfection that Carol wondered how they could bear to use them, came and talked to Madge. She introduced Carol to all of them, but with one or two there seemed to be a note of triumph in her voice and a certain light in her eye that was not there when she spoke to the others. Having said good-bye to a friend who seemed to Carol to be put out by the whole encounter, although nothing she said would have supported that view, she turned to Carol and noted the heavy-lidded eyes.

'Oh, dear!' she said. 'Too much claret! I know what you need. Come!'

With gentle imperiousness, she led the way to the saunas. 'Have you ever had a sauna?' she asked.

Carol shook her head.

'You'll love it. It's more fun if you have it together. D'you mind stripping off in front of other women? You can have a towel if you do.'

After the daily turmoil of communal washing in the back kitchen at Mugsley Street, Carol didn't mind stripping off in front of a bus queue in Park Lane. They went naked into the dry heat of the Finnish pine cabinet together. Madge had a beautiful body, very curvaceous and feminine. She was, perhaps, seven pounds overweight, but it was so evenly distributed it simply made her rounder and more huggable.

Her pubic hair, Carol noticed, was black, as against the chestnut of her head. Madge noticed her noticing and laughed. 'I know,' she said. 'I've often thought of getting it matched, but I'd feel so ridiculous!'

She looked at Carol's gleaming blonde curls down there. 'At least you have no problem,' she said. Her eyes seemed to linger just a fraction too long and Carol wondered briefly if she should have chosen a towel after all.

Then more water was thrown on the stones and she had enough to do just breathing to the bottom of her lungs without thinking about anything else. All her life, she had been accustomed to living in the cold. Her metabolism had adapted to it. This bloody ridiculous heat she could do without. 'Where's the cold bath?' she gasped to Madge. 'I always heard you plunged into a cold bath from one of these things.'

'Oh, we don't have that system here, my dear. We're not all Nordic-type goddesses like you.' She followed with a finger a bead of sweat that was running down Carol's gleaming flank. Carol moved away on the pretence of examining something on her left foot. She could have been mistaken. All her life she had led a tactile kind of existence in which everyone rubbed against and touched everyone else all the time. Why should this touch have felt so different? Why did she imagine a certain look in Madge's eye that accompanied it? And why did she feel Madge was crowding her now as they sat alone, side by side, on the wooden-slatted seats?

'I think I've had enough,' she said, getting up, slipping on a wrap and going outside.

Madge followed her swiftly. 'Now you're all teed-up for the massage,' she said.

'Massage?'

'After the sauna, the massage,' she said with gentle bossiness. 'Some people like it the other way round, but they're wrong. The sauna relaxes the muscles, opens the blood flow. Come.' There it was again, that subtle imperiousness. Perhaps it was merely thirty-five speaking to eighteen, but Carol felt that there was more to it than that.

They padded along to the massage cubicles. Carol half-expected them to be communal, but they weren't and she began to feel a little ashamed of her nascent suspicions.

They split up into cubicles next door to each other, separated by a plastic division. Carol lay down on the spotless white linen of her massage table and her masseuse, a pretty girl slightly older than herself with a hockey captain's good looks and a cellist's arm muscles, covered her across the hips with a towel and began to smooth warmed oil over her body. She started to palpate and press and dig and sweep and stroke.

'Just relax,' she told Carol.

'If I relax any more,' said Carol, 'I'll drip off the edge of this table like warm wax.'

The girl's fingers had the knowingness of Stewart Crown's, even to their awareness of the sensitivity of the toes, their separations and joints, and the secret lairs inside her hips on either side of the subtle swell of the smooth round belly. But they didn't have the snaking, vibratory ropes of masculinity pulsing through them and Carol's hormone brigades failed to respond, remaining resolutely in barracks. All the same, the sensations were extremely pleasant.

'Turn over, please,' said pretty hockey-sticks. Obediently, Carol rolled over on to her tummy, her bouncy round breasts squashing just bearably on the slightly padded table. This time there was no towel across her haunches. The oil was smeared aromatically all over her again, from her neck down her shapely back, over the jutting rubber-firm buttocks and down the long yet compact thighs and calves.

Having smoothed on the oil, the girl seemed to take a slight breather before starting again. Carol, now deliciously relaxed, allowed herself to indulge in fantasy. Now that she couldn't see hockey-sticks' pretty, square-jawed face, she abandoned herself to the pretence that these really were Stewart's strong brown hands upon her, working on her the sensual necromancy that had first taught her what her own body was all about.

The chemistry of her longing for Stewart had been lingering on in her blood. Now, such was its power and that of her imagination that the hands actually felt different, less impersonal, more loving, as Stewart's used to do. They probed and teased and kneaded her just like his; not so stirringly, perhaps, but still, it was uncanny.

She half rolled over and looked up - straight into the flushed face of Madge Smith. Her cheeks were hectic, her eyes brilliant. Of the masseuse there was no sign.

'Oh, no!' groaned Carol, her anger mixed with astonishment. She swung completely around and sat up.

'Please!' begged Madge, her pretty face contorted by the

power of her pleading. She pressed Carol back down on the table, kissing her wherever she could reach, kissing her breasts, her neck, her stomach. 'I've never wanted anyone, anything, so much in my life,' Madge whispered desperately, 'from the minute I saw the pictures . . . I'll give you anything, I'll make you famous, I'll make you rich, I'll put you beyond the reach of any other model in the world!' She was rambling, her lovely chestnut hair tossed over her face, the rash of arousal spread across her smooth, creamy stomach.

Carol was paralysed by a combination of shock and inadequacy. She had genuinely liked this woman and there was nothing she could do for her. And she shouldn't beg like this. It . . . diminished her.

Madge was now forcing her down on her back again, scrambling on top of her, trying to force one of her thighs between Carol's. Their oiled limbs slithered and slid together. Finally, Carol's dammed-up sense of outrage was released. 'No!' she said again, with a quiet power more shattering than any shout. All her athletic strength was unlocked and she flung Madge off her like a slippery, climaxing doll, dumping her unceremoniously on her sweet, oily little arse with her back against the wall.

She slid from the massage table and stood over Madge. For one delirious moment, Madge persuaded herself that this flawless blonde fury was going to pounce on her. Instead, Carol spoke in the same low voice. 'I'm sorry,' she said. 'I liked you. I thought we were going to get on well together. But I'm not like that. You should have asked me and I'd have told you and we could have been friends. But . . . I mean . . . this! Well, it's just sort of letting yourself down. I'm sorry.'

Madge was weeping silently, one of the rare women who didn't spoil her looks when she cried, the tears scalding down her cheeks. 'I mean it,' she sobbed, 'the centre-page spread – everything. It wasn't just a come-on.'

'I know,' said Carol, 'but it just wouldn't work now, would it? We both know that.'

'It started the minute I saw your pictures,' said Madge

again, starting to sob in a way that left her needing great shuddering intakes of breath, like a child.

'Don't! Please don't!' begged Carol. She wanted to kiss Madge but, although she didn't know the word, she knew instinctively it would look patronising.

She left swiftly for the showers.

That night when Michael got home he found her cardboard suitcase, packed only with the threadbare garments she had brought with her to London and which she had never allowed Mrs Pinkney to throw away, already standing in the hall.

Carol herself was waiting for him in the drawing room. She was wearing the flea-market sweater and skirt in which she had first arrived. She looked like some fallen angel.

'You knew, didn't you!' she challenged him, before he could even open his mouth or plant his usual chaste kiss on her forehead.

'Know? Know what? What are you talking about, dear heart?'

'You bloody knew that Madge Smith was dikey!'

'Well, if I'd realised you took such a strong moral attitude—'

'I don't take any attitude. It's up to people what they want to do. What I do take a fucking attitude to is being leaped on and practically raped!'

'She didn't!' Michael seemed genuinely shaken.

'She did and I've practically got the teeth marks to prove it!'

'Not Madge Smith!'

'Who the bloody hell else did you send me to see?'

In her tatty old clothes, with her new superb face, enraged and swearing like a trooper, Michael found her totally fascinating, so much so that he temporarily forgot the seriousness of the crisis he was in. The memory of seeing the cardboard case with the string round it down in the hall brought it back to him. He decided it was time for him to go on the attack. 'What's the idea of the Little Nell costume?' he asked, pointing at her clothes.

'I'm bloody off,' she said, 'and I don't want anything of yours with me, that's what the idea is.'

'Would it be in order to ask a simple why?' he enquired.

'Because I don't want an agent who thinks I'll become a tart – and a bent bloody tart at that – to get my picture printed; that's about the simplest fucking why I can give you. The only reason I've stayed till now is to settle up with you for the money you've laid out on me so far. Tell me what I owe you and and I'll be on my way.'

Michael paused, deliberately slowing the tempo. He took a pace or two up and down before he spoke. 'D'you think you're being quite fair to me?'

'About as fair as you were to me.'

'Would you believe me if I told you I had no idea Madge Smith would make that kind of pass?'

'Oh, come on! You know everyone's little likes and dislikes. I bet you keep a file. If only you'd told me; I could have headed her off, there are a thousand ways; it need never have happened.'

He crossed to her and put his hands on her shoulders. She shrugged them off. 'Look,' he said, more earnestly than she had ever heard him say anything, 'of course I knew that Madge Smith is lesbian. But lots of people are . . . lots of things. It doesn't affect their work. It doesn't prevent them functioning. Good God, if we knew what some of our parsons did in bed we'd never go to church again!'

'They don't jump on top of people on massage tables,' said Carol tartly.

'Is that what she did?' Michael struggled desperately to keep the laughter out of his face. Madge Smith! And he'd always thought she was the submissive type. This alien angel of his was going to have a lot of fighting off to do if she could turn gentle Madge on like that. The image of Madge the predator recurred in his mind and this time he couldn't resist the laughter. Carol looked at him as if he were mad. 'I'm sorry,' he gasped, 'it's just the thought of darling Madge – gentle, sweet, violet-eyed Madge . . . !'

'You didn't have her squirming all over you, covered in oil,' retorted Carol. This made Michael's spasm of laughter even worse. He had a contagious laugh, his elegant frame creasing neatly in the middle, a lock of the immaculately layered hair falling over his forehead. Despite herself, Carol found herself joining in. It was Michael's laughter that convinced her of his innocence. She knew – and not from Shakespeare – that a man could smile and smile and be a villain yet: but she also knew the clean, abandoned sound of laughter without guilt, laughter that couldn't be stayed, and she was hearing it now.

He recovered himself somewhat and put his hands on her shoulders again. This time she didn't shrug them off. 'Now would you please get out of those ridiculous clothes, which I happen to find extremely sexy, and get into something civilised?'

A sensation crept through her body. She tried to reject it, but it was no use. The Francis episode, the physical nostalgia for Stewart, the stimulation of the sauna and massage, the reverberations set up, even, by the rotund and slippery limbs of Madge Smith slithering all over her like vaselined pythons: all these stimuli had triggered disturbances in her. She realised now that she'd always quietly fancied Michael. 'If I get out of these clothes,' she said, 'I shan't be getting into any others . . . tonight.'

'I never make love to my clients,' he said firmly.

'I'm not your client yet,' she said. 'You haven't got me one lousy job since I've been here.' She slid out of her skirt, exposing the superb legs in cheap stockings and suspenders she had bought on her angry way back that afternoon, determined to take away with her nothing that Michael had bought her.

'For God's sake!' hissed Michael. 'What if Mrs Pinkney were to come in?'

'Then you'd better get me upstairs quickly, hadn't you?' she answered, starting to shrug out of her sweater.

'If you think with my delicate constitution I'm going to scoop you in my arms and sweep you up the stairs,' he said, 'you're vastly mistaken. You skip up yourself like a good little girl. Off you go!' He picked up a bamboo backscratcher, which he sometimes drew slowly up and down his spine, looking like a sensual cat, and ran at her, whacking her bottom with it lightly.

She squealed and dashed out and up the stairs with him pursuing her, giving her shrewd little twitches in indecorous places with the scratcher, until he had herded her into his own bedroom, magnificent with its seven-foot bed, its Matisses and Dürers and two definitely kinky early Allen Joneses, its mirrored ceiling and the deep brown lambswool carpet that came up around her ankles the minute she'd taken her shoes off.

She started by imagining, with her not untypically vivid female erotic imagination, that he was Stewart Crown. He soon, unwittingly, put a stop to that. He proved to be a lover of startling inventiveness, starting with the bath he insisted on their taking together in his huge round bath adjoining the bedroom, in which he had installed a miniature jacuzzi. He held her against it at an angle where the powerful jet created sensations in the whole of her pelvic area that were new to her. Then he insisted that they got out of the scented water and hurl themselves on the bed without drying. 'What about the sheets?' gurgled Carol, through a kiss.

'The hell with sheets!' he said. 'Sheets are for changing' – and slipped on to his finger what looked like a leather ring with soft bristles sticking out all around it.

'What's—' she asked, before she felt it stroking, first, her swollen outer lips and then, as they opened like succulent plants, the inner ones, and finally the heart of the flower, which extended and quivered to the stimulation of the soft, caressing hairs.

'You look just like a Nuits de Young down there,' he said, just before he started his first smooth slide into her.

'Don't be disgusting,' she murmured, like an endearment.

'It's the name of a deep red rose,' he protested.

'Then don't be wet,' she said.

'I'm not the one who's wet.'

'Don't be disgusting.'

After he had filled her and she had locked her legs

around him with an anticipatory shudder and a grip that nearly ruptured his left kidney, he rolled them over on their sides, reached for and opened a drawer in his bedside table, produced something from it that she couldn't see and expertly slid it up her arse.

She quivered with shock. 'What's the hell's that?'she demanded, suddenly alert.

'Just a little something I got in Japan.'

'Then it's either a transistor, a camera or a Datsun and I want it out.'

'All in good time,' he said soothingly.

She started to protest again, but her vagina had tightened round him and her buttocks had fired into spasmodic clenching and pushing, and the warm waves of blood that set her body alight had already started their slowly mounting assault on her pleasure centres. Just as the final tides had started to crash through, the rolling breakers churning her towards the core of that exquisitely precious sensation, he pulled something attached to whatever it was he'd slid up her bottom and the orgasm was compounded by a stimulation that felt as if a never-ending reel of twine were being unravelled inside her. She let out a shriek of enjoyment that would have been heard by passing aircraft, had he not clapped a hand over her mouth until it was finished.

'What *was* that?' she demanded, dreamily, as she sank back into his cradling arm, already laid out along the pillow to receive her.

'I told you,' he said, 'just a little something I got in Japan. Devilishly clever, these Japanese. Well, it's Chinese in origin, actually: they've had it for five thousand years, but naturally the Japanese appropriated it and improved it.'

'Yes, but what *is* it?' she persisted.

'Oh, don't let's go into technicalities now,' he reproved her. 'Post-coital melancholy is bad enough without that, don't you think?'

Michael Willoughby suffered from *post coitus tristus* to an unusual degree, which was one of the reasons he was, quietly, so sexually active. The only way he could drive out the demons was by inhabiting the lovely body of a woman, after which the whole thing started again. There was one other remedy and that was work, and as he lay cuddling the smooth warm form of this odd protégée of his, a name leaped into his mind – *Haute,* a magazine based in New York, but with editions all over Europe. It was as fat and glossy as a mating seal and it started trends as easily as pouring water downhill. It had style. What was more, it had Diana Fremantle.

Diana Fremantle was a young woman with the body and the hair of a ballerina, a lovely generous mouth and big melting brown eyes that she hid behind glasses to prevent people noticing that they weren't melting at all: they were lasering you up into handy sections and analysing the pieces.

She was now editor-in-chief of *Haute* with a reputation for spotting what was new and exciting almost before the concept was out of its creator's womb. She had recently published a picture of a fat, pasty-faced youth with a mouth like the loading bay of an air car-ferry in the rain, called Mick Jagger.

Her fellow editors had thought her mad, but if Diana Fremantle thought he was worth a picture, had he been a horse Michael would have put money on him on his next time out.

And Diana Fremantle owed him.

He pulled over Carol's face, on which its high-cheek-boned shadowed beauty seemed to have settled permanently now, with or without Gregoriou's subtleties, and kissed her on her upper lip. 'We're going to New York,' he announced.

'Great,' she said drowsily. 'Just let me get my knickers on.'

10

Of New York and Carol it is literally possible to say that she took that city of glittering, man-made stalagmites by storm. The moment she walked into Diana Fremantle's office, wearing a silver silk-crocheted dress and a close-fitting silver cap which came to points at her temples and let the glistening, white-blonde hair stream downwards, a thunderstorm hit: a magnificent maelstrom of light and energy, seen to enormous advantage through the huge, thirty-sixth floor glass wall that flanked Diana's desk. At the same moment all the lights in the office went out, and Carol stood illuminated by great blue snarls of crackling, searing light. She looked like a beautiful apparition. Anyone making an entrance to the accompaniment of that kind of special effects must have been impressive. Carol was spectacular.

The lights went on again and Diana Fremantle let out a noise that sounded as if she had been holding her breath. She stared at Carol with those gamma-ray brown eyes that looked so soft. She switched them to Michael, who had taken great care to stay in the shadows during the storm, so as not to distract from Carol. 'You told me you were bringing me a phenomenon,' she said. 'You didn't tell me it was Artemis! How did you arrange that entrance, anyway? Storms are one thing, but to have the fuses pulled in this building?'

She held out her hand to Carol and Carol moved to take it, her dress shimmering as she moved. Diana took her hand warmly in what Carol was to learn was a typically open and embracing American fashion.

That night, Diana whistled up a party for Carol. Carol

was amazed at the speed with which such things could be arranged in New York. Diana automatic-pistolled a stream of telephone numbers through the inter-com to her secretary and that seemed to be it. Apart from one or two specials, she didn't seem to have to lassoo any of her guests personally. Such was this young woman's power that the invitation seemed to be enough.

The guest Diana most wanted Carol to meet was photographer Dick Swann, a grey-flannelled faun with a way of moving like Fred Astaire. He was silvering at the temples.

'Don't you think this apartment is staggering?' he asked. 'Who but Diana could get away with putting that Louis Comfort Tiffany glass against a Eugene Michel vase?'

'I'm sorry,' said Carol, 'but I wouldn't know a Eugene Michel vase if they gave me one to throw up in on a rough flight.'

Swann's laughter was so full and so genuine that it gave all those other guests who had been longing to join the great-looking pair the chance to move in on the tête-à-tête and demand what the joke was.

'The joke,' said Swann, 'remains our private property, but by all means invade my private devotions.'

From that moment on, the party revolved around Carol. Her naïveté was taken for wit, her ignorance for kindly muted criticism. She drank only orange juice under the prior directions of Michael who, knowing the kind of life she had been leading just a few months ago, watched her like an anxious hawk from the fringes. Several times he choked on his martini at some horrifying gaffe, but always the unfathomable blue Blair eyes, the strange beauty that one couldn't quite categorise as beauty and the blinding smile transformed it, in the minds of the company, into an insight which they assumed they hadn't quite grasped.

Carol, whose native intelligence was light years beyond anything the nuns had ever detected, knew perfectly well that she was out of her depth, but she also knew she was getting away with it.

It was a matchless time. No city in the world responds to the new face quite like New York. There had been a mixture of social big cats and media people at Diana's party and Carol could have spent every day and every night at parties or on television and radio had she wished. But Michael's brain was turning over as shrewdly as ever. 'You'd be just another starlet, dear heart. What are you going to say when they ask you what you've done? There's no more self-destructive phrase in the English language than 'Well, I'm just about to . . . ' Wait till you've done it, *then* watch our after-burn!'

Accordingly, she gracefully declined all invitations. Instead, she worked exhaustively with Diana Fremantle and Dick Swann. Dick flew her from state to state in a chartered executive jet, inside which was rack upon rack of American-designed clothes, for Diana had spotted in Carol a quality that would fuse with the new young indigenous designers' feeling for change and revolt. Dick had refused point-blank to have a fashion editor along. 'If I don't know what to do with girls and clothes by now you'd better shoot me for dog food,' he said. But he couldn't refuse to have Michael. Michael was with them every step of the way. Anything he didn't like didn't get done.

This chafed at Swann's ego. It came to a head in South Bend, Indiana, where he wanted to shoot Carol against what was left of the long-defunct Studebaker factory. They had just reconnoitred the location while Carol changed in the plane and were driving back.

'No,' said Michael.

'What do you mean, no?' demanded Dick. 'It's no just because you say it's no?'

'You could put it like that.'

'I want a feeling of glamour against depression,' Dick insisted.

'I do not want my model associated with depression.'

'What do you want?' shouted the normally gentlemanly Swann. 'The whole fucking world to be Disneyland?'

'If at all possible – yes,' said Michael equably.

'I could always take my camera and go home, you interfering prick!'

'You could equally well stuff it up your arse and save the fare!'

'There are other models,' Swann threatened.

At that moment they reached the plane and Carol came down the steps in the soft, woollen, eye-matching dress she was to wear.

They both gazed at her.

'Other models?' repeated Michael, softly.

Dick Swann sighed. 'I never really did like that location,' he said.

They found snow bears at Aspen, wild ponies in Arizona, Pacific dolphins – supplied by a Hollywood animal trainer – in California. The shot of Carol walking out of the sea like Aphrodite in diamonds, her Thai silk evening gown water-glued to her body, a froth of surf around her thighs and a dolphin arched in the air behind her, remains pinned to many a picture editor's mind to this day.

It was an exhausting month, a rolling panorama of landing strips, big cars, hotels, improvised dressing rooms and endless changing, changing, changing. Often, Dick would have her up at dawn to catch a certain light, or keep her up until 3 a.m. to get a sky quality he called 'starshine'.

Naturally, the word got around. Dick Swann couldn't work for a solid month with the same model and keep it a secret. Just as movie producers know that the best time to sell an idea for a new project is before the one you're just finishing is shown, so the best time to sell a model is when she's working with someone else, preferably prestigious. The bandwagon had started to roll. And at that point, Michael again showed why he was the best. The moment the assignment with Swann was completed, he snatched Carol away.

'What happens now?' she asked as they strapped themselves into the Boeing for the flight back to London.

'Now we wait,' said Michael. 'We wait for the June issue of *Haute*.'

'What am I supposed to do with this?' she demanded, handing him the cheque for fifteen thousand dollars which was the unprecedented first-time fee he had negotiated for her. She had, as yet, no real concept of that kind of money, despite the luxury in which she had been lapped ever since she left Liverpool.

'Bank it, give me ten per cent, keep half for tax and have fun with the rest,' said Michael. 'It's only just the beginning, funny-face.'

The June 1963 issue of *Haute* is still talked about in the business. Carol's first sight of it was in her suite at the Sherry Netherlands, high over Central Park. She and Michael had flown over two days before publication date.

About four in the afternoon, Michael came in from his suite next door with a copy of the magazine, which Diana Fremantle had sent round to him by special messenger. He looked as if his shoes were full of hydrogen, so high was he stepping, and his face was a sun. He flung the magazine on to the polished glass top of a table near Carol without a word.

On the front cover was a close shot of her that was fabulous beyond her wildest imaginings. But there was more. Carol leafed through page after fat, glossy page, struck completely mute. Diana Fremantle had nailed her colours to the nose cone and shot for the moon. For the first time in the history of the magazine, or any magazine, every single fashion shot in the entire issue was of one model – Carol.

And just like Robert Marshall and David Hales before him, Dick Swann had been inspired. The pictures were sublime. Carol looked unsurpassably stunning. She had exploded upon the scene with the kind of starburst Michael had planned and for which he had prayed.

When she had reached the last page, she looked up at Michael, as if in a plea for help. His eyes were luminous with conquest. 'Now!' he said, almost aggressively, '*now* they can have you for as much TV and as many parties as they like.'

For the next months she was on every talk show on the screen. Since her general knowledge was abysmal, she relied on her native wit and the Liverpudlian's gift of making quite ordinary events sound amusing to get her through. Also, her face had the quality of making quite simple statements sound profound.

She was interviewed solemnly by the *New York Times* as 'a contemporary phenomenon'. *Woman's Wear Daily* called her 'the ultimate model' and *Time* said, 'Carol Blair is the face in a misty light of every man's adolescent dreams – and not just the face!'

And all the time, the work was pouring in. Michael winched up her fee to unheard-of heights, and the higher they went the louder the customers screamed with pain and the more they liked it.

Michael handled her social life beautifully. She went to few premières and no night clubs. Occasionally she was to be seen at a concert or the ballet – and then usually on the arm of some rising young politician, or banker, sometimes a distinguished academic; never a film star, ball player or leather-faced old stud.

Even in this ambience, her ignorance and largely untutored mind caused her no problems except those of a stomach constantly fluttering like a nest of sparrows. She very quickly learned that what most men want is to do the talking themselves, and largely about themselves; so she became an expert listener. It gave her an air of tranquil, detached authority and it gave her the opportunity to learn. Her mind was like some voracious cerebral sponge, sucking in information on which her native intelligence could work at leisure.

Slowly, however, as her assignment-graph soared, she had to abandon social life almost completely. Her work began to take over. It seemed that every magazine, every photographer, every agency of any distinction wanted her – usually on the same day.

She was still living in the Sherry Netherlands. Michael had taken an apartment nearby: he didn't want any crap publicity about their living together. The hotel suited her. She would come home, have an omelette or a plain steak sent up to her suite, then fall into bed, exhausted, at about nine o'clock. And every morning's post would bring some new demand on her, dreamed up by the limitless fertility of American inventiveness.

She became, for instance, the first girl ever to be asked by a famous men's magazine if they could photograph her with her clothes *on*. They wanted to do a fourteen-page spread on her, showing nothing more provoking than, perhaps, a knee, accompanied by a learned piece about her by a fearsomely authoritative, Galbraithian figure from Cornell, whose subject was anthropology. He had some theory about her representing a tribal longing for a harvest goddess.

The magazine's owner and editor-in-chief was a gentleman. Jackson looked like a ravaged Peter Pan. He had tried everything and mostly liked it. He had a sex drive that the space programme could have used for propulsion and he was also a wickedly inventive and elaborate sexual practical joker.

He had once bought a friend, a famous Middle European film director, a camper which he had encouraged him to use in the studio as well as on location. It had a roll-back canvas top. Jackson waited for the director to get used to it. Then one day, during a break, Jackson sent in to the director in his camper a girl whose mouth was beautiful, bold and adventurous, which was just how his Austrian friend liked it. He lay on his back on his bunk with a sigh and Jackson's beautiful fellatio exponent bent her head and went to work on him. Both became absorbed.

At that point, by prior arrangement, Jackson had the canvas top of the camper rolled back suddenly and completely, leaving the celebrated director staring directly upwards into the interested eyes of a dozen or so lighting technicians up in the flies, looking down on him. His own eyes bugged, his colour traffic-lighted from red to green and back again. Finally, he looked at the girl who, head down, was still blithely unaware and happily engaged at her task. He struck an attitude as if he had only just noticed her. Flapping his arms like a duck, he roared to her, 'Get avay from there! Vat you think you doing down there!'

Jackson, perched up among the electricians, was lucky to get away with his life. He laughed so much he nearly fell.

What he wanted from Carol was a preliminary talk about the spread and then, perhaps, to take her to dinner. Michael, who knew Jackson's reputation, was against it. But Carol was uninfluenced. She knew Michael was beginning to believe in the image he had created for her. She knew she was still the tough little kid with a wicked left hook from Scottie Road and she was intrigued by what she'd heard of this joker.

Jackson sent his limousine for her at six in the evening. She'd told him she couldn't have dinner with him. It was one of her rare nights out and she was being squired by Jonathan P. Cabot to the Lincoln Center.

The elevator whisked her directly into the living room of the fortieth-floor penthouse where Jackson lived at the top of his office building. Carol was ushered in to find him having his second shave of the day. His barber was a shimmering, black-haired Amazon, whose breasts, like an extra pair of hands, steadied his head as she scraped away. He was swathed in a voluminous pale blue nylon sheet. The brunette, whose tunic was in the same shade and material, seemed to merge with it. They looked like some bizarre, androgynous centaur.

With one hand, Jackson was holding some proof pages of his own magazine, reading one of the articles. Carol had to presume, since it was nowhere in sight, that the other hand was under the sheet. A certain expression of smug complicity on the face of the brunette led her to suspect that the sheet wasn't the only thing it was under.

'Hello there,' he said. 'Come in, fix yourself a drink. I'll be with you in one minute.'

He surveyed her curiously, her demurely sheathed, lithe body moving like a gymnast's, and that haunting face unreadable. He'd had so much success with girls that this British chick, with that effortless cool that breathed out of her, was a challenge.

Although he didn't realise it, Carol had taken an equally interested appraisal of him. Against everything she had expected, she had felt a familiar stirring. He had something in common with Stewart and Michael. an air of ease and confidence and command. And his ravaged, young-old face had a hooded Rex Harrison quality about the eyes that made her feel like smiling.

'I can't stay long,' she said. 'Jonathan Cabot's taking me to a concert.'

Trust the bloody British, though Jackson. J.P. Cabot's father had seven hundred million dollars at the last count and would be very useful right now for an expansion scheme Jackson was pushing, but he couldn't get near him. This cool-assed piece of British provocation drifting across his shaggy white carpet could probably wrap the bastard up in her snatch and carry him home to Mummy.

'Thanks, honey, that'll be fine,' he told his barber, and she shimmered from the room like a nylon-sheathed puma. Jackson turned to Carol. 'I'll tell you why I want you with your clothes on,' he began.

'Because you knew you hadn't got a hope in hell of me taking them off,' said Carol.

Jackson grinned. 'I was about to give you a lot of crap about mystery,' he confessed.

'I know.' She'd decided she liked him. He was no shitter, at least. Who knows what turn their relationship might have taken if she hadn't seen the plastic circlets on his desk? 'What are these?' she asked idly.

'Oh, they're the new plastic handcuffs New York's Finest are trying out,' he explained. 'No keys, about ten-thousandth the weight and so cheap you can throw 'em away after each bust. We're doing a piece on them – "The Hygienic Bracelets!" '

She dangled the strips of thin notched plastic. Her father would tear them apart. 'I can't see these holding the kind of thugs they'd be used on,' she said.

'They're good,' Jackson assured her. 'Here, let me show you.' Before she could say anything, he had laughingly clipped her beautifully boned wrists behind her.

'You see?'

'Good heavens!'

He reached over to release them, but before he could do it his private line rang. Again, if it hadn't been for that fateful call, he would have unclipped the strips of plastic and they would probably have finished their talk in a civilised fashion. But he picked up the telephone and forgot all about Carol for the moment because, on the other end of the line, his European circulation manager was telling him that his magazine's sales had just outstripped *Playboy's* for the first time. A tide of warmth from some mysterious happy-gland flooded through Jackson as he and his circulation manager congratulated each other.

Carol came towards him, miming that she wanted him to release the handcuffs. She turned her back to him and presented her wrists. But the happy-gland had released more than happiness into Jackson's bloodstream. It had also released the sexual mischief that was never far away. He had no idea he was going to do it until he did, but, instead of releasing her, he goosed her, his hand slipping under her skirt and feeling the cool, rubber-ball firmness of those buttocks.

She reared like a mare and tried to get away, but he pushed his hand right through between her thighs and raised three fingers in front of her. She kept her cool, he had to grant her that. She stopped struggling and said, in a very loud voice, so that anyone on the other end of the line would be able to hear, 'Stop that, Mr Jackson, you dirty old man!'

She'd chosen her tactics well: it wasn't the 'dirty' that hurt Jackson, it was the 'old'. In Europe they thought of him, rightly, as a young swinger. He stifled the mouthpiece of the receiver against his chest and relaxed his fingers just enough to allow her to pull free across his fingertips. Did he feel a sudden moisture as he did so?

She marched instantly towards the elevator doors, a slightly absurd picture of affronted dignity, her hands behind her giving her a sort of prancing walk. He pressed the button on his desk and she heard the electronic security bolt slide home before she reached the elevator. She didn't even bother to press the call button, but turned exasperatedly and faced him. Jackson fancied that, despite herself, the neatness of his operation etched a slight smile over her irritation.

He finished quickly with his European man. 'Okay, Jack, thank you – it's a shot in the arm just to listen to you. And it's all just fine, huh? Thanks a lot, Jack – be seeing you. Oh, and regards to Miriam!'

He put down the receiver. The contact with that fantastic body and the good news from his man in Europe had combined to make him as horny as a rhinoceros. 'Well now, Miss Carol Blair, we seem to have got ourselves a situation here.'

She still kept that beautiful British cool. 'There is no situation. I am simply becoming late for my date with Jonathan Cabot and you can stuff your fourteen-page spread as of now!'

He smiled. 'Well now, that's not such a bad idea at that: that kind of rubs out the patron-client relationship between us and we can be just good friends.'

'Just take these things off or I'll scream this building down to the ground.'

'Wouldn't do any good, Carol. Everyone gone home. Besides, you don't really want to scream. Not really . . . . do you?' He advanced towards her and she backed away.

Afterwards, he was never able to decide what he would have done had things remained on that level. But it was at this point that he got lucky. He reached for her, sliding his hands under her armpits, and to his astonishment she went to pieces. She buckled and shrieked, stamping her feet in agonised laughter, banging her heels against the floor. 'No, please! Please! Don't do that! Please don't do that! Please! Please!'

Hallelujah! Who'd have thought it? This Rolls Royce of chicks was ticklish!

It had been Jackson's experience that the defences of chicks who were ticklish were penetrable. It was only a matter of time before the tickling sensations modulated into the erotic, and although they generally fought to a finish they were always ready when he put Old Mose to them at the last. Besides, what about that tell-tale dewiness when he had goosed her?

He tickled her standing up, he tickled her when she sank to her haunches, he tickled her while she tried to screw herself into a ball like a hedgehog, her bound hands beating a tattoo behind her against the wall. Then he picked her up, sat on the barber's chair on which he always had his shaves, put her on his knee and tickled her again.

He got rid of her pants without difficulty and after that it was his birthday all the way. He lifted her up and set her down again astride his lap. Exhausted, she made only a token resistance. Then he unzipped himself and freed Old Mose, who had for several minutes been trying to tear his trousers apart. Old Mose was like iron. As always, with every girl's first sight of him, Carol's eyes widened like a cat's. He put his hands under her buttocks, lifted her in his passion as if she weighed nothing, then slowly, slowly lowered her, gradually staking her on Old Mose. As he'd expected, she was very ready.

When he was fully implanted, he jacked the barber's chair up with the lever until her feet were five or six inches from the floor. Then he leaned back in the chair, clasped his hands behind his head and grinned at her.

Her face was flushed and running with sweat, her hair was tossed, her immaculate teeth were showing through slightly parted lips. She couldn't use her hands: with her feet off the floor she could find no leverage from them. She squirmed there, impaled and immobilised. She was as fixed as a drilled china figure swivelling on a rod.

Jackson's smile broadened. 'Now then,' he said, 'let's see how badly you want to keep your date. There's just one way you're going to get off Old Mose here and that is to bring him down to size.'

She twitched and kicked, trying to reach the floor with her feet, trying to get some upward leverage from the muscles on the insides of her thighs. 'You perverted bastard!' she gasped.

'Not perverted, honey,' he replied, 'just fanciful. I never

did this before in my life.' He winced with pleasure at her movements.

She noticed, stopped squirming and sat absolutely still. 'You'll get tired before I do,' she said. 'If you think I'm going to ride you off, you're insane.'

This girl had evidently been around, he reflected. She knew how a cold and clinical policy of non-cooperation could turn off a man like him quicker than a twisted ball. And it was at that point that Jackson got lucky for the second time that evening.

He opened her dress and started very gently on her breasts which, her arms being behind her, were thrust out in particularly fetching rotundity. They proved, with Carol, to be the crucial point where tickling merged with exponential speed into stimulation, erotic blast-off and sexual detonation. Half-laughing, half-cursing, sometimes mixing in endearments, she chomped, gripped, crushed, wrung and squeezed Old Mose as dry as the sands of Nevada. By the time she had finished and slid triumphantly off, Old Mose looked like a flag that's been hoisted on a windless day. Jackson's face, drained as a moon landscape, looked as if she'd got most of his blood as well; he'd never met any girl anywhere with that kind of control over her genital muscles.

With weary hands, he slipped the plastic cuffs off her. Slumped in the chair, he held out his fist to shake hers in a gesture of peace. 'No hard feelings?'

'You tell me,' she replied, as she looked at the flaccid morsel of flesh that had once been the omnipotent Old Mose.

He started to laugh and she laughed treacherously with him as she casually slipped the notched plastic around his wrist. Before he knew what was afoot, she fastened the other end to a bar under the chair, completely inaccessible to his other hand. She then jacked the chair up as far as it would go, pressed the bolt-release button for the lift doors and made towards them.

'Hey!' he yelled.

'I admire your sense of humour, Mr Jackson,' she said.

'Laugh that one off.' She pressed the down button. With any luck, they wouldn't find him till morning.

They didn't. But Jackson was a generous loser. She heard him starting to laugh as the elevator doors closed. Next day she got a gigantic, anonymous bouquet of flowers at the Sherry Netherlands in the shape of two circlets. She also, some months later, got her fourteen-page spread in Howard T. Jackson's magazine.

At the concert J.P. Cabot, in the middle of L.V. Beethoven, proposed to her for the fifth time. She turned him down as usual.

She had been in America for a year and away from home for eighteen months. Next day she announced to Michael that she was going back to Liverpool. 'There's something I have to do', she said.

A week later, Francis delivered her to the Adelphi Hotel in Liverpool. The lights in the portico glittered on her hair, the car, and Francis's livery to compose a picture that had the lobby staff straining their necks for a glimpse before she even got inside.

She had toyed with the idea of slipping into her old sweater and skirt and going down by train with her old cardboard suitcase. But she had decided to start as she meant to go on. She was determined to keep close contact with her family and she didn't see why she should become a split personality or lead a double life to do it. Besides, whose susceptibilities would she be offending, turning up in high style like this? Not Janet's, not Martha's, not Tony's: they'd be delighted for her. Her father would be the only one to be outraged. Well, sod him.

The only thing she had insisted on with Francis was that she would walk to Scotland Road from the Adelphi. It might be the best hotel in town, but it wasn't far away and her legs didn't only look great, they worked. Francis protested, but she was adamant: the presence of another man – even sitting outside in a car – would be a red rag to her father and she wanted to keep this cool. The hotel staff in the lobby were amazed to see her step out into the night unaccompanied: no chauffeur, no taxi. The shoes and the handbag alone made her a mark.

Heads turned to the point of spinal dislocation as she swung down Lime Street with the athletic grace that had now developed in her, but she was not molested. Nor did she expect to be. This was her city. She knew its every stone.

It was just after she had entered home ground and the street lighting became sporadic pools in the surrounding darkness that it happened. She had had a feeling that someone was following her, but she could see no one. Then, from round a corner in front of her stepped four youths, two white, two black. They surrounded her. She looked around. The street was empty. It was weirdly like the ambush she ran into on her first day at Marshall's. That felt like a hundred years ago now.

'Let's have the handbag,' said one of the black ones. She handed it over. They took the fifty pounds it contained and flung the handbag away. One of the white ones pushed closer to her, his sour breath coming through the smell of the gum he was chewing.

'You got nice tits,' he said. So it wasn't going to be just a simple mugging.

'You've got bad breath,' she said.

'Don't be like that, darling,' he said, reaching out and squeezing one of her breasts. 'You're a long way from home.'

'Wrong!' she spat, kneeing him crunchingly in the balls and drawing her spiked heel viciously down the shin of the one behind her. As they went down, moaning, she turned to run, but the other two had her, one with an arm across her windpipe, the other stuffing something into her mouth: and the one whose shin she'd sheared was coming on again, hate on his face. Despair drenched her as she tried in vain to find another target for her heels.

Then, suddenly, it was all over. The arm melted away from her throat, the youth facing her slumped to the floor, the one with the shin followed. She went down, suddenly dizzy with relief, her knees gone.

And there he was, bending over her, his face concerned – Tony! 'Are you all right, miss?' he enquired anxiously.

Her eyes sparkled with the enjoyment of it. 'Yes, thanks, Tone,' she said.

He started and peered closer into her face in the dim light. 'Carol?' he asked, disbelieving. 'Car? It *is* you! Bloody hell! You look like a film star!'

He helped her to her feet, staring at her. She grinned. 'When are you going to stop rescuing me, Tone?'

'I was just coming home from karate class,' he said.

'Well, you obviously haven't been wasting your time there,' she said, indicating the supine heaps on the ground, just beginning to groan back into life. She retrieved her handbag, then bent down and ripped the money from the pocket of the one who'd taken it.

'I didn't take 'em all out myself,' Tony said. 'There was this other bloke – blond, very smooth – he got one of them with a car spanner before I arrived.' He looked around him. 'He must have beat it when he saw I could cope.'

'Yes,' agreed Carol. So Francis had followed her after all.

They started to walk on.

'I've come to get you out of the Mersey Docks and Harbour Board and into art school,' she said. He stopped in his tracks. She saw the hope blaze into his eyes, then die.

He shook his head and resumed walking. 'I've missed my chance of a scholarship now. It'd cost money.'

'I've got money.'

He shook his head again. 'I can't hang on to your skirt.'

Now it was her turn to stop. 'Look,' she said, 'all my life you've been rescuing me. Don't you think it's time you let me rescue you? Are you so unsure of yourself you can't let your sister help you?'

They discussed it the rest of the way to Mugsley Street, Carol demolishing her brother's arguments one by one. By the time they reached the house, he had only one left, referring to their father: 'That bastard'll never stand for it.'

'Leave him to me,' Carol said.

As they walked into the kitchen, Janet and Martha were sitting in front of the meagre fire watching television. They turned round casually. There was a moment's pause. Then uproar broke out. Janet flung herself at Carol, hugging the breath out of her. 'Oh, love, love, love!' was all she could say.

Martha grabbed her next. 'It's good to see you, love,' she said quietly, her arms trembling at the intensity of her feeling.

Then both women held her at arm's length. 'Here, let's look at you, then,' said Janet.

They appraised her as women and their eyes gradually widened as they took her in. From the tip of her toes to the top of her shining head, she had the stamp of quality and difference all over her. Standing there, taller than they'd ever seen her in her high heels, in that pinched, deprived kitchen, she blazed like some archangel; and they realised the magnitude of the shift she had made in her world.

Finally, Janet said: 'It's all true, then, what you've been writing in your letters.'

Carol laughed. 'Of course it's true. I've never been that good a liar—'

She was interrupted by the sound of heavy boots outside and a key in the door. Everyone in the little room looked at each other. Except Carol. Heart thudding, she turned to face the door.

Jack Blair came into the kitchen and stopped as if he'd walked into a wall.

He'd often rehearsed the things he would say to this little bitch if he ever got the chance. Now he had the chance and, staring at her, trying to work out what had happened to her, he couldn't say any of them. Eventually, he tore his eyes away and threw down his cap and coat. 'What the hell do you want here?' he asked. 'Your fancy man found himself a new whore, has he? If you think you can crawl back here—'

Carol silently called the articulate spirits of Stewart Crown and Michael to her aid. 'I have no fancy man,' she said calmly. 'If I wanted one, I've no doubt I could get one easily enough, but I don't. I'm a fashion model now and I seem to be rather good at it.'

Even her voice was different, he thought – but nothing you could get hold of to ridicule. 'Fashion model,' he sneered. 'A tart's job if ever I heard one!'

'There may be some tarts who call themselves fashion models, just as there are some layabouts who call themselves dockers,' she answered, 'but mostly they're just girls doing a very hard job of work.'

Her refusal to get riled confounded Jack. He was at his best when the guns were roaring and the air was full of the smell of verbal cordite. At the same time, deep down where he didn't even realise it yet, there was a sense of grudging pride at the giant strides she had taken in eighteen months. Christ, the way she looked, too! She made Royalty look like peasants! 'What the hell have you come here for?' he asked finally.

'I've come about Tony,' she said. 'I want him to go to art college.'

'*You* want!' She'd taken his breath away.

'And he wants, Mam wants, Martha wants. You know that.'

'Aye, well I don't want!'

'If you don't let him go, he'll just take off. I did it. He can do the same.'

'Just let the bugger try.'

'Once I decided to go,' said Tony, 'there'd be sod-all you could do about it.'

Jack lashed out at him. His son's head moved with a lightning-fast reaction and the blow spent itself in the air. He looked at Tony curiously; he'd used that trick a lot lately, in fact, he couldn't remember when he'd last managed to land a blow on him. But he had no time to ponder at the moment: he was too anxious to play his hole card. He turned to Carol.

'You made a mistake coming back here,' he said. As if to emphasise his meaning he went over and closed the door. 'You're a minor. I'm keeping you here from now on. I'm not having any daughter of mine making a whore of herself in photographs.'

Despite her resolve to stay cool, Carol felt the Blair blood sizzle inside her, the Blair obscenities, which had been part of the first sixteen years of her life, leaping to her tongue. 'You're so fucking dim!' she shouted. 'It's a wonder you know how to draw breath! You try that and I'll hit you with a team of lawyers that'll stretch from here to the Pier Head. By the time I've finished with you, the world'll know you're not fit to be in charge of pigs, let alone children!'

'Carol, love—' Janet began, anxiously conciliatory as usual.

'No, Mam, leave her be,' interrupted Martha. 'He's got no idea how far and fast our Carol's travelled since she left. It's time he learned.'

'She's *someone* now, you thick bastard!' Tony exclaimed. 'She could have you for breakfast!'

'If she's such a bloody big potato let her pay for you to go to bleeding art school, then!' he said, his miserliness dropping him straight into Carol's trap.

'That's just what I came to suggest,' she said quietly. 'I want to pay his fees.'

'He's bringing a wage into this house,' Jack said. 'Where's that going to come from while he's loafing about at bloody art school?'

'I'll pay it you,' said Carol. 'I'll pay it into this house every week of every year he's studying.'

Martha said quietly, 'No, you won't. You'll pay half. I'll pay the other half.' Carol tried to speak, but Martha interrupted her. 'I want to, Car.'

Tony, who had found himself too full to take any part in the discussion, went abruptly into the back kitchen. What his father had never been able to do with his fists, his sisters had just done with their love – they'd brought sodding tears to his eyes.

During the next few days, while the arrangements for Tony's admission to the College of Art were being made, Carol took Janet to the finest boutiques and women's shops in the city. Janet refused to let her buy her a thing. Her logic was impregnable. 'When would I wear them, love? I'd look like a parrot in a pigeon loft.'

Carol eventually persuaded her to accept a little money. 'There must be things you do want,' she said, 'things that wouldn't make you look out of place.'

Martha took her along to meet George Ironstile. Carol discovered, to her astonishment, that her sister had given up the security of her job in the Inland Revenue and thrown in her lot with Ironstile. 'We're partners,' she explained, 'fifty-fifty. He knows metals, I know money. It works out pretty well.'

George had moved out of the squeezed, sooty-black terraced house he used to inhabit in Preston to a detached house at Hoylake, small lawn at the front, bigger lawn at the back.

His brilliant red face turned, if possible, a shade redder and the teddy-bear-button brown eyes became yet brighter as Martha introduced Carol to him there.

'Martha's shown me your pictures in the magazines,' he said, 'but seeing you in the flesh, well . . . you don't happen to have a blood pressure pill on you, do you?'

They now had a couple more trucks and a much bigger yard. 'Earnings up three hundred per cent last year,' exulted George, 'on a turnover up five hundred per cent, so we must be doing something right. I'll tell you something – it's that sister of yours. She should be head of the bloody Treasury or something. Figures and money are her meat and drink.'

They were walking quietly on George's modest, suburban lawn. George cleared his throat: 'There's something else, though. We've been . . . like . . . going steady now . . . I mean apart from being business partners . . . for about a year. But, well . . . ' He paused, seeming embarrassed. He kicked at some invisible object on the grass, then went on: 'Well, she doesn't seem interested in taking things any further than just business and friendship. She doesn't . . . you know . . . seem to want anything to do with anything . . . physical.'

'Well, have you thought she might not be interested in you in that way?' asked Carol with brutal home-town directness.

'No, it's not that,' said George. 'I feel she is, but she doesn't seem to want to do anything about it. It's almost as if she's . . . afraid.'

'She probably is,' said Carol. 'The way Dad goes on is enough to put anyone off it for life.'

'Aye,' said George, ruefully. He'd had one disastrous meeting with Jack Blair a year ago, bull meeting bull. Jack had tried the Fred trick on him, taking him down to the pub and tanking him up with drink. When they'd got back to the house, it was George who'd had to take the wavering key from Jack's hand and put it in the lock. Jack had never forgiven him for that. They hadn't met since.

'Will you have a talk with her?' asked George.

'I can't,' said Carol. 'We've never talked about that kind of thing. It's just not something we can do. Martha would curl up like a hedgehog.'

George hesitated. 'God knows I love the bloody woman! I want to marry her!'

But it was to be five years before George began to break through towards that ambition. Five years during which all that held him and Martha together at times was the phenomenal success of their mutual business chemistry. They were born to make money together, if nothing else.

During those five years, Carol became the equivalent of *prima ballerina assoluta* of her world. She had the inevitable and repeated approaches from film companies, but she knew she couldn't act and she didn't want to suffer the fate of other famous beauties she had seen turn into creatures of wood on the screen.

Michael explained that her tax situation forced her to live out of Britain. It didn't have to be an actual tax haven like Jersey or the Isle of Man or Monaco, so long as she spent most of her time out of the country. Diana Fremantle advised Paris: 'It excites fashion editors to have a model fly in from Paris rather than California.' Diana's choice was the chic discretion of the Avenue Gabriel, the Faubourg St Honoré or the Avenue Foch. Instead, Carol chose the lovely loud glitter of the Champs Elysées. She took an apartment on the fifth floor of a building largely given over to lawyers and fat-cat accountants, with a gorgeous old clanking open-barred elevator.

She loved to be in the centre of bustle and activity and from the window of her superb, Empire-style drawing room she could look down and see the chaotic magic of that indiscreet, almost vulgar, but mighty boulevard.

She hired a French housekeeper, Claudine, the widow of an Italian naval officer, from whom she picked up flawless Parisian French and French-accented Italian.

Her relationships with men were singular, even in the light of the tide of the times that was flowing. She simply chose from the abundance that was offered to her. Sometimes she turned up at a function or a restaurant with a man, sometimes without. Head waiters from Chasen's in Los Angeles to Raffle's in Singapore became accustomed to seeing her walk into their restaurants unaccompanied – and usually un-booked – stirring up a mild typhoon of chatter among those already seated.

The truth was that, although she adored men and almost everything about them, she realised, by thinking back on her own father, that they had the best of it. They had an independence and an ascendancy, largely for economic reasons, which were very pleasant. She didn't for one minute, with the exception of her father, begrudge it them, but she didn't see why she shouldn't have it too.

The aura which by now surrounded her bestowed it upon her. Walking into a party or gathering of any kind she felt a little like an Empress being carried in her palanquin into a male flesh market, from which she was expected to make her selection. She enjoyed some of the best love-makers of the decade, only one of them a movie star. She had an instinct for sexual excellence. The best cocksman she met during that time was a small, balding cellist with the Vienna Philharmonic. His chromosomes were XYY and he should, by rights, have been a violent criminal or a boxer. Instead, he spent his energies on Brahms, Beethoven and beautiful women and he remained a staunch friend of Carol's to the end of his life, which came suddenly, driving in a storm from a concert in Munich to see another lady friend at Scuol in the wild east of Switzerland and hitting a Volvo forty-four-tonner head-on along the side of a mountain.

Kurt, the cellist, had been a bachelor with a family trapped in East Germany. After he flattened himself against the truck it was left to his colleagues, organised by Carol, to cremate what was left of him, in accordance with a letter left in his flat off the Karntnerstrasse. Then, strictly against a local bye-law, they scattered his ashes and their tears in the Vienna Woods.

Still weeping for her roly-poly little tiger, Carol was driven by a First Violin straight from the bizarre little ceremony in the Wiener Wald to the airport. She was due in New York for a meeting with *Vogue*.

She walked across the tarmac towards the plane and it was then that she saw him. There could be no mistake. She knew it was him the minute she saw the heavy, black hair, whipped up by the airfield breeze, falling back into place on the shapely head in front of her as he went up the aircraft steps.

After nearly six years that never-to-be-forgotten bastard Stewart Crown, as lordly as ever.

Hastily she wiped her face and her eyes. She was damned if he was going to catch her at a disadvantage. As if by telepathy he turned his head and looked past the dozen or so people separating them, straight into her face. The sun, low in the sky behind her, shone full into the big-cat eyes, making him look like some beautiful mythical man-beast from an old legend. Despite herself, she felt all the old sensations he had stirred in her the first time he had walked into Marshall & Nephew, a lifetime ago.

His lips curved into the kind of muted, closed-mouth smile that established instantly a conspiracy between them. First, it banished everyone else to some limbo where they ceased to intrude. Secondly, it abolished time: it was as if the six years between them had evaporated. The third and most insidious thing it did was somehow to conjure up every libidinous encounter they had ever had: every trick, twitch, posture and pleasure in which they had indulged each other.

She felt the hinges go in her knees and the drumbeat start between her thighs. The arrogance of the sod! How bloody dare he!

She decided that when she got on the plane she would walk past him, straight past, as if he didn't exist, to her favourite seat with the extra leg room at the front of first class, which she always managed to book. She looked forward to the pleasure of cutting him cold.

Escorted by her perfumed-hipped stewardess – that's where she knew the crafty sirens wore it, because it was on that level they wafted past the passengers – she looked in vain for the expensively layered head on either side of the aisle. She didn't see it until she reached her own seat. He was sitting, with all his chiselled composure, in the seat next to it.

She decided to be first in with her attack. 'Where's the passenger who's supposed to be sitting here?' she demanded, without preamble.

'I did a deal with him,' said Stewart Crown.

'Let me guess,' said Carol, ironically. 'He gets all your free liquor and you help him sue the airline when he falls down the steps getting off.'

'He gets to sit next to my secretary,' said Crown, 'and I get to sit next to you. Of course, he hadn't seen you when we made the deal.'

He glanced backwards up the aisle and she followed his eyes. A pleasant-looking young American was chatting animatedly to a leggy, shining brunette. She looked as if she'd just come from the beautician rather than an exhausting three-day seminar in Vienna on Human Rights and the Law, at which Crown had been one of the principal speakers.

'Why so keen?' demanded Carol. 'You weren't six years ago. So far as I was concerned, you just pissed off the face of the planet. Had you never seen a slum before, is that what it was? Did it revolt your delicate sensibilities? Is it all right now that I'm a kind of star?'

Had he denied it, given her some story which, with his gifts, she knew he could have made extremely plausible, that would have been that. She would have been arctically polite to him until they reached New York and then she would have dismissed him from her mind. But Crown had not become one of the sovereign figures of the English Bar without a deep sense of empathy. Taking a line from the scrawny, disturbing kid he used to know through to the goddess he had watched blossoming in the glossies, he knew infallibly that she hadn't changed. Bullshit was out.

'I was shaken, yes,' he admitted. 'I hadn't quite realised how far apart we were. I hadn't honestly known how you lived.'

'You didn't want to know,' she accused him. 'When did you ever ask me about my home or my family?'

'I didn't think it was important between us. It's not Death that's the great leveller, it's sex. On that we dealt with each other as equals. I didn't force myself to think any further.'

'You didn't want to.'

'No, I didn't.'

The jets bellowed into full voice and they trundled forwards, the machine gathering itself for take-off. Carol's hand twitched, instinctively wanting to be held. It was the tiniest movement, but Crown spotted it and enfolded her ivory hand in his brown one. It was a protective gesture, completely asexual but full, instead, of friendship.

'That night,' he said, 'when I saw how you lived, I realised two things. The first was that I was on the edge of being in love with you. The second was that we were completely incompatible. You just wouldn't have fitted into my career.'

'Maybe you wouldn't have fitted into mine,' she retorted.

'Yes,' he said judiciously, 'I dare say I deserved that. By the way, the photograph – the one on the front of the magazine that night – did you know—?'

'No,' she interrupted, 'not that it was going to be published. But I'm glad it was. Without that I'd probably still be behind the counter at Marshall & Nephew.'

He opened his mouth to frame another question, as delicately as he could, but she anticipated him. 'And no,' she said, 'I never did. Not with Robert Marshall. He had his own little ways.'

They talked incessantly until they landed at New York; he was now reading for the American Bar as a Visiting Fellow at Harvard Law School. Out of the Seventh Circle of the Inferno that was Kennedy Airport, Carol's large chauffeur magically emerged, having straightened every official in sight, ready to whisk her to the brownstone she shared with a cousin of Diana Fremantle.

'Can I give you a lift?' she asked Stewart. His secretary had already been swept off by the young businessman she'd sat next to on the flight.

He answered entirely on impulse. 'I've got a cabin up in Vermont,' he said. 'I meant to crash out there for a week when I got back; do a bit of fishing and a lot of lying around. Why not come? You said on the plane you had a free ten days. Do come!'

He was intoxicated with her. Often he had marvelled at her pictures, but on the plane he had discovered they were only echoes of the creature she had turned into. Their proximity during the flight had exposed him to the full potency of her. She was treated by the cabin staff like a kind of lay royalty. Her sexual magnetism was of an order he had rarely encountered before. No one knew better than he that it had always been there, but now it was fired by a fully developed female chemistry that was almost a vibration in the air.

For Carol his power was still as strong as ever. His complete honesty had utterly demolished the resentment she had harboured. At the same time, she wondered if she weren't letting him off too easily. Had the face not been so moulded and the body so finely framed, would she have been willing to grant him amnesty so freely? A plan began to half-form in her mind. Would justice not be served if, this time, she were the one to disappear?

The cabin was log-constructed. It sat on the edge of a

mirror-like dark blue lake and looked as if it had seeded itself and grown there. It was the end of summer. The days were broiling hot, the lake had lost its chill but was still cool. They hung their wine in it and ate barbecues and salads. They bought their provisions in the village, rowing across the lake instead of driving around it. Except for shopping, they got into the habit of living without clothes. It seemed natural to plunge into the lake first thing in the morning, then dry off in the warm air, naked, and stay that way. The only clothing they needed was the glow of the sun on their beautiful bodies. They were Adam and Eve with oil lamps and a Cadillac.

They made love in the lake, at the edge of the lake, on the lake in the ancient rowing boat. They couldn't get enough of each other, two perfectly matched creatures. Their relationship was of a kind that not a great many people experience. They discovered the comfortableness of deep erotic compatibility without love. Their time together had a quality of innocence and trust that being in love, with its turbulence and contradictions, can never confer. And their love-making had a relaxation and fondness about it unique in Carol's experience.

They had meant to spend ten days together. It had stretched to four weeks. The leaves were beginning to drift down in their reds and golds. As the sun sank at night a new chill claimed the air and instinct told Carol it was time to tell the best friend she would ever have goodbye.

She slid out of the big bed like a snake and moved silently in her bare feet through to the rudimentary bureau in the next room. She sat down, took paper and biro and began to write. She had long ago abandoned all thought of revenge. She was going to tell him, from the heart of her, that he was the most man she had ever met, but if they went on like this they would end up marrying and that would be disaster for both of them. She didn't know why: she only knew it would.

She had got as far as 'Dearest, darling Stewart' when she saw the envelope addressed to her.

She ripped it open and read: 'Sweetheart mine, by the

time you read this I will be gone. We have had a sublime high. The only way to go from here would be down. I don't want that to happen. Neither do you. Let's "fix" what we've had. As the girl said in the old movie, any time you need me, all you have to do is whistle. Yours adoringly, Stewart.'

She tore up the page she had begun. In the big, bold, schoolgirl hand she had never lost she scrawled across the bottom of his letter: 'As always, you say everything better. I agree, darling lion. I will whistle. All my love, Carol.'

She replaced the letter, padded softly back into the bedroom, saw that the discreet wristwatch alarm on his brown arm was set for 4 a.m. Thanking the Lord that he slept like the dead, she packed a few things in a single overnight bag, leaving the rest behind. Then she took the boat, rowed over to the village and rousted out the only taxi in town to take her, for an exorbitant fare, to the airport. She wept, half-happily, all the way.

Stewart Crown woke as scheduled at 4 a.m., saw her note and smiled, with an aching fondness.

Was Carol Blair happy? It was a question she asked herself against the cushioned luxury of exotic locations all over the world: the kind of places she had dreamed about in that freezing backyard in Mugsley Street.

She was moderately sure she wasn't happy. She was the highest paid and most illustrious model there had ever been, at the pinnacle of her world, and yet there was something absent from the celebrations. She couldn't tell what it was. She only knew that the thing she had sensed coming towards her all her life had not yet arrived. Maybe the thing was happiness, or would bring happiness in its wake; maybe it would bring something completely different. All she knew was that she couldn't rest until the thing had come. Was rest happiness? She didn't know that, either.

Just now she was on a cable car coming down from Nob Hill in San Francisco, and a man was watching her every movement. Partly this was because she was behaving in the most extraordinary fashion and partly it wasn't.

She was standing on the platform at the front, hanging on to the rail and leaning out into the street with one arm and one leg extended. She was wearing a cerise silk gown that streamed in the breeze like a banner of triumph in Ancient Rome and on her face was a beatific smile.

To a spectator widening his field of view, the reason for her behaviour became clear. Preceding the cable car down the hill, his top half sticking out of the open sun-roof of a hired Carey Cadillac, was Dick Swann. He'd had a concept and the concept was San Francisco plus Carol. He'd already had her on Fisherman's Wharf in a plastic bubble inside a glass tank of live lobster, her hair streaming like a mermaid's; streaking into camera with her natural runner's action across the man-made cobweb of the Bridge in a Lycra second-skin track suit; he'd shot her in a fog, out in the bay, the droplets of moisture glittering on the ends of her lashes, condensing into diamonds on her skin, her eyes, behind the veils of vapour, like lures to fetch sailors to their doom.

Carol was conscious of the man who was watching her for a number of reasons. First, because he was watching her far more intently than the rest of the passengers on the cable car who, as good San Franciscans, were both too blasé and too polite to stare; secondly, because he had also been at Fisherman's Wharf and on the Bridge; and thirdly because she couldn't get rid of the impression that she had met him before at some other time, in some other place.

She was puzzling out the conundrum, without in the least disturbing the splendour of her smile, when, a mile away, the winch controlling the car's cable coughed and jammed and the car came to a jolting and utterly unexpected stop.

Carol lost her grip and was thrown out on to the steeply inclined street, straight into the path of a Lincoln Continental roughly eighty yards away being driven by its owner's eighteen-year-old son, whose reflexes were splendid and experience nil. He hit the brakes instantly, but neglected to over-ride his automatic box and go into low to back them up. There was no way his two-ton vehicle could avoid the tossing cerise and blonde vision that had just tumbled into his path.

While Dick Swann, mouth opened with horror, instinctively continued to fire off film with the dedication of a *Time Life* photographer under bombardment, the Watcher hurled himself from the cable car like an Olympic sprint swimmer, hit Carol like a missile, and bowled her out of the path of the oncoming Lincoln. He took the brunt of the impact as they crashed against the side of a house bordering the street.

She was conscious of the discreet San Franciscan crowd gathering, of the flashing-crystal stridency of ambulances, and of the face of the Watcher bending over her before she passed out.

And in that split second before she lost consciousness, it came to her who he was.

When she woke up in a hospital room smelling of flowers, there he was still, as if he had never moved. She smiled straight up into his face. 'Ike,' she said. 'Ike Palmer.' She lifted a knee, tenting up the bedclothes. Grinning, he jumped back as if in alarm, protecting his balls with his hands.

She laughed. 'Don't be foul,' she said, 'you deserved it.' Her mind swam. 'How long ago was that back alley doorway? Eight years? Ten?'

He still looked like the young Henry Fonda, thin, male, vulnerable. The little steel-rimmed spectacles had been replaced now by heavy black frames. He was tall and his face had taken on intellectual authority.

'I did deserve it,' he grinned, 'but let me tell you something: if I had you in that doorway again right now, I'd do the same thing.' He had a slight American accent.

The brazen admission, coming from the distinctly professorial countenance, made her laugh, which made her wince. She seemed to have done something to her ribs.

'I want to thank you for what you did,' she said. 'If it hadn't been for you—'

He interrupted her. 'It was just an excuse for jumping on

you,' he smiled. 'I've been following you around for days, hoping you'd fall off something!'

Dick Swann moved into her field of vision and so did a pretty and imperious black nurse. 'I told you two gentlemen you could stay until Miss Blair woke up,' she said, 'and then you'd have to go. Well, she's woke up, so get!'

'I will be back,' said Ike.

'Who d'you think you are?' asked the nurse. 'Macarthur?'

But he was back, and back, and back. Carol was in for a week's observation: there was the possibility of a hairline fracture of a rib. Anyone less fit would have suffered a great deal more damage, they told her. Ike came twice a day.

He by no means had her to himself. Whenever Beatrice, the pretty black nurse, wasn't about, Dick Swann was prowling around her bed like an immaculate cat, taking available-light pictures. He called it his broken butterfly album. Her reply was friendly but monosyllabic, and not polite.

Michael Willoughby, who'd got to hear about it as he got to hear everything about his clients, flew over, bawled out both her and Dick Swann, gave her an enormous teddy bear and flew out again.

Friends drove down from L.A. and Santa Monica. Movie stars dropped in with zany, expensive gifts. They would look curiously at the serious bespectacled figure in the corner, who seemed content just to watch and listen. He would look back with that friendly, non-committal Fonda smile and just go on sitting.

Carol had liked him the minute she had opened her eyes and seen the boy in the man and the kind of man the boy had become. But now she found herself liking him more and more. She gathered that he had followed her career from the start, could practically chart it mathematically. He didn't seem greatly surprised by it. 'Everyone knows you're great now,' he said, 'but I was the very first.' And that, plus the fact that he was at UCLA doing post-doctorate work in physics, was about all she had time to get out of him amid the flood of other well-wishers and champagne-bearers. She knew her friends were impressed by him; some of them were impressed by anyone who didn't look as if he needed a brain implant. She occasionally giggled inside herself, conjecturing how all these rich and beautiful people would react if they knew the background from which she and Ike had sprung; if they could somehow play back to them that last encounter in the back alley.

On the Sunday, some of the cast of *Hair,* the revolutionary new musical that had just opened on Broadway, flew in, turned her room and the entire wing of the hospital into writhing, musical chaos and flew out again. She was pronounced fit forty-eight hours later. She had a suspicion that the visitation from *Hair* speeded up a decision which – at this hospital's prices – could have taken far longer.

She and Ike moved into a penthouse overlooking the bay. It had been lent to her by Gore Vidal, whose bestseller *Myra Breckenridge* was, much to his brilliantly articulate disgust, just being overtaken by Arthur Haley's *Airport* in the lists. There, amid the serious, cool-it luxury with which Vidal liked to surround himself, Carol learned for the first time who and what Ike was.

He was a doctor: what she called a real doctor and he called an MD. He was also, she discovered, a Doctor of Philosophy. Finally, he was Jewish. And that she found out without any discussion at all.

They were lying, clothesless and complicated, on top of the bed as they talked. She'd found he liked to discuss quite serious issues during foreplay. He always took his glasses off, but still retained that academic look and she found a delicious piquancy in the contrast between what he talked about with his young professorial face and what he did to her while they were talking.

He was talking about fossil fuels and how they were going to run out sooner or later and nobody seemed to care very much, with the exception of himself and a few others. 'We've got about forty years of oil left, maybe fifty if we can find more; and about a couple of hundreds of years of coal if we can hold our present rate of usage, which we can't—'

Just then she rubbed her nipple across the glistening tip of his penis and he lost the track. He'd have lost everything else as well if she hadn't grabbed him between her fingers and thumb near the top and squeezed.

'Thanks,' he said. 'Ehee! What were we talking about?'

'Fossil fuels,' she said, slithering back up alongside him.

'Fuck fossil fuels,' he said, sliding salaciously into her.

'No,' she said, 'it was in-ter-est-ing . . . '

It was at this point that he reached underneath her with his physician's middle finger and stroked her sphincter, the velvety-textured opening between her buttocks that she referred to as her 'cat's eye'. It was as if his hand were electrified. She reared with delicious shock, shuddered, and started the inexorable build-up to the bursting of the dam.

There was no more discussion of fossil fuels for some time.

'You were saying?' she asked later.

He was in a deep blue terry-towelling robe and only when she glanced down at his bare calves as he paced about while he talked was his authority just marginally undermined.

The only two alternatives that are really viable are hydrogen and nuclear. The rest are crap. Well, not crap, but not the answer.'

'What is the answer?' asked Carol, reaching out to stroke one of his legs as he passed the rug on which she was lying in front of the fire. It suddenly occurred to her that for the last five years she had been getting all her information about the world from men who really knew what they were talking about: the top men in their field.

'Hydrogen's pretty interesting, but I think nuclear,' he was saying. 'Not fission: there's only enough uranium on land to last about a century. That means breeder-reactors and pollution and the rest of it and . . . anyway, I don't see that as the answer.'

'What do you see?' she asked, this time grabbing hold of a leg as he passed and stopping him in his stride.

'Not fission, but fusion,' he answered. 'Anyway, that's

what I'm working on; without too much support, I might tell you.'

'What's the difference between fission and fusion?' Now she was cuddling his leg, her hand venturing above the knee, stroking up his thigh.

'In fission, in order to get energy, one splits atoms. In fusion one melds them together: the nuclei of deuterium and tritium, to be exact. The energy release is almost inconceivable in power, and the sources of deuterium and tritium are practically inexhaustible. If we could get it together . . . !' His enthusiasm was mounting. 'We'd have enough energy to last man the rest of his time on earth! If we can only get a grip on it!'

Carol had now reached up and got a grip on something else. 'Here endeth the first lesson,' said Ike as he descended upon her on the rug, and fusion took place with no help whatsoever from deuterium or tritium.

He had taken a two-week sabbatical to come to San Francisco after reading in some gossip column that she was due there on an assignment. Now he had to be back and they climbed into his battered Volkswagen and did it the slow way, keeping the sapphire and cream Pacific mostly in sight, picnicking and making love on beaches, staying and making love in motels.

It was an idyll. And on the last day he spoiled it.

They were lying on a beach, sun-drenched, breeze-cooled, thirty miles south of Los Angeles. He lifted himself up on his elbow. 'Marry me,' he said.

For some seconds she was mute. It was as if her emotional responses had seized up. She had taken it for granted that because they came from the same background, practically the same street, they thought the same way. No ties. No parallels to what they had gone through and seen happening at home.

What she couldn't know was that Ike had had a happy childhood, in a home as deprived as her own but warmed by love. Marriage never entered her head. To Ike it was the natural state.

She took her time, gathering her thoughts. She knew

there was proud masculinity behind that professorial exterior and a mind that could spot bullshit in a swamp.

'I don't believe in marriage, Ike,' she said.

'You really mean that? It's not that you don't love me?'

The superb sweep of his masculine ego stopped her breath again. When had she ever said that she loved him? When had he said he loved her? *Did* she love him? She didn't know: the whole thing was being thrown at her like shock-therapy.

'Ike, I don't know if I love you. I've never thought about it.'

'Never thought—!'

'I love your body. I adore the way you make love. I admire your mind. Does that add up to love? If I have to ask the question, it seems to me it doesn't.'

'Oh, fine,' said Ike. 'So all I am to you is a good fuck, is that what you're saying?'

'Ike, look, we knew each other as kids and we weren't the best of friends. Don't let's spoil what we've got now. We'll live together if you like–'

'*Live* together?' He turned to the blue ocean and the sky as if appealing to them. 'Christ, the kid's patronising me!' He turned back to Carol. 'Listen, do you have any idea what I was offering when I asked you to marry me? The amount of shit that would hit the rabbinical fan? The rending of clothes and tearing of hair in my family? We're Orthodox, practically Hassidic! What I'd have to go through? The tears, tantrums, torment, the threatened maternal heart attacks?'

'You're arguing on my side,' said Carol. 'Why go through all that when we can be together without it?'

'Because I want you to be mine, that's why!' He almost snarled it. And that, though she had been calm until then, was what lit the fuse in her blood.

'Yes, that's it, isn't it?' she ripped back at him. ' "Mine". Possession. Mine, mine, mine. Well, let me tell you something, you fucking Old Testament chauvinist! I was possessed by a man for the first sixteen years of my life. By my father. My mother is still possessed by him. For all I know my sister too. I've had enough of "mine". To me "mine" is a four-letter word. If "mine" is the magic word that turns you on, then piss off, Ike Palmer! We got each other all wrong!'

Without another word he got up, rising straight from the sand, she couldn't help noticing, without having to lever himself with his hands, and went, in his ragged-kneed, sawn-off jeans, his brown back sweating with fury. Maybe it was just respect. But did he respect her? A strange question, she knew, to ask about a man who'd asked her to marry him. With what she had earned by now she could buy him a thousand times over. But she would never have tried to possess him in that way, though he wouldn't hesitate to possess her by force of law and custom. Fuck him, then! She heard the Volkswagen start up on the highway. *And* he'd left her to get a taxi, the bastard!

11

As Ike stomped away across that burnished Californian beach, six thousand miles away somebody else was having trouble with a Blair female.

Knutsford, Cheshire, a pretty little town with its black and white flower-badged houses had been the model for *Cranford*, Mrs Gaskell's Victorian novel. It now, however, had another claim to fame.

Just outside the town, at Greensleeves Manor, within sixty-four acres of rolling parkland, lived George Ironstile, the fastest-growing tycoon in the north of England. Word in the neighbourhood had it that he'd started with a scrap-yard just outside Preston and that, magically, he had worked his way up in short order to being the third or fourth largest steel stockholder in the country.

Word also had it that, apart from Ironstile's own uncanny feeling for metal – he felt about steel the way jewellers feel about diamonds – a major ingredient of the magic formula was a dumpy, broad-faced, tweed-skirted, flat-shoed partner, who could make figures perform tricks that would fill a circus Big Top every night for a year.

At this moment, the two ingredients of the magic formula were ensconced in the superb interior of Greensleeves Manor, about as cosy with each other as a mongoose and a snake. To be precise, they were in the 'snug', a small glowing den of comfort just off the panelled drawing room, and they were arguing about motor cars. Except that they weren't really arguing about motor cars at all, but something a great deal more fundamental.

'There was nothing bloody wrong with my Ford when I arrived here this afternoon, that's all I'm saying!' Martha Blair was shouting.

'Well there's something bloody wrong with it now,' George Ironstile shouted back, 'because it won't bloody start and you've killed the battery trying!'

'That car's never failed to start in its life!' yelled Martha. 'Not since the day I got it!'

'There's a first time for everything,' roared George. 'What the hell am I supposed to do about it?'

'You can run me home in the Rolls.'

'The Rolls is in Chester, being serviced.'

'Very bloody convenient!' Martha was not prepared, just at that point, to say what that was supposed to mean. It would lead on to dangerous ground, where she was not prepared to venture; which had not, however, prevented her, woman-like, from hinting. 'Get the AA then, or the local breakdown service,' she said.

'You heard me telephone both of them an hour ago,' bawled George, with a great burst of exasperation. 'It's a bad night: there's a four-hour delay!'

His face had escalated from its usual scarlet to a deep and stormy crimson. His teddy-bear eyes were flashing lightning. George Ironstile was lying in his teeth and he was doing it magnificently. Martha's car wouldn't start for the simple reason that, while she had been raking his personal tax accounts with her formidable eye earlier, he had sneaked out and removed the rotor arm from the distributor. He had also, while pretending to telephone the AA and the local breakdown service, dialled two non-existent numbers and held animated conversations with the 'unobtainable' tone. George was that most dangerous of combinations, a man who was in love, frustrated, desperate and resourceful.

During the five years he and Martha had spent building up Ironstile Holdings, they had discovered in each other the perfect complementary business partner. Martha had proved to be something of a financial prodigy. The company's profit before tax was already £1.4 million a year. By shrewd buying of capital equipment, operating in Government-aided development areas and using all the legitimate devices available to her from her own years in the Revenue, Martha had so far managed to reduce the tax charge to zero.

The house belonged to the company, so that it was, in theory, half Martha's. Apart from having hired 'Town and Country' to furnish and decorate it, she never bothered with it.

'Why not?' George had once asked.

'We bought the house for the company,' she explained patiently. 'You have to entertain a lot of overseas suppliers and clients – that's tax-deductible. You can have a decent household staff to look after you: they go on the company payroll. It's important to have a good front. Also, the house is an appreciating asset.'

'But what about you? Here's me living the life of Riley: manservant, cook/housekeeper, gardeners, Rolls; what are you getting out of it? You won't even pay yourself a decent wage. And you're still living in that bloody awful hole in Liverpool. I rattle around in this great house on my own like a dried pea in a box. Well, I just think there could be a better arrangement.'

'Like what?'

'Like . . . well . . . like bloody marriage, for instance.'

It wasn't the most elegant proposal in the world, but then it wasn't the first one he had made to her either. He pelted onwards. 'It makes sense,' he said, 'you must admit it. Instead of you slogging backwards and forwards every day, we'd both be here, on the spot, partners in business and partners in life.'

'Don't get fancy, George,' she said drily, 'it doesn't suit you. And the answer's no, it always will be no, so save your breath and your energy and get out and sell some steel.'

Now Martha was as sure as she could be, without actual proof, that he was behind the non-starting of her car, sitting out there in the drive, dead and desolate as an empty salmon tin.

'I'll get a cab,' she said, 'or a hire car.'

'Don't be daft,' said George. 'You'll not get anyone turning out for you this time of night, not when they find out where you want to go: Scottie Road, Liverpool! You might as well ask to go to Vietnam!'

'Then what do you suggest?' she asked, with an edge of irony to her voice that would have sheared through tank armour.

'Stay here,' suggested George. 'God knows there are spare rooms enough!'

'What about nightclothes, hair brush, toothbrush, housecoat, tiny little details like that?'

'No problem,' said George, nonchalantly pressing a bell button. Fifteen seconds later, his manservant appeared, trained in some of the best houses in England, devoted to George for the speed at which George had learned. 'Oh, Muir, get a spare room ready for Miss Blair, would you? She'll need pyjamas, toothbrush, things like that. I dare say we can rustle something up?'

'Certainly, sir. Will that be all?'

'Before you get on to it, you might put a bottle of champers on ice. The Krug we gave those Spaniards the other night wasn't bad.'

'Very well, sir.'

Martha felt off balance. In the first place, it was becoming increasingly clear that this was a planned seduction. And in the second place, George was handling it with considerable polish. She unbent so far as to sit down, countering the concession by saying, 'And if you think I'm having any of that champagne, you've got another think coming.'

'In Greensleeves Manor,' said George, 'property of Ironstile Holdings, partners Martha Blair and George Ironstile, nobody has to do anything they don't want. Those who wish to retire to bed early with a volume of *The Lives of the Saints* are at liberty to do so, provided they do not disturb those who wish to swing naked from the chandeliers.'

He was tapping a vein of badinage she hadn't heard him use before and he was doing it well. In fact, looking at him now, standing in front of the big log fire, his ruddy face contrasting with his well-cut greeny-brown tweed suit, his checked shirt and woollen tie immaculate, the teddy-bear eyes twinkling, she had to admit he was all right. They'd been so busy building up the business, they hadn't had time to take stock of each other for years. She hadn't realised how he'd come on from the clodhopper who clumped in his big boots into her office that day.

He, for his part, looked at her, at her sensible skirt and her sensible blouse and her sensible brown brogue shoes and the rather pudgy square face with the make-up not very well applied and he saw what only the perceptive saw: the essential vulnerable femininity beneath it all. He knew that when she was eighty years old, there would still be for him this lost, hidden maidenliness about her, which gripped his emotions every time he saw her again after an interval.

'I'll have to ring Mum,' she said. Both she and Carol had insisted they put a telephone in at home, the installation and running expenses of which they paid. She dialled the number. 'Hello? Mum, It's Martha. Listen, my car's broken down, so I'm having to stay the night at Greensleeves.'

'I see, love.' Martha could have sworn she could detect a smile in Janet's voice and it infuriated her.

'I'll be able to get someone to fix it in the morning,' she said flatly, a baleful eye on George, who was beaming at her while lighting a cigar, 'so I'll see you then. Explain to Dad, will you?'

'I'll try, love,' answered Janet, the smile still there. 'Goodnight . . . and good luck!'

The last two words, with their conspiratorial feminine overtones, filled Martha's cup of wrath to overflowing. She slammed down the telephone and looked up at George. 'Why don't you go and get knotted, you great smug red-faced pudding!' she roared.

'What—'

'Just shut up!' She felt trapped, manipulated and misunderstood.

Muir came in, wheeling a trolley on which were a bottle of Krug in an ice bucket and two glasses. 'Shall I open it now, sir?' he asked George.

'Aye, if you would,'George said.

'And then would you get some orange squash for me?' asked Martha.

Muir merely blinked, but there was eloquence in his blink. George choked slightly on his cigar. Martha felt that she had wrested the initiative for the first time.

Muir recovered before George: 'Certainly, madam,' he said, as he smoothly thumbed the cork from the Krug and stifled the explosion with the napkin. He put down the bottle without pouring and went, returning almost immediately with a tray on which sat a whole jug of fresh orange juice – not squash – a glass and some ice. 'I thought you might prefer fresh orange juice, madam,' he said, setting it down alongside the champagne.

'You're dead right,' said Martha, 'I would. Thank you very much.'

Without being asked, Muir poured first a glass of orange juice for Martha and then a glass of champagne for George. That done, he left the room as noiselessly as a cat.

George raised his glass; 'Well then, here's to the Mistress of Greensleeves Manor,' he proclaimed.

'You what?' asked Martha, suspiciously.

'Well, you are, aren't you?' asked George patiently. 'Articles of partnership, fifty-fifty. If I'm the master of this flash four-hundred-year-old status symbol, then you must be the Mistress.'

'Yes,' Martha gave him, grudgingly, 'I suppose in that sense you're right.'

'So, cheers!' He clinked his glass against hers and drained it in one gulp. 'If I'm going to get through this bottle on my own, I'm going to have to get on with it, aren't I?' he said, refilling his glass. 'I honestly don't understand why you stay in that dump.' He raised a hand to forestall her indignation. 'You know it's a dump and I know it's a dump, because I used to live in one, too, remember?' She made to open her mouth and he again over-rode her. 'And it's not just a crafty way of getting round again to suggesting we get wed or owt like that. But you could get yourself a nice flat, you can well afford it. It doesn't make sense.'

'I don't want to leave Mum alone.'

'She won't be alone. She's got your dad and she's got Tony.'

'Tony's not going to be there much longer, and it's leaving her alone with Dad I'm worried about.'

George finished his champagne and re-filled his glass again. He offered Martha more orange juice, but she had hardly made a dent in her first glassful yet.

'He's not likely to beat her up or anything like that, is he?'

'No, he'd never lay a finger on her that way! But there's not much between them, no real binding. Oh, there is on her part. She loves him . . . still. But I'd swear he just . . . uses her. No, I can't say that. I just don't know. I do know he's worn her out, that she's been a kind of slave.'

'Why d'you think Tony's likely to be off?'

'Well, he's finished his course at art college. He came out top of his year. Picasso's an also-ran if you heard his teachers talk.'

'Aye, I remember you telling me.' George poured himself another glass of champagne. Martha noticed that the bottle was more than half finished.

'Well, Carol and me, romantic little souls that we are, wanted to go on staking him so that he could spend his time painting. I mean, like Carol said, all she can do is look pretty and all I can do is conjure with money: he's the one with the real gift, it's the least we can do to help him realise it. Could he see that? Could he hell! D'you know what he's gone and done?'

'No,' said George, trying to keep his eye on her while he poured more champagne.

'He's only gone and got himself a job as an art teacher, that's all. He's got some bee in his bonnet about paying Carol and me back for staking him through college and he's breaking his arse to do it by teaching snotty little kids in some comprehensive school how to daub crayon on cartridge paper. A man with a gift like his! And then he gives us so much a week out of his pay. He's got no bloody chance to do any painting of his own!'

'Can't he do it in his spare time?' asked George, quaffing

yet another glass of champagne.

'If you work out what teachers get paid and the pound of flesh Dad will be clawing off him every week, you'll see he won't even have enough left to buy paints and canvas. Me and Carol have offered to set him up in a proper studio of his own with everything he needs, but he won't even hear of it.'

'Masculine pride,' said George, sinking yet another glass of Krug. Martha noticed that he had slight difficulty with the enunciation of 'masculine'.

She found she was enjoying their talk, comfortable by the crackling log fire in the great hearth, with George looking so tweedy and tailored and colourful and becoming more amiable by the minute as he drank his champagne. She realised she liked to see a man with champagne and a cigar. And she realised, too, how much she had missed those chats they used to have right at the beginning in the warm, greasy exhalations of suburban restaurants that had, at the time, represented social promotion for them.

They still had meals together, in far more exalted restaurants, but since the business had begun to boom business was all they seemed to talk about. There was always so much to discuss, so many problems to resolve, and they both loved it so much. Everything else had got crowded out.

She glanced at the champagne bottle. It was empty. Magically, George was now cradling a brandy balloon which, together with the decanter, Muir had tactfully left on a lower level of the trolley. In the balloon there was a more than generous measure of fine cognac, which she hadn't even noticed George pour out. He rose to his feet and lifted the glass, his articulation that of a man whose tongue is valiantly trying to interpret the signals from his brain, but only partially succeeding.

'I drink a toast,' he said, 'I drink a toast to the new Picasso, the new Michelangelo: the bloody big new painter of our day. To Tony Blair, more power to his palette!'

He poured the cognac down his gullet, carefully replaced the glass on the trolley and, as far as it was possible for a man of his build, sank gracefully to the floor, his head reclining on the carpet. He began to snore, gently.

For a stunned moment Martha sat there paralysed. Then she leaped to her feet and rang for Muir. A minute went by. Ninety seconds. No Muir. George snored bubblingly.

She rang the bell again, this time keeping her broad thumb on it for a long, nail-blanching stretch. She waited. George snored. No Muir. Perhaps he'd gone to bed? Well, if he had, he could bloody well get up again! She pressed the bell once more. Again to no effect. Perhaps he slept somewhere he couldn't hear it; well, what sort of a bloody stupid arrangement was that? Or perhaps, more likely, there was an arrangement between George and Muir that, after a certain hour, no matter how many times the bell rang, Muir was to ignore it.

George snored on.

As always with Martha, frustration led to action. It was action she was going to enjoy. She went over to the drinks table, picked up a soda syphon and came back to George. She'd often seen it done on television, but never in real life. She sent a jet of hissing soda water smacking straight into George's blissfully placid face.

For a second nothing happened. Then George started to splutter. He coughed; his eyes opened and he spoke with perfect lucidity. 'Sorry about that,' he said, 'going suddenly off like that; it's supposed to mean you've developed an allergy to alcohol. What a bloody awful thought! Here, help us up, would you?'

He put out a hand, she seized it and helped him to his feet and he was instantly drunk again. He staggered against her. 'Whoops!' he cried. 'Would somebody please keep this blurry boat still!' He started to subside to the floor again. She got her thickset strength under his shoulders, her arm supporting him.

'Stand up, will you, you daft bastard!' she cursed, as he reeled about.

'Give us a kiss,' he said, his voice blurred, his face lurching towards her like a big, soft dog, his intoxicated eyes unfocused.

'I'll give you a thick ear in a minute,' she threatened, trying not to laugh. 'Come on, bed's the best place for you, though I don't know where the hell you sleep.'

'You nav'gate, I'll drive . . . ' he said, lurching off in the direction of the door leading to the hall. 'That is, I mean t'say . . . I'll nav'gate, you drive.'

He stumbled out of her steadying clutch and nearly went clean over a small coffee table. She grabbed him again. 'You couldn't navigate a toy boat on a kid's paddling pool,' she said.

'I can nav'gate my way to my own blurry bedroom!' he exclaimed, gratefully letting her take his weight again. 'Give us a kiss!'

'Give over!' she snapped irritably, as she somehow opened the drawing-room door and shoehorned him through it.

They heaved out, like an ill-assorted pair of Siamese twins, into the imposing hall with its coats of arms built into the panelling and its heraldic windows. 'Up th'stairs, 'long the corridor, second door on left,' George directed boldly.

Somehow, they negotiated the stairs in a style which, had it been filmed, would have ranked with the best of Laurel and Hardy. The great breadth of the stairs and the shallowness of their rises helped. Martha's strength helped more than somewhat, too. There was power in that broad, sturdy frame and she needed all of it to prevent George from missing his step and rolling back on to the unyielding chessboard marble tiles of the floor of the great hall.

Eventually, like an indomitable tug with a liner, she got him into his bedroom. The luxury of it staggered her. She had instructed 'Town and Country' not to hold back; but this! There was a small indoor garden behind a sliding window, mainly succulents and evergreens. They got their light from a cleverly devised glass ceiling outside the room and were spotlit when the bedroom lights came on. Martha got a strange feeling deep down inside her body when she saw the plants; she didn't immediately know why.

She unloaded George like a sack of coal on to the imperial-sized bed and he flopped, boneless, on to the silk and cashmere coverlet. He looked very young, suddenly, and vulnerable.

As she gazed down at him, his eyes opened hazily and he looked up at her as if through a mist. 'Thanks, Martha lass,' he said. 'I don't know what I'd do without you.'

It was said with genuine affection and lucidity, then the brown eyes hazed over again and closed. He looked young and vulnerable once more.

On an impulse, Martha bent over and kissed the mouth that had just opened again on the overture to a snore. There was no response, but the lips were pleasantly warm and unexpectedly pliant.

Apart from Tony's, when he was little, they were the first male lips she had ever kissed and she found the experience instructive. She couldn't decide whether the slight tingle she felt in her own lips was real or imagined. She hesitated, then tried again. No, it wasn't imaginary: there was a definite buzz.

George mumbled and threw out a robust and random arm. It landed across the back of Martha's neck, trapping her in an awkward stooping position with her face against his.

'George!' she said. 'George!' He remained in serene oblivion.

The arm lay across her more heavily; she was developing a crick in her back. Strong as she was, she found it impossible to break free. She sank to her knees to ease her back, and as she did so George's mouth opened again in that childlike fashion, as if someone had just removed a soother from it, and she found her lips pressed against his far more firmly than she had dared to do it the first time. She felt a stream of sensation, long denied, course through her nervous system.

Contrary to all her expectations, she felt a curious lack of guilt. Perhaps it had something to do with George's unawareness. Perhaps it wasn't a lack of guilt at all, but merely a lack of embarrassment and self-consciousness.

She had little time to ponder the matter, for the next minute George rolled slowly off the edge of the bed like some insensible, humanoid oak tree and subsided gently on top of her, pressing her into the densely welcoming pile of the lambswool rug that lay beside the bed.

She wriggled experimentally. No result. She heaved. Couldn't budge him.

'Get off! Get off, you daft bastard!' she shouted.

His face remained happily dormant. She became aware that she wasn't at all sure she wanted him off her. There was an indefinable deliciousness about having the weight of him on top of her that was the stuff of some of her dreams.

Gradually, arousal had grown in her, stealing through her body, an insidious stimulant. In her helplessness underneath George she wriggled again and now there was concrete, definable and fairly localised pleasure in it.

George's eyes opened sleepily. They were slumbrous and infinitely kind. He began to pass his hands over her as if she were a child and to kiss her, not only on the lips, but all over her face: little, soft, affectionate kisses.

More and more her body was softening. Muscles that felt as if they had been rigid for years were relaxing: even her blood seemed to be flowing more freely.

She half remembered Shakespeare's dictum about drink making men feel loving, while rendering them incapable of doing anything about it. But she could feel by George's body that he was an exception. The brown eyes that were usually so sharply bright were veiled and misted, but the pupils were widened by excitement and she could feel the hardness of him growing and pressing insistently down on her. It was as if she had been released from some kind of iron restraint. She felt free and bold and innocent. 'Wait,' she said softly. 'Roll over.'

Without a word, he took his weight off her and swiftly she stripped naked. She had a strong, square, firmly planted body like a peasant woman, yet with that same mysteriously conveyed femininity that George could always see in her face. She knelt by the side of him and stripped him, too. He was as she'd imagined him, hard and textured like a tree, cord and muscle seaming him like the knots and sinews in the bark of an oak.

'It's the very first—'

'I know that, love,' he interrupted, stopping her with a kiss.

The sight of his body, so uncompromising, like her father's, in its masculinity, might have been expected to re-create her lifelong tension. It did the reverse. She became more receptive, more open than ever, and ready for the final surprise, which was that George Ironstile, hard man, hard swearer, former terror of the scrapyards, killer of businesses that got in his way, had the touch and tenderness of a mother bathing her baby.

Martha, by her nature, was no firecracker: she was slow, a steady builder. Her nerves were quite deep beneath a skin that was substantial. All this, George seemed to know. He gathered Martha up, almost, it seemed, nerve by nerve, to a peak surpassing her most complex dreams. And when he used the peak to which he'd built her to puncture her, it seemed that she skied down the mountain in a series of swamping spasms that washed through to the tips of her toes while at the same time the peak, which was George, exploded and leaped inside her like a volcano. It was as though dream and reality had fused and that hard-headed, stubborn, bull-necked chauvinist George was the sorcerer who had done it.

It wasn't until three o'clock in the morning that she awoke suddenly, the sound of his steady contented breathing beside her, to the memory that he had once out-drunk her father, the man with the best head for liquor she had ever seen, and remained as sober as a tight-rope walker.

12

The helicopter thrashed to rest in a miniature storm of dust and grass-cuttings on the lawn that sloped down from the terrace of the Locatelli villa in the foothills outside Turin. Carol got out, followed by her husband, Prince Leopoldo Locatelli, member of the Black Aristocracy of Rome and the Vatican, director of the latter's own bank. He and his wife, the Princess Carol, had been skiing in the mountains one could see behind the villa, as one had been able to see them on the canvases of Renaissance artists for the last five centuries.

They had been skiing the rich man's way. The helicopter would lift them to the top of the run, whirl down and pick them up at the bottom, then sweep them up again for another hissing, spuming, thigh-testing descent. Carol was in a brilliant, blood-red ski suit, her helmet off and her hair flashing in the winter sun; Leopoldo was in lean-looking, efficient black. At that moment, any agency in the world would have paid them a million dollars to endorse anything.

It was five years since Carol had climbed off the beach in California. As she had reached the road that day and made to cross to a pay-phone on the other side, a large white bullet had snarled out of the heat haze and snapped past like a cracking whip within a yard of her. Then there was the smell of hot steel as the brake discs hit the drums and of rubber being heat-smeared on to the road. A hundred and fifty yards further on a white Lamborghini screamed to a halt and began to reverse.

The driver was dressed in a white cotton racing suit. Even with the wrap-around sun-glasses he was wearing and the strained angle of his head as he twisted round in his seat, Carol could see he was exceptional. He had the face of a beautiful predator, a hawk, maybe, or a falcon. It was deeply tanned, with unexpected creases in the cheeks. His hair was as black and glossy as Stewart Crown's. He would be thirty.

He jumped out of the car and took off his sun-glasses. Christ, she'd heard of green eyes!

'I am so sorry,' he said instantly in perfect Italian-accented English. 'You were in no danger, but I must have frightened you.'

'You did,' answered Carol. 'I didn't think you were allowed to fly so low.'

'Touché!' Christ, he'd heard of blue eyes! And with the blue denim ragged shorts and those legs! 'Allow me to introduce myself,' he said. 'My name is Leopoldo Locatelli.'

'And mine is—'

He interrupted her. 'Carol Blair. The best-known face since Helen of Troy: better, in fact. Nine-tenths of the men who died for her never even saw her. Don't you think that's ironic?'

'Are you going to stand here talking history or' – she pointed in the direction he'd been travelling – 'give me a lift to San Diego?' She gave him her poleaxing smile.

Locatelli laughed and led her without further words to the passenger seat of the Lamborghini.

His driving was fast, dexterous and – thanks to an eagle eye for Highway Patrollers and an illegal device on the dashboard for detecting radar traps – free from interference.

She got his history out of him. He was an aristocrat, head of one of the largest industrial complexes in Italy, and people said he was irresponsible. 'Just because I like to enjoy myself. I like to race cars. I have just driven in the Indianapolis 500. I came second. Of course I would have liked to be first, but I have never driven in it before . . . ' He shrugged. 'Graham Hill won it at his first attempt two years ago, so I thought why not me?'

'Graham Hill was British,' grinned Carol.

'Chauvinist!' he grinned back.

They were on the outskirts of San Diego. 'Where do you stay in San Diego?' he asked. She gave him the address of a house belonging to the Paul Newmans.

'And you?'

'Oh, I'm not staying here,' he said. 'I have a little place in San Francisco.'

She gasped. 'But you were headed this way!' she said.

'That was only because I had found a stretch of road that the Highway Patrol seemed to ignore and I was trying out my baby. I'd been backwards and forwards along it three or four times.'

'You mean you really wanted to go to San Francisco?'

'Yes, I will still go.'

'But you've come two hundred miles in the opposite direction!'

'Those poor fellows went much further for Helen of Troy and they had never even seen her.'

It was style. Undeniable twenty-four carat style. And it was kindness. What was a girl to do? Especially to an emerald-eyed Prince with creases in his cheeks and a small bottom in his tight driving suit that you wanted to dig your heels into while lying on your back? They had dinner – and much else – at home. He was fantastic: demonic almost. He was charged with an energy that might almost have come from some outside source. Her glossy, round, golden body with its glistening contours and warm come-on girl fragrances seemed to drive him mad, and his obsessiveness triggered off a sensual power in her to match his own.

Sometimes he liked to take her with her favourite knee-high boots on and she came to enjoy the almost cruel purchase the leather gave her legs on his slim, beautifully defined body as she helped to drive him deeper.

They didn't go out for a week. At the end of that time, he was a spent battery and she, for the first time in her life, was sore. She was to wonder, very much later, if there had been any tenderness in either of them.

The reasons why she married him were complex. Certainly the utter physical compatibility was a potent factor, his kindness, consideration, his superb appearance. They all came into it, but they weren't decisive.

There was, of course, the fact that he was a prince and would make her a princess. For a girl from Mugsley Street, no matter how far she'd travelled, it would have been stupid to deny the lure of the Cinderella syndrome.

What finally clinched it, however, she was later to believe, was something he said to her on the seventh day.

She was naked, making orange juice for breakfast, the sunshine like gold sovereigns in her hair. He came up behind her, damp from the shower, put his arms around her and clasped her breasts. 'A goddess needs a worshipper. Let me be yours. Marry me.'

It wasn't the flattery, though she loved it: it was that she had no sense of his taking her over as a piece of property. If anything, the feeling was the opposite, that he was willing to make himself over to her.

She didn't realise it, but she was still bouncing about like a squash ball on the rebound from Ike Palmer.

She saw Ike again on the concourse at Los Angeles airport as she was leaving with Leo for Rome. Leo had gone to buy magazines. Ike came up behind her. He was on his way to a scientific convention at MIT.

'Where are you going with him?' he asked in his usual direct fashion, glancing over at the Italianate elegance of the suit at the magazine stand.

'Rome.'

'Why?'

'I'm going to marry him.'

Ike paused, struggling to conceal the effort he was making to adjust. 'I thought you were the girl who didn't believe in marriage,' he said finally, without sarcasm.

'I suppose there's always someone who can change our minds about anything,' said Carol.

Ike studied the striking back and profile of Leo again, then turned to her, an unfathomable expression in the beautiful wise eyes behind the spectacles.

'You'll be sorry,' he said. Then he went. There was a seriousness about Ike that was different. It was as if he were a seer or a prophet. For some reason,she shivered. She hurried over to Leo and took his arm. It felt warm and hard and reassuring through the silk sleeve.

He looked at her questioningly. 'Cara?'

'Nothing,' she said. 'Love you.'

'And I adore you,' he answered.

They made their way through the crush to the VIP lounge, then on to the Boeing. She tried to exorcise the memory of Ike's last look with a couple of Bellinis – fresh pears whipped in a blender and mixed with champagne – but the haunting image remained undimmed.

At Leonardo da Vinci they were met by Leo's younger brother Stefano, as cruelly good-looking as Leo, but without the iron beneath the skin that gave Leo's looks credibility. It was the first time she had stepped off an aircraft straight into a Rolls waiting on the tarmac by the bottom of the steps and it was her first intimation of what conveniences power and riches in Italy can buy.

The Rolls, driven immaculately by one of the family chauffeurs, insinuated them noiselessly through the suicidal Roman traffic to a stunningly restored villa on the Appian Way.

In the pillared, chandeliered entrance hall eight indoor staff were lined up: a butler, three footmen, the housekeeper, a cook and two maids.

With that incomparably boned face Carol was already one of Nature's princesses, but she was being brought increasingly to an understanding of what it meant, if the money was there, to be a prince in Italy. To the most discerning eye she was flawlessly gracious as she ran the gauntlet, but inside she felt like the valley of the butterflies at Lindos where Dick Swann, ever inventive, had once photographed her.

She thanked heaven as she went on Leo's arm up the broad stairs, branching out on to a golden, picture-studded landing, that the glowing cream silk in which she was draped was not silk at all, but a cunning, experimental man-made fibre from her friend Boussac, which had not picked up a single crease all the way from Los Angeles.

That night, after dinner, just the two of them in an exquisite small dining room off the palatial main one, they tumbled into separate beds in separate bedrooms – 'There is no one so puritanical as a Roman servant,' said Leo – and slept as deeply as children.

Perhaps, had Carol thought about it next morning, she might have been perturbed. It might have occurred to her that those who are fleetingly in possession of perfect happiness do not want to sleep, for fear of missing a second of it.

That day she spent most of her time with the designer Valentino. She had wardrobes scattered all over the world, but she had brought very little with her. She was to be a bride, and the one man in the world who knew how to dramatise romance was Valentino. She had modelled his designs before he was known; indeed, she had helped to get him off the runway with a spread in *Elle*.

The media had got hold of the wedding and she was met as she came out by a riot of 'paparazzi' from the newspapers and men from television, carrying the mis-named 'hand-held' cameras on their shoulders like some physical deformity. She stepped into the Rolls and Franco whisked her back to the villa with the newsmen buzzing behind in their Fiats like minnows in the wake of a whale.

She was glad, on reflection, that her family was not coming to the wedding. Faced with harassment like this, her father would have strewn the pavements of the Eternal City with felled photographers like Zulus at Yorke's Drift.

In addition to the normal calls home which she made every week, wherever she was, she had called Janet several times from California, pleading with her to come. She had also spoken to Martha and Tony. They had all been obdurate. 'We'd stick out like a razor in a convent,' was Tony's summation. She hadn't even talked to her father. She already knew from Martha that to Jack Blair the magnificent being who was Prince Leopoldo Locatelli was 'that Wop'.

Secretly, although he made the appropriate noises, Leo was relieved. There's no snob like an Italian aristocrat and although he recognised that the gods had made Carol a masterpiece, he doubted if they had been as generous to the rest of her family.

The wedding was held, not in Rome, but in Leo's own domain outside Turin. It was from here that he ran his industrial empire; and after they had flown up there in his Lear jet Carol began to realise what he had meant in California when he had told her that some people considered him irresponsible.

He controlled an empire stretching from steel to petrochemicals to civil engineering to electronics. It had been built up by his father, who had died doing it. His mother also was dead. There was a flock of cousins and there was Stefano. If anything happened to Leopoldo, it would be Stefano who would have to take over; and Stefano, even he knew it, was a lieutenant and not a general. Yet Leo refused to abandon his passion for motor-racing. He didn't want to be a tycoon: he wanted to be World Champion. Even though he knew that thousands of workers' livelihoods depended on him, he persisted in pushing himself to the ultimate against the Jimmy Clarks, Jackie Stewarts, Denny Hulmes and Graham Hills – the best there were – in a car of his own design and manufacture. Marie Small Pegler, one of the most perceptive writers about motor racing in the world, once said of him: 'Glamorous, dangerous, handsome as the Devil and rich as Croesus, Prince Locatelli could possibly be breaking a pattern. Most drivers drive to live. Does His Highness drive to die?'

For the wedding the surrounding villages treated Leo like the feudal seigneur he was. Produce from the fields and vineyards and orchards was delivered by cart and piled up in the outhouses and paddocks of the villa. Flowers by the sheaf were delivered to the tiny sixteenth-century church belonging to the villa where Leo had chosen to be married. Everything – frescoes, triptyches, statues, the altar itself – was obliterated by a mass of floral white and yellow, the colours of the Locatelli arms.

The day of the wedding presented the media with unrepeatable riches. Ferraris, Maseratis, Lamborghinis, Rolls Royces and Aston Martins littered the lawns, lanes and fields around the villa like toys. The motor racing fraternity was there in force, as was the Italian aristocracy. Both contingents spent most of their waiting time with their heads immersed in each other's engines, while their wives got the Kleenex out to wipe the oil from their men's hands and morning coats in time for the service. Graham Hill was only barely persuaded from removing the bridal Rolls to some hiding place and replacing it with a rusty old beribboned tractor.

Into this setting glided, as if on castors, the Cardinal Archbishop Locatelli who, as yet another cousin, would have conducted the ceremony even had Leopoldo not been on the lay staff of the Vatican. He had arrived the previous evening. 'I used to play with his son,' Leo had whispered to Carol as they welcomed the Cardinal in the villa's great hall. He and his retinue were to spend the night there before the wedding.

'What!' Carol demanded, shaken as only a lapsed Liverpudlian Catholic could be.

'Sssh!' hissed Leo, delighted to have rocked, even momentarily, the composure of his Elf-Queen. She nevertheless kissed the glowing four-hundred-year-old ruby on the Cardinal's hand with incomparable grace and set His Eminence to thinking briefly about making another son.

Now, next morning, as she paced her measured way across the shaved lawns of the villa to the church, handmaidens from the village strewed flower petals before her. Six stalwart lads, who weren't above taking in her beauty out of the corners of their eyes, held a canopy of olive branches above her head.

Leo, hand-tailored to his ancestral ear-lobes, was waiting for her at the church, which was stuffed with his kin. The rest of the guests – to look at the women was to risk diamond-blindness – were packed outside, standing on the grass, on tombstones, some of the young ones halfway up trees.

The crowd, sated and sophisticated as they were, gasped at the sight of her. The women discarded envy and exulted in her as a triumph of her sex. The men cursed Leopoldo Locatelli.

A second gasp went up as something like an 'incident' threatened to develop at the church gate. A cab, its horn blaring, was bullying its way through the crush. The Italian driver, a committed Communist, his face ablaze with delight, kept his thumb on the horn and his foot on the throttle as Contessas and Principes and bourgeois millionaires leapt for their lives.

The cab forced its way through to Carol, standing at the church entrance looking like something from a child's fairytale as she clung to the arm of Leo's massive cousin Alvaro, who was to give her away. The cab stopped: a man catapulted out.

Alvaro moved forward, a massive fist bunched, and doubled up gasping as the mysterious new arrival did something very fast with stiffened, stabbing fingers – and there stood Tony! Her Tony! Her eternal rescuer, bringing family flesh and blood to her wedding after all. In a morning coat and trousers that gave even Leo's a run for their stylish money, a grey topper in his hand, looking more like Montgomery Clift than ever, he sent a buzz sizzling through the crowd.

Their embrace was fierce and their conversation short.

'You look fantastic, Car.'

'So do you – where d'you get the gear?'

'Rented. Moss Bros finest.'

As they entered the church, Leo, who was standing with Stefano at the altar, could not resist turning around. His heart felt as if it had been punched at the sight of his bride. She was so entirely lovely, so precious, that the dark face quivered for an instant and the green eyes blurred briefly with tears.

It was only when they cleared that he realised she wasn't on the arm of Alvaro, but of . . . it could only be her brother! *Lacrima Christi*, if the whole family looked like these two, he wished now they'd all come!

It wasn't until after the ceremony that Carol had a chance to question Tony. They were in a corner of the resplendent salon in the villa, which had once housed the Medicis. The speeches which, thanks to Italian good manners and accomplishment, had all been in English, were over. Carol had thrown a brilliancy over the reception with her grace. Tony had met a great many lustrous feminine eyes that were saying more than '*Buon giorno*'.

'What's it all about, Tone?'

'I just suddenly realised what you must be feeling like, all on your own with no Blairs around, so I grabbed a few days off, got an advance and came to hold your tiny little hand.'

'I'll pay you back for the fare and everything.'

'Like hell you will! If I can't pay my way to my own kid sister's wedding . . .'

She laughed. 'Come with us on honeymoon!' she said impulsively. 'We're going cruising in the Mediterranean for two weeks, then Leo's going to race in the Monaco Grand Prix.'

'Oh, yeah?' Tony grinned. 'That would make me really popular. I'd just have to be the biggest gooseberry of all time.'

'Don't be a nit,' said Carol. 'There won't be just Leo and me. The Italians say a man's yacht should be one foot long for every year of his life. Leo's multiplied the ration by four. His is a hundred and thirty feet, ten cabins with bathrooms, crew of five terrific Yugoslavs. We're taking a party. I'm sure we can squeeze you in.'

'Car,' he said, 'there's nothing I'd like better. But I've got a new job, textile designer for Courtaulds. They were very good about giving me the time off to come to this shenanigan when they found out who you were, but I don't think they'd wear me taking another two weeks off to swan around the Med.'

'Textile design? Is that what you want?

'There's more money in it than teaching. I'll be able to pay you and Martha back quicker.'

'Will you for God's sake forget about that! We want you to paint!'

'I'll paint – honest. When I'm ready.'

Carol saw him on to the plane at Turin airport before boarding Leo's executive jet, which was to fly them and his party to San Remo where his yacht was berthed.

With him, Tony took a film of the wedding and the reception, together with a screen and projector. It had taken Carol a long time to prevail upon him to accept them. Only her argument about how much it would mean to Janet convinced him.

Leo watched their parting and felt a pang of jealousy. The two heads, so beautiful, so close, riveted together by a past that excluded him.

The first sight of the motor yacht *Contessa* took Carol's breath away. It glistened, dolphin-sleek and white, against the green-shuttered, cobalt-watered harbour of San Remo. It was a practical, working port and the contrast was to the advantage of the yacht.

To Leo it represented beauty but, more importantly, freedom. He explained this aspect of it to her with great seriousness. 'When I was small I was always on ships and planes and wherever they wanted to take me, that was where I had to go. D'you know what I said to my Captain the first time we took out the *Contessa*? I had her built by Camper&Nicholsons at Southampton in England. We took her out into the Solent. I waited until we were well out, then I went to my Captain and said, 'Turn round.' The luxury of being able to say that, that is what having your own boat is all about. Or your own plane. You are in charge. No one has you in his power.'

'Have you ever tangled with an air traffic controller who's missed his lunch?' demanded Carol, grinning.

'Everything is relative!' he smiled, ruffling her hair.

There was only one place on the boat to which access was forbidden to everyone but Carol, Leo and his four mechanics: the sun-deck. There, strapped and bolted down and covered most of the time by tarpaulins, was Leo's racing car. In its white and yellow livery it should have looked cheerful. To Carol, whenever she saw it, it seemed sinister. She shivered. Also, there was one of the mechanics she didn't like, a curly-haired blond youth called Angelo. The other three obvously adored her. There was a look in Angelo's black eyes that seemed to convey the reverse whenever she looked at him. She said nothing to Leo. There seemed nothing that wouldn't sound silly.

The party of ten had a late dinner on the after-deck, then one of the twin thousand-horsepower Perkins diesels kicked into life and slowly they nosed out, watched with mariners' interest by every other boat within eyeshot.

The diesel fuel fired more than the Perkins. The smell of it drifted down the convoluted passages of Carol's memory and connected with a quiet sizzle with the smell of the paraffin lamp which had watched over her earliest childish love dreams. Suddenly she felt randy. One look from her to Leo was enough to bring him off his yellow canvas chair as if it were electrified and they went down to the Stateroom cabin, leaving a trail of indulgent smiles behind them.

At about the same time that the *Contessa* was passing, on her starboard side, the Customs House which marks the Riviera border between Italy and France, a world away in Mugsley Street Tony had set up the screen and projector in the kitchen and was running the film of the wedding, delivering a running commentary to Janet and Martha. The light was out.

Janet, eyes shining, was saying, 'It's just like Princess Grace getting wed!' when the sound they had all learned to associate with dread, the key in the front door, grated in their ears.

Jack Blair came in. He took one look at the screen, assessed instantly what was going on, and switched on the light.

'What's all this about, then?' he demanded, already moving in for destruction.

'It's our Carol's wedding,' said Janet, trying to hide her fear behind a pathetic veneer of bright cheerfulness.

'We want want no Wop-whore weddings in this house,' he said, launching a massive fist at the projector. Had it landed, it must have reduced the machine to so much scrap. But Tony had anticipated it. Moving too fast for Janet or Martha to follow he deflected Jack's blow with a rising forearm block and followed by using his blocking arm to deliver an elbow strike to his father's chest. Jack staggered back against the wall, agony and astonishment mingled on his face; he felt as if he'd been hit by an iron spike.

'Get those things out of here – quick!' Tony shouted to his mother and sister. Without a word, the two women grabbed the screen and the projector and scuttled out into the hall. Before she closed the door behind her, Janet released one last anguished look of appeal at her two men. But neither was looking at her. They were staring at each other.

Jack was now fifty-four. But the years and the docks had only put extra iron-cladding on to him. To hit him was like hitting a wall. He'd lost his speed, but his punch was still like the hammer of Thor. If anything, it was even more lethal now he had an extra fourteen pounds riding on it. Tony was twenty-four. He was thin, blade-shouldered, sinewy, two inches shorter than his father and at least seventy pounds lighter. But he thought he had two things going for him. He had been training for this fight since he was sixteen years old and he was now a karate black belt. The latter was, perhaps, not so big an advantage as he thought it was; Jack hadn't street-fought all his life without learning a thing or two that aren't taught in gyms.

Tony stood relaxed in the horse-stance: legs apart, knees pointing slightly outwards. He had not yet lifted his arms. Jack moved a table out of the way. 'Been learning some fancy-fighting, have we?' he sneered.

'Enough to take care of you, you fat old bastard,' said Tony. It was part of his game-plan to make Jack furious while he himself kept cool. He reckoned that part of it would be easy, since he knew there'd always been something about him that made his father angry just to look at him.

Sure enough, the blood rose in Jack's face and he lunged forwards with a straight right-hand punch which would have finished the fight instantly had it connected. Instead, Tony swept both arms into a straight-up knife-hand posture and moved his right foot back at an angle. With his left hand he deflected the punch, sending it whistling past his ear, while he brought the edge of his right hand scything down across the side of Jack's neck. Swivelling on his left foot, he followed up instantly with a roundhouse knee-strike crashing into Jack's midriff.

With anyone else that should have been enough, but the hardened edge of Tony's hand had felt the corded muscle on the side of that trunk-like neck and his knee had felt the hardness of the stomach wall and he knew it wasn't over yet.

For his part, Jack knew that he was in the fight of his life and that if he were to win it, it was going to have to be short. No one had ever hurt him like this.

He bulled in, head down, to butt Tony in the face. Tony managed to take the blow on his shoulder, which felt as if it had been reduced to pulp. He struck his father twice with the heel of his hand. Jack, momentarily blinded with pain, let loose two upper-cuts, of which Tony had not seen many and which he only half-rode. Even the half-impact he had to take was enough to shake him to his toes and only an instinctive hard-fist to his father's liver gave him time by driving Jack back. He hard-fisted again as Jack retreated, this time to the jaw, but he could tell by the feeling of his fist bouncing off that rocky chin that it was going to have to be his feet, not his fists, that finished this job.

'Just what I thought,' he cried, keeping Jack mentally off balance. 'Fat!'

The goad brought him his chance a second later. Jack came in, kicking for the groin. Tony scooped the kick off course with a circular arm block, throwing Jack off balance, and instantly countered, kicking three times with snake-strike speed, the loose, trained leg swinging with vicious effortlessness as his shoe-clad heel smashed into Jack's ribs, his left bicep and the side of his head.

Jack went reeling across a chair, which crumpled under his weight. He had a broken rib and a fractured cheekbone and to breathe was agony. Dimly, he saw Tony coming for him, patricide on his face. As his son raised another knife-edge hand above him, which Jack knew was aimed at his throat, he managed to strike upwards with the broken chair leg. He caught Tony across the side of his skull and the last image on his retina was of Tony going down and out. Then he himself lost consciousness for the first time in his life.

Jack was in hospital for a week and off work for a month. He made only one comment about it. It was when Jack O'Riordan visited him in hospital and asked him, incredulously, who had done it.

'My son,' said Jack, without a trace of a smile, but with . . . was there, thought O'Riordan, a trace of pride? Jack's next remark confirmed O'Riordan's suspicion. 'You're never going to believe this,' added Jack, indicating his bandages, 'but it was a draw.'

13

The *Contessa,* sleek as a sea-going jaguar, nosed its way into the harbour at Monte Carlo. From the wheelhouse, where she stood with Leo and Captain Milko, Carol could see to her left the Royal palace, high up on its cliff, from this side austere but for the rosiness of its stone in the sunshine. Soaring up ahead were the Casino with its green roof, the tower of the Hotel de Paris and the functionally elegant semi-circular spread of glass and dark grey concrete, dominating the foreground, which Leo told her was Loew's Hotel.

But the nonsensical toy-shop iced-cake fantasy of Monte Carlo rising from the sea, unseen underpinnings of financial girders holding up all the spun sugar, failed to lift Carol's heart. That wedding day two weeks before, when the neon signals in her eyes had effortlessly lured Leo to their white-and-gold bedroom in the *Contessa,* nothing had happened.

He had caressed her and stroked her and spoken with passion, but there had been no significant flicker of movement in his body. She had used all her considerable arts to strike a spark in him, but there was none. He had had a curious, drained look in his face and something she could have sworn was fear in his eyes.

'Carissima,' he said, 'I am sorry. It is something that sometimes happens to me. An American doctor has told me that I am not good at dealing with certain kinds of stress.'

'Darling mine,' she had said, 'please don't worry about it. It can happen to men. It means nothing.'

She lay with a superbly modelled leg flung carelessly

across him, her hand stroking his face, the muscles of which were as taut as a drawn cross-bow.

She couldn't resist asking gently, 'What kind of stress?'

'The marriage, the preparation of the car, wondering if it will be good enough this year, if we can stand up to the works teams. Also, there are certain business problems.' He was sweating, the drops crystallising on his temples and rolling down his cheeks.

She was distressed at his distress. 'Sweetheart, relax. It's not the end of the world.'

He hurled himself from the bed in a rage. 'Don't baby me!' he shouted. 'Don't nurse me!'

He strode into the bathroom and slammed the door. Almost instantly she heard him turn on the shower. Was it, she wondered, to hide another noise? The sound of crying?

For the next two weeks the glistening ship creamed its way across a glassy blue Mediterranean, anchoring every now and then to let down the diving platform so that the party could swim like porpoises around it. They ate luncheon on board, Leo's cook producing meals from his sophisticated electronic galley that would have brought a flush of competitiveness to the neck of every chef along the Côte d'Azur.

At night they berthed in the resorts strung along the coast like a continuous strip of the good life – Nice, Cannes, Antibes, Beaulieu, St Tropez – sipping their drinks on the after-deck, the milling panorama of the quayside life like opening scenes from old Gene Kelly musicals.

Carol turned a polished light-honey colour all over, against which her eyes and hair took on the power to stop all rational thought momentarily in the beholder. Yet still Leo, the sexual tiger of that explosive interlude in California, was unable to respond.

He wanted to, she could see that. He loved her, she knew that. But it was as if someone had turned off a switch. He would lie glistening with sweat, cursing in Italian, while Carol pretended it didn't matter. She had inherited all her father's sensuality; it did matter.

Finally, they turned back towards Monte Carlo for the Monaco Grand Prix. Leo immersed himself with maniacal concentration in the final preparation of his car.

From the start of his motor-racing career he had rejected the Cosworth engine used by most of the other teams and designed and developed his own at his own works, together with the chassis, suspension and body shell.

The engine was brilliant but erratic, and he and his mechanics were now working on it. They stripped it and re-stripped it, micrometers re-measuring tolerances, hawk-eyes scrutinising linkages, ears listening like stethoscopes for missed heartbeats.

It happened the night before they were due to reach Monte Carlo. Carol, pretending to be asleep, watched Leo's gleaming body twitching and turning on the other bed, plagued by demons she didn't understand. Suddenly, quietly, he swung from the bed and made silently for the door.

'Leo,' she whispered, 'where are you going?'

'There is something wrong with the engine,' he said. 'I feel it.'

'Leo, you've stripped that engine five times—'

'I am sorry,' he said. 'Try to sleep.'

He went, perfectionist, obsessive. Escaping, wondered Carol, from a problem he couldn't face to one he could?

No one on board got any sleep that night. Leo rigged up a bench test for the engine on the sun deck. Under blazing arc lights, which he had had installed for just such an emergency, he and his mechanics, half-naked and smeared with oil, the whole scene reminiscent of something from the Inferno, moved about amid the roar of the chained devil as if it were their lord and master.

The mechanics were used to these sudden psychic flashes of Leo's. They knew they were not mere caprice, but were usually right. He was proved right again this time. The engine had been singing *bel canto* ever since it left the test track at Turin, but now every time it was asked to deliver maximum revs it stuttered and lost heart. Leo's hunch had been providential. It was the kind of shortcoming likely to show up only under maximum pressure during a race.

They worked through the night, stripping down the engine, and by dawn they had found it – a small split-pin intermittently blocking a non-return valve in the fuel system when the throttle was wide open.

'Who last examined the fuel feed?' asked Leo.

Three pairs of eyes turned towards the blond-haired, black-eyed Angelo. In a racing team there is no mercy.

'How did that pin get in there?' asked Leo quietly in Italian. 'What would you be using such a pin for, anyway?'

In the dawn light, with his oil-smeared body and his hawk's face, he looked like some primitive, barbaric chieftain about to pronounce death. Carol had come up on deck and was standing in the shadows, watching. A number of the rest of the party, having despaired of sleep, had done the same.

Angelo replied as quietly as Leo: 'That pin got in there because I put it there. I put it there to fuck up your engine.'

'Why?'

'A year ago you hired Sophia Gennaro as a maid. You screwed her, made her pregnant, then fired her. She was my cousin. If I could have sent you out into that race with no brakes, I would have done it!'

Leo turned to Captain Milko, who was one of the watchers in the shadows. The sun was coming up over the milled edge of the sea, setting the bizarre tableau of car, sun-deck, oily mechanics and half-clad watchers ablaze. 'Lower the rubber dinghy.'

He turned back to Angelo. 'Sophia was pregnant when she came to me. I took her in because her family had thrown her out. After she'd had her child, I sent her back. There is no room for babies in my servants' quarters.'

The rubber dinghy was being winched down into the water. 'Get in,' Leo ordered, looking at Angelo.

'I have my things below decks,' the mechanic protested.

'Get in,' Leo repeated. His body looked like a spring under tension, the sinews highlighted by the oil.

Angelo turned, hammered down the companionway to the after-deck, and climbed into the dinghy just before it hit the oily, gently heaving dawn waters. As it settled into the sea, Angelo pulled the jump-cord of the powerful outboard motor, starting it up. The dinghy began to growl away.

Angelo shouted in Italian up to Leo on the sun deck: 'Your mother was a whore and your womenfolk are on the streets of Naples!'

Leo seized the twelve-bore he used for skeet-shooting on calm days from its waterproof case. He loaded it with one cartridge from the proofed box below and blasted a hole the size of a melon in the rubber fabric of the dinghy about an inch above the water-line.

'You're about half a mile off shore,' he shouted. 'If you hurry, you'll just make it!'

They reached Monte Carlo three days before the race. Already the place was thick with white-belted revolvered police busily sealing off roads.

Leo first checked that his spare engine and body shell had arrived by road at the cavernous Renault garage just outside the perimeter of the course, and then pulled strings to get permission to drive Carol around the course in a comparatively sedate Alfa Romeo saloon.

The race at Monte Carlo is run on the public roads, which are taped off tightly for the race to the enormous inconvenience, but rich profit, of the Monegasques.

Leo took her through it: along the inner promenade on the sea front, turning right to the end of the harbour, then up the vertiginous rock face to the Casino, dropping down through the gears again, winding round neck-grinding bends all the time, lean brown hands totally certain in their movements, to the sea wall, through the tunnel and back to the harbour, this time along the outer promenade to a chicane followed by a vicious hairpin where the gasometer used to be, leading back to the starting line.

It was the tunnel that frightened Carol most. Shooting out of eye-splitting sunshine into total blackness, hoping blindly that nothing had stopped and blocked the road in front of you, then shooting back out again into Mediterranean light, the wavelength blasting the back of your eyes.

It was just past the tunnel, she knew, that Lorenzo Bandini, the works Ferrari driver and a friend of Leo's, had died horribly the year before, in a spectacular crash.

Nobody liked the tunnel. Everyone, with a solitary exception, always instinctively eased fractionally off the throttle as they went in. The exception was Graham Hill, five times winner of the race, who went in with his throttle foot hard down and usually came out going more quickly than he went in.

She had noticed Leo flinch and swerve slightly as he came out of the tunnel back into the light; she remembered a celebrated eye surgeon, David Darby, telling her once that the pigmentation of some green eyes could make them more susceptible to sudden extremes of light

Leo had not exceeded forty miles an hour throughout the whole course – the first-ever Grand Prix there in 1929 had been won by 'Horse' Williams in a Bugatti at an average of fifty – yet Carol was appalled. She knew what speeds Leo would be pushing on the day of the race. At any time she would have been frightened at the thought of her man throwing himself in a bombshell on wheels around a killer course against the best in the world. But now everything seemed to be magnified. Ridiculous little things made her want to cry. She discovered, for the first time in her life, that a sexual block made every other problem loom larger and more ominously.

'Christ!' she exclaimed as she got out of the car.

'You didn't enjoy it?' His face was stricken.

'Why do you do it, for God's sake?'

Leo shrugged. 'I like it,' he said.

The killing demands of the Monaco Grand Prix, with its eighteen hundred gear changes, its constant bends, the difficulty in passing other drivers, are compensated for in some part by the fact that the drivers are given three days' practice before the race.

The race had been cut down from one hundred laps to eighty in an attempt to reduce the pressure on the drivers. But drivers are put under pressure largely by other drivers and on the second day of practice Jackie Stewart, clever tactician that he was, screwed the lid down tight on everyone else. He slapped on a pair of scrubbed tyres and flew round the circuit half a second faster than the lap record. The tyres wouldn't have lasted for anything like the race proper, but temporarily they gave instant, leech-like grip.

The day of the race was oven-hot, the sun like a great brass gong. Leo was on the front row of the grid, having put up the second fastest practice time. He was an object of great interest to the crowd, as always. With his privately financed car, his great yacht in the harbour and his aristocratic good looks, he was a glamorous figure in a glamorous game.

Carol was in the pits with the rest of the party. At Monte Carlo, the pits are simply spaces painted on the roadside. They were, as on all racing circuits, packed with beautiful girls in tight jeans.

Prince Rainier did a sedate lap of honour in an Italian car, then the drivers shoehorned themselves into their cockpits. Leo was the last to get in, as if trying to establish a psychological ascendancy. Finally, he pulled his visored Bell-Star helmet over his face and raised a lordly hand as if giving permission for the race to start.

The flag dropped and the field surged forwards like a pack of hungry tigers. On some of the drivers Leo's tactics had the desired effect. An Argentinian spun into the straw bales at the first corner, narrowly missing taking Chris Amon with him, and Jack Brabham took the hairpin sideways which, however, was not all that unusual for him.

The race was one of the hairiest Leo could remember, with drivers bouncing off the chicane, finding the bends cracking up their steering. Surtees lost his oil pressure, Stewart's engine blew up. Leo was slipstreaming Chris Amon, who was driving his usual immaculate race, with Jo Siffert pressing him from behind. His plan was to let Amon tow him until the last ten laps when he would make his move to take him.

But he was having the trouble that Carol had noticed. The sun was now like a laser. On every lap, roaring out of the tunnel, he momentarily lost vision. Even despite the visor, the sun seemed to pierce his eyes and go straight through to the back of his head like an internal hammer.

On the forty-fourth lap it led to disaster. Leo followed Amon into the tunnel, the crackle of their exhausts booming off the walls. In front of him he could hear the snarl of Amon changing down into fourth. What he could not know was that in the tunnel Amon, his night sight as sharp as an owl's, had lapped a tail-ender, who was still trailing to the left as Leo came out of the tunnel. His sights on Amon, accelerating along the promenade, Leo's blind spot hit him and washed the tail-ender into invisibility at the precise moment Leo's eyes should have picked him up to his left.

He clipped the rear of the South American as he passed. At that speed the resulting deflection of Leo's car had an effect on his direction and controllability out of all proportion to the actual impact, and his car took wings. It sailed with a terrible grace towards the straw bales protecting the drivers from stone and rock and sea, and the crowd screamed in half-pain, half-ecstasy as the car atomised the bales, crunched into the railings and burst into a ball of flame.

Carol, with everyone else in the pits, saw it happen as if in slow motion. She saw the armed torpedo in which Leo had been travelling arc into the air then crash down on its back like an exploding shark.

She opened her mouth and started to scream. She felt, as in a nightmare, as if her lungs were bursting, but she was making no noise. She started to move forwards like a robot. Helen Stewart and Nina Rindt, who'd had to live with the possibility of this moment in their own lives, tried to hold her back, but she tore herself free and ran. Marshals and policemen tried to stop her, but she was an irresistible force, crashing through all barriers, defying all authority.

'Leo! Leo!' She ran towards the inferno, her heart bursting her throat. It seemed to her that nothing could survive that maelstrom of black and orange heat.

Then she saw him. He was already outside the circle of danger. He was not even singed. By one of those inexplicable chances that motor racing sometimes throws up, he had been hurled out of a cockpit that fitted him like a tight glove and into which he was securely belted. Perhaps it was the fact that he always refused to wear the part of the harness that came up between his legs that had allowed him to be thrown clear and saved his life. His face was slightly smoke-blackened, as was his driving suit, and he had no helmet. That was all.

They smacked together like a magnet on iron, the tears streaming down her cheeks and he kissed her; and it was back. The stream of power was there again, searing the inside of her lips, sending streams of molten gold down the hidden pathways of her thighs. Then he broke off the kiss and his eyes closed and he crumpled in her arms.

Carol's screams brought the ambulancemen, already jumping from their vehicle, running like Olympic sprinters. Within a minute Leo was in the big white Grand Prix Drivers' Medical Mobile Unit with doctors and nurses bending over him and drip-feeds standing like cranes in the background. Dr Laret finished a skull-to-toe examination while Carol stood by, her stomach churning like a spin drier.

Finally he looked up. 'He has concussion, nothing more. His helmet must have come off before he hit the ground.'

Carol grabbed Dr Laret and kissed him. 'You lovely, lovely man!' she shouted.

'Some of my colleagues would describe him as unconscious. I prefer to say he is sleeping,' he went on. 'He is a lucky man to have such an angel to watch over his dreams. I will look in again in about an hour.Come out and call me if he wakes before.'

He did wake before. He awoke, to be precise, five minutes after the doctor left. He opened his eyes and looked at her steadily. 'What happened?'

'You had a little argument with the crash barriers,' said Carol.

'No, I remember all about that. I seem to recall something more pleasant afterwards.'

'You mean this?' She leaned over him and joined her

warm, loving mouth to his and she found that the first time had been no freak.

Hastily, she rushed over and jammed the door with stools.

'Quick, help me with this damn thing!' Leo was struggling with his asbestos under-suit, which Laret had replaced. They chuckled uncontrollably as they stripped off this modern knight's armour. 'My God!' he gasped. 'A man could come out of sheer suspense!'

Finally, he was naked and she was naked enough and they climbed on to the hospital stretcher-table on which he had been examined and at last she felt again the lean weight on top of her, the flat hard stomach rippling as it began to power its way to sweet contact.

There was no time for much finesse or groundwork. They knew that at any minute the nurse or doctor might come back. In any case, Carol was in no need of being brought along gently. She had been smouldering for more than two weeks and she started her orgasms from the minute his body touched her.

His mood was the same and he married with her slippery tightness with an elegant effortlessness. It was a weird deepening of pleasure, knowing that they were in the middle of half a million people, cars roaring past within yards of them, radio, television, the whole majestic lunacy of the Monaco Grand Prix surrounding them. They were touchy, electric. All they had to do was to move a leg to a marginally different position or shift their sun-painted bodies an inch either way and a new sensation would be offered to them . . .

They took the yacht and their guests back to San Remo. They had a week of sensual glory together, just like the first time, his dark brown body cleaving to her honey-gold with a magnetism that was inexhaustible.

One afternoon they hit a force seven wind in the Baie des Anges just as he had eased his way into her in a connection so snug that it made a racing car motor look about as well engineered as an orange crate. The yacht started to buck like a horse with a burr under its saddle.

Leo and Carol were both excellent sailors.

'I should be above-decks, helping my guests,' murmured Leo, not meaning a word of it.

'What could you do for them?' whispered Carol, chewing his ear. 'Help them to the rails?'

'You are right,' said Leo solemnly. 'Anyway, it would only embarrass them for me to see them like that.' He shifted exquisitely inside her. She started to move her roundly resilient buttocks gently.

'No, don't do that,' he said. 'I have an idea. Let us do nothing. Let us lie here and permit the sea to do it for us. Hold me tight.'

They locked themselves together, his hard arms encircling her shining body, her thighs gripping his slim haunches, and while others were dashing for their bathrooms or agonising over the side they let the force seven sea rock and swing and buffet them to a force ten climax. They ended up on the floor, between the beds, still clamped together, stifling their cries as best they could in a kiss. They had forgotten the gale.

'Listen,' said Carol, 'if this were to get out, it could put Dramamine out of business!'

Ten days later, Leo was impotent again.

They were back at the Turin villa, and for the first time Carol learned the nature of the problem she faced. It was exactly the same as the first time: an almost inexhaustible discharge of energy and then nothing. No trace, no spark.

This time he talked about it. He was lying in their beautiful fifteenth-century bedroom, his eyes on the looking-glass above their canopied bed. He was glistening with sweat as before, looking at himself as if it were someone else reflected up there

'I can only do it after a race,' he said. 'The time we met, you remember, it was just after the Indianapolis 500. I was filled with the race. That's it, that's what racing does to me: it fills me with sex, with desire, for about ten days or two weeks. Then it goes. Nothing. I am like an empty pitcher.'

'Have you been to see people about it?'

'I have seen everyone who is known to be discreet. They all have their theories. Most of them are as lunatic as the condition. Stimulation of the adrenal glands, the gonads, vibration of the testicles – if I didn't come out of their consulting rooms laughing, I would come out crying!'

'Have you got any ideas yourself?'

'I have one. It is as crazy as all the others.' He shrugged. 'I think I respond to risk, physical danger. I remember once, when I was fourteen, I climbed up on to the roof of a big high church near our villa in Rome. I was up there among the gargoyles and the turrets and I climbed out on to the parapet and looked down. I didn't want to: I'm terrified of heights. I don't know why I climbed up there in the first place.' The sweat was running off him as if he were lying in a mist, condensing on him. 'As I looked down, I got a long, swinging stab of panic that went right through me. I thought I was going to fall and at the same time I knew I was going to have an orgasm. And I knew that if I had the orgasm, I *would* fall.'

'What happened?'

'The orgasm happened. But I managed to throw myself backwards instead of falling forwards.'

'We'd better not ever go up the Eiffel Tower,' said Carol, trying for the lightness she didn't feel, hating to see the suffering on Leo's face.

'Please don't make jokes,' said Leo. 'I am thinking of you as much as me. Before, it was all right. I could pick up a charming girl after a race – there is never any shortage of them on the circuits – and we could have our fling and when I shut off, it didn't matter. But now I have a wife I love. I have you and I have to consider you. It's not fair.'

Carol rolled over towards him and kissed him. 'Thank you for telling me,' she said. 'We'll find a way, darling.'

During the next five years they were about the most glamorous couple in the world. They could hardly help it with their looks, his riches, his death-or-glory style of driving. She gave up modelling and became simply Princess Locatelli, though she could hardly have been photographed more. They did not, however, find a way.

Carol rationalised that, in a sense, they were lucky. An intermittent conflagration was preferable to mild, if constant, central heating. It also gave their unbridled encounters a sense of occasion, which familiarity would certainly have dulled.

Gradually, however, she became aware of another aspect of Leo's sexual metabolism which threatened disaster. The aphrodisiac of physical danger seemed to be subject to a law of gradually diminishing returns. Like any hard drug he needed more and more of it. His driving became increasingly more reckless.

'What is it with you?' she cried when he crashed at Zandvoort, trying to out-brake Pedro Rodriguez on a tight corner. 'You must have known you couldn't do it!'

'You don't know one end of a car from the other,' he snapped at her. 'Don't tell me how to drive!'

'Somebody had better tell you,' she shouted. 'You seem to have forgotten!'

She cursed herself the minute the words were out. Never criticise a man's love-making nor his driving – especially that of a racing driver. He remained away from her for three days, even though this could have been one of their good times. It was the first of a series of estrangements that were to become more and more frequent.

'When you're not racing, you're hang-gliding, or ski-jumping or bob-sleighing,' she said another time, hating herself but unable to hold back: 'anything that's dangerous. You're hooked on danger! You've got a death wish!'

'You like what happens afterwards, don't you?' he asked mildly.

'You need more and more sick danger to make it happen!' she cried back, slamming out.

But always, sick or not, the physical reconciliation made up for all.

Now, five years after their marriage, as they stepped from their helicopter, she in her red ski suit, he in his black, and Maria, the nanny, brought four-year-old green-eyed Pietro and three-year-old blue-eyed Lucilla squealing across the lawn to meet them, they had a new problem.

He had told her about it halfway down the ski run. She thought he'd been looking strained for some time, the clefts in his cheeks deeper. Now, taking a turn around a clump of firs, a manoeuvre he could normally have taken on one ski, he fell heavily and awkwardly.

She shirred up to him and flinging herself on her knees did the routine check for broken limbs. He was only winded, like a racehorse. In her relief, she scolded him as a mother scolds a child who has narrowly missed being flattened by a truck. 'You're not yourself,' she said. 'I keep telling you! You skied that turn like an idiot! How many more times have I got to ask you? When are you going to see a doctor?'

'No doctor can help me.'

'Oh, don't be so bloody dramatic! This isn't Puccini!' The acidity of the tongue in that lovely face when she chose to let fly amused him, as always, and some of the weariness went from his eyes. But it came back as his face straightened. He came out with it, not trying to wrap it up.

'I have stolen millions from my companies,' he said, 'and I can't hide it any longer.'

'How d'you mean, stolen? I thought they were your companies; you just said so. How can you steal from your own companies?'

'I have shareholders. They have rights. If I divert money for purposes they don't know about, which are personal to me, that is stealing.

'What have you spent this money on?

'Motor racing is an expensive pastime.'

'But Enzo Ferrari spends millions of company money on motor racing.'

'Enzo Ferrari is entitled to. He sells motor cars. I don't.'

'Anyway, I thought it was all your private money.'

'It was until it ran out. I've been racing since I was twenty-three. That's twelve years. I started to channel a little off here, a little off there. At first I thought, like you, that I had a right to do it; at least I fooled myself I did. Now

I can't fool myself any longer. Or anybody else.

'I told you years ago you should have got sponsorships,' Carol accused him. 'God knows you had enough offers.'

He turned on the arrogance which she both loved and disliked in him. 'Locatelli does not sell his back or his car to be plastered with advertising slogans like a public wall,' he snapped.

'No, he just steals!' she snapped back.

He said nothing, but jumped around on his skis and set off down the slope. Neither of them uttered again until they were indoors in après-ski before a blazing fire.

'I'm sorry,' she said.

'No, you are right,' he answered. 'How can I be angry with you for telling the truth?'

'How much have you taken?'

'Ten and a half billion lire.'

'How much is that in real money?'

Her habitual joke when confronted with a hail of Italian zeros for once did not make him smile. 'Seven million pounds,' he replied.

She sat up abruptly. 'Can you borrow it?'

'If it became known that I was trying to borrow a sum like that from the banks, questions would start being asked.'

'What about your rich friends? Your Vatican bank? In some way or other you must be connected to half the money in Italy.'

Something like a trace of contempt shaded Leo's face briefly. 'If they were so much as to suspect I was in trouble they would forget how to spell my name.'

It was not until the middle of the night, as she lay wide-awake beside a wide-awake Leo, that a possible solution occurred to her.

14

It was four years and six months since Martha had become George Ironstile's mistress. She had announced her intentions at home with typical directness. 'I'm moving in with George,' she said one night, just as Janet was about to switch on the television.

Janet's hand froze on its way to the set. 'You mean you're going to marry him?' she asked, the fearfulness in her voice showing that she knew Martha meant no such thing.

Jack slowly lowered his copy of the *Echo*.

'No,' said Martha equably, looking up from the copy of the *TV Times* through which she'd been leafing, 'I'm just going to live with him.'

'Over my dead bloody body!' roared Jack, his great leathern fist crashing down on the table.

'Dad,' said Martha, still mildly, 'it's got nothing to do with you. I'm thirty-four years old, I can behave as I like, and there's nothing you can do about it.'

'I can cripple George Ironstile for a start,' said Jack.

'Dad,' said Martha patiently, 'you can't even do that. I've told you before, there's a whole world outside Mugsley Street where you can't do that to people any more and get away with it. You're a dinosaur.'

Jack's colour was rising dangerously. Janet spoke up: 'But can't he marry you, love? I'm sure if you explained how we feel–'

'It's not him, Mum, it's me. George wants to marry me. I won't marry him.'

'D'you love him?'

'Yes, I do.'

'Well, then.'

Martha was silent. How could she tell Janet that it was watching marriage slowly corrode the vital young Welsh beauty with the swinging walk to this broken bundle of twitching dependence that had made her swear never to put herself in the power of a man in that way?

Jack rose to his feet, towering like an Old Testament prophet, overturning the table on which Janet had her one precious possession: the little tea service she had bought at a sale and kept intact for twenty-five years. 'What the hell have I done to end up with two whores for daughters?' he demanded.

'You've just been your own fucking self,' said Martha.

Jack knocked her cold.

Ironstile Holdings had flourished mightily. Under Martha's singularly abstract mind and George's titanic energy and feeling for 'things', it had grown into one of the most powerful conglomerates in the country. As well as specialist steel, it was now into electronics, clothing, stores, civil engineering and construction and it had a stake in the exploration of the Forties oil field in the North Sea. None of this particularly impressed Locatelli as his private jet set down on the landing strip at Manchester airport and he and Carol were picked up by the Ironstile Rolls.

Like most people who had inherited their fortunes, he had a curious lack of respect for those who had made their own, and he was of the opinion that he could pick out *nouveaux riches* in the dark. Even the endless broad acres the Rolls cruised through on the way to the mansion – George had been buying land and the park was now more the size of a small county – made no impression on him. What he hadn't grasped was quite how *riches* these *nouveaux* were.

George and Martha were both millionaires many times over. They had gone public with a floating by Hambros and such was the City reputation of these two hard-headed, hard-mouthed Northerners that the issue had been spectacularly oversubscribed.

Leo had met George and Martha once, when Carol had asked them to the villa in Rome for a visit, and he disliked them on two scores. He had a passion for beautiful things and beautiful they were not. He also prized good manners and the rough bluntness of theirs set his teeth on edge. It had, in fact, taken an almighty row to get him to come over now. Initially, he had refused point-blank.

'If you think I'm going cap in hand to ask that pork-faced peasant to bail me out, you must be crazy.'

'That pork-faced peasant happens to be practically my brother-in-law. In any case, thieves can't afford to be too choosy.'

'That's the second time you've called me a thief! The third time will be the last!'

'What word would you like me to use? Some nice Italian euphemism to smooth it all out like one of your Cerutti suits? You told me, remember. I didn't ask. And now when I try to help you you suddenly turn into a stainless aristocrat who can afford to call my relatives peasants! Well, I am a peasant and never forget it! I call things by their names. And when I steal, I know I'm a thief!'

They were in the small dining room having breakfast. The cherubs on the painted ceiling looked down unmoved, accustomed to five centuries of beautiful people rowing.

'Do you know what it is to be a Locatelli?' Leo demanded.

'Do you know what it is to be a Blair?' she retorted. 'We may not have ripped off the world five hundred years ago and grabbed our stake like the Locatellis, but we know what family means. And when family is in trouble, we mobilise. We close ranks – or is that not an expression you bloody Italians would understand? Well, you may not want the help of the Blairs. To have to feel grateful to someone you feel should be cleaning your boots may be too high a price to pay to stay out of jail. Well, if it is, go to fucking jail!'

She rose and left the table so violently that she tipped his coffee in his lap.

'Bitch!' he shouted after her. It wasn't for a couple of

minutes that he realised that she had flung the whole tirade at him in flawless Italian.

Later, he came to her in her dressing room. 'I'm sorry,' he said, with a simple grace that washed the blackness straight out of her. 'It's just that I'm ashamed of what I've done. I'm angry with myself. So I become angry with everyone else.'

'I'm sorry, too,' she said, putting her scented arms around him and her cheek against his. 'I'm frightened for you. I want you to get out of this mess. I want to help.' She felt her tears running down her cheeks.

'I know, my darling, I know.' He patted her satiny back gently.

'Then you'll come? You'll see Martha and George?'

He held her away from him and looked into her eyes, made even more luminous by her tears.

'Si,' he said.

They were in the great hall of the lovely house in Cheshire, the manservants bringing in the luggage. Carol and Martha clung to each other, wordless, while George and Locatelli shook hands warily.

Leo's eyes took in the undoubtedly exquisite English Georgian decor. What fashionable designer, he wondered cynically, had been paid a small fortune to sell Ironstile his taste?

'I am delighted to see you again,' he said.

'Likewise,' said George, who reciprocated Leo's dislike heartily. Scented, silk-suited prick, he thought dispassionately.

They got down to base rock that evening in the library, a room with an amber lustre that came largely from the panelling. Leo grudgingly admitted to himself that, unlike most *nouveaux*, they had no portraits among the excellent pictures.

'Now then,' said Martha, settling herself down briskly behind her desk in her best tax officer fashion, 'if we could all sit down.'

They sat. Carol, who had never watched her sister in

action before, was fascinated.

Martha took a file from a drawer and cast her slate-green eyes over the first sheet of paper in it. She handed it to Leo.

'I think you'll find that's a comprehensive list of your major and associated companies in Italy, your holdings and your properties.'

Leo stared at it, astonished. 'How did you put this together?'

'It wasn't easy,' Martha parried deftly. 'I'd like to draw your attention to the company with a star against it, Lombardi Engineering.'

'Yes?' said Leo, looking up from the paper, wondering what was coming.

'Am I right in my belief that it's the only company outside the Group umbrella? That it is, in fact, still owned privately by you?'

'Yes,' said Leo.

'Why is that?'

'Because,' said Leo slowly, feeling as if he were being interrogated by this mud-faced oracle, 'it was the first company my grandfather started and it has sentimental associations.'

'We'll buy it,' said George abruptly.

'I would never sell it,' said Leo hotly. 'Never!'

'It's worth seven million quid to us,' said George.

Leo paused. 'So that is it. You're willing to help me, but you want to humiliate me in the process.'

'Now listen, Romeo-' said George, the crimson surging in his face.

'My name is Leopoldo!' raged Leo. 'Prince Leopoldo Locatelli!'

'Then get out and sell ice cream,' said George. 'You'd do well with a name like that.'

'I will not stay here and be insulted by an . . . an . . . English warthog!' shouted Leo, rising and knocking over his chair.

George sprang to his feet too. It was left to the women to behave like adults.

'Leo,' said Carol, 'will you sit down and stop behaving

like someone out of *Tosca*.'

'George,' said Martha, 'simmer down or your face'll catch fire.'

The men sensed the absurdity of their situation, so beautifully de-fused by their clever wives, and sat down, still glaring at each other. Finally, Leo said, 'It's worth nine million.'

'That's if you're selling,' said George. 'We're buying.'

'Eight million,' said Leo.

'Done,' said George.

'On one condition,' added Martha.

'What is that?' asked Leo.

'We don't want to pay the premium for buying it in foreign currency. It would cost us half as much again.'

'How do you propose to get around it?' asked Leo.

Martha gave George the floor. 'We do a lot of business in Italy,' he explained, 'but we don't have a commercial agent there—'

Leo, who could see which way George was heading, exploded: 'I am nobody's commercial lackey—'

Martha took over, the intelligent eyes having a curiously sedative effect on Leopoldo.

'What we thought,' she said patiently, 'was that if you acted as our agent just for a time, you could collect all the monies due to us. What more natural, since we're family? You wouldn't pass the money on to us. You'd keep it until you'd got eight million, which wouldn't take long at the rate we're going in Italy. You pay no tax on the eight million because you're collecting it on someone else's behalf, and we get Lombardi Engineering without paying the premium. You pay back the monies that you have 'borrowed' from your companies – and don't forget I might be able to show you a few tricks there – and everybody is happy. Yes?'

Leo knew a high-flying business sense when he saw it and he didn't hesitate. 'Yes,' he agreed.

Next day, Carol made the short journey to see Janet in Liverpool. Her heart ached as she saw the deathly weariness in her stepmother's face as she opened the door.

'Carol, love!' – the eternal greeting that meant exactly what it said and that never failed to renew Carol and her sense of belonging. George's Rolls and chauffeur, standing outside, were causing the usual commotion among the street's window curtains.

'How's Dad?'

'Oh, you know your father. He doesn't change.'

'Is that why you still haven't moved?'

Now, in 1973, the old Scotland Road had crumbled about their ears. People had been moved out to taller and more spirit-crushing slums in the suburbs, newly built for instant degradation. Their old brick jungle was being demolished all around the Blairs. Again and again both Carol and Martha had offered to buy them a new house, out in the kind of greenery in which Janet, the doe-eyed country girl, had grown up. Jack had set his face against it like an Easter Island statue.

'I'm not living off Wop money,' was all he had to say the last time they'd discussed it.

'Dad, it's got nothing to do with Leo,' Carol had protested. 'It's my money. Money I earned.'

'It's whore's money, then.'

'Dad, modelling isn't whoring – oh, what the hell's the use!' She'd given up, just as Martha had given up.

Carol looked about her now at the familiar kitchen. The bastard obviously hadn't allowed Janet to spend any of the money she and Martha kept sending her to have the place done up. It was a dump.

'How's Tony?' she asked, hoping to divert Janet from reading her face.

Janet hesitated for a second: 'Tony's not here any more. He's living with some girl in Aigburth. German, I think she is.'

It had only just happened. More suddenly than Janet realised. Senta with the golden loins, the spectacular legs and the neatly cut pelvis was the German girl.

It was chemical, just as it had been for Janet with Jack. Tony had encountered her in a dim, distant basement of the Picton Library, a place where sound dropped and died within a foot of its origin. He had gone there researching Victorian newspaper advertisements for ideas for a new textile design. Senta, a sociology post-graduate, had been seeking out old BBC Yearbooks.

She was standing on a perilous ladder and he had looked up the back of her gleaming legs to the perfect bottom that surmounted them. She was very blonde, very blue-eyed, very tanned, with a moist lubricity about her golden flesh that was more than just baby-oil rubbed into the skin. Her face had the full, shapely, rather brutal cheeks that always go with a finished perfection of roundness in the limbs. She had looked down as he looked up: their eyes met. They had both known instantly.

In that hushed, secret place it was as if they were out of time and everything was permissible. He had taken her on top of a heap of dry and dusty files, which had collapsed under the intensity of their collision, pistoning into her with the tight but lubricated precision of perfect tolerances, the inside top of one of her stockings curiously harsh on his hip, rubbing a raw mark there. Inside, she had a firm, viscous, sliding grip like ridged rubber.

They had been disturbed by the warning of the lift bringing someone down to their lair and he had come, helplessly, joltingly, as a little old lady stepped out of the lift and instantly fell back in, her short, shocked little arms making imprecise gestures.

Tony's laughter brought Senta on again and he thought he was going to die – but happy.

She had taken him home to her flat. For a week they had scarcely gone out. It was a possession, a sickness almost; like Carol's and Leo's first time in San Diego, but more so. And Tony, his father's formidable genes throbbing in the engine room, had not run out of steam.

Carol rang the bell of the semi-detached house in Aigburth. Senta opened the door and Carol knew immediately that Tony had his hands full. Senta was spectacular.

She smiled, showing strong white teeth. 'You are Carol! The princess! Please come into our charcoal-burner's hut. I am the charcoal burner's wife, Senta.'

It was said in a friendly, humorous way, but was there the faintest hint of malice or mockery there? Or was Carol looking for nuances, finding them where they weren't intended? After all, she had been accustomed to being Tony's treasure all her life and now she had been replaced. No girl takes kindly to that even if the man concerned *is* her brother.

'Car!' Tony was rushing out of the living room, arms outstretched, thin as ever but looking well and happy. 'Car, you really should try to get home more often; we need a bit of class in the family.' They hugged long and hard. 'God, you're looking great!' he said. As they broke off he turned to Senta. 'And you've met Senta, of course.'

'Oh!' cried Senta, with that friendly laugh that yet had the effect of keeping one off balance, 'I'm glad someone remembered me at last!'

Tony hurried over and kissed her. 'Tiger-girl,' he said, 'how could anyone ever forget you?' So it was the animal thing, thought Carol; it was sometimes hard for a woman to be sure.

'Senta said something about "wife", Tony,' Carol said, as he was pouring drinks in the small, unremarkable sitting room.She noticed that Senta had already got him serving Liebfraumilch as an aperitif. There was no choice of anything else.

'Ah . . . yes . . . well,' said Tony, giving a creditable impersonation of a long line of situation-comedians, 'that does . . . in fact . . . happen to be true.' Carol sensed his discomfort. 'Yes, it does happen that the little lady and I' – 'little!' thought Carol – 'tied the knot, as you might say, yesterday.'

So it was too late to do anything about it. In any case what business was it of hers? She was thinking like a possessive mother. Furthermore, what could even a possessive mother have done against someone who looked like that, emanating jungle vibrations all around the room?

'You might have invited me,' she said reproachfully.

'We did, Car,' he said. 'Even though we didn't think

you'd be too keen on turning up to a draughty Liverpool register office at nine o'clock in the morning.'

'You got to mine,' retorted Carol. 'I'd have got to yours.'

'Yes, Tony told me about that,' said Senta. Carol had to admit her accent was delicious – Marlene Dietrich on the rocks. 'It was very romantic,' she added. Again, was there a slight edge of satire there?

'We sent you a cable three days ago,' said Tony. 'Honest!'

'We were already travelling then,' said Carol. 'We stopped off at Paris first. But what about Martha, Mum, everyone?'

'Martha doesn't believe in marriage; Mum isn't lapsed like the rest of us, and I didn't want to give her a problem, her son's wedding not sanctified by the church and all that; and as for Dad, I'd as soon ask him as an insurance detective to an arson.'

'But Mum doesn't even know you're married.'

For the first time he looked shamefaced. 'I know. I'm in trouble there. She hasn't even met Senta yet.

'It was my fault,' said Senta. 'My study permit was about to expire. I would have had to go back to Germany. But now I can stay and we have no problems.'

Was that all it was about? wondered Carol. Just a way for Senta to stay in England? Then she looked at them together, recognised the obvious love between them and the almost tangible physical bond, and she felt ashamed of herself. Nevertheless, as she drove away, her psychic antennae were buzzing with a signal that a dark star was spinning somewhere in the void and it would affect all three of them.

From Martha and George they drove straight up to London. Leo had some business there.

They stayed at Claridge's, as always, in the suite that they always had, which looked as it always did even down to the yellow and white roses. Claridge's, reflected Carol, undoubtedly had the most meticulous 'black book' in the hotel world. There wasn't a preference, a habit or a detail of diet about valued clients that wasn't recorded in it.

One of the hotel's few equals in meticulousness was Michael Willoughby. Michael, a long-time subscriber to *Celebrity Bulletin,* had spotted their arrival instantly and they were greeted in their suite by a magnum of Moët et Chandon, blue-beribboned. His note said, 'Either you come to my party tonight or I'll tell Claridge's you've got small-pox.'

'I can't go, cara,' said Leo. 'I have to meet my Americans. If I get through in time, I'll come on. But, please, I want you to go. I know what a good friend Michael has been to you.'

So it was that Carol found herself once more in the house in Montpelier Square. Michael had changed by the mere addition of three grey hairs to each temple, which she was sure he put there himself.

The 'darlings' flew back and forth like a flock of rooks disturbed by a cat. As always, Michael's party was a mixture of high society and the beautiful people, most of whom Carol knew well, with a sprinkling of journalists, TV people and writers whom she didn't. Michael's tongue was as scything as ever as he introduced her to the flora and fauna of that night's jungle.

'You see the little chap over there – the one with the barbed-wire hair and the mouth that looks as if it were designed for scooping up oil slicks? He's a journalist here to try and corner an energy-expert boffin; then he wants to go home and be walked on by a tall girl.

'The lady over there with the tits jacked up on hydraulic ramps, she wrote one of those everything-you-didn't-want-to-know-about-sex-but-I'm-going-to-tell-you-anyway books and now she can't get anyone to go to bed with her.

'The woman over there, with the face beginning to drop off the bones: watch her. She's an Irish novelist who'll try and get confidences out of you. Then she'll either use them in one of her misty books or threaten you with them if you start getting the better of her on a TV discussion show.'

'Michael, you are the most waspish—'

He ignored her, which was easy because something had

happened to her. 'And over there,' he said 'is the guest of honour. He's the energy boffin whom little blubber-mouth is trying to corner at the moment–'

But Carol already knew. What had happened to her was that she had looked over Michael's shoulder and seen him already. Ike Palmer, looking as donnish, as slightly untidy, as Henry Fonda-ish and as stubborn as ever. His suit was certainly a better one, but she noticed he hadn't changed his spectacle frames in the last five years.

It was so unexpected, seeing him in this kind of ambience, that her surprise evidently showed on her face and was instantly picked up by Michael.

'D'you know Professor Palmer?' he asked. 'Or, if you don't, would you like to? He's got a reputation for far more than his brains.'

'Oh, no, thank you,' said Carol. 'I mean, yes, we do know each other.' She was flustered. She felt the slight flutter at the base of her throat.

Ike had seen her at the same moment and was already carving his gracefully loose-limbed way towards her through the crush. Aware of the warmth of feeling arcing between them, Michael left them to it.

'There's not a day goes by that I don't think what a damn fool I was walking off that beach at L.A.,' Ike said without preamble.

'I shouldn't have spoken to you the way I did,' said Carol. 'I suppose my father's made me paranoid about certain attitudes . . . maybe they're just phrases, even. I react like one of Pavlov's dogs.' She was anxious to change the subject. 'Anyway, what are you doing here? This isn't exactly your kind of party.'

He looked around at the thrash of stars, peers, famous hairdressers, dress designers and property developers. 'Oh, didn't you know?' he asked, with just, she thought, a hint of bitterness. 'I've been taken up. I'm fashionable. I'm the pundit they pull out whenever they get in a panic about the energy shortage. I've been warning people about it for years, trying to get my research funded. Now it's 1973 and people are just starting to get mildly upset about it.'

'Where are you now, Ike?' asked Carol, inexplicably excited by the red spots that fired the tips of Ike's cheekbones as he warmed to his theme.

'I'm in Israel,' he said. 'University of Tel Aviv. They're the country looking hardest for an alternative to oil, for obvious reasons.'

'Why are you looking so down, then?'

'They can't afford to finance the research properly. D'you know what shape their economy's in? Their inflation rate?'

'Then go and do your research somewhere else,' said Carol. 'If you're fashionable, you're bankable. You could get yourself set up wherever you want.'

'It's not like that. I have feelings, loyalties.'

'Feelings don't buy lasers, deuterium, tritium.'

His eyes widened. 'How the devil do you know about all that?'

Carol grinned.' 'The deuterium and tritium you told me about yourself. Besides, you're not the only genius I've talked to in the last few years. I don't spend my *entire* life surrounded by idiots.'

'Listen,' he said, 'what d'you say we get out of here and have something to eat?'

'Leo said he might come on here after his meeting.'

'We'll tell Michael where Leo can find us.'

She hesitated just fractionally. 'All right.'

They went to Mr Chow's in Knightsbridge. As they left Michael's house several of the gossip-column photographers outside flashed them. It was an occurrence so much part of Carol's life that she hardly noticed it any more. Had she known what the consequences of this particular image were to be she might have paid more attention.

Over dinner up the glittering staircase at Mr Chow's Carol realised that she was not the only one being stared at. Ike, too, was treated with particular respect.

'Not been married yet?' she asked.

'You're not available.'

'No, seriously.'

'I am being serious,' he said. 'I decided when I was seventeen in Liverpool that one day I'd get my lecherous hands on you legally.' His American accent was stronger than it had been five years ago. He switched on a mock-passionate tone. 'Knowing you has spoiled me for all other women—'

'Shut up and eat your duck,' she said, flashing her incomparable smile at the adolescent-looking Duke of Grosvenor, who hadn't taken his eyes off her since she came in and seemed ready to lay most of Belgravia, which he owned, at her feet.

'You still happy with the Prince?' asked Ike.

'Very.'

'I guess I was wrong. He looked like trouble to me.'

'You were wrong. Tell me about this process of yours, the one you're working on.'

'It's not really mine. It's a problem everyone in the world is trying to crack.' He started to assemble instruments on the table, the red spots appearing in his cheeks as he got excited again. 'Now the salt here – this is the deuterium – that's an isotype of hydrogen, but you obviously know all about that.'

'I never stop talking about it,' Carol smiled.

He went on, unconscious of her gentle irony. 'The pepper is the tritium – that's super-heavy hydrogen that you make from the deuterium. Now then, we need heat.'

He reached for the candle on the table. By this time Carol was raptly attentive and conversations were beginning to stop at other tables too. Ike was oblivious to everything but his theme. 'Now say we put these two little old atoms together and lay a temperature of a hundred million degrees centigrade on them' – he smiled, as if it were Christmas – 'they fuse! And the process sends out an unimaginable amount of energy. It's how the sun works, giving us all that heat and light for millions of years, giving the earth life. Well, I think we could make our own little suns down here and have limitless energy till the end of time.'

'So what's the snag?'

'A box to keep the suns in.'

'A box?'

'When the deuterium and tritium fuse they generate an order of heat that no known substance in the world can withstand. If you dropped, say, an aircraft carrier or a skyscraper into that sort of heat, it would make a little spitty noise like a drop of water hitting a furnace and then it would cease to be, instantly.'

'I think I've got the problem. Before I get indigestion, what's the answer?

'You get a pellet of deuterium and tritium and you hit it with laser beams. These beams have such tremendous intensity that they produce fusion instantly, but you have to put forty to fifty times more energy into the pellet than you get out of it. That's what I'm working on now.' His eyes went hazy. 'You know,' he said, 'we used to have a much cosier way of discussing these things. I go back to Israel tomorrow.'

He reached out and covered her hands with his. She felt the old force streaming through them, remembered the feel of them on her body. Gently, she disengaged her hands and looked him in the face. 'I don't cheat, Ike,' she said softly.

'Is this the way it's going to be?' he asked. 'Bumping into each other every five years?'

'That's the way it seems to be.'

He made a fist, looked as if he were about to smash it down on the table, then thought better of it. 'Sometimes I wish,' he said, 'I really wish that neither of us had ever left home. At least then I could have had you, I know I could. I'd have stayed on your tail, stayed after you until you gave in out of sheer exhaustion. I'd probably be an electrician and you'd be a shop assistant. We'd have a couple of kids and be living in a council house on some estate and dammit if I don't think I'd be a happier man than I am now!'

'Ike—'

'D'you think that a day goes by without my thinking of you? D'you want to know something? I look through the newspapers and magazines every day first, *before* I look at my scientific journals, in case there's a picture of you in there somewhere!'

'Ike, it's no good. That's not sensible. You have to get on with what you've got.'

'What the hell else d'you think I do? Why d'you think I'm such a good physicist? I sublimate it all in my work.'

And you, my lovely long-lashed Ike, are a bloody liar, thought Carol next morning as she looked at the William Hickey gossip column in the *Daily Express* over her breakfast coffee at Claridge's.

For there, as the lead story, was a very clear picture of her leaving Michael Willoughby's with Ike the previous evening, under the headline: THE CASANOVA GENIUS AND THE PRINCESS. And the body of the story was devoted to the previous exploits of Ike Palmer.

'Professor "Ike" Palmer, equally well-known as an atom-smasher and a ladykiller, walked out of model-agency czar Michael Willoughby's jet-set party last night with the prize of his life on his arm. No less than the brain-stunning beauty, Princess Locatelli . . .

'The cerebral Professor's previous companions have included . . .

'The Professor is, of course, an authority on nuclear fusion. There seemed to be some kind of fusion in process at the table for two he shared with the spectacular princess later in the evening.'

Just as Carol had flung the paper away in disgust – whether at the insinuating tone of the column or the insight it gave her into Ike, she wasn't sure – Leo stormed in, carrying a copy of the paper opened at the identical page. His face was disturbingly pale and he spoke with the softness of an assassin. 'What is all this about?' he demanded, his eyes like witch's emeralds.

She rose, to touch him and soothe him, but he evaded her. 'Leo, it's just a gossip column. Nobody pays any attention to gossip columns. Who would pay one minute's attention to that rubbish? It's written for people who don't know, not for people who do!'

She floated towards him, her eyes and housecoat merging in the same mesmeric blue. But she wasn't mesmerising Leo, not this morning. He still looked like an eagle with kill on its face.

'I don't know what you're so upset about,' she continued, laying her hands on his arms. 'When we left the party we told them the name of the restaurant we were going to. If you'd come to the party you could have joined us there and none of this would have happened. Anyway, they've printed far worse things about us in Italy.'

He picked up a delicate blue-tapestried Louis XVI fauteuil and slammed it down again so hard that she feared for its safety. 'That's another thing – this will be picked up and printed, with embellishments, in Italy!'

'And our friends will laugh,' she said. 'D'you think they will believe it for one minute?'

Leo paced the blue and gold suite, seeing the justice of her words, not wanting to admit them. He turned on her, suddenly. 'This is the man you told me about in California. The thug who would leave a girl stranded on a highway!'

Light dawned in her mind: 'So that's what this is all about! It's this particular man. You dislike him!'

'I dislike ignorant peasants who would desert a girl like that – yes!'

'Leo, I wasn't exactly a helpless little ingénue; I wasn't going to starve or get lost—'

'So you defend him now? He wasn't so bad in California after all, eh? You begin to have nostalgic feelings for him!' He hurled the paper at her as if it were a grenade.

He was not to be placated. He flung out and did not reappear for the rest of the day.

The next week he was due to race in the U.S. Grand Prix at Watkins Glen. They made the flight to New York in total silence. Carol had a core of obstinacy in her equal to Leo's.

Leo asked a stewardess for the Italian papers. They both opened a copy of the *Corriere della Sera*. The first thing they both saw was a pick-up from the Hickey column; with embellishments, as he had predicted. He crumpled the paper savagely and threw it under his seat.

Just to annoy him, Carol read the piece calmly through to

the finish, then turned to the rest of the paper and, with apparent serenity, read that. She knew that Leo couldn't be in a worse position. Normally, his instinct would have been to roar off somewhere in a fury. In a transatlantic jet where was there to go – the lavatory?

At New York they checked into the St Regis hotel, their current favourite, and went straight to bed to try and get un-lagged. Next morning, the first thing they saw in the *New York Times* was a paragraph linking the names of noted physicist Dr Palmer and society queen the Princess Locatelli. That was enough to poison the day for both of them and reinforce their common silence to the point where it looked as if they'd have to start writing each other notes.

Watkins Glen motor racing track in New York State, although the inhabitants would stoutly deny it, was possibly the most dreary venue in the whole racing calendar. It looked like an abandoned Marine training camp that the Marines decided to kick apart before they left. On the other hand, it enshrined the truest spirit of racing in the game. The marshals worked for nothing and the Trust that ran the track was non-profit-making, so that all the money – particularly the prize money – went back into the sport.

Italian engineers being the perfectionists they are, Leo's team had already prepared his car to near-faultlessness, altering the suspension and the engine's torque to combat the 'G' and other forces that would be combining to try and rip apart its fragile shell at every corner. Brandino, Leo's test driver, had done everything in his considerable power to break the car's back and it hadn't broken.

Leo shoehorned himself into the cockpit and took her round. It was like driving a spoonful of honey round a butter-bowl. It slid where it ought and stuck where it should. There was only one corner out of the eight on the course that worried him. It was the one they called the 'hard right', the last corner before one shot past the starting line again.

It wasn't only Leo the corner worried. It worried everyone. It was a right-handed bend with a left-handed camber. Instead of sloping into the side of the road it sloped back into the centre, throwing the weight of the car off balance.

To add to the joy of life, having negotiated it moderately safely, the driver had to contend immediately with a 'ramp' or hump in the road, which left the front wheel on the driver's side four inches in the air and completely out of contact with the road at exactly that point where the driver was punching the power back into his rear wheels to complete his slide around the corner.

Leo practised and practised, as did Fittipaldi, the 1970 winner of the race, Stewart and the rest of the circus. By the day of the race he had fought his way on to the front rank of the grid alongside his old friend Stewart. He had to come better than third to maintain his place in the World Championship, which he had more chance of winning this year than he had ever had in his life.

The day of the race a mean little zip fastener opened itself in the clouds and a steady light drizzle enshrouded New York State. Even normally it would have made Leo, who didn't enjoy driving on rain tyres, morose.

What made it infinitely worse was an early edition of the *New York Daily News,* which had shown great enterprise in tracking down a copy of the front cover of the photographic journal in which Carol had first burst upon an astonished world.

She was greatly more beautiful now, at twenty-eight, than she had been at sixteen, but the picture, nevertheless, was still enough to knock your eye out; particularly now that it was a shot of an Italian princess rather than a Liverpudlian ragamuffin.

They had also had the inspiration to print an inset picture of Ike Palmer, who appeared to be appreciating the lavish charms of the naked, pubescent princess.

Leo, his beautiful strong dark face flushed, stalked from the dressing room where he had been sleeping and dashed the paper on Carol's bed, upsetting her breakfast tray, coffee and milk all over the coverlet.

'This,' said Leo, 'is what you said is nothing!'

'Leo, that's bullshit and you know it,' she said. 'Palmer is probably as outraged about it as you are. He's a distinguished man. You'd like him.'

'He's a distinguished fucking womaniser,' said Leo, his face like roughened parchment, 'and you have yourself spread across the newspapers with him like a whore on your back.'

The pin came out of her emotional grenade. The Blair blood took over, exploding at the confluence of all the interlocking injustices to which she'd been subjected and she spoke the words that could never be taken back.

'At least if I *had* been on my back he'd have been able to do something about it,' she spat out, spearing him with it, knowing the minute the words were out that she had opened a wound that could never be healed.

Leo turned on his heel and left the room.

He drove straight to Watkins Glen, making no request to Carol to accompany him as he usually did. She was determined not to go anywhere near the track, then, an hour too late, she found herself scrambling into her rented red Lamborghini and pointing its nose towards Watkins Glen.

It was one of those days. Fifth was a solid mass of immovable metal; the roads out of town – once you got to them – were fit only for helicopters; and by the time she was able to rip the silk and let the Lamborghini go – and the hell with radar traps – the race had already started.

She had it on the radio, which only made her tension worse, but she couldn't resist it. She had the doomwatch pulsing away in the pit of her stomach.

She was still a quarter of a mile from the track when it happened. They were on the ninty-ninth lap of the one-hundred-and-eight-lap race. Leo had been driving like a demonic force. Carol knew the wish to retain his place at the top of the championship table could have accounted for the remorseless ferocity of his driving; but she knew, too, that there was a cold fury against her, a shame against himself, that could be partly assuaged by furious action.

He was now in the same position Jackie Stewart had been in in the same race three or four years earlier, before his engine had blown up. He was so far ahead of the field that no one had a ghost of a chance of catching him. Perhaps that's what caused him to relax that one or two per cent of the one hundred per cent concentration a racing driver must maintain. Perhaps it was the oil on the corner.

As he approached the 'hard right', the ribbon of road rushing at him like a wind, Carol's face leaped unbidden into his mind and the words she was saying were the last words she had said that morning.

He drifted the corner, bundled the hump, his right front wheel out of contact with the road as usual, and as he poured on the power again his rear left wheel hit the patch of oil.

The car became a snake in his hands. It wasn't a car any more, it was a bundle of conflicting forces. He hit the safety barrier, the car disintegrating like tinfoil in a slow-motion explosion. He was thrown fifteen feet up into a tree.

Carol was approaching the edge of the circuit among the caravans and the campers and the hucksters and the notices advertising firewood for sale when she heard it on the radio. She wrenched the wheel round and roared between them, marshals jumping for their lives as she punched the red Lamborghini through the rails on to the track itself.

She knew the track by now. She knew exactly where the 'hard right' was and she drove for it now at the very limit of her skill. Cars screamed past her, their drivers hardly able to believe their eyes. She passed two tail-enders nursing sick engines and then she saw the pall of smoke, the ambulance, the marshals warning off the other cars.

She screamed to a stop right in the middle of it and jumped out. They had already got Leo down from the tree and had him on a stretcher. They were taking him to the Arnott Ogden Hospital at Elmira. There wasn't a mark on his beautiful body, but all the life-sensors indicated that he was dying, very quickly.

She flung herself on her knees beside him in the ambulance as it screamed its frightening way off the track. 'Leo, Leo! The thing I said this morning. I didn't mean it. I said it to hurt.'

He looked up at her, the fine eyes full not of fear or pain but of compassion. 'I know, cara mia,' he said as he gripped the hand she held out to him.

'You're going to be fine,' she said with desperate calm. 'The Locatellis have always been hard to kill.'

'I know,' he smiled. 'We will go for a cruise in the boat next week. Would you like that?'

She nodded, trying to swallow back the tears as she felt his grip on her hand weakening. She tried to pour into him all the strength and vitality of her own magnificent constitution.

His eyes closed momentarily, then opened again suddenly. They were sparkling with mischief. He grinned at her. 'Today was a race day,' he said. 'We could have—' Then he died.

15

For a long time Carol was emotionally paralysed. It did not seem possible that Leo could cease to be, that the presence he had imprinted on their surroundings would not bring her beloved husband through some door, his arms outstretched, at any minute.

She countered the pain with a frenzy of activity. She personally organised every last detail of Leo's funeral. She was sufficiently at home now in Italian society to manage it all impeccably, in the little church where they had been married, next to the villa at Turin. This had been Leo's kingdom. This was where he would want to lie. But behind the black veil there was a frozen woman. With her two beautiful children, one on either side of her, neither really understanding, she looked, as she walked up the church, like some exquisite moving statue.

A bitchy cousin, Contessa Padovicini, described her as 'a commercial for grief'.

It was the cousins who were going to give her the trouble, Carol knew that. The day after the funeral, Carol had a visit from a lawyer representing the family. Leo had made a will leaving everything he prized to her: the villas in Rome and Turin, the yacht, the family jewellery. And he had made her, together with his brother Stefano, joint manager of his sprawling business empire. 'I know that Stefano will listen to her advice,' he wrote, 'and I know and trust those to whom she will go for hers.'

'The family,' said the lawyer, a pleasant grey-haired patrician, 'will dispute the will as inequitable, especially insofar as the management of the business is concerned.'

With him was the prime mover in the family insurgency,

Contessa Padovicini. She had been the beauty of the family until Carol arrived, when she had been incontestably relegated to second place. She was also greedy. She had not come off badly in the division of the considerable estate that lay outside Carol's portion, and she stood to flourish as the business flourished; but she wanted it all.

They were seated amid the Old Master decor of the library in the villa in Rome. Carol was sitting in a crimson velvet chair which perfectly set off her gold, black and ivory beauty and in which the Contessa now wished she had sat herself.

The lawyer, Dr Luccini, continued: 'With all due respect, you have no experience of business management, Principessa, and the family is naturally concerned about the wisdom of leaving its financial futures in your hands—'

'I learned a very great deal from my late husband,' said Carol, 'and I also have recourse to a calibre of advice which would be known and respected throughout the business world.' She turned to the carmine-faced man and dough-faced woman who were sitting quietly behind her. 'May I introduce Mr George Ironstile and my sister Martha, joint Chairmen and Chief Executives of Ironstile Holdings.'

The good Luccini was largely a commercial lawyer and the name of Ironstile Holdings was as familiar to him as Fiat Motors and almost as prestigious. Besides, he was aware that Ironstile had already bought the late Prince Locatelli's private company and had transformed both its output and its prospects in an impressively short space of time. Carol's introduction altered Luccini's whole outlook and strategy. His case, as he had foreseen it, rested on the incompetence of Carol and her inability to back up Stefano. With Ironstile Holdings behind her, he doubted if he had a whisper of a chance of breaking the will. What was more, as a faithful adviser to the family for many years, he was not sure it was in its interests even to try.

He ushered the Contessa to a window, where they had a whispered consultation. Then he turned to Carol. 'In the light of the new information now available to us, Principessa,' he said, 'we would like your permission to withdraw and reconsider our position.'

When she saw that they were safely gone, she walked to a magnificent Renaissance cross-framed chair which had been Leo's favourite despite its hardness, leaned on it and started to cry. She cried like a child, torrentially, without restraint, for the first time since Leo's death. The ice had therapeutically cracked at last.

George, who'd sooner trap his hand in a hydraulic press than be exposed to a woman's tears, crossed to a window on the other side of the room, upset beyond expression. Martha went to the tall, lovely girl she still thought of as her kid sister and took her to her ample breasts; Martha was becoming even more comfortable-looking with the years.

'Cry, love,' she said, 'cry. I thought you were never going to!' That was all she said; simply kept on hugging and rocking gently as long as the convulsion of delayed affliction lasted.

Gradually the intervals between the spasms grew longer and Carol began to say something. Martha couldn't make out the words. Carol repeated them again and again between the sobs. It was George who picked them up first.

'She's saying she wants to go home,' he said.

'Of course you can, love,' Martha said. 'You can come and live with George and me.'

'No, home . . . home,' Carol gasped between sobs like a child. 'I mean I want to go home.'

Again it was George who got it first. 'Mugsley Street!' he exclaimed, bewildered. 'She means she wants to go to Mugsley Street!'

'To *stay*, you mean?' Martha asked, wanting to make sure she'd got this bizarre request right. 'To *stay* in Mugsley Street?'

George and Martha remained behind in Italy to sort out the tangle of the Locatelli empire. They had no worries about Carol's being in safe guardianship. Michael Willoughby arrived that evening. He flew back with her to London, uttering not a word, simply holding her hand for most of the way across. At Heathrow Michael put her on his own executive jet, which flew her to Speke, just outside Liverpool. There she was met by Michael's chauffeur Francis, better looking than ever with a few wrinkles around his eyes. Looking at her face, he took her in his arms and held her silently for a long time.

The reunion with Janet was unbuttoned, but quiet. Janet had wept for her daughter's loss by herself, when her husband was out. He wouldn't go to the funeral, nor would he let her go. Now she and her stepdaughter stood together in the hall, a few tears rolling silently down their cheeks. No words. Not yet.

Janet had understood better than anyone what Carol wanted. As soon as she got the call from Martha three days ago, Janet had set about making Carol's old room exactly as it was when Carol last saw it, even down to the little paraffin lamp.

'It's new!' said Carol, laughing a little for the first time since Leo's death. 'The sheets are new, the bedspread's new, even the little lamp is new!'

'Get away with you,' Janet protested. 'I bought that lamp in 1939. I just polished it up, that's all. Where d'you think you could find a new one today?'

'You're a marvel!' exclaimed Carol, holding it up and admiring it. She would never be able to analyse what this lamp meant to her, but it was like a talisman. As soon as she cupped it in her hands she began to feel calmer, safer. Janet watched her face and sent up a silent prayer for the magic of tactile things.

If the feel and smell of things have a memory, so, certainly, has sound. And the metallic ring of the steel hoops her father wore on the heels and toe-caps of his boots sent a chill through her, despite herself, as she heard them from her room, striking the pavement like weapons as he came up the street.

She was unpacking the one case she had brought with her and trying to fit the contents into the totally inadequate space. She heard the rumble of her father's voice and the soothing sound of Janet's. Then his footsteps again and the kitchen door to the stairs being flung open.

'Come on, then!' he shouted. 'Let's be having you!' The phrase that her childhood had burned into her brain.

She started downstairs and found that her knees were trembling. She tried to tell herself that she was the Princess Locatelli, that she owned two massive villas, an enormous yacht and half of one of the biggest business empires in Europe.

On the outside, that's exactly what she looked like. She had chosen her simplest dress and no jewellery, but the quality of the dress told the whole story. Nevertheless, on the inside, she was still the skinny little tousled-flax scrag-end being called down to account for some transgression, real or imaginary.

She walked into the kitchen feeling as if she were fumbling her way through the door as she did as a child. He was standing there, as he always had, legs apart, massive, the carved-stone features as colour-stained as Roman statues once were. He didn't seem to have changed in the last twenty years.

He knew suffering when he saw it and he read it now as clearly as newsprint in Carol's face. Every prompting of his male instinct made him want to take this stricken, lovely daughter of his in his arms and ease the anguish away with his strength and love.

'Hello, Dad,' she said simply, in a tone that was an invitation to a new beginning. She knew that if she could only make the tiniest crack in the dam, the past, or at least its bitter after-taste, could be swept away in a flood.

But the years and their sourness stood mercilessly between them. Jack felt trapped in a role he had created for himself and his pride would not allow him to step out of character. So all he said was, 'You've given your mother a hell of a lot of trouble getting that room ready for you.'

Instantly the clamps snapped back over her antagonism and she answered coolly: 'So long as I didn't put you to any.'

'Why couldn't you stay at one of those fancy hotels of yours?' he asked. 'Now you're a Wop princess I wouldn't have thought we were good enough for you.'

'I wanted to be with my mother,' she said simply. Jack winced inside. Janet wasn't her mother yet there was real family love in his daughter's voice, which he had never heard her use towards him.

They sat in silence at their evening meal. Janet had bought a shoulder of lamb in celebration of Carol's home-coming. Janet had the touch: she could make fried bread and bacon taste like a banquet. Carol couldn't help thinking that she had never enjoyed lamb as much as this at the hands of any chef in the world.

She told Janet so and her stepmother flushed with pleasure. Carol reflected again what a pretty woman she was. Her skin had almost the same texture it had had at twenty-five. Only the abandoned look in her eyes when she thought no one was looking gave her the mask of sadness that twisted Carol's heart. There was something else, too, in those eyes. Janet had a secret of some kind. She was haunted. It wasn't sickness, Carol was pretty sure of that. It wasn't until next day that she discovered, entirely by accident, what it was.

She awoke at about ten. The house seemed to her strangely, almost ominously, silent. She wrapped her robe about her and went downstairs. There was a note from Janet on the kitchen table: 'Gone shopping, love. Didn't want to wake you.'

Carol made herself some coffee and toast and began to prowl around the tiny, empty house. She was curious to see the front room, which she had hardly ever been let into by Jack as a child. She knew where the key was kept, above the door.

It was just as she'd remembered it from her few brief glimpses: the pianola given to them by Jack's uncle, which Jack would never permit anyone to play; the fire grate, still the original Victorian iron, never with a fire in it.

She had a sudden fancy to play the pianola, something she had always longed to do as a child. The pianola rolls were kept in the deep cupboard, constructed by the simple means of boarding across a recess in the wall by the side of the fireplace. She opened the cupboard and started to rummage among the rolls – *Poet and Peasant, Tiptoe through the Tulips,* selections from some long-lost musical called *Our Miss Gibbs.*

She decided to play *Our Miss Gibbs* and slid out the box. As she did so, something that glittered caught her eye in the dark recesses of the cupboard. Curious, she reached in for it and brought it out. It was a beautifully packaged, very expensive jar of Estée Lauder skin cream. Carol was puzzled. She had never know Janet to need any skin supplement in her life.

She moved more of the rolls and gaped. At the back of the cupboard there was an Aladdin's cave of gleaming boxes, none of them open, bearing the priciest and most exclusive names in the world of scents and cosmetics: Coty, Patou, Guerlain, Dior, Worth; a roll-call of illusion, seduction and money. Yet Janet had never been interested in that kind of glamour. And all the boxes were unopened.

There was more. On a second shelf, behind stacks of old magazines of Martha's, there were other things. Lingerie of a kind Janet never wore, costume jewellery, filmy nightgowns, all of them new, none of them worn. Was this how Janet spent the money Carol and Martha regularly sent her to make her life more comfortable? Why?

At that moment, Janet was in her favourite downtown store. She loved the warmth of it, the luxury, the alluring smells. Usually she went there when she was low, which was most of the time now. Today she was there because she was on a high. Having Carol home had fired her with euphoria and she wanted to prolong it, luxuriate in it, build it to a peak.

So her motive for her actions at this moment was different from the usual one. What she was doing was resting her shopping bag on a counter full of hand-stitched leather gloves while she apparently fumbled in it for something she was looking for.

But she wasn't looking for anything. She was opening one of the two sprung and hinged halves into which the stiff trick bottom of her bag was split, and pulling in a pair of gloves. Already in the bag were a box of expensive soap and a crystal scent atomiser, for neither of which she had paid.

From behind and slightly to the left, a pair of cynically dispassionate grey eyes suddenly slid around and picked her up. They belonged to one of the store detectives, O'Hara. He had not seen Janet do anything, but his antennae were twitching. Casually, her heart beating so that it shook her chest, Janet turned away from the counter and started out of the shop. O'Hara slowly followed.

It was a big store and a long way to the door and right up to the last moment O'Hara could not decide what to do. On the one hand, his itch told him he had got a shop-lifter. On the other hand, he had not actually seen her take anything. If he stopped her outside the store he might find he was wrong. She would kick up a fuss. The store hated the bad publicity of false accusations. In the end, cross with himself, he watched her go through the doors and out into the day. But he stored away Janet's face in a special compartment of his filing-cabinet mind, and the next time she set foot in that store he would haunt her like a soft breeze.

Janet went straight home. As she opened the front door she called Carol's name. There was no reply. Maybe she'd gone out, or perhaps she was still asleep. She had looked in need of a good rest last night.

Quietly Janet opened the parlour door. She crossed over and knelt by the cupboard where the pianola rolls were kept. She removed the first two rows and revealed her treasures. Lovingly she took her three new ones out of her bag and put them among the things already there. So engrossed was she that she didn't hear Carol come in behind her. The first thing she was aware of was Carol's puzzled 'Mum?' She jumped violently and whipped round like a cat caught at an open refrigerator. She could think of nothing to say. Her eyes were wide and wild.

'What is it, Mum? What is all this?'

'They're . . . they're just things I've bought,' Janet gasped. She looked like the guilty child and Carol the mother.

Carol looked down at the things Janet had taken from her bag. 'Why are there no wrappings on them?'

'I . . . I . . . well, you see, I opened them on the bus, love.'

'What did you do with the paper?'

'I . . . I threw it away.'

'What? On the bus? What did the conductor have to say about that?'

'I kept it until I got off the bus then put it in a rubbish bin.'

Carol pressed her remorselessly. 'There aren't any garbage bins between here and the bus stop,' she said.

'Well then, I threw it away in the road – what does it matter!' cried Janet desperately.

'You didn't pay for them, did you?' asked Carol gently. 'That's why they're not wrapped.' She knelt and took Janet's flushed cheeks between her soft hands. 'Did you?'

Janet's tears, which started to roll, were admission enough.

'You must have been doing it for quite a long time?'

'Yes.' It was a mere whisper.

'Why?' Carol murmured.

'You've all gone,' said Janet, still crying silently, 'you and Tony and Martha and it's as if there's no use for me any more.'

'Of course there is!' Carol exclaimed. 'To begin with, Jack needs you.'

'He needs me in one way. He's still a . . . passionate man. But I sometimes think anyone would do, not just me.'

'That's not true!' Carol protested. 'No matter what kind of a brute he's been to the rest of us, he's never lifted a hand to you. With a man like him that means respect.'

'I don't think it's respect I want.'

'Anyway,' Carol persisted, 'we all need you as well. Look at me. Something goes wrong I come running home to you. I'm sure it's the same with Tony and Martha. We need you. We all need you.'

She took her through to the kitchen, sat her by the fire and made her some strong tea before she pressed Janet further. 'Even when you do feel like that, why does it make you steal?'

'When I'm down,' said Janet slowly, explaining it as much to herself as to Carol, 'if I steal something from a shop without getting caught I feel I've achieved something. I feel that the day counts in my life, that it hasn't been wasted.'

'Even though you don't want what you've taken?'

'It's not the thing I've taken that counts, it's taking it.'

'You can get addicted, you know. Whatever reason you started doing it for, you end up doing it for its own sake.'

'It's not like that with me,' said Janet earnestly. 'I can stop it easily. This is the last time I'll ever do it.'

'Promise?'

'I swear, love.'

She really did mean it at that moment.

Carol went to a shop in London Road, bought a large cheap suitcase, hid it in her room and waited for nightfall.

Jack came in, made a sarcastic remark about 'Her Highness' still being there and went out to the pub. Carol and Janet packed all the stolen goods into the suitcase. Carol's intention was to call a taxi to go to the Pier Head, take a ferry across the Mersey and drop the suitcase in halfway across.

The flaw in the plan became obvious the minute they'd got the case filled. Neither of them could carry it. When the front doorbell rang, Carol and Janet looked at each other like the Macbeths hearing the knocking on the castle door. What if it were Jack, having forgotten his key? Carol finally unfroze and went and opened the front door. There stood Ike Palmer.

He was due to speak at a Congress on Energy at the Philharmonic Hall. He had already, in Tel Aviv, sealed the letter turning down the invitation when he read about Leo's death. He promptly wrote another one, accepting. His motives were mixed. He knew his wounded dove would make for home and he wanted to be there with her and comfort her. He also felt she would be vulnerable and, if she were, he intended to take shameless advantage of it.

There he stood, the shy smile as appealing as ever, and found himself stepping into a conspiracy to compound a felony.

'Ike!' Carol's embrace was as warm and open as a log fire. 'Have you got a car with you?' When he nodded, she pointed to the suitcase. 'Put that in it. It's urgent.'

Without question, Ike picked up the suitcase and loaded it into the car. The next thing he knew, Carol was in beside him. 'Pier Head,' she said.

It was only on the way there that she explained the situation, with the total candour that only fellow-inhabitants of their ghetto could appreciate, respect and protect. The bond was absolute.

Halfway across the river on the way to New Brighton they went to the deserted stern of the ship. And there the Principessa Locatelli and Professor Isaac Palmer tipped a load of stolen goods into the Mersey and promptly collapsed into the giggles, which by degrees turned into unbuckled laughter.

'Why is it you're always so much fun?' Ike asked when they'd recovered their breath.

'Because you think I am,' Carol answered.

They stayed on board at the New Brighton turn-around, the smell of kelp and seaweed reminding them both of brief one-day holiday outings when they were kids. The *Iris* backed off from the jetty, threshed through an impeccable turn and started its rhythmic, bucking beat back to Liverpool. There was a full moon. It was chopped up by the river's small, sharp waves into a glittering, motion-filled field of moonstones. Carol and Ike were in sympathy. Ike was not a man to miss an opportunity.

They were leaning against the rail, the breeze from the Bar ruffling their hair. 'I haven't had a chance to say I'm sorry about Leo,' said Ike.

'I didn't give you any opportunity, did I?' Carol answered with a smile. 'Throwing you straight into a criminal conspiracy.'

'If you wanted to, you could drag me into a plan to steal

planet Earth,' said Ike. He moved closer to her, the moon lighting up the landscape of her face, showing up the suffering beneath her eyes.

She sensed his mood. 'Ike,' she said. It was an admonition. But Ike was a man, as contemporaries in his field had noted, not easily to be put off.

'You need someone,' he persisted, 'that's why you came here.' She felt the pressure of his personality, as she had always done. And, as ever, she was aware of its hunger to take her over, something she would not allow.

'Ike, we've been through this.'

'I've changed, Carol. I don't have to own everything.'

'I know that's what you think, Ike–'

'Look,' he said, 'you need peace; a rest. Let's go away somewhere remote. I'll take a sabbatical. No pressures, no demands, no commitments. Any time you want to finish it, you can finish it. Just two friends from Scottie Road having a good time. What do you say?'

He'd lost none of his charm. It had grown, if anything, with the wrinkles beginning at the corners of his eyes and the depth that profound concentration on a discipline can lend to a face. He was having a powerful physical effect on her. The familiar moist warmth was threatening to burgeon. She had to stop this now.

'Ike,' she said, 'Leo's hardly been gone five minutes. What do you think I'm made of?'

'The dead are dead,' answered Ike implacably.

'Leo's not dead to me yet,' she said. 'Not in his spirit, in what he left of himself behind, in the resonances of himself he left in me. Can't you understand that?'

'No,' said Ike stubbornly. ' "The past is gone, let it go," says the book.'

He started to move in on her, stroking her shoulders. She decided she had to be brutal. 'I was married to Leo for five years,' she said. 'I screwed you for two weeks. What makes you think you can step in and take his place?'

The old Ike would have detonated nicely and probably tried furiously to stalk off the boat into the river. The new Ike was wilier. His mercury stayed down. 'We've known each other since we were two years old,' he said. 'What's five years against that?'

She could see she was not going to be able to make him angry; she decided to change her tactics. 'Ike, you're probably the best friend I have—'

'Friend!'

'No, please let me finish. I need to be with people I care for, but I can't stand up to any conflicts. I don't want to have to make decisions. I don't want to have to do anything I feel would be a betrayal of Leo. Please let me be with you for a few days, but please don't want me to ask anything of you, and please don't ask anything of me. D'you understand what I'm talking about?'

'I believe so,' Ike said cautiously.

'You're a medicine for me,' she went on. 'Just to be with you, to see that serious face of yours, to remember you as a kid with glasses, sprayed with pimples—'

'I never had pimples!' he interrupted indignantly.

'You were covered in them,' she said mischievously. 'You looked as if you had the plague most of the time.'

'That's a goddamned lie!' shouted Ike. This was better, thought Carol. She had shifted them on to safer ground.

They went home to Ike's parents. Ike's father was an outworker for a fashionable tailor in Bold Street. The parlour was dominated by a large industrial sewing machine. Ike's mother, a touchingly faded blue-eyed beauty with a French-Yiddish-Liverpool accent that had to be heard to be believed, fed them delicately but remorselessly into a state of semi-torpor.

Carol asked Ike how his energy research was going.

'I *know* I've got the answer with the laser and the fuel pellet,' he said. 'The ratio to power-in, power-out is coming down steadily. Pretty soon I'll be able to *prove* that this is where the world's fuel supply is going to come from in the future. That's if I'm not closed out first.'

'Closed out?'

'You've got to be a politician. The Appropriations Committee only has so much money to hand out. If one of the other guys sells himself better than I do, they'll lay all the money on his project and I'll be mending fuses for a living. And the world will be a cold place to live in next century because I *know* I'm right and they're all wrong.'

He had been watching Carol's face. He saw her thawing out. This was what she needed: involvement with him. She could lean on him and when the time was right he would marry her. It would be soon.

16

Tony's marriage to the sumptuous Senta was not a happy one. Senta undoubtedly had beautiful legs, but their preferred position was wide apart. She had an itch which could only be relieved in one way. Tony, with the sexual drive he had inherited from Jack, was uncommonly happy and able to accommodate her. But as he rose in his firm he started having to go away for a day or two at a time to demonstrate new designs his team had created.

At first Senta objected, pouting and sulking. Then, it seemed, quite suddenly she accommodated herself to it. She saw Tony lovingly off on his trips and greeted him even more lovingly on his return.

It was, naturally, a variety of good friends who brought Tony the bad news. They had moved from Aigburth to a large, pleasant semi-detached house on the groomed and rural Wirral peninsula across the river. It seemed that, during Tony's absences, Senta was becoming quite well known in the better country clubs and hotels lounges within a radius of some miles.

For months, Tony did nothing. His whole life up to then seemed to have been one long battle and he didn't feel equal to facing another one. He also knew he had his father's dark violence latent in him and he daren't start anything that might trigger it. And he happened to be both desperately in love and sexually infatuated with his wife and he didn't want to lose her.

It was inevitable that there should come the confrontation he could not ignore. He came home unexpectedly early one evening from a conference in Stockport to find another man's car in his drive. Carefully, he parked in such a way as not to block it with his own, revved his engine loudly and made a great to-do of opening and shutting his doors.

As he made towards the house, his tact was rewarded by the emergence of Brian Smithers, the kind of man who wore a blazer with a golf club badge, a silk cravat and suede shoes at country hotels all over the county every Sunday of his life. 'Just given your wife a lift home from town,' he shouted with desperate jauntiness to Tony as he jumped into his car and switched on the engine almost in one motion. 'See you at the club on Sunday!'

'Yeah,' said Tony, as the Ford with the cosmetic alloy wheel trim spun down the drive. He went into the house. Senta's broad-boned cheeks were flushed, her hair, hastily patted down, hopelessly mussed. Despite a quick dowsing of 'Madame Rochas' the scent of sex was unmistakable.

'Hello, darling,' she said, rushing up to kiss him so that he shouldn't have time to scrutinise her too impersonally from a distance. 'I was just doing some shopping in town.'

'Yeah . . . he told me,' said Tony. He was frightened. He could feel his control going. He'd always believed himself incapable of hitting a woman. Now he couldn't be sure.

She tried to make the kiss deepen and scramble him, but he brushed past her and went upstairs to the bedroom. She hadn't had time to change the sheets.

He came slowly downstairs again. She was now in the living room, pouring a powerful whisky with which she intended to de-fuse him. His face was expressionless as he came steadily towards her. She saw some fore-shadowing in his eyes of what was coming, and flung the whisky in his face. He caught her wrist with a hand like a steel trap, sat on a chair and flipped her struggling body face down across his knees. His father had used a strap. Tony needed no strap. While Senta shrieked oaths, pleas and imprecations in a mixture of accented English and filthy German, he tanned her generous arse with a hand made as hard as wood from karate until it was as rosy as an apple in high summer. He went on and on and on, releasing all the resentments and tensions his months of restraint had dammed up. Senta had never been hurt so much in her life.

When he judged that she had had enough, he stopped. She slid from his knees, sobbing, her head cradled on her arms on the floor.

Tony stood up. 'And next time I catch you, or even hear a whisper,' he said, 'you'll get the same again.'

'Big man!' she yelled from the floor, tossing her mane of hair, sobs momentarily stifled. 'You can beat a woman. I noticed you didn't try to do anything to Brian!'

'He'll get his,' said Tony comfortably, walking from the room.

Brian Smithers, in fact, got his the following Sunday. Tony drove Senta to 'the club', the roadhouse known as the Spider's Web five miles down the lanes.

They met in the bar with the usual crowd. There was a noticeable hush as Senta and Tony came in. Smithers had not, of course, been able to keep his mouth shut.

Tony's attitude to Smithers was ingratiating, almost sycophantic. Smithers' attitude to Tony became more and more patronising. He was a big man, a keep-fit fanatic, forever slapping his flat, hard gut. Tony took a particular interest in that today, his admiration being interpreted by Smithers as the equivalent of a dog's rolling over on its back to signal surrender. In the end he invited Tony, as he had invited many men in the past, to take a punch at his impregnable, muscle-ribbed belly.

Tony did. They carted Smithers off to hospital with a ruptured spleen and internal bleeding.

Senta, however, had her revenge. They had not been able to have children, and investigations had shown it to be Tony's fault. This gave Senta the perfect weapon. Every argument they had – and they started to become frequent – ended with the swingeing, unanswerable, 'Big Man! You can't even give me a baby!'

They went to adoption societies, but found that the pill and easier abortion had dried up the supply of unwanted babies. Also, they had a mixed marriage, Catholic and Lutheran, which put them in trouble with both the main religious societies. Finally, they settled for a system of external fostering, taking an older child out from nearby Carter's Hill Orphanage once a week for a treat. It could be the cinema, the zoo, or perhaps for tea in a restaurant. It could mean just taking the child home to watch television or play with them for a day.

The orphan they chose was Jacqueline, a pretty little girl of ten with long grey eyes and the arms and legs of a Victorian doll – perfect, but so that you could see their construction. At first she was withdrawn and suspicious as most institutionalised children are by that age. They know that no one wants to adopt them properly; everyone wants to adopt babies.

By the time she was thirteen she was blossoming into genuine beauty, totally secure in her relationship with Senta and Tony, more secure in her relationships with other people as well, and with only a residual trace of that tendency to slyness that institutions breed.

At this time Senta had to go to Germany to visit her mother, who was seriously ill. Despite the orphanage's strict rule that girl children taken out for treats must be accompanied by both parents, Tony turned up at Carter's Hill on the usual day and collected Jacqueline, saying that his wife was waiting for them in town. He never knew whether it was habit, affection or need that made him do it.

He took her into Chester and they went for a walk right around the broad Roman wall that encircles the city. When they reached the end of the wall and looked over the ancient, lovely city, Jacqueline snuggled up to him a little against the freshening breeze.

'What would you like now?' asked Tony. 'Tea at Smollett's? Dirty great cream cakes?'

'No,' said Jacqueline, 'I'd rather go home with you and watch telly.'

'Okay,' said Tony, 'I'll whip you up some tea there. Let's get back to the car. Last one back's a cissy!'

They raced back along the wall and down into the streets and back to the car, Jacqueline laughing and yelling; and Tony just beat her to it.

After tea the roof of the ordered world fell in on Tony Blair. They were sitting on the sofa, watching a pink panther cartoon. Jacqueline was sprawled in her usual careless fashion next to him. Almost absent-mindedly, it seemed, she took hold of his left hand. Tony, half-dozing, took little notice. Then, without taking her eyes off the screen, she transferred his hand firmly to cup one of her more than nascent breasts.

Tony jumped as if someone had put a million volts through the sofa. He snatched his hand away. 'What the devil d'you think you're doing, Jackie?' he blurted.

She smiled. 'What you've been wanting to do.'

'What I've been wanting . . . ' His mind wouldn't seem to focus.

'Of course you have.' Her voice was soothing, complaisant. 'I don't mind. I want it. I've wanted to be nice to you for a long time now.'

'Jacqueline, I don't want you to be nice to me; not in the way you mean. I'm in the position of your father. You're a child—'

'Why did you tell the orphanage that you were meeting your wife when you weren't, then?'

'I didn't want you to miss your outing.' He had risen to his feet and was pacing, appalled at what his thoughtlessness had created.

'Well then, I'm not going to miss it, am I?' replied Jacqueline. 'In fact it's going to be the best outing ever!'

She sprawled back on the sofa, her tousled skirt way up her thighs. He looked at her in amazement. It wasn't the kid he knew. Had this other creature been lurking inside little Jacqueline all this time?

He grabbed hold of her inviting, outstretched hand and yanked her to her feet. 'You're coming back with me to Carter's Hill right now, young lady. I don't know whose fault this mess is, but it stops right here.'

He drove her back to the orphanage, talking to her gently all the way, explaining the law, trying to explain that she was unusually advanced for a thirteen-year-old, attempting to make her see his responsibility and how despicable he would be if he betrayed it. At the same time, he was careful to stress his affection for her. She maintained a stubborn silence.

As he dropped her at the portals of the orphanage, she spoke for the first time. 'Will you be here next week?' she asked.

'If my wife is back and can come with me, yes.'

Without another word, she turned and went inside.

Carol listened to the story with acute attention and without interrupting once. Senta was still away. They were in the living room of Tony's house.

Now she spoke for the first time. 'And that's when you got the call from the superintendent of the orphanage.'

'After I missed the next visit a week ago. Senta wasn't back, so I didn't go. He said Jacqueline had accused me of sexually assaulting her. I can see how she must have made it sound.'

'So can I,' said Carol grimly.

'They asked me to come and see them. I did.'

'You shouldn't have gone without a lawyer.'

'Then I'd have been admitting I had something to defend. I haven't! Anyway, they interviewed me separately and then together with Jacqueline. It was horrible. Every word that kid said – well, she has a way of putting things that would make a game of dominoes sound suspicious! Now they're talking about the police. I can hear their boots tramping over the horizon, outraged fathers to a man!'

'We've got to head it off now, before it goes any further,' said Carol.

'Yes, but how?'

Carol had seen enough to know how such things are done. 'By subversion, corruption, bribery and anything else that may be necessary,' she said happily.

'But I'm innocent!'

'Exactly. Which is why you'll surely go to jail if you play it according to the rules. 'Anyway, look, Tone – supposing you do get off. Suppose, in court, on the day, your lawyer happens to be in better form than hers, or you're more convincing than she is and you get acquitted. What then? You know people. There'll always be someone to point a finger, talk behind the back of his hand. It will still ruin your career – and your life.'

He knew she was right. 'What *do* I do, then?' he asked.

'You, darling brother, do nothing. What's this superintendent like?'

'He's a bastard.'

'Good. That makes it easier.'

A week later, suitably pre-announced by a cable and a telephone call from two of her secretaries in Turin, Princess Locatelli scrunched up the drive of Carter's Hill in a hired chauffeur-driven Rolls Royce. She was wearing a simple long-sleeved cream woollen dress, a single strand of pearls and eight hundred pounds' worth of handbag and shoes. She had had the whole ensemble flown over from Rome, together with one or two other items not immediately apparent.

'As my secretary told you,' she explained to an overwhelmed Superintendent Grindly, a man with the face and disposition of a Chieftain tank, 'under the terms of my family's charitable trust we are now empowered to make donations to institutions in this country as well as on the mainland of Europe.'

'I see,' said Grindly, his eyes bugging slightly. He could already see the money stacking up behind her exotic presence.

'If I might just have a look around,' she suggested, 'see some of the classrooms.'

It was in the third classroom that Carol saw her. She couldn't miss her from Tony's description: a truly remarkable face with its wide grey eyes. Besides, she made the rest of her class look like five-year-olds.

'That's a sweet child,' she remarked casually to Grindly, as they looked in from the corridor. 'What's her name?'

'Jacqueline Jameson.'

'I think I'd like her to show me round the grounds.'

'I'm sure she'd be delighted,' beamed Grindly, his face like a buckling tin can.

In the gardens, Carol was aware of Jacqueline's covert study. 'You're very beautiful,' said Jacqueline at last. She was at that stage of development when girls find lovely older females an object of fascination, a preview of something to which they could aspire themselves.

'You're very beautiful yourself,' answered Carol.

'Not like you. Not yet.' She plucked the head off a dahlia. 'I'll bet you can get anything you want.'

'I dare say I could get more than you could,' said Carol provocatively. She saw the beginnings of a pout on Jacqueline's lips and was triumphant.

'I get quite a lot of things I want,' the child retorted. She paused. Carol waited. She looked up at Carol and added, 'Have you had a lot of men in love with you?'

'Hundreds,' said Carol carelessly.

'So have I,' replied Jacqueline competitively.

'Not hundreds,' said Carol scornfully, 'you're not old enough. What are you – ten? eleven? You're not old enough to know what love is!'

'I'm thirteen!' asserted the child, undoubtedly pouting now. 'And I do know what love is!'

'What is it, then?' Carol teased, with a sweet smile.

'It's when you . . . do things with each other.'

'With whom?'

'Some of the older boys in this place. They're crazy about me.'

'What kind of things do you do?'

And it all came tumbling out, as it would never have done to a man. Jacqueline hadn't been a virgin since she was eleven and a half years old. 'I know how to turn boys on,' she concluded proudly.

'It's funny, though, isn't it,' said Carol. 'There's always one you can't turn on.'

Jacqueline looked at her in amazement. 'D'you mean that happens to *you* too?'

'Sometimes,' said Carol, not to make too much of it.

Jacqueline scuffed the gravel path. 'Mind you, mine's a grown-up man. Maybe they're different from boys. Maybe I did something wrong.'

'Tell me what you did,' said Carol, with apparently casual interest, but in reality as taut as a kite string. 'Let's sit down.'

They sat on the garden bench in that blossom-drenched garden and Jacqueline told the whole story of her abortive attempt to seduce Tony Blair, straight into the watch-like wrist microphone that led up Carol's sleeve to the tiny tape recorder in her handbag.

Ten minutes later, Mr Grindly was listening to it, in the presence of Carol and an increasingly white-faced Jacqueline, who was absorbing her first realisation that she wasn't as smart as she thought she was. The tape finished and Grindly, grey-cheeked himself, turned to Carol. 'You're a private detective, I suppose, working for Blair.'

'No,' she said gently, 'I am Princess Locatelli. I am also Mr Blair's sister.' He sagged visibly. 'And if I were you,' she went on, 'I'd pay more attention to getting that little tramp sorted out than to ruining innocent men. I'd also have a thought about how to turn this place back into an orphanage rather than a teeny-bopper's bordello. Mr Blair will expect your written apology within the week.'

She snatched up the tiny recorder, popped it back in her handbag, and disappeared through the door.

Tony duly got his grovellingly apologetic letter.

'That's one I owe you, Car,' he said, after he'd given it to Carol to read.

'I've got about ninety-nine to go to square the score,' grinned Carol.

Ike had flown back to Israel. He'd heard that one of his rivals for finance appropriations for the coming year was pulling more than his share. A realist, having failed in what he thought would be the definitive assault on Carol, Ike plunged back into the scientific politics of what he sincerely believed in as the future survival of the planet.

Carol said a tearful farewell to Janet and a mutually grunting goodbye to her father and flew back to Italy to the villa in Turin, still echoing, it seemed, to the sound of Leo's presence. Her children, Pietro and Lucilla, greeted her ecstatically. Pietro was becoming so like Leo that it was heart-bruising to look at him.

For the next two years Carol, Martha and George worked unceasingly to interlock the empires of Ironstile and Locatelli. Carol, with her title, her languages, her beauty and her connections was the tranquillising angel who soothed the frequently ruffled feathers of Ministers and senior EEC officials. If there was a problem there would be a party, in the Roman villa or Turin. After the party, there would usually be no problem. Despite the steadily worsening oil crisis, Ironstile-Locatelli finally docked with each other in 1977 with a clang that was heard throughout the boardrooms of the world. And Carol saw Ike with increasing frequency, sometimes in Paris, sometimes in Tel Aviv and once in the villa in Rome.

It was not that she loved Ike, she was sure of that; there was still something in her nature which rebelled against something in his. But they were fluent and compatible lovers, who gave each other a great deal of pleasure – he had just introduced her to the 'spinning wheel' – and it was comforting to be with someone, apart from family, who had the same roots as herself. She knew he was in the highest class as a scientist and something in her, more than affection or local pride, wanted to see him succeed.

When she finally left again for England, neither guessed that the next time they met it would be in the presence of the most formidable rival Ike had yet encountered.

Patrick Clarence O'Hara – he never told anybody about the Clarence – had woken up in high good humour. She'd been in again yesterday. For over two years – nothing. Then suddenly, a week ago, there she was, pushing in through her favourite door.

He never forgot a face. Especially one that had got away.

She had wandered around, a little paler, a little more worn, gazing about her with that look on her face like an alcoholic in a liquor store. She hadn't given him an opportunity to pounce, then. But O'Hara felt in his bones that today was going to be the day.

She came in at half past eleven and O'Hara's adrenalin started to pump.

Janet hadn't forgotten her promise to Carol, but she had returned to the black forests of depression. Jack was becoming more and more remote. He had found another photograph of Claire and had now put that up in the kitchen as well. She felt unwanted and useless. The pills the doctor gave her made her feel as if she were wearing lead boots and she gave them up. Only one thing would do, but she had not yet been able to screw herself up to it. Was today the day?

As always, Janet had no idea what she was going to take. She moved forwards from the door, waiting for something bright and life-enhancing to catch her eye. She didn't see the grey-suited shadow who fell in, muffle-footed, about ten yards behind her, moving down other aisles, sometimes in other directions, but always keeping her in clear sight.

Using her trick bag, she stole a cashmere sweater, a silk square and a pretty tub of bath salts. She had remarkable peripheral vision: she could see very clearly to the sides while apparently looking straight ahead, but she didn't spot her hunter. The first she saw of him was when she stepped outside into the street, the familiar feeling of elation starting to rise, and felt a firm hand on her arm.

She looked up into the triumphant red face of Patrick Clarence O'Hara.

The Gulfstream private jet streaked across Europe at its maximum of four hundred and seventy-five miles an hour, boosted by a forty-knot tail wind to over five hundred. In it were Carol and Martha and George.

Janet had used the telephone call allowed her to ring Carol to say she'd been arrested and was being held overnight at Hope Street Police Station.

Carol had tried desperately to get in touch with Stewart Crown. But he was fully qualified in America now as well as Britain and was currently in court in New York in the middle of a huge suit between two computer giants.

The plane landed at Speke Airport and George dragged

one of Ironstile-Locatelli's brightest young lawyers, Peter Fineman, away from his dinner with orders to meet them at Hope Street. As the big Mercedes, which had been telexed forward from Turin, rolled to a stop outside the police station, Carol, George and Martha saw with sinking hearts an all too familiar figure striding towards them from the opposite direction. Jack, on the unfailing Liverpool bush telegraph, had heard. His fists were clenched like bludgeons. His face could have cracked a bank vault.

George leaped out of the car and barred his way, followed by Carol and Martha. Jack, for once, showed genuine astonishment. 'How the hell did you get here? How did you know?'

'We flew. Janet phoned us,' said George.

Jack grunted and made to push through them. They closed ranks.

'Just what are you thinking of doing in there?' asked Martha.

'I'm going to ask those buggers what they think they're doing to my wife.' He tried to push past again.

'And what'll happen,' said George, 'is that you'll go spare, deck two or three coppers and instead of just one of you being inside, there'll be two!'

'Get out of my way,' said Jack.

Carol spoke. 'Dad, we've got a lawyer on to it. Now you've *seen* how good they can be.' Her eyes, holding his, forced him to remember and acknowledge what Stewart Crown had once, against all the odds, donc for him. 'If you screw things up, Mum could be in real trouble – and it'll be doubly your fault.'

The 'doubly' was not lost on Jack. He took the nuance that, in some way, he had driven Janet to this. It subdued him. 'Get in there with your fancy bloody lawyer, then, and get her out of there,' he said. He leaned back against the wall of the police station, one knee bent, the sole of his boot flat against the bricks, thumbs hooked into his belt.

Fineman was not only fancy, he was really fancy. He had taken the precaution of dragging his uncle, one of the most distinguished physicians in Rodney Street, away from his own dinner and had brought him along with him. Nephew and uncle were already inside doing a number on Liverpool's finest. Sir Howard Fineman had given it as his opinion that Janet was completely unfitted to undergo a night in custody. Fineman Junior added that should any harm befall her from such an experience they might expect a noise not unlike the start of the Third World War.

The constabulary was already rocky on its feet when in walked the Chairman and Chief Executive of the giant Ironstile-Locatelli enterprise, enquiring as to the whereabouts of their beloved relative, one Janet Blair. George, moreover, was, to their certain knowledge, a constant golfing partner of the Chief Constable of Lancashire.

Within fifteen minutes Janet was released into their custody, on bail of five hundred pounds. As they streamed out of the station Superintendent Sutton, who had batted for the police side, looked up from his desk at his inspector in bewilderment. 'What the fuck just happened here?' he asked. 'We pick up a little shoplifter and suddenly we're hit by an armoured column!'

'It's family,' the inspector reminded him.

'Aye,' said the superintendent, recognising an immutable fact of Liverpool life as he gazed disconsolately into the mug of tea his sergeant had just placed tactfully in front of him.

Outside, young Fineman was having a whispered consultation with George. 'If it comes to court, our best chance is a plea of mental confusion,' said Fineman. 'Her attitude since she was brought in will support that.' He paused. 'There's only one spike in our eye.'

'What's that?'

'She used a trick bag. It's a professional's tool.'

'Aye,' said George heavily. He and the rest of the family climbed into the Mercedes. Jack, still leaning against the wall, watched them without a word. As they were about to drive off Janet caught sight of him. 'Jack!' she shouted hysterically through the window.

'I'll walk,' he said.

'You'll have a hell of a long walk, then,' said George.

'We're going to my place.'

Jack hesitated, then shoved himself easily off from the wall with his foot and climbed into the car. He sat bolt upright, determined to be unimpressed by the monstrous vehicle; and, indeed, perhaps he was.

When they arrived, George went straight to his cloistered, glowing study and had a quiet word on the telephone with another golfing companion, the Chairman of the group of stores to which the Liverpool branch Janet had looted belonged. It was a brief and friendly conversation in a kind of shorthand.

In the drawing room Carol was in the process of stripping Jack to the bone. Jack was shouting, half in rage, half in pain, 'She goes on shoplifting binges and it's all my bloody fault, that's the story, is it?'

'Yes, it bloody is!' shouted Carol, her beautifully modulated voice sounding strange wrapped round the barbed obscenities which were the only currency Jack respected. 'You've steadily destroyed that beautiful woman's spirit since the day you married her. If Martha and I hadn't got away, you'd have destroyed us, too. Even so, you left your mark on us!'

'I could still leave my mark on you now, you Wop-loving alehouse poke!' roared Jack, moving towards her.

'Just you fucking try!' said Carol, picking up a perfectly weighted brass poker from the fireplace, where the log fire crackled as ever. She had the weird experience of being able to wonder with one half of her brain what her elegant Italian friends, who regarded her as the quintessence of aristocratic cool, would think of her now.

Jack paused as George came into the room. 'I thought you'd all like to know,' he said, 'that the store will be dropping all charges and you've got nothing more to worry about, Janet love.'

There was a babble of delight. Martha embraced George in a bear hug, kissing his bristly red cheeks as if they were peaches. Janet looked as if she were about to faint. Carol snatched up a decanter and poured her a powerful brandy. Janet drank some, coughed and smiled through her spluttering like a child. Then she leaped up and kissed George.

Martha's voice rang round the room. 'It isn't all over, you know. George has managed to square it this time, but what about next time? And the time after that?

'There won't be a next time, Martha, I swear it.'

'Mum, you swore it to me two years ago,' said Carol. 'With you, it's not something you can control just like that. We all know who drives you to it. You've got to get away from him.'

Jack's face became almost as red as George's. 'You interfering little bitch!' he roared. 'Who the hell do you think you are? You think you can come over here and order people's lives for them! Piss off back to your Wops and your fornicating before you get driven into the ground like a bloody nail!'

He made another move towards her and again she raised the poker. The anger that this man was capable of arousing in her privately terrified her.

Martha tried to introduce a more rational note. Addressing herself to both Jack and Janet, she said: 'It can't do either of you any good to go on living in that house. The whole area's being pulled down around your ears, anyway. We've asked you often enough – why don't you come and live here? There's that beautiful cottage in the grounds, central heating, two bathrooms, the lot.'

A look of longing crossed Janet's face, to be wiped off instantly by Jack. 'I'm taking no man's charity to put a roof over my head, and I've got a house of my own,' he said.

'It wouldn't be charity. You could pay us rent,' said Martha.

'With what? I wouldn't be able to get in to the docks every day from out here.'

'There's plenty of work around here,' said George. 'You could work in one of my steel yards, come to that.'

'Oh, right! And pull my bloody forelock every time you lorded your way through it? Yes sir, no sir, kiss your bloody arse, sir! Be known as the boss's tame hand-out relative? Get stuffed! I've made my own bloody way all my life and no tomato-faced get-rich-quickie is going to change that!'

'Don't you come that with me, you ignorant git!' said George. 'I've worked as hard as you ever did – and with my back as well as my head. It just happens I've got something inside my skull instead of the turnip you use for a brain.'

'It's my daughter's brains you live off, soft-gut. If it wasn't for her, you'd be shovelling horseshit.'

George hit his flashpoint and tensed, ready to go for Jack. Jack prayed that he would. What he wanted now more than anything else was release through physical action.

Martha laid gently restraining fingers on George's arm. She knew that even now Jack could thrash any three of the best men you cared to put against him. Instead, she made another reasonable suggestion. 'Then let Janet stay here with us for a bit. She needs a rest. You could look after yourself for a few weeks, couldn't you? Buy yourself a few TV dinners? You'd get by.'

Jack took a deep breath. 'Listen,' he said, 'shall we just have a look what's happened here? My wife gets nicked for shoplifting. Not me. Her. But suddenly she's getting all the sympathy and I'm getting all the flak. In some mysterious bloody way it's all my fault. Well, I don't buy that. I didn't ask her to shoplift. I didn't know she was doing it. I'm not taking any part of the blame. And I'll tell you something else. I don't know how it is with the high-class riff-raff you all mix with now, but where we come from we marry, we stay married and we stick together. Where the man goes the wife goes too, and tomorrow I'm going home to Mugsley Street.' He turned to Janet. 'You can either come with me or you can stay here. If you don't come tomorrow, don't bother to come at all.'

The door opened and Muir, the butler, came in.

'Dinner is served, madam,' he said to Martha.

'I'll eat no food under this roof,' said Jack. 'Just show me where I sleep.'

Wordlessly Martha showed him along to the luxurious suite which had been prepared for him and Janet. A pair of George's pyjamas and a dressing-gown and slippers had been laid out ready for him. Jack flung the pyjamas and dressing-gown on the floor, ripped the counterpane off the bed, kicked the slippers into a corner and flung the window wide open.

Martha stared at him, her eyes like split flint. 'One day you're going to get your come-uppance,' she said. 'I pray God I'm there to see it.' She went out and slammed the door before he had a chance to come back at her.

Carol flew back to Italy the next day feeling deeply depressed. Janet had gone back to Mugsley Street with Jack. Of course, she'd sworn that never again . . .

But Janet was sick and her sickness was Jack and sooner or later she would be driven back to the duel with O'Hara, or some other O'Hara in some other store.

George and Martha stayed on at the manor. Carol had the jet to herself, a lonely princess in the clouds wrapped in her own forebodings.

17

Countess Lucia Livorna would have been scandalised had anyone ever suggested that what she ran in her huge and impeccably kept villa was anything other than the longest running, most exclusive house-party in Rome.

Drop in, provided you were *persona grata*, at any time you cared, and you could find what seemed to be the loveliest girls in Rome taking tea in the salons, some apparently having forgotten to put anything on over their elaborate underwear; or playing badminton in the ballroom, naked to the waist; or, failing the overt presence of men, taking part in the gymnasium in the ancient sport of *callista* without benefit of clothes at all. These were, as it were, the public displays. What happened in the luxurious bedrooms – and other chambers which it would be difficult to categorise – was limited only by the farther reaches of the imaginations of Lucia's guests.

What Carol was doing there at three in the afternoon twenty-four hours after her return to Italy she couldn't readily have told you. She was apparently taking tea with her good friend the Countess. She liked Lucia. She liked her hedonistic, almost pagan, approach to sexual *mores*, and she found it relaxing to be with her. She had never been, as it were, a member of her house party.

'It is a long time that you have not been to visit me,' Lucia was chiding. 'To have friends it takes application, it must be worked at.'

'Friendship is in the mind,' said Carol. 'If my friend is in my mind she's still my friend no matter how long we've been apart.'

Just then, Vittorio, six feet seven inches of Calabrian

concrete, ushered in Conn Fordinger, four inches shorter, with a battered, broken-nosed beauty which was the result of football at Choate, bob-sledding at La Rosaye and boxing at Yale.

Fordinger money was old money. There was a story that the Fordingers had had the best berths on the *Mayflower* and dined with the Captain every night. They had been rich for a long time before they left for the New World and they saw no reason to abandon a winning streak just because they'd come three thousand stomach-chucking miles in order to be able to think how they wanted to think.

The Fordingers now ran like a fat vein of platinum through the financial geology of the country: through oils, coal, banks, high technology, fission research, pharmaceuticals and a phalanx of Foundations and Trusts.

They had not seen actual money for generations. The world was one large charge account. Every store owner, jeweller, picture dealer, hotelier or restaurateur of any consequence knew that the Fordinger financial comptroller, fulfilling something of the same function as his counterpart in a Royal Household, received, examined, and paid the accounts.

Carol looked at the current head of this imperial dynasty curiously as he came in. She had met him at numerous social functions in the past, but had never found him attractive. She wondered why. He was certainly a striking-enough figure, always immaculately tailored, with a rugged impressiveness in the slightly broken, powerful face.

'Contessa!' he said, 'I simply wanted to say goodbye.'

Lucia's eyes twinkled. 'That's most charming,' she said. 'I've never known you do it before, but then I've never had the Princess Locatelli with me before.'

The strongly cut mouth curved in amusement as he answered. 'See what a position you leave me in. If I deny your soft impeachment I shall be showing discourtesy to the princess. If I accept it, I admit that I followed her in here.'

Charlton Heston couldn't have done it better, thought Carol. 'Soft impeachment!' Christ, he should be in the theatre!

'You have a third alternative,' she said.

'What is that, Princess?' he smiled, the big white teeth showing easily.

'You could say goodbye as you intended.'

She wouldn't normally have been so rude, but something in Fordinger's physical presence had suddenly forced her to admit to herself what she was there for. She wanted a release from tension. She wanted a therapeutic faceless fuck with no emotional entanglements. The recognition of the fact, with Fordinger's blue-black eyes on her, had made her embarrassed. She could feel prickles of sweat all over.

'Oh, come now,' said Lucia. 'Do sit down, my dear Conn, and take tea with us.'

Conn sat down and she handed him a cup, his large brown hand dwarfing it.

'Did you know I'd got another Bosch?' she asked.

'No! Which one? Where is it? May I see it?'

Bosch's paintings held a curious fascination for Conn. He had four himself, bought at auctions for enormous sums in the teeth of the world. He never tired of gazing at them.

'Carol knows where it is. She saw it before you came. You'll show Conn, won't you, Carol darling?'

Carol paused for a moment, succeding in making her consent precious. 'I want to see it again myself,' she said, finally.

She rose and started out of the room in one ripplingly continuous movement. Conn Fordinger, a not ungraceful man despite his size, was nevertheless left giving the impression of lumbering submissively in her wake.

'What are you doing in Rome?' he asked, as he followed her hypnotic choreography along the hushed, soft-carpeted corridor.

'Trying to make Vittoccini see sense,' she said. It had been in all the newspapers.

'Of course,' said Conn, 'you've been trying to take them over and the old man's been resisting.'

'He's somehow massaged his shares up to a ridiculous price. We'd have to pay three times what the company's worth.'

'So you're pulling out?'

Too late she remembered that stock market operations were Conn Fordinger's hobby. He played the market in preference to playing chess or doing crosswords – and in much the same spirit.

Her brain raced. She stopped and turned to face him. 'I didn't say that,' she said brusquely.

'No, of course you didn't,' said Conn with a grin.

'It's not for anyone to know.'

'Oh, come on, I wouldn't—'

'We're locked into a sizeable bundle of Vittoccini shares. All it needs is one big seller, selling short, and the price will crash and we'll lose millions. We intend to unwind out of them slowly without making any fuss. If someone like you were to go into the market and sell just now—'

'I've told you I wouldn't! Anyway, how could I? What am I going to do – try and call my broker now while you hack off my head with a nail file?'

She gazed at him steadily. Suddenly she smiled and Conn had the dazed impression that someone had shone a torch in his eyes. 'Make no mistake about it,' she said. 'I would.'

The Bosch was in one of the glowing little bedrooms. Carol pushed open the heavy door, quilted with plump, rose-silk padding on the inside – and there it was on the opposite wall, the familiar nightmare of a technicoloured teeming maggot-heap of tormented humanity in a hell that was at once defined and yet limitless.

It never failed to arouse in Conn the crawl and creep of a fascinated terror very close to pleasure. As always he had the sudden illusion that he was on the brink of some truth about himself.

The door swung shut behind them, its perfect fit creating a hushed punch of compression in the air. Instantly they were enclosed in an atmosphere of total intimacy and Carol suddenly scented danger. Her radar had already told her that beneath this immaculately clothed, aristocratic jock with his primitive vibrations there was an extremely complex man.

He walked slowly over to the Bosch, never taking his

eyes from it. A detail leaped out: two tiny bodies, a man and a woman, knotted around each other, both perfectly realised, being drawn into the mouth of a mammoth red demon. The demon's head was sliced off across the top and other copulating figures were tumbling into its crimson glow.

Carol looked at his intent, craggy profile. 'Is that what you think is going to happen to you?' she asked quietly.

Conn dragged his eyes from the picture. 'What are you talking about?' he demanded irritably. 'What are you, a priest or a shrink or something?'

'What's the matter? Are you afraid I'll steal your soul?'

'My soul can take care of itself,' he snapped.

'Bosch didn't think so.'

Fordinger realised he couldn't match Carol on this ground. He could feel the grip of her mind tightening on his, gaining ascendancy over him.

He decided to change the arena to one he understood. He grabbed her polished shoulders, crushing her to him, his mouth on hers, strong hands sliding down beneath her taut buttocks and lifting her off her feet as he turned towards the bed.

The pain started in the vertebrae at the back of his neck and travelled down his spine, almost paralysing him. His arms fell away from Carol and the pain stopped.

Carol shook her shining hair and smiled at him. 'Pressure point,' she said. 'My brother taught me.'

Conn's eyes were blurred with pain and rage. 'What the hell's the matter with you? Don't try to tell me you're not ready for it.'

'Not as an act of war to win an argument,' she answered. 'You're out of date.'

'Are you trying to tell me you come here looking for love and romance?'

She laughed outright, genuinely amused. 'Mr Fordinger, even your sneers are old-fashioned.'

This enraged Conn more than anything else she could have said. She made the mistake of turning contemptuously away to tidy her hair in a mirror, and he grabbed her again from behind. This time he made sure he had her arms inside the bear hug, crushed helplessly against her sides.

'There's an old-fashioned way to deal with cock-teasers, too,' he said furiously.

This time the pain started just below his right knee and travelled all the way down to his foot as she scraped her heel down the length of his shin. It was unbearable, but he bore it, yelling with outrage but tightening his arms. She started on the other shin.

It was too much. He let go, intending to spin her round and slap her. As he grabbed her hand and pulled she spun all right, but somehow she kept on spinning, taking his arm with her until suddenly he was down on his knees with his wrist somewhere up by his shoulder blades. Bully for her fucking brother! he thought wryly to himself. He countered by rolling forwards in the direction of her twist and sweeping her beautiful legs from under her with his right foot.

He had expected her to collapse into his arms. Instead, she fell the wrong way and hit her head on the brass rail at the end of the exquisite early Victorian bed. She lay there, dazed, and Conn looked down at her, breathing a little heavily. He knew what he was going to do.

He bent down and picked her up, carried her round the side of the glittering brass bedstead and laid her gently down on the bed. Using a silk scarf that was in her hair and another that floated vaguely around her throat, he fastened her wrists to the brass rails on the bedhead. He worked quickly; her eyelids were beginning to flutter. Then, breathing deeply and slowly, he undressed unhurriedly and completely. When she opened her eyes a minute later, he was standing over her, rampant.

'You lost,' he said.

She tried to catapult from the bed before she realised she was tied. Her first reaction was to thrash about like a landed trout, her body leaping convulsively, to be tugged back by her fastened wrists. Her second reaction was to shout, 'You lucky bastard! My brother could take you to pieces! Lucia!'

Conn grinned. 'He probably could. But he's not here. And it's no good shouting for Lucia. You know nobody outside this room can hear a thing.'

She thrashed again, like someone being given electric shocks. 'Girl fighter!' she hurled at him.

'Every time,' he grinned, 'if the girl is worth fighting.' He reached down and flipped up her skirt. She was wearing nothing on the glossy bronzed legs, just a pair of sleek pants made of some soft, tough material. They wouldn't rip. He tried to drag them down. She spread her thighs, preventing him.

'Okay,' he said. He got off the bed, went over to the dressing table, riffled through the drawers. He returned with a pair of nail scissors.

Carol's eyes widened.

'It's all right,' he said, 'I'm a shit, not a nut-case.' He snipped neatly across the stretched crotch of the pants from leg to leg. The material fell down limply, exposing her sweet construction to his gaze. He stroked it lovingly. 'Some day I'm going to have Cartier make me a watch just like you,' he said.

She struck up viciously with a knee, almost catching him, but he moved back just in time. 'Leave my Excalibur alone,' he chided. 'Pretty soon it's going to be in you right up to your fabulous eyes and there's not a thing you can do about it.'

The struggle, the satisfaction of her own earlier violence, the hatred, and now the helplessness, had all – despite herself – prepared her for him: she was glistening like a peeled grape. He used his massive strength to force her clenched thighs apart and slid into her smoothly like a salmon plunging upstream.

He took his time. He was slow and gentle, easing himself inwards while he suppressed her struggles with his weight, avoided her teeth, turned his head away while she spat at him. He had no wish to be brutal; his revenge was to be of another dimension. He waited until Excalibur was fully sheathed in her. He paused and gazed down into her hate-filled eyes as she lay there, trying the trick of being completely inert. Then he raised himself on one arm and reached for the bedside telephone. He called his Rome office and asked for his local financial controller.

'Luigi? This is Conn Fordinger. Get through to London and New York—'

She opened her mouth to scream. He pressed a muscular forearm across her throat. He looked down at her, the blood pounding in his neck, buried the telephone momentarily in the pillow, whispered to her. 'To screw you while I'm screwing you – Christ!'

He lifted the telephone again, spoke to the patient, dry little man who could never in a thousand years have conceived what was going on at the other end of his telephone. 'Tell my brokers to sell every piece of Vittoccini stock we've got. No limit – whatever price they can get. When they've dumped it all, tell them to go short on another million.'

He put down the receiver and started to shudder, taking his arm from her throat. She screamed electrifyingly with rage, strained at her bound wrists as if she must wrench out of the bars, and gave one last gigantic thrust with her buttocks. Then her legs snapped around him and they exploded, simultaneously, in the most piercing, comprehensively shattering orgasm either of them had ever known. It came in wave after rending, building wave like the thousand-year climax promised to the faithful Muslim, seeming to trigger every synapse, touch every nerve-ending, accelerate every neurone in their bodies.

As it finally ebbed away, Conn collapsed on her breasts. 'That must have been the most expensive fuck in history,' he murmured and came again, quietly, sweetly, a kind of afterglow as her insides gripped and neatly shifted him a millimetre for her own further satisfaction. He untied her wrists and let her draw her nails down his back, slowly and savagely while she came again and again.

They lay there for a long time not speaking. Then he got out of her and off her and looked down at her face. Her eyes were open wide: sapphire irises without expression, almost as if they were mirrors reflecting a Southern sky.

Her sensual face was drained and impassive. She rose in one movement like an athlete and walked without looking at him into the bathroom. He heard her lock the door and turn on the water. Then he fell into a contented sleep.

He awoke an hour later, feeling slightly cold and with a note stuck between the first and second toes of his right foot. He bent his leg up and snicked it out. It read: 'Who screwed whom? Check the price of Vittoccini.'

He snatched up the telephone stark naked as he was and checked with Luigi. The Vittoccini share price had doubled. Ironstile-Locatelli had been into the market, soaking up every share in sight at the depressed price Conn's operation had forced them down to and announced it now had a controlling interest in Vittoccini. As a take-over exercise it would not have passed muster in the City of London, but this wasn't the City of London.

Carol had got what she wanted and Fordinger was going to be out roughly a million dollars.

He showered swiftly, dressed, said a swift goodbye to Lucia and stormed in his Maserati to the Locatelli villa.

As he was announced, Carol was descending the main staircase into the hall, her exquisite children on either side of her, each holding a hand. She looked the picture of fragrantly demure motherhood. 'Run along now, sweet-hearts,' she said, 'Mummy has a little something to attend to.' Then she turned to Fordinger with the sweetest of smiles.

'A little something!' said Conn thirty seconds later in the gilded library, dominated by portraits of six former Locatelli cardinals and one schismatic Pope. 'You just cost me a million dollars!'

'Then you'll have to cut down on buying neckties for a while,' said Carol.

Conn pointed an accusatory finger at her; 'You told me you'd pulled out of the Vittoccini deal.'

'I did not,' said Carol. '*You* told *me*! All I said was that it wasn't for anybody to know. If you'll recall, I denied it.'

'You meant me to think you'd pulled out.'

'I admit it did occur to me that if I let you talk yourself into believing that we had, you might play exactly the kind of dirty trick you did play. The circumstances in which you played it, of course, I admit I did not foresee.

The memory of the exquisite pleasure of that moment, even though he now realised that he had been the dupe and not she, brought a reminiscent smile to his lips despite himself. She knew what the smile was about and it awakened her own bodily memories.

'Tell me,' she asked softly, 'why did you have to do that? I mean score off me mentally as well as physically?'

'You've always given me such a hard time,' he said. 'I wanted to do something crushing to you.'

'D'you still feel like that?'

He paused. 'I want you to marry me,' he said.

Conn Fordinger was forty-one. He had never married because he had never met a woman yet who couldn't be bought for as long as he wanted her. This woman he had wanted from the second he set eyes on her and he had known instinctively that she was not for sale. It was not merely that she was already married to Leo the first time he saw her; it was something in her aura that told him that she was utterly her own person and anyone who tried to buy her would be shrivelled by her derision.

She was in his thoughts constantly. After Leo's death he had redoubled the clandestine efforts he made to be in the same places as her, at the same functions, just for a few words, perhaps to sip a glass of champagne together. The fact that she was invariably cool towards him made no difference.

What Conn Fordinger didn't realise was that he was in love as well as in lust. Now that he had actually tasted her, he was turning on the spit of his own craving.

Carol, for her part, was in a state of utter emotional confusion. So much so, in fact, that she had completely forgotten she had invited Ike Palmer for lunch that day.

Ike had lost his battle with his academic competitors in Tel Aviv and was now at Princeton in America, where they still had sufficient faith in the fuel pellet-laser principle to offer him a research Professorship and limited facilities. He and Fordinger had met each other on the international circuit. Fordinger had respected Ike as one of the foremost physicists of the day and Ike had respected Conn for the enlightened way in which the immense Fordinger fortune was used for the advancement of the sciences and the arts.

Today, however, as Ike entered the sumptuous amber, red and parchment-coloured room, the hackles of both men rose.

Ike enfolded Carol in a social embrace into which he artfully injected something that was a little more than social, a fact that was not lost on Conn. Then the two men shook hands with scandalously false bonhomie.

'Good to see you,' said Ike. 'What are you doing in Rome?'

'Just at this moment,' answered Conn, going for the knock-out, 'I'm proposing to Princess Locatelli.'

Ike affected to take it as a joke. 'Oh,' he said, with an ease he did not feel, 'you'll find that becomes an annual event. I shouldn't take it too seriously.'

Conn stiffened. 'I take it very seriously indeed. I'm not in the habit of playing games about such matters.' He dismissed Ike in a manner which only the imperially rich can bring off and turned to Carol. 'Well?' he demanded briskly. It wasn't the best approach he could have chosen.

Carol bristled. 'Well what?'

'I asked you a question.'

'I wasn't aware you'd asked me a question. You merely told me what *you* wanted.'

Ike, watching the exchange, began to feel more comfortable. If this was his approach, Conn Fordinger had about as much chance as a positron hitting a neutron.

'I'm deeply sorry,' Conn said, 'I put it clumsily. What I wanted to say, what I'm saying now, is that I'm desperately in love with you and I would like, more than anything else in the world, to marry you if you'll have me.'

Ike, watching Carol's face, saw that Conn had surprised and touched her. Swiftly he intervened. 'Of course she won't marry you. She doesn't need you, she doesn't love you, she certainly doesn't want to be just a trophy on the Fordinger shelf—'

Conn took a step towards him, big hands clenching. 'What the hell's it got to do with you?'

'You'd love that, wouldn't you?' Ike swept on. 'The most desirable, richest, most beautiful, most stylish woman in Europe! At last you've found someone you think is worthy of you, so you graciously offer to elevate her to your throne. Well, you can just bug off, King Fordinger, she's not interested!'

Carol was torn. It took guts to talk to a Fordinger like that, knowing the power they wielded. On the other hand, there it was again: that deep tug of total possessiveness inside Ike. He was acting as though she were incapable of speaking for herself. He might be right: Conn Fordinger might want her for an empress. But Ike wanted her for a puppet.

Almost involuntarily, she spoke. 'Yes, Conn, I'll marry you.'

And Ike Palmer, with the agonising conviction that he had helped to stampede her towards disaster, walked away from her for the third time in his life.

18

The marriage of Conn Fordinger to Princess Locatelli was the stuff of which the dreams of media men are made.

Carol made the mistake of telling Lucia, which was as good as putting posters up all over Rome. By the third day after Conn's proposal, every large newspaper and television company in Europe and America had telephoned or cabled. Conn, however, remained equal to the occasion. He knew something about evasiveness where newsgatherers were concerned.

First, he had his jet fuelled up and serviced with discreet ostentation at Leonardo da Vinci. Second, he booked and paid for tickets on scheduled flights to twelve different destinations, knowing that they would all be leaked. Third, he asked one of his secretaries in Rome to send some important documents to his chateau in Indre-et-Loire and a secretary in New York to telex him at a certain date at his villa at Cap d'Antibes. Having reduced the best sleuths in the world to total confusion he and Carol caught a plane to Boston. There they were married by a Justice of the Peace, who was also a Fordinger, in a room of such flawless black and white simplicity that it could have been built by the Pilgrim Fathers.

Afterwards they climbed back into the black-windowed Lincoln and drove to the airport.

'Where now?' asked Carol, who loved surprises.

'You'll see,' grinned Conn.

They passed all barriers and checks and security clearances without let or hindrance and emerged on to an isolated runway removed from the main complex.

Standing there was a Boeing jumbo jet. The car delivered them to the bottom of the steps where they were met and greeted by the granite-faced Captain. Then they boarded.

Carol gasped. The giant's huge interior had been converted into a duplex apartment. Muted elegance, flowing space and unlimited artificial sunshine had created an ambience that lifted the heart the minute one entered it. They walked straight into the sitting room, with its sense of glitter and lightness, its enfolding, creamily reassuring sofas and banquettes sinking into the silk-soft carpet, the walls covered by fabric of the same shade of yellow-amber. A Van Gogh cornfield blazed over a false fireplace filled with flowers.

Carol toured a kitchen to make a chef jump on his hat for joy, a velvet-walled dining room dominated by an obscure rosy-cheeked squire and his lady by Gainsborough, two marble bathrooms and a complete guest suite. There were also quarters for two stewards and a chef. Up the stairs, the cocktail lounge had been transformed into a bedroom of such closeted, rose-mirrored intimacy that it was an aphrodisiac in itself.

'Conn!' she exclaimed. 'How long have you had this?'

'I had work started on it two years ago,' he said, 'the minute I decided seriously to lay siege to you. It's your wedding present.'

'Mine! You mean this magic carpet is mine?'

'Yours to do whatever you want with, to go wherever you want to go.'

'Let's go round the world!' she cried impulsively.

'I'll go and instruct the Captain,' he said.

They flew around the world and they loved each other, in their physical infatuation, over every major continent and sea on the globe.

Conn had had an ingenious system devised whereby a television camera on the flight deck projected pictures of whatever they were flying over on to a huge screen which covered the whole of one bedroom wall. It added a singular new dimension to watch the Himalayas pass slowly across their vision as they snugly pleasured each other thirty-five thousand feet up in the air.

The honeymoon lasted a month. Strictly speaking, it was over before that.

Carol received her first jolt in Raffles Hotel. She had been in touch by telex with Martha in England, outlining her itinerary. Now, enjoying the best whisky sour in Singapore while waiting for Conn in the bar, a telex from her sister was brought to her by a bellboy. It read simply: 'Fordinger nominees been buying Ironstile-Locatelli very heavily in the market. Please explain.'

She confronted Conn with it the minute he joined her. He laughed easily. 'Sure, I've been buying them. You're a good company and it looks like a sound investment.'

'This isn't investment-buying,' said Carol. 'It looks more like a bid for control.'

Conn shrugged. 'I don't mind admitting I wouldn't object to having Ironstile-Locatelli inside the Fordinger fold.'

All of Carol's inbuilt revulsion to being owned surged up in her. So he was at it too now! Her voice was freezing. 'There is no way you're going to get your hands on that company.'

'Come on, honey,' he said cajolingly, 'there's no need to get so spiky. It's only business. There's nothing personal.'

'Then why be so sneaky about it?'

'I wasn't being sneaky—'

'You've been buying shares in my company without telling me, under cover of nominees, right through the honeymoon and you don't call that sneaky? I think I'd better tell you something, Conn. You ever try to take me over in *any* way, business or otherwise, and we're finished.'

He was angry now too. 'If I wanted to, I'm in a position to put in a bid for Ironstile-Locatelli tomorrow.'

'You haven't done your homework,' she flung back at him contemptuously. 'Every single voting share in the company is held by the family.'

'I've still bought myself enough clout to have a hell of a stink created at the next annual general meeting.'

'About what?'

'I'll think of something.'

Carol spoke very flatly. 'Conn, I think you'd better put those shares back on the market. Or else.'

'Or else what?' he shouted mockingly after her as she left the bar and went up to their suite.

She didn't know what, but Martha, when she telephoned her, did. Carol told her everything that had been said and Martha listened intently. At the end she made one comment: 'Master Fordinger's going to find that we've got a bit of clout too.'

Martha hadn't been an Inland Revenue officer for nothing. Fordinger had various charitable trusts in England as well as everywhere else. They were admirable in their aims and gave a great deal of help in areas where it was much needed. But Martha knew from experience there was never a charitable trust created that could stand up to a really beady-eyed scrutiny from an ill-intentioned Inland Revenue man. Sometimes by carelessness, sometimes not, certain expenses would have been charged which were not strictly allowable. Sometimes, mostly by oversight, certain types of investments, forbidden under the terms of the trust, would have been made. There were a hundred and one trip wires about which the Revenue did not unduly exercise itself because there was little deliberate fraud.

But now Martha called in one of her erstwhile colleagues who had risen to impressive heights in the dread Special Department of the Revenue. Obligingly he put a brilliant young ferret, just down from Cambridge, on to one of the Fordinger trusts in England.

The cable reached Conn in Bangkok. They were staying in the Noël Coward suite at the Oriental. His face bleached as he read it. The Fordinger image of almost puritan probity was in danger of being completely overturned. 'Are you behind this?' he demanded.

'Yes,' she said.

He called London, got a senior partner out of bed and told him to start selling his stake in Ironstile-Locatelli discreetly first thing next morning, London style.

Then he raped Carol.

Afterwards, he was genial and very charming. 'I'm sorry about that,' he said. 'I guess I didn't realise you weren't feeling like I did. And once I get started, I don't seem to be able to stop.'

It was a lie and she knew it, but she didn't mind too much. He had used only strength to overpower her, no threats, nor injury, nor pain; and towards the end she had quite enjoyed it, especially when she sank her beautiful teeth into his flesh.

But there was the shadow of something hovering over the rim of her mind's horizon and she couldn't coax it out into the open.

'I take it you'll call the hounds off me back in London now?' he asked later.

'Of course,' said Carol.

The next incident was at Keith's restaurant in Bahrain. They had flown there on a whim because Conn had taken a sudden violent fancy for Keith's particular way with a fillet steak and his Bahrain prawns with Sauce Louis.

Carol, like all blondes in an Arab country, had been the target for glittering charcoal eyes on every side since they came off the airstrip in the air-conditioned Daimler which would whisk them to the old Bedouin house that concealed Keith's tiny, white-washed, candle-lit restaurant.

There, they had never seen such a blonde. Even Keith's Arab staff peered out of the rear quarters at her, looking, in the shadows, as if their faces were made of charred parchment with two pieces of jet stuck in for eyes.

'Stand up,' said Conn to her suddenly. 'Stand up and let them see what a real golden beauty looks like.'

At first Carol thought he was joking. 'I'll throw in a belly dance as well if you like,' she said.

'No, come on,' Conn urged, grasping her elbow. 'Get up and let them see you.' She resisted the pressure on her elbow and he increased it. He meant it!

'Get fucked!' she said. It was the first time she had ever sworn in his presence and it stunned him. She followed it up by tipping his dinner in his lap and stormed out to commandeer the Daimler to take her back to her plane.

He came raging back after her in a clapped-out Arab taxi, his temper as filthy as a Moroccan sewer. She was sitting in the living room of the plane when he marched up the steps and in, his face like a thunderhead, his impressiveness somewhat undercut by his dinner-polluted trousers.

'You bitch!' he hissed. 'You ever speak to me like that again or do anything like that to me again and I'll pull your fingers off!'

She was ready for him, met him almost with joy. 'And you *ever* ask me to put on a public exhibition for a collection of Arab voyeurs again and you'd better bring an intensive care unit with you. You are, without exception, the most disgusting male pig I have ever met and, believe me, where I come from, one meets them all!'

He raped her again.

This time it took longer. She had revived in her mind a great many more of the tricks Tony had taught her over the years and Conn was to bear for days the bruises on his belly, throat and kidneys which were the price he had had to pay for his final Pyrrhic victory.

As ever, when he finally stormed her curly golden citadel, it was good for both of them. But Carol knew that it was only her body that was satisfied. Her mind was deep under cloud and she knew that if only she could disperse it she would have the answer.

The third time it happened, although 'it' did not yet have a precise definition in her mind, was in Haiti just outside Port au Prince. Carol had thought it would be interesting to go to a native festival that was not just for tourists but was not too heavy either.

Their coal-black driver took them to exactly what they wanted: a kind of beach party where everyone was rum-high but no higher; there was rhythm, not religion, in the drumming; and joy, not possession, in the dancing.

The beach fires flickered on gleaming, hairless black

bodies; eyes and teeth gleamed: the patois was musical. Conn and Carol wrestled with their roast suckling pig, burning their fingers, dipping them in white rum to soothe the hurt, happy to watch in the warm black night how people can learn to relax even under tyranny.

The trouble started with the limbo dancers. Unlike some of the other West Indian islands, in Haiti the star limbo dancers are female. They are pretty, their faces a confection of chocolate and roses, and their bodies round, supple and gleaming beyond belief.

The 'vedette' of the evening was a compact little madam, Carol thought, about five-six with a short torso and the thighs of a Praxiteles statue; and when she splayed them to wriggle under the lowest bar of the evening they were as taut and perfect a piece of feminine geometry as the sculptor himself could have imagined.

It was at that point that Conn leaped to his feet, confident in the anonymity of the occasion, dragging Carol up with him. 'My wife can do better than that,' he shouted in his Swiss-French, a legacy from his years at Le Rosaye: 'my wife is the snake-muscled wonder of the Western world. Come on, honey, show 'em what you can do!'

Carol looked at him in astonishment. This wasn't the Conn Fordinger she thought she knew. Even in Bahrain he had been discreet about his request. Yet he wasn't drunk: she knew damn well he wasn't. Suddenly, the clouds started to swirl and part in her brain. She caught a tantalising glimpse of the truth.

There was no time to do more because now he was dragging her towards the fires and the limbo bar and the crowds were clapping and chanting, encouraging her. She struggled against the big, hard hand clamped on her wrist. He was dragging her past a fire on which a suckling pig was being roast on a spit. She said to the cook, very swiftly in French, 'Give me a pair of gloves and the pig.'

The spit-turner threw her a pair of the rush-woven gloves, the equivalent of oven-gloves. She put them on and then he deftly slid the bubbling pig off the spit into her hands. Conn watched, baffled; but not for long. No sooner did she have the sizzling pig in her gloved hands than, with an irresistible smile, she offered it to Conn. Lost in whatever corner of the particular fantasy he was playing out, he took it, unthinking.

He screamed as the scorching hide and flesh adhered to his hands. He was instantly surrounded by concerned helpers, ministering to him with salves of palm oil, coconut oil, coconut milk and dock leaves. Meanwhile, Carol slipped away like a blonde wraith, found their waiting taxi, and ordered its peeled-almond-toothed driver, who hadn't missed a moment of the drama, back to the Boeing.

The almond teeth were much in evidence all the way back. He had evidently enjoyed the whole episode enormously. He enjoyed even more the lowering of small arms and the lifting of barriers at the airfield when the bastards who guarded it recognised his passenger. Delivering her at the plane, he refused all payment, begging only a signed photograph which he immediately sellotaped to the dashboard of his cab.

Conn, driven by the same cabbie, arrived forty minutes later, his hands heavily bandaged. He stomped into the living room. Carol saw his swathed hands and struck instantly. It was becoming clearer all the time.

'Sorry about the pig,' she said. 'I just thought you'd get on well together.' He said nothing. 'This is when you would have pounced, isn't it?' she asked. It was a rhetorical question: they both knew the answer. 'What is it, Conn? If it hadn't been for your hands you'd have come back here and raped me. Why does it have to be like that? Is it because that's what it was like the first time at Lucia's? Did that fixate you? Imprint you? Or has it always been like that with you?'

She was beginning to see through the enigma more clearly now. Each encounter with him had been a scenario, set up and directed by him, in which he provoked her into some dramatic action as an excuse for violating her.

Conn's reply was perhaps predictable from any other man, but not from him. 'I don't want to talk about it,' he said. 'You behaved very badly tonight. Let's forget it.'

She knew that she'd scored an absolute dead centre bullseye, but she had no sense of triumph. He looked so destroyed and so vulnerable, this big man with his baby-mittened bandaged hands, that she took him upstairs to bed and consoled him as only she could. She consoled him with her mouth, her flower-petal hands, her whole, educated body, bringing them both to such a peak of pleasure that she hoped she had exorcised his previous predilections. He came for the second time just as the Boeing pointed its snout into the moonlit sky for lift-off.

She grinned, the urchin back in her face, regarding the double uplift as an omen.

At Princeton, at about the same time, the fifteenth in a planned series of sixteen nuclear fusion experiments overlorded by Professor Isaac Palmer failed, nearly blinding a technician. The technician had, by a million-to-one chance, angled a sheet of polished steel in such a way that one of the laser bolts had been reflected back very nearly into his eyes.

It wasn't absolutely direct and the technician had been wearing dark goggles, but it was a close thing.

In the mansion in the lush greenwoods and meadows of Cheshire in England, again within hours of the same time, a momentous decision was being taken.

George and Martha were lying in their William and Mary bed, a blazing log fire crackling in the handsome Georgian fireplace, watching a re-run of *Love is a Many-Splendoured Thing* on a large television set at the end of the bed. Simple souls, albeit encased in tempered-steel chain mail, they had been touched. As the credits rolled, Martha turned to George, tears running down her homely cheeks. 'Love,' she said, 'let's get wed!'

The next minute it was as if the bed had exploded. The bedclothes were soaring towards the ornate ceiling and George was doing a kind of Zulu war dance on the king-sized mattress, in imminent danger of bouncing straight off and cracking his head against something.

'I've been saying that for the last ten years!' he shouted.

'If you carry on like that,' remarked Martha drily, 'you won't last another ten minutes.'

It had worked between George and her. He was that rare creature, a naturally good man with a heart as big as a gong. He had long ago expunged the fear of marriage with which her father had left her. Now that she had made her mind up, she coudn't think what had taken her so long; they'd been so busy becoming multi-millionaires, she supposed.

The wedding was set for the week before Christmas, 1978. Martha, a battleaxe even to the most charitable eye, was in fact an extremely sentimental woman. Like all the Blair children, she had never known what it was to have a happy Christmas as a child; Jack Blair had seen to that. They'd been the only house in the street with no paper chains or decorations of any kind. He had done his damndest to reduce it to just another day in the calendar. Martha was determined now to link the season emotionally with happiness.

A month before the date she brought in an army of workmen and electricians. Multi-coloured fairy-lights were strung along the branches of every tree lining the impressive drive. An enormous Christmas tree was somehow manoeuvred into the hall and drenched with lights and baubles. She ransacked the county for holly and mistletoe. She bought a Christmas present for every single guest and every member of staff, both indoors and outdoors. She had them superbly gift-wrapped and piled around the tree . . .

Martha was happier than she had been for a long time. Carol had never been so miserable in her life. She could no longer fool herself. There was something very wrong with Conn, something of which she, with all her skills, could not cure him. He didn't want to love, he wanted to violate.

She was perfectly willing to co-operate in playing it as a game, to give him a hard fight before he won her. But Conn was not interested in games. The only thing that engaged him was the real thing. There had to be real conflict, preferably with Carol winning the argument while ending up hating him; and then he would take his revenge. And it seemed to be progressive. Each time he used a little more violence.

Had she come all this way, she asked herself, to end up as she had started: the favoured victim of a violent man?

It was in Rio that she decided she had not. After a particularly stressful submission to him, she waited for him to go to the bathroom. She then threw on some clothes, took a taxi to the airfield, and took off in the Boeing for Liverpool. The cold December blasts coming off the Mersey hit her like knives after the heat of Rio, but she was grateful for them. They brought reality and a sea-kelp smell of home.

Jack was beginning to grey at last. But his heart was as hard as ever and so was his body. A couple of years ago they had offered him voluntary retirement with a compensatory sweetener of four thousand pounds. Hundreds of dockers had accepted. Jack had told them where they could stick their money. One of his pleasures in life still was pitting his bone and sinew against the force of gravity, and even with mechanisation muscle was still needed on the docks.

'Come home to find a shoulder to cry on again?' he asked Carol. 'What is it this time – somebody nicked one of your yachts?'

Carol looked into his eyes and thought she caught a shadow of something, as she had once before. What it was, although she couldn't know, was puzzlement. Why did she come back to this place like a homing pigeon when he had seen pictures in the magazines and papers of how she lived normally? Again, too, seeing the lost look on her face, he felt as he had done at the time of Leo's death. He was like a man wanting to take a step towards her and finding his feet set in concrete of his own laying.

Janet was Carol's solace. The overwhelming warmth of that Celtic heart was like a brazier at which Carol could warm herself. She told Janet everything, as she had always done. Janet, out of the wisdom that starts to reach its subtlest peaks of perceptiveness in women of her age, began by not criticising Conn.

'There are men like that, love,' she said. 'They can't help it. They need aggravation, opposition.'

'Dad's like that, but he doesn't take it out on you in bed.'

'No, he doesn't, I'll say that for him. He gets rid of most of it down at the docks. D'you love this Conn Fordinger?'

'When he's not being a Nazi in the bedroom, he's the sweetest man on earth.'

'Carol, love, he's not unique,' said Janet. 'The daytime man and the bedtime man seem to be two different people. If we only knew what goes on inside the heads of bank managers!'

'Why bank managers?' Carol started to laugh, which had been Janet's intention.

'Well, they're so pious! I bet when they get home they expect their wives to be swinging from the light fittings wearing nothing but a fireman's helmet!'

Carol's laugh deepened. Just for a minute, Janet had succeeded in reducing Conn to a cartoon.

They were sitting high up in a tower block. The Blairs had been re-housed by the Council when the rest of the street had been knocked down about their ears. It had taken an eviction order and five bailiffs to get Jack out. The block was a stack of concrete egg boxes piled on top of one another in which to package people. Grey, soulless, without human feeling; but for the Liverpool skyline one could have been on the outskirts of Moscow.

Inside, Janet, with her home-making instinct, had made it a nest. But she hated the cold, dark landings, the graffiti-covered, urine-smelling lifts. Muggers lurked on the landings and around the corners of the stairs, except in the section where the Blairs lived. Jack's presence there was enough to keep it free at least of human garbage.

'Guess who's on the landing above,' Janet said the next day. 'The Palmers!'

'No!'

'They got re-housed at the same time.'

'Has Ike been home?'

'They're expecting him for the holidays.'

That night Ike arrived home. Then minutes later, after

he'd been nearly strangled in embraces and been told fifteen times how handsome he was, yet at the same time how ill and under-nourished, his mother said: 'Guess who's on the landing below. The Blairs!'

'Carol?'

There was a triumphant pause as Mrs Palmer's chubby little face beamed and her husband cast his eyes up to the heavens, then: 'She's here now!' she revealed.

Two minutes later, Ike was tumbling down the stairs and knocking on the door. Carol herself answered it. They looked at each other and for one dizzy moment they felt that they were going to fall into each other's arms as in the movies and everything that was wrong in their lives was going to be put right.

'Ike!' she said. 'How lovely!'

'Princess . . . ' he answered, smiling.

'Oh, shut up, Ike,' she said as he gave her a smacking kiss on both cheeks.

They talked as old friends, he and Carol and Janet. Even Jack fractured his customary taciturnity to join in. Ike Palmer was one of the younger members of the ghetto for whom he had always had time. There'd always been a 'Stuff you!' look in his eyes as he looked at the world, even through his spectacles, that Jack had liked. Now he thought he detected a hardening of the lines of the whole face. Again he approved.

'How's the research coming?' asked Carol.

Ike rubbed his hands wearily over his face. 'They're going to close me out,' he said. 'Oh, they say that all they're going to do is cut my budget for next year, but the project can barely keep ticking on what we're getting now. To cut it is the equivalent of putting me out of business.'

'Have you got enemies?' asked Jack, looking at the world as he knew it.

'Jack,' said Ike, 'the only way to stay safe in science is to work with your back against a solid wall – and even then some bastard'll invent a knife that slices through brick. And I'm so near! I've got the input-output power ratio down to one point one to one. I'm on the edge of a breakthrough, I know I am! Once we crack it, we're through our version of the black hole and out the other side in a different dimension of power-generation!'

'How much d'you need to complete the experiment?' asked Carol.

'I could get by on half a billion dollars,' he answered casually. Money, figures, had long since ceased to have any reality for him unless they related directly to his theory.

'I see,' said Carol thoughtfully; 'say two hundred-odd million pounds.' The first shoots were beginning to thrust up in her fertile mind of a plan that was to lead to the most lunatically memorable and potentially disastrous Christmas of her entire life.

At Greensleeves, Martha pressed on with her wedding preparations. Typically, she'd given Carol a free hand to invite anyone she wanted. Carol stuck to her tried and true friends. She gave Martha a short list of names and addresses. On it were Ike, Stewart Crown, Michael Willoughby, Diana Fremantle, David Hales, Richard Swann and Countess Lucia. All accepted instantly.

She had Harry Winston fly over to London by Concorde, accompanied by two of the largest men she had ever seen, and in the VIP lounge at London Heathrow they had enjoyed themselves beyond measure haggling over a diamond like a frozen tear. She finally bought it as a wedding present for Martha, then commissioned for George a model of a scrapyard at night, executed in gold and quartz and rubies by Garrards, the Royal Jewellers.

When Carol got back to Greensleeves, Martha was testing the lights and lanterns in the trees. The effect was magical. As she was swept up the bejewelled drive, alien lights appeared in the sky to add to the display, a winking red and a winking blue and a powerful spotlight directed towards the ground. The noise soon made it clear what it was. A private helicopter, in jet-black livery like a bird of ill omen, was chattering its way down on to the front lawn, thrashing up the few leaves that George's assiduous gardeners had not yet gathered. Out of it, as Carol's Silver

Shadow whispered past, stepped Conn Fordinger, only his Savile Row tailoring preventing him from looking like a rock-fall waiting for someone to drop on.

By the time Conn had reached the front door, Carol was floating down the graceful stairs into the hall in a long, soft, eye-matching woollen dress conjured up by Melz in his address-less tower outside Florence. Her hair was loose. Ferociously angry as he was, the sight of her melted Conn down to warm tallow.

He was nevertheless determined not to be undermined. 'Where the hell have you been?'

Carol came softly towards Conn and linked her arms around his neck: 'Darling, you were so foul to me in Rio I thought you'd prefer me out of the way for a bit, so I came home. I'm surprised it took you so long to work it out.'

'You just pick up and leave without a word to me. You . . . What are you planning to do here, anyway?'

'My sister's getting married. I'm a guest. You're invited.'

Conn strode to the front door, made a gesture into the night and a minute later his man strode in carrying his bags.

'Muir!' shouted Carol, knowing perfectly well he'd be riveted behind the green door, not missing a syllable.

He appeared as if by electronic magic. 'Madam?'

'Take Mr Fordinger's things to the Blue Suite.' She turned to Conn. 'I should think you could do with a drink,' she said with one of her most corrupting smiles. 'Let's go and meet George and Martha.'

In the yellow room she introduced him to his hosts. The well-tweeded rude health of George, the money hopelessly wasted on Martha's oil-rig stockiness, were reassuring to him. These were people to whom he could relate. They were folk who would have done well in Connecticut or Virginia in the sixteenth and seventeenth centuries.

'I'm sorry,' he said. 'I know you weren't expecting me.'

'Rubbish,' said Martha. 'Wherever Carol goes, her man is sure to follow.'

Clever, thought Conn. He couldn't possibly take objection to it as a compliment to his wife, yet it somehow subtly reduced him to the level of a gun-dog.

Later, in the Blue Suite before dinner, Carol let Conn take it out on her. Ten days of frustration, anger and desire. He didn't even wait for her to get her dress off and she gave him the best contest he'd had from her so far. Afterwards, she could tell that his curious concept of male honour as well as his sexual drive had been satisfied. This could have been a good time to start to put her plan into operation, but instinct told her it would be too obvious. She held off. Gently, gently, catchee monkey: was that how it went?

During the next two days, those who were to be house guests, as opposed to those simply coming to the wedding, started to arrive.

First a ferociously beautiful Panther de Ville growled up the drive to disgorge David Hales. His wedding present to George and Martha was to be an album of pictures of the whole event from beginning to end, shot by himself. He shook hands in his quick, friendly, terrier-like way while giving the impression that he'd already started shooting with his free hand. He was a little plumper, but his black eyes were still as merry and his movements as rapid.

Next, Dick Swann flew in from New York, his hair now so transcendently silver it could have been auctioned at Sotheby's. He'd planned an album, too, but on learning of Hales's plans resorted to his fall-back gift: a tiny Fabergé egg into each half of which he was going to insert a bridal photograph, Martha one side, George the other. 'And bugger you, Dave,' he grinned triumphantly as he showed it to Hales.

'Your pictures always did look better small,' Hales grinned back.

Countess Lucia turned up with a flurry of Italian maids; there were actually only two, but they managed to make a noise like an argument in a Neapolitan market. They were promptly despatched by Martha to stay at the local inn. 'I'm not having my house turned into a rehearsal for *Tosca*,' she said.

Lucia took one look at her face and knew she'd met her match.

Next came Michael Willoughby, his suit more cunningly crafted than ever, his light blue eyes as shrewdly compassionate. He swept Carol into his immaculately sleeved arms. 'Darling!' he said. 'I could sign you up for a million pounds with Revlon tomorrow!'

She smiled at him with great affection. 'Michael,' she said, 'you made me rich once; don't you think that's enough?'

Diana Fremantle came next, California-burnished and with a portmanteau the size of a small truck, and then Stewart Crown. A dark green Rolls Corniche sighed up the drive and out he stepped, the lawyer who was now as famous in America as he was in England.

He looked magnificent, thought Carol. If ever a man had actually improved with age it was Stewart, a full-grown lion, king of the jungle. The honey-coloured eyes now had a depth of authority that antagonists in and out of court found daunting and juries irresistible. And the raven hair had started to silver at the temples in a way that Vidal Sassoon's finest colourist couldn't have managed.

There is nothing a first lover ever needs to say to a woman. He simply hugged her with the same kind of authority that was in his eyes and she warmed down to the furthermost tips of her toes.

At this procession of undeniably attractive and celebrated men from Carol's past, all of them either unmarried or divorced, Conn got more and more beady-eyed. Goddammit! he thought, as Tony arrived. Even her brother had to look like that! Then Tony helped Senta out of the other side of the car and Conn's spirits rose.

If any girl ever looked like a tigress, this one did. She rippled towards the house and her bold blue eyes did not waver as they met the probe of Fordinger's.

Last came Ike Palmer. He arrived in an old banger he had hired from somewhere and no man ever managed to get his collar as crumpled as he had; all he carried was one suitcase, and the reflections on his glasses hid the stunning intelligence that lay behind them. On the face of it, he was the least impressive of Carol's guests. Except to one person. And that person was Conn Fordinger.

He remembered Ike from his encounter with him in Rome when he had felt so strongly the vibrations between this man and Carol. No man ever forgets a threesome like that. And as he watched Ike's loose-limbed arrival from an oriel window on a landing next to his dressing room, he could have sworn he heard himself growl.

Carol broached her plan in one of the miniature four-wheel-drive jeeps that George had provided for his guests as an amusing way of getting out and about and seeing the enormous estate, which held its traps for normal vehicles in the winter.

'Hell, I'd like to help, honey,' said Conn hypocritically, as they rattled over a cattle-grid into a meadow brittle with frost, 'but all the Foundations are fully extended.'

'But with interest rates the way they are, the cash must be piling up! Conn, the Foundations have never been so liquid.'

'Should be, honey, should be,' he countered blandly, 'but inflation's taking care of that. It's all we can do to keep pace with the projects we've got already.'

'Conn, you've got money in those Trusts that's doing nothing but make more and you know it! What are you going to be, the first man in history to drown in dollar bills? You're always looking for new projects to back. You *should* be into alternative energy sources – it's the future!'

'Carol, I'll level with you,' he said, spiritually donning his most conservative Wall Street suit. 'We have been examining alternative energy and frankly we just don't go with the fuel pellet-laser system. We don't believe in it. I'd be crazy to recommend that kind of investment in a concept I've got no confidence in.'

Carol, who was driving, unconsciously in her anger let her foot rest more and more heavily on the throttle. In a mini-jeep, speed feels as if it's double what it is. Conn had the impression they were hurtling towards an impenetrable stand of conifers at eighty miles an hour. 'You spend hundreds of millions on projects you don't believe in,' she shouted, 'just to keep the money circulating, yet you won't back one of the most brilliant physicists in the world! Why?'

Conn, seeing the trees rushing towards him as if he were sitting in the front row of the movies, hurled himself sideways out of the doorless little truck and rolled expertly over and over in the mud, coming to no harm. Carol slewed to a stop and reversed towards him. She was laughing helplessly. She knew she was only further damaging her own cause, but she couldn't help it. She reached Conn, his clothes a mess, his face a mask of mud, and started to apologise. He didn't even hear her.

'Because said brilliant fucking physicist happens to be your ex-fucking boyfriend, that's why!' he shouted. 'And over my dead body, which you appear just now to have tried to arrange, will he get any money from the Fordingers! Now take me back to the house. If I want to get killed I can try for the Indianapolis 500!'

The wedding took place in the village church of St Botolph three miles away. David Hales and Dick Swann groaned silently as they shot reel after reel of Martha in an inspiredly conservative Zandra Rhodes, which looked on her like curtaining material draped round a wrestler, and George in a six-hundred-pound morning suit from Huntsman's that, on him, looked as if it were made of asbestos. 'I told you my body only took to tweeds,' he had complained to Martha that morning.

Jack had conceded to come down to the wedding, by bus, in his best dark serge suit, and had even agreed to stay at Greensleeves until Christmas. His sole reason – although runaway tugboats couldn't have dragged it out of him – was that he simply couldn't stand being without Janet. For the first time, while she had been at Greensleeves, he had realised, in that soul-sapping tower block in Liverpool, how necessary to him she was.

Carol had never had anything but contempt for women who used the withholding of sex as a weapon. In any case, that wouldn't have worked with Conn. He'd only have enjoyed the extra obstacle and taken his pleasure anyway.

She did, however, following their discussion in the jeep, refuse to fight or struggle or be difficult.

Conn was a perfectly competent lover without the sadistic overtones and that was what he had to content himself with. He seemed to be curiously complaisant about it, as if it were his apology for not helping Ike.

After the wedding, snow fell persistently the week before Christmas, filling Carol's children with delight. And when the fairy lights were switched on in the park at night there wasn't one of the house party who didn't stand silently at a window, rapt in the pure, dream-like beauty of the white-shrouded, crystalline colours that enveloped the grounds.

On Christmas Eve, helped by Martha, George grunted his way into a Santa Claus costume, complete with beard and whiskers. With his signal-red face he looked superb. He then trudged a quarter of a mile through the snow to an outlying barn where a sleigh-belled mini-jeep had already been piled with glamorously wrapped presents sticking out of sacks. At midnight, bells tinkling, he drove it slowly to the house. As he approached, two small faces were flattened hard against the windows, and by the time he reached the house two pyjama'd figures were shrieking out into the snow.

Within five minutes every grown-up in the house, with the exception of Jack, was up too. There followed a present-opening orgy in the great hall under the Christmas tree, where George had taken care to see that the log fire was kept built up. It was the kind of chaos, excitement and goodwill that Martha had dreamed of all her life. She had to retire precipitately to the cloakroom, where she blew her nose vigorously, called herself a damned old fool in the mirror, and made sure the mascara hadn't run from her stubby little eyelashes. George followed her in and a glorious scuffle ended in his giving her a great whiskery kiss.

It was the prelude to a perfect Christmas and it couldn't last.

The day after Boxing Day, in the middle of the afternoon, Carol caught Conn in bed with Senta.

Senta was straddling Conn, sitting back with him inside her while he massaged her smooth and marbled stomach with a powerful electric vibrator, a process which was evidently sending hitherto undiscovered sensations through both of them.

Carol had sometimes wondered what she would do in circumstances like this. Withdraw with extreme dignity? Scream with fury? Attack one or both with her nails? In the event, she did none of these things. She grabbed a fire extinguisher from its bracket outside the door and sculpted them from head to foot in white foam, freezing them in their remarkable posture. She then slammed the door, totally at a loss what to do next.

As it happened, matters were taken out of her hands by the immediate arrival of Tony. He saw Carol, looking vacant, standing outside his bedroom with a fire extinguisher still dribbling foam.

'What in God's name—'

'Don't go in there!' she tried to bar his way.

He pushed her aside, thinking there'd been a fire and she was in shock. He flung open the door. The sight that met him was surrealistic. Two figures, one of them his wife, covered from top to toe in glutinous foam, which they were vainly trying to wipe off with bedsheets, covers, anything that came to hand, handicapped because some of it had got into their eyes and they couldn't see very well. His wife's breasts looked like two Fontainebleau meringues with too much Chantilly cream on them, and as he watched a blob of foam dropped off the end of Fordinger's decidedly dejected-looking prick.

Carol watched Tony, ready to try and get between them if he made for Conn, whom he might conceivably kill. Instead, unpredictable as all the Blairs, that last blob of foam did it for Tony. He started to laugh, deeply and uncontrollably. He laughed until he had to hold his ribs.

It hurt Conn Fordinger more than if he'd been blasted with a twelve-bore. 'Now listen here—' he started.

'You'd just better shut up,' said Tony, with sufficient authority, despite the tears of mirth running down his cheeks, to chop off one of the unseen emperors of the world in mid-sentence.

He turned to Senta, her mane of hair a sodden draggle, who was peering at him with fascinated horror through the eye that was not still covered with foam. 'As for you, we'll be discussing this later.'

It was her first transgression since he had so comprehensively spanked her. She knew now for a certainty that, after he'd finished with her tonight, it would be her last.

Tony slammed the door and brother and sister went downstairs for a large Delamain each. As they sipped it, Carol's thoughts were on a quiet divorce, Tony's on whether his hand would still be harder than a hairbrush on his wife's apple-perfect backside.

It was Conn's reaction that nobody foresaw.

19

Over dinner that evening nobody would have noticed that there was anything particularly amiss. Conn and Carol were charming to each other, as were Tony and Senta. After dinner they played with a diabolical computer toy – a prototype which Dick had brought from New York – and then they went, blissfully tired, up to their rooms.

It was then that Carol got the surprise of her life. She sat at the dressing table and started the nightly ritual of brushing her shining hair.

'I want a divorce,' she said conversationally.

'The Fordingers do not divorce,' Conn said calmly, meticulously removing his cuff-links. 'That's why they take so long to marry.'

'I don't give a damn what a bunch of lapsed Quakers do or do not do,' she retorted, her knuckles whitening on the handle of her hairbrush, 'but the Blairs do not stay married to adulterers!'

He crossed the room in a stride, grabbed her by the hair and yanked her head back, staring down into her upturned face. 'What the hell are you talking about?' he snarled. 'There isn't a man in this house party you haven't screwed at some time or other!'

'That was before I was married!'

'That makes a difference, does it?'

'Of course it does, you corkscrewed pig! And don't try defending yourself by attacking me. And let go of my hair!'

He tightened his grip on it. The pain was agonising. She lunged back with an elbow as Tony had taught her and drove it into his lower abdomen. He released his grip and sank to his knees, gasping. She sprang up from the dressing table, but he grabbed her ankle, bringing her down. To her utter disbelief, he started his customary violation routine. What she didn't understand was that his obsession clouded all rational considerations and that to take her against her will when he was so totally in the wrong was all that he could see in the situation.

However, there was something he didn't understand, either. On previous occasions she had been fighting at perhaps seventy per cent of her capability. Now she turned on the full hundred. He found he couldn't prevail. In fury and desperation, he started beating that incomparable face. She felt her nose crunch and a cheekbone break, a lip splitting. And in that terrible moment she had a flash of insight and she knew what she had to do and what she had been waiting for.

She kicked Conn in the balls with the precision of a pro footballer and grabbed the house-telephone. 'Stewart? My room – quick!'

Forty seconds later Stewart Crown, dressing-gowned, was bursting into the room, his face draining as he looked at the wreck of her face. Conn still lay curled up, hugging his genitals.

'Stewart,' she said, 'it's about a divorce.'

Crown picked up the telephone and dialled two in-house numbers in quick succession: 'David? Dick? Carol's room now. And bring your camera.'

David Hales and Dick Swann, knots of pain between their eyebrows, shot her broken face from every conceivable angle. Conn had locked himself in the bathroom.

Next morning, after the discreet local doctor had seen her and the contusions and blackenings and swellings had had time to ripen, Crown had Dick and David shoot her again. She stayed in her room and had sworn the three of them to secrecy. She was terrified of what Tony would do if he found out. Conn had moved to a spare room and was packing.

In the event, it was Martha who found out. In the garden after breakfast, she happened to look up just as Carol was looking out of her window. She stopped as if paralysed and then came rushing indoors. She hammered on Carol's door until Carol had to let her in and then she wept at the ruin of that exquisite face.

'Martha, sweetheart, don't worry,' pleaded Carol, hugging her elder sister as if she were the one who was hurt. 'It's mostly bruising, it'll go down. And the rest the plastic surgeons can put right.'

'You've got to charge him,' said Martha. 'Grievous bodily harm. He's got to pay!'

'He's going to pay,' said Carol quietly, 'but not in a wasteful way like that.'

Martha's swollen eyelids after she'd left Carol's room were noted by everyone in the party which, like every house party, was one multi-faceted detective. It was Tony who got it out of her first. He turned and headed like a guided missile in the direction of Conn Fordinger's new room. On the way he met his father.

Jack had instinctively picked up all he needed to know. He, too, was on his way to Conn Fordinger. He met Tony on the landing outside Conn's door.

'Look,' said Jack, with a logic Tony had never heard him use before, 'we could fight each other for the privilege of clobbering Mr bloody Fordinger; and by the time we'd finished we'd neither of us be in a fit state to stun a rabbit. She's my daughter and it's my fight, so get out of the fucking way.'

Tony got out of the way and Jack kicked down Conn Fordinger's door.

Fordinger knew what he'd come for and he wasn't too worried. After all, he'd boxed for Yale, he was almost as tall as Blair if not quite as wide, he was twenty years younger and he'd kept in shape in the gym. He'd smashed two big-fisted right hands to Jack's head and one to his midriff before Jack had landed a punch. That was when he learned that staying in shape in the gym was not the same as working on the docks. He felt as if he were hitting mahogany. Jack was slow now, but when he landed his first punch, a little too high, Fordinger realised that Jack was in a fearsomely different physical dimension that had nothing to do with size. Conn's balance went, only his superb condition bracing his knees and he started desperately to box. He slipped punches, blocked them, moved inside others, hammering away at Jack's middle where, at his age, he *must* be vulnerable. Jack took it all and kept hitting with the heavy mortars that were his fists. He hit about half as often as Fordinger, but each time those huge bunches of bone landed Fordinger felt fear and defeat and inexpressible pain. He went down in stages, first to his knees, then to his backside, finally to his back.

Tony was waiting on the landing as Jack staggered out of the room. He took his father anxiously by the elbow. Jack shook him off and lurched away down the landing. Tony peered inside. Conn Fordinger, king of the world, was flat on his broad back, deeply unconscious. He looked as if he had been through a metal crusher.

Later that night, Jack had a stroke. He woke up in the local cottage hospital in the next bed to Conn Fordinger. He had the satisfaction of noting that Fordinger appeared to be still unconscious. He needed all the consolation he could get because he discovered that nothing on the left side of him worked.

Forty-three floors above Manhattan Stewart Crown faced a cavalry platoon of Fordinger lawyers, including three Englishmen who would have commanded respect in any court in the United Kingdom.

'It's very simple,' said Crown, skilfully giving the impression that he was trying hard not to be patronising. 'My client, Mrs Conn Fordinger, proposes to sue for divorce on the grounds of adultery and cruelty.'

Jacouth Bright, Fordinger's aptly-named principal litigation attorney, intervened. 'Your witnesses to adultery consist of your client's brother and the lady who is alleged to have taken part in the alleged adultery, namely his wife. Not a very convincing array in a suit where the division of community property is likely to be argued into the billions.'

Crown smiled graciously. 'We'll come to the sordid question of billions later. At the moment I think you had better make an unofficial preliminary examination of our evidence for cruelty.'

He nodded to his junior, who rapidly distributed packets of eight-by-ten glossies to the opposition. They sat in a stern line, dark walnut panelling behind them, while Crown and his aide sat facing them, almost as if they were on trial. It was not a fortuitous arrangement, but it made about as much impression on Crown as a water pistol on a cruiser.

The pictures were arranged in pairs. One of each pair showed Carol at her peak of beauty; the others were the shots that Dick and David had taken after Conn had beaten her up. The poker faces opposite struggled to avoid showing their automatic human reaction.

'These injuries are distressing,' said Jacouth Bright smoothly, 'but there is no evidence in the pictures that our client caused them.'

'Those pictures,' said Crown, 'were taken by two of the most distinguished photographers in the world while my client's blood was still on your client's fists and your client was still in the room. They will give evidence to that effect.' He let his words soak through and watched the nerves start to twitch in their faces. 'Furthermore,' he continued relentlessly, 'we have other photographs illustrating the fact.'

His junior distributed a further batch of pictures showing Crown himself ministering to Carol while Fordinger, his fists bloody, crawled away to the bathroom. Crown watched the twitches turn into winces. He decided to go for the kill with a professional foul.

'I'd hate to think of pictures like that getting into the hands of the press,' he said, at his silkiest. 'They know there's been a split between our clients and we all know how persistent and ingenious they can be.'

There was a pause. Glances were exchanged along the table.

'We would appreciate a short recess so that we may confer,' said Jacouth Bright.

'Naturally,' agreed Crown, in his friendliest tone.

'My secretary will bring you some coffee,' said Jacouth,

as he and his colleagues rose and filed into the next room.

Three thousand miles away, on the terrace at Greensleeves, Jack Blair, watched anxiously by Janet and Martha and George, grabbed once again at the crutches by the side of his wheelchair and made a herculean effort. He heaved, the veins standing out on his tree-like neck, and slowly his great frame rose on the crutches like a magnificent, propped-up film-set façade.

'I'm better!' he roared. 'We can go home!' Then he crashed back into his chair, panting triumphantly.

He had been convalescing at Greensleeves for the past six weeks and for Janet it had been a time of bliss. Waited on, laundered, fed and respected for the first time in her life, it had been – her distress for Jack apart – a revelation of what living could be. This was what George and Martha had been urgently offering her for years and Jack had been refusing. And this was where she had to make her stand. She had to fight for it now if she were not, for the remainder of her life, to be drained to a nothing by this demanding giant in front of her.

'Home?' she demanded. 'Back to the Lubyanka? And what d'you think's going to happen to us there?'

'We're going home, woman,' he roared. 'I'm taking no man's charity!'

'No,' retorted Janet, 'but you'll take a woman's.'

'What the hell does that mean?'

'Who's going to bring in the money?' she asked. 'You can't work, so I'll have to be the breadwinner. Right? That means I'll have to go out to work every day. Right? Who the hell d'you think is going to look after you?'

'Martha can,' he said tersely.

Janet laughed. 'Now it's two women's charity! Anyway, don't be bloody daft!' Oh, the unfairness of hitting him like this when he was at a disadvantage! But oh, after thirty-odd years of containing herself, the utter blissful bloody joy of it! 'Martha's a big businesswoman,' she continued, 'a tycoon. She's not going to fart about looking after the likes of you! And if I'm not going to be there and she's not going to be there, you're going to be on your own all day. That means the Welfare. Meals on Wheels to bring you your food. Social workers to help you to the lavatory. The District Nurse in every other day to give you a bath!'

She saw Jack's face drain. She had never been cruel to him in her life and it was half pain and half luxury. She knew that every stroke in the picture she presented to him was a whiplash. But she had to win; it was her life. 'Is that what you want? To be a pauper in the hands of the Social Services while I go out and earn the money?'

He sat there, silent, like a great oak felled. Then with his massive good right arm, he grabbed his crutches and hurled them into the rhododendron bushes a good thirty yards away. He swivelled his head to look at George, who hadn't said a word. 'Right, you bastard!' he shouted. 'I've a fancy to see the trout stream. Push me there!'

George grinned and grasped the handles of the chair. He'd get an electric one for him next week. He had a feeling that it wouldn't be long before Jack would be able to make do with just a stick, anyway.

As they disappeared across the lawn, Janet and Martha hugged each other silently.

High above Manhattan, Jacouth Bright and his colleagues filed solemnly back into the room.

'Do you wish to fight or settle?' asked Crown, with his most dangerous smile.

'Settle,' said Bright.

'Now then,' said Crown, 'as to the billions. I think I may have a surprise for you there.' He leaned forward.

It was five o'clock on 10 December, 1982, in the Concert Hall in Stockholm. Outside, it was dark and snowing. Inside, it was warm and drenched with flowers. Carol was in the front row of the auditorium, her not quite perfectly restored face somehow more fascinating than ever.

On the platform, on little gilt chairs, sat the Swedish Royal Family, surrounded by current and previous Laureates. Professor Isaac Palmer was among them. He had been awarded the Nobel Prize for Physics for a significant breakthrough in the production and harnessing of power from nuclear fusion.

At the back of the hall sat Conn Fordinger. It was the Fordinger half-billion, funnelled to Ike through Princeton, that had enabled Ike to make the breakthrough. It had been the most civilised, sensible and creative divorce settlement there had ever been. There had only been one condition, That Ike never knew. So far as he was concerned, it was simply an enlightened example of the famous Fordinger philanthropy. And sitting there at the back, Conn had to admit that this was some woman, to let him walk off with the credit for something she'd had to twist his arm to do.

For her part, in a mysterious way, the gesture had broken Carol's fear of being possessed by Ike. Now she had done this for him, he could have all of her. Last night had proved that. The meek were going to inherit the earth after all. Ike, the least violent man she had ever known, had turned out to be the strongest. He was going to give something precious to the world. Perhaps she could be part of it.

The young Swedish King, flawless in his white tie and tails, was stepping to the microphone to begin the presentations. She looked at Ike, up there on the platform, his Adam's apple working under his stiff winged collar as he searched the audience anxiously for her.

As he found her, he smiled that shy, yet confident smile. She was pretty sure it was going to be all right.